SKIN
OF THE
SEA

SKIN
OF THE
SEA

NATASHA BOWEN

RANDOM HOUSE 🏠 NEW YORK

This is a work of fiction. Names, characters, places, and incidents either are the product of the author's imagination or are used fictitiously. Any resemblance to actual persons, living or dead, events, or locales is entirely coincidental.

Text copyright © 2021 by Natasha Bowen
Jacket art copyright © 2021 by Jeff Manning

All rights reserved. Published in the United States by Random House Children's Books, a division of Penguin Random House LLC, New York.

Random House and the colophon are registered trademarks of Penguin Random House LLC.

Visit us on the Web! GetUnderlined.com

Educators and librarians, for a variety of teaching tools, visit us at RHTeachersLibrarians.com

Library of Congress Cataloging-in-Publication Data
Names: Bowen, Natasha, author.
Title: Skin of the sea / Natasha Bowen.
Description: First edition. | New York: Random House Children's Books, [2021] | Series: Skin of the sea; 1 | Summary: Transformed by the goddess Yemoja into a Mami Wata, an African mermaid charged with collecting the souls of those who die at sea, Simi goes against the gods to save a living boy, Kola, from drowning.
Identifiers: LCCN 2020043962 (print) | LCCN 2020043963 (ebook) | ISBN 978-0-593-12094-1 (hardcover) | ISBN 978-0-593-12095-8 (lib. bdg.) | ISBN 978-0-593-12096-5 (ebook)
Subjects: CYAC: Mermaids—Fiction. | Gods, Yoruba—Fiction. | Yoruba (African people)—Fiction. | Death—Fiction. | Soul—Fiction.
Classification: LCC PZ7.1.B6847 Ski 2021 (print) | LCC PZ7.1.B6847 (ebook) | DDC [Fic]—dc23

ISBN 978-0-593-56505-6 (B&N edition)

Printed in the United States of America
10 9 8 7 6 5 4 3 2 1
2021 Barnes & Noble Edition

Random House Children's Books supports the First Amendment and celebrates the right to read.

Penguin Random House LLC supports copyright. Copyright fuels creativity, encourages diverse voices, promotes free speech, and creates a vibrant culture. Thank you for buying an authorized edition of this book and for complying with copyright laws by not reproducing, scanning, or distributing any part in any form without permission. You are supporting writers and allowing Penguin Random House to publish books for every reader.

To my mum,

who couldn't read very well

but made sure I did.

CONTENT NOTE

Before you begin reading, please be aware that parts of this book may be triggering for some readers. *Skin of the Sea* blends fifteenth-century history with fantasy, and there are depictions of violence, enslavement, death, and suicide.

SKIN OF THE SEA

CHAPTER ONE

I CIRCLE THE ship with the sharks, slipping between dark waves. The water is layered with cold currents, sea creatures, and a ship that slices through it with cargo holds full of stolen people. I swim underneath the swells, away from the gaze of men and just out of the reach of jaws.

Waiting.

The hull of the vessel is a shadow above me, and as I follow the line of the keel, my chest tightens, hot rage building against my rib cage. I spin away as fish flit around me, stretching my fingers up toward watery sunbeams. It has been weeks since I have felt the burn of a midday sun. I miss basking in its light, letting the heat soak into my bones. Closing my eyes, I reach for a memory that twists and coils like smoke. *I'm sitting on red-brown earth under the dappled shade of a mahogany tree, splashes of sun on my hot skin.* Eagerly, I grasp for more, but as usual, the vision fades.

My stomach churns with disappointment as sharp as red coral. Every time, the loss feels the same, as if a part of me is within reach, only to dissolve like mist on the tops of the waves.

I turn in the water, a shiver of skin and coils, of hair and scales that flash like buried treasure. Embracing the current, I let trails of seaweed run through my hands, feel the wisps of memories fade away. I pause for a moment as the shoal once again spirals around me, glittering yellow with delicate stripes of pink, letting the beauty of the fish soothe me.

Diving down, I head farther away from the ship. I know I'll need to go back, but for now I close my eyes against the velvet slip of the water, its coolness sliding along my skin. This part of the sea is darker, and I welcome being cloaked in an enfolding gloom.

Below me, an eel slinks through the depths, its muscular body only slightly blacker than the water surrounding it.

Go, I tell the creature, and in one inky slither it moves away from me. I sink deeper. Enough for the cold to seep into my bones. Enough for the glint of my tail to be swallowed by the dark.

I feel the pull of a current, and for a moment, I consider letting it take me, but then I remember the ship and I tip my face toward the surface, toward the sun and the domain of humans who breathe air. I swim up once again, my task fresh in my mind as I see the wooden hull of the ship plowing through the ocean. I'm reluctant to drift too close in case I am seen by humankind; instead I lurk in the midnight shade of the sea, the bellies of the great whites gleaming above me. They glide closer, flat obsidian eyes and teeth ready. I shudder, turning away from their large bodies as they track the ship, even though I am doing the same as they are. We both seek those that enter our domain.

As the creak of the ship echoes in the deep, I stroke the gold chain that hangs heavy around my neck, its links cold against my skin. My fingers move over the sapphire that gleams in the murk.

And then, there it is, the water crashing and hissing with the force of a body entering. Bubbles rise and pop, leaving only the descent of splayed limbs and crimson-stained skin. I swim faster as a shark darts forward. Blood curls in the sea, red ribbons unspooling in the deep. Pushing my way upward, I try to ignore the copper tang in the water as I swim between the gray-and-white creatures.

Wait, I command them as the body sinks. They circle impatiently, black eyes flashing. I turn to the person, catching a glimpse of their unseeing eyes and an open mouth, bruised and swollen.

A woman, her skin a dark brown in the water. Black tufts of hair wave in the current, revealing more wounds on the side of her face. She spins slowly and something in the line of her body speaks to me. There was no easy death here, I think, closing my eyes briefly. But then there never is.

As I take hold of a hand the same size as mine, rage swells at the thought of another death that the sea will hide. The woman's body knocks against me as I hold her close, closer, until our hair intertwines. Cupping her chin, I look at her face and pause.

The tilt of her mouth is familiar, with generous lips framed by full cheeks. Her hair floats free from rows of the kòlẹ́sẹ̀ style, black tendrils that I want to touch, to neaten. I look again and a memory stirs. She reminds me of . . . I try to focus, to tease the edges of it out, but it will not come and the sharks glide closer. They will only listen to me for so long.

My gaze rakes over the woman once more, but the feeling of familiarity has passed. I let it go and remind myself that it doesn't matter. It is better this way, I think, echoing the words of Yemoja. To not remember who I was before. Leaning closer, I focus on the small glow that emanates from the woman's chest, just above her heart. I reach for the swirl of gold that grows brighter as it breaks free from her body. When my fingertips touch the essence, I close my eyes in preparation.

"Mo gbà yín. Ní àpéjọ, ìwọ yóò rí ìbùkún nípasẹ̀ẹ̀ Ìyá Yemoja tí yóo ṣe ìrọ̀rùn ìrìn àjò rẹ. Kí Olodumare mú ọ dé ilé ní àìléwu àti àláfíà," I say, and then repeat the prayer that will glean the woman's soul. "I welcome you. Gathered, you will be blessed by Mother Yemoja, who will ease your journey. May Olodumare take you home to safety and peace. Come forth."

The warmth of the woman's life floods my mind. I see her as a child, laughing when she winds her arms around the neck of her mother. Then she's older, eyes alight with a different kind of love as she holds out a bowl of rice and peppered catfish. With shining dark skin and a wide smile, the man before her is beautiful. I feel her heart lift as he takes the food and their fingers brush. Later, she's tilling a small field next to a village. Fingers sprinkling seeds into the grooves she's created in the earth, as she sings a song to Oko, the orisa of crops. Her voice is sweet and high, rising with the heat of the day. And then she's holding a baby with the same grin as hers. She presses her face into the folds of the girl's neck, inhaling the child's milky scent. I smile, feeling all the jubilation she has felt and the love that fills her soul.

When I open my eyes, the woman's essence hovers in the cradle of my fingers. I focus on the joy in her memories as I coax forth her soul, guiding it toward the sapphire of my necklace. The stone absorbs her essence, growing warm against the hollow of my throat. I hold the images of the woman's life in my mind and wonder if the village she came from still stands. If her people continue to wait for her, checking the horizon every day to see if she will return.

Tatters of her wrapper drift in the water, a faded orange that was once as bright as the midafternoon sun. I look down at the hand still in mine, with its torn pale nails and jagged scars. She will receive Yemoja's blessing before she returns to Olodumare; it is the one thing I am able to do for her.

May you be at peace, sister. Yemoja will ease your journey back home.

Releasing the woman's fingers, I turn away, not watching as her body sinks into the depths.

A daughter, a wife, a mother.

My tears join the salt of the sea.

...

Yemoja can only be summoned on the seventh day, but I swim to her island the afternoon before. A small outcropping of sand, rock, and tufts of trees, it will afford me a brief rest from the sea and all it swallows. I still like to feel the sun on my legs, on my hair, to sleep and dream sometimes.

A flick of a caudal fin stops me as I get closer to the island. I pause, the sapphire in my necklace glowing gently to let me know that another of my kind is close.

"Simidele." The voice is like a vine, snaking through the water and teasing out the hint of a smile from me.

I turn, sweeping my arms through the water in arcs, taking in the deep purple scales and round face of Folasade. Remade by Yemoja when the first people were stolen early this year, Folasade is small, but her smile is large, her eyes reflecting every feeling that ripples through her.

"It is good to see you, Simidele," she says, pressing her hand

5

against her chest as the fans of our tails touch gently in the water, scales glinting. "Although your search does not usually include this part of the sea."

I mirror her welcoming gesture before cupping my jewel gently. "I know. I'm returning with a soul to be blessed."

Folasade nods, her short curls in a soft, round black halo. "Praise Yemoja for her unbounded love." She touches the matching sapphire at her throat and then cocks her head to one side, peering at me closely. "What is the matter? You look . . . not yourself."

"It's just . . ." But the words won't come and instead I find myself saying nothing, trying to keep my lips from trembling. The sapphire is cool in my grip as I look down at it, remembering the woman.

Folasade floats nearer as my hair waves in front of us. "May I?" she asks.

Nodding, I let Folasade sweep my curls away so that we can see each other's faces clearly. Her eyes are almost black in the water, but they shine with a reverence I know is missing from mine.

"I know you find this hard, Simidele." Folasade pauses, thinking carefully before speaking again. "But gathering the souls of those who pass in the sea is a way to honor them and bless their journey back to our Creator, Olodumare." She nods in encouragement, her smile beatific. "It is important to focus on this and not be distracted by other doubts."

"Yes," I say, but my eyes don't meet Folasade's and there are still echoes of grief in me.

"Where are you heading to now? It is not the seventh day, you can't summon Yemoja yet."

"I know, but I'm going to her island. To—" I stop myself, knowing what Folasade will say, what she has said to me before.

"You are going to change. To lie on the sand and mull over memories of your life before. Why must you keep doing this, Simidele? It has been three months since you have been remade."

"I like to feel . . . like myself." I try to keep the petulance out of my tone, but I know it is still there. None of the other six Mami Wata change unless they have to.

"You mean, you like to pretend you are still human," says Folasade, her mouth pursed.

I stay silent, glancing up at the watery sunlight. I'm still craving the heat of it on my skin and the way it will settle deep into my bones.

"But you are not a girl anymore." Folasade grips my shoulder, forcing my gaze to hers. "You are more than that. We are more than that. Gathering souls to bless is what we were created to do. It is easier to leave who you were behind. Rejoice in that, sister. Let the sea swallow your memories, and embrace what you are now."

I lift my chin and nod. I think of the woman again, of her memories, her family. Folasade is right.

"I only remind you of this to make it easier. The others all agree, Simidele." She holds me closer before releasing me, floating backward, melting into the darkness. "Let your past go."

Folasade's faith in Yemoja, in our task, should inspire me. I should let myself sink down, let the depths soothe me until it is time to summon Yemoja.

But I don't. I can't. I wait until I can no longer see the purple of her scales or the black of her hair, and then I look up at the sun that pierces the surface. With a push from my tail, I propel myself toward the light.

My head splits the gentle waves of the sea, revealing the island. I swim to the beach, pull myself carefully across the shallows, and lie on the sand, letting the sun dry me. Two legs split from the curve of my tail as the gold-and-dusty-pink scales elongate, growing into a wrapper that tucks around my body. Small feet complete my human form, a dark brown that matches the rest of my skin.

I blink against the bright clean of the day, thinking about the woman I found in the water. There was something about her that makes me think of wrappers spun with gold and the taste of yams, of rich voices echoing in the night.

I spread my hair over the white of the beach and close my eyes. With the sun burning my skin and my hands grasping fistfuls of sand, I let myself dream in a way I never can in the sea.

I run my fingers over the uneven walls of my home, warm from the heat of the day. The floor is freshly swept, and as I walk outside, the red sun sets the rest of the city on fire. I can see no one, but I can hear the voices that drift on the cooler breeze of the evening and I know where everyone will be.

I weave through the neat streets, feeling the contentment that comes with safety. The city is cocooned by forest, set out in concentric spirals that begin with the Aláàfin's palace and end with the great wall that encircles it all. When I reach the outer compound, I am greeted with the sight of the people. Most are seated around the smaller fires or gathered in groups, talking and laughing before the storyteller begins the tales of the day.

My age mates gather around the mahogany tree in the main meeting space. The girls with their hair in ìpàkọ́ ẹlẹ́dẹ̀ style, flicking the ends of their braids off their shiny foreheads while boys crouch around games of Ayòayò. All dazzle in wrappers of yellow, indigo, and red. Elders sit closer to the fire, most of them clutching dried papaya and fried plantain, late-night snacks offered by the Aláàfin's market that fill the air with spice. It is only as I venture farther into the crowd, closer to the seventeenth gate, that I see my mother. She's standing against the tree, backlit by the fire. Her wrapper is midnight blue with stars picked out in silver and gold, repeating patterns that sparkle in the last rays of the day. As the principal storyteller, she will tell a story about Olodumare tonight. She always wears that outfit when speaking about the Creator, telling me that the fabric reminds people of when the world was made.

She spots me weaving through the crowd and greets me with a huge smile, cheeks full over a large mouth, her brown eyes wide-set, the same as mine. "What is it, Simidele? Is there a stain?" She cranes her head, twisting to check the sides and back of her wrapper.

"No. You look beautiful, ìyá."

She walks to me, lifting both hands so that she can cradle my face. "And so do you, ọmọbìnrin ìn mi." Releasing me, my mother twirls away before throwing a look over her shoulder. "Are you staying for my performance this evening?"

I nod and she smiles again, dimples puckering the smoothness of her cheeks, a beauty mark next to the corner of her mouth. I watch as she settles down in front of the crowd, clasping her hands together and lifting her chin.

"Here is a story. Story it is . . ."

• • •

There are curls across the sky and salt in my mouth when I wake on the seventh day.

My mother.

The woman whose soul I gathered looked just like her.

Hair slides from my face as I blink into the hazy pink dawn, my mother's features stamped upon my mind. On land, the memory does not snake away from me, and I hold it close, remembering the split of her smile and the dimples that would crinkle on either cheek when she laughed.

My mother.

In front of me stretches the sea, thick with waves. I sit up, smiling into the bones of my knees, happy at remembering her, if only for a while. I wipe the sheen of sweat from my face and look out to the open water where the sky is hanging low, clouds scraping the tips of the waves. I could stand, if I wanted. But I don't. Instead, I close my eyes, hold out a hand, and trace the curve of my mother's imagined cheek, the quirk of her lips. The giddiness of remembering almost makes me forget what I am here for.

But the sea reminds me, and the surge and crash of giant swells bring me back. I take a deep breath, tuck the memory away, and hope that it stays. Hope that, when I am back in the water, I can still recall her face. Hope that the sea will not erase this, even though it always does.

CHAPTER TWO

I STAND WITH the sun on my back and the waves behind me as I face the tree line. The sapphire of my necklace sparkles as I focus my thoughts on the soul inside. And then I am moving once again, doing what is needed in order to bless the woman's essence.

Banana leaves hang down over tan trunks, their green a vivid lime against the white sand. Ignoring them, I bend down toward the low bushes with their spiky leaves and blooms of white and blue.

Yemoja's colors.

Each flower has a splash of gold at its center and a sweet honey scent that grows stronger as I touch my fingertip to a waxy petal, stroking the softness. Carefully, I select seven of the flowers, snapping off their thick stems and holding them loosely so that they are not crushed. The walk back to the sea is slow, my legs not used to the motion now required of them. We honor the people whose souls we gather by blessing them in human form, so I don't complain as I feel the pops of small bones accompany each step. I stop when I reach the hard damp sand, the breeze from the ocean stirring my curls. As I release the flowers into the shallow water, I lift my head to the sky, mouth pursed. Orisas can only be summoned with certain prayers and offerings. Unless called upon, they remain hidden from human eyes, granting blessings when they see fit, governed only by Olodumare.

"Yemoja, mo bu ọlá fún ọ pẹ̀lú àwọn òdòdó wọnyí," I call, my voice high enough to be heard over the rush of waves. "Jọ̀wọ́ bùkún ùn mi pẹ̀lú wíwáà rẹ. Fi ore-ọ̀fẹ́ fún mi pẹ̀lú ìfẹ́ tí o ní fún gbogbo àwọn ọmọọ̀ rẹ. Ẹ tẹ̀ s'íwájú."

The flowers fall into the water, each one gently floating on the tide. I stand back, digging my toes into the warm sand, and repeat my call. "Yemoja, I honor you with these blooms. Please bless me with your presence. Grace me with the love you have for all your children. Come forth."

Five more times I say this, seven in total, until the sea swells and then recedes, drawing back from the land as if scalded. Shells and seaweed and red crabs dot the bare sand as I run my gaze over unveiled black rocks. My heart races just a little bit faster, as it does every time I get ready to face Yemoja. I slow it down by taking deep breaths of humid air, savoring the feeling, one I won't have when I return to the sea. The exposed sand is marked with complicated swirls, fashioned by the tides and now seen by the sun. The waves draw out farther and farther, and I examine the slope of beach, struck by its beauty as always.

I wait as the line of now-distant water begins to grow. The jewel at my throat is heavy. I run a fingernail over the facets, re-membering the woman's unraveling hair, the memories her soul showed me. A flare of grief burns through me. *She will be blessed,* I vow, and lay the sapphire down against the heat of my skin. Push-ing back my shoulders, I match my posture and expression in signs of respect.

I hold my position as the sea reaches the height of the banana trees before it surges forward. The wave is a giant tumble of teal, indigo, and turquoise as it rushes toward the shore. A cacophony of water and rocks fills the air, blotting out the calls of birds and, for a moment, even the sun. The day momentarily darkens, and my skin itches in the heat. The sea calls to me, promising to soothe me with its coolness, and I push back the urge to run forward, to plunge myself into the wall of water. I must be ready to greet Yemoja. And just as it seems as if the wave will crash against the shore, destroying all in its path, the water pulses and then draws backward, retreating into a gentler swell that covers the bedrock, lacing the sand with white foam and strands of seaweed.

The beach glistens, its newly decorated expanse leading to the clear shallows. I scan the sudden calm line of the sea, searching, my breath catching as I spot a ripple that grows larger. The sea undulates, shifting and flexing almost like a serpent. And then I see it. The tip of a golden crown. It splits the gentle waves, followed by obsidian coils shining with water. The orisa moves closer to the shore as she emerges from the sea. Thick shoulders and onyx skin glow in the sun as she takes a step onto dry land, her dark blue scales shifting to form a white and indigo wrapper with threads of gold throughout.

"Simidele." Her voice is both rough and smooth, like satin and sand and smoke. Twin combs hold back the mass of her hair, while a veil of milky pearls obscures the middle of her face. The smells of violets and coconut fill the air. She's so close that I can see the cowrie shells and sharks' teeth that are woven in among her curls.

I place my hand on my chest before bowing deeply, my forehead nearly pressing into the hot sand. "Mother Yemoja."

When I straighten up the orisa smiles, teeth that are sharp points emerging from her generous mouth. She beckons me closer, the delicate white gold that encircles her wrists and twines up to the tops of her arms glinting.

"I am blessed to see you. It has been a while since you have summoned me," Yemoja says as she takes a step toward me, pearls clinking. She smiles, flashing curved lips. "Praise Olodumare."

I look up; the gleam of her black-and-silver gaze reaches me as I clutch my necklace. The jewel is warm in my palm, the only hint of what it contains. As the orisa reaches for the sapphire, I think of the woman's eyes, so similar to my mother's.

"Something troubles you," murmurs Yemoja, drawing her hand back. Her head tilts, hair tumbling down her shoulders, a bulbous emerald glinting from the coils.

For a moment, I can't speak. All I can think about is the woman's face and her life memories.

"This soul . . . ," I say, swallowing hard. I think of the brown of my mother's eyes, the fullness of her lower lip. "She reminded me of someone."

Yemoja drifts closer, the scent of violets growing stronger. "And this has upset you." She doesn't ask me who the woman called to mind and I don't offer. Instead, I look down at my bare feet, though I know my feelings are there to hear in the tightness of my words.

"Yes," I manage as I grasp at the memory I claimed and kept. Of my mother in her star-splashed wrapper and of her smile.

Yemoja lifts my chin with one elongated finger, tipping my gaze to hers. Her eyes soften with sympathy, the silver muted now. "I am sure you remember what I told you when you were remade just months ago, but let me remind you." The orisa's voice lowers as she opens her hands, palms to the sun. "The òyìnbó first came to our lands this year, greedy for power and resources. I watched as they began to steal people, taking them away on their giant ships. And so I left the rivers and streams of our lands and made the sea my home, following the people whose lives were fractured, taken and forced on a different type of journey . . ." Yemoja pauses here, her voice cracking in pain. She takes a moment, breathing deeply as the pearls in her veil sway lightly. "A journey that is eternally horrifying. Enslaved and stripped of their homeland— I wanted to ensure that those who lose their lives on the sea receive comfort and our prayers before they return home to join Olodumare. This I can do through the creation of Mami Wata." When she drops her gaze to me, her eyes glitter with fervor. "It is not everything, but it is something. It is our honor."

Questions grow inside my head at her words. Why do we not smash the ships to pieces? Why do we not drag down those who sail them to the black parts of the sea? Yemoja has always been plain-speaking, leaving little room for discussion, but now I open my mouth to speak. The sharpness of the orisa's glare stops me.

"Tell me, Simidele. Do you trust me and trust in the task I have given you?" Yemoja stares down at me, her dark curls swaying in the breeze.

I nod. My faith in the orisa knows no bounds, but it is always easier to surrender to her guidance in the sea when my memories ebb away, pulled by the tides. She runs a hand down my arm, lightly scraping the skin with her long nails.

"Do you understand all that I ask of you?" Her fingers dig into the soft skin under my chin again, but I don't wince or pull away, staring back at the orisa. Her pupils are large, slashes in her metallic eyes.

"Yes," I say. I realize my hands are in fists and force myself to unclench them.

"This is good," says Yemoja. She pulls me to her and presses her lips against my forehead, holding me in place with warm hands. "All that you need to do, all that you must do, is to gather any souls of those who pass in the sea, and we will say a prayer to bless them on their journey back to Olodumare. This is your purpose. Nothing more, nothing less." The orisa pulls away and looks down at me. "I need to know that you understand this, Simidele. It is important."

"Nothing more, nothing less," I repeat, nodding my head and dipping my gaze in respect.

"Good," Yemoja says, her silver-and-black eyes still on me. "Now, let the water set your memories afloat. Let it set you free from the pain of the past, of what once was. Focus on your task." The pearls of her veil clink together as she squeezes me tighter, so tight that my chest is crushed and for a moment, I can't breathe.

Blackness blooms at the edge of my vision and silver stars, the same shade as Yemoja's eyes, sprinkle across the creeping dark. I know she is right.

"Of course." Using the last of my voice, I muster a scraped whisper. "To bless their souls is an honor."

The pressure disappears as the orisa releases me. My lungs fill once again. I look up to the curve of Yemoja's mouth as she smiles down at me, to the sharp points of her teeth. "True words indeed, Simidele. Come now, let us say a prayer to release this soul together."

Yemoja stands before me, the white and indigo folds of her wrapper luminous in the sun. She holds out her large palms, beckoning me closer. I take a step forward and then another, until the orisa towers over me. She hooks a nail under the chain of my necklace so that the sapphire is held between us. It spins lazily in the sun, sparkles scattering on my skin. The orisa presses her fingers to the gem and I do the same. Together we cradle the jewel, its blue brighter than the sky above us.

At the thought of the soul being blessed, I feel a calm spread through me. Better this, I think. Better an easing of her journey. Yemoja smiles and I join her.

"Are you ready?" she asks.

"Yes, Mother Yemoja."

"Then let us begin." The orisa angles her face to the heavens, her rich voice strong. "Arábìnrin a gbà ẹ́. Àláfíà ni tìrẹ báàyí."

"We welcome you, sister. Peace is yours now," I repeat, thinking of the woman's faded orange wrapper.

"Olodumare ń pè, pẹ̀lú àdúrà yìí, á ṣe ìrìn-àjò rẹ padà sí ilé ní ìrọ̀rùn, adẹ́dàá rẹ, ìbẹ̀rẹ̀ àti òpin ìn rẹ."

"Olodumare is calling, and with this prayer, we ease your journey back home, to your maker, your beginning and your end." I think of her kissing her child.

"A bùkún fún ọ arábìnrin."

"We bless you, sister," I murmur over and over again, until the sapphire releases the soul inside, a gleam of light gold, a shimmer of essence that hovers in the air above us.

"May Olodumare bless you," we finish, as the soul spirals away from us and a sense of calm envelops the island.

With our words, the woman is sent on her way home to Olodumare, the Supreme Creator.

• • •

The jewel feels colder at my throat as Yemoja turns to me. Her smile is sharp beneath her veil, but her voice is soft. She strokes the sapphire of my necklace once and then bends down to embrace me.

"May Olodumare bless your search, Simidele."

Before I can answer, the orisa steps into the sea in a flash of gold and pearls and brown arms that slice the surface. All that is left is the scent of violets and coconut, a sweetness that permeates the air as my gaze roams over the water. The trails of Yemoja's curls, spread out across the waves, are the last thing I see as she sinks back into the depths.

I stand on the warm sand as the sun slides across the sky, crowning my hair with light. Breathing out, I thank Olodumare. Blessing the woman's soul has gone some way to calm me, but as I contemplate the sea before me, I linger once more over the memory the woman invoked.

Stars on a midnight-blue wrapper and eyes alight with love. Full cheeks and a voice that spins words like silk.

My mother.

I step toward the sea, holding her face in my mind. As the water washes over my feet and the scales begin to form, I feel the seeping of details. Pale gold and pink fabric turns to scales and I can no longer recall the color of her wrapper. The sea reaches my thighs, stealing my skin and legs as well as the wideness of my mother's smile. As I dip under the waves, the sound of her voice fades and I embrace the coolness, a balm to my sun-soaked skin.

The sea takes me and I let it, but this time I don't allow it to have everything. The brown of my mother's eyes stays with me. I take it and tuck it away, bury it in the back of my mind and hope that, if I want to, if I need to, I can return to it. And with it, I join the salty currents and the creatures I now belong with.

CHAPTER THREE

THERE IS NO sleep for me in the sea and so, when I break the surface to search for ships, the sun and moon are my constant companions. Sometimes, I swim downward, taking comfort from the deep. From its darkness and the viperfish that often dart out of sight.

Occasionally I think I see flashes of a star-scattered wrapper, remember the smooth flow of words that spin images in minds. But it is never for long. Instead my thoughts stay simple, merging with the sea and the creatures in it. It is easier to swim between the shifting blues, to skirt the dolphins that nudge me, calling me to play before I head back to the sky and the air to search.

On the last day before Yemoja's seventh, I rise from the depths to discover that the sea and the sky have decided to conspire with each other. Clouds press low against slate-gray waves that rise and fall in growing peaks, and the air has a thickness to it, a fresh musk that I can almost taste. I want to dive back down, to ignore the growing storm and the havoc it will bring, but it is then that I spot the sail. A flash of white in the meager light.

A ship.

I bob for a moment, letting myself be carried high by a wave.

Even from far away I can see that the vessel is larger than the one I found before. Its mainsail snaps in the wind as it rocks from side to side.

I swallow as my heart lurches with the sea.

The wind picks up, throwing thin needles of rain that sting my skin. I wait, the heavy wetness of my hair cloaking my shoulders.

Yemoja's words echo in my mind. Honor. It is our honor.

I swim toward the ship, fighting against the strong currents, choosing to slip just under the waves where the rain shatters the surface but doesn't pepper my skin. Sharks glide beneath me, twisting and turning, but I don't pay them any attention, nor they me. I am not what they want.

When I emerge, the wind is sharper, rising with peaked waves that grow to the size of small mountains. The vessel is ahead of me, the curve of its dark hull scoring the surface as it cuts through the water. Faint shouts carry on the wind and I make sure I stay close to the ship, just enough to watch but not to be seen.

And wait.

The day pulls out, clouds and waves whipped together so that it is hard to tell where the sky ends and the sea begins. I keep my position, watching as the waves, shot through with white foam, batter the ship relentlessly, wondering if the mass of shifting water will sink the vessel. Shuddering, I imagine shards of masts and sails and limbs and blood in the sea.

A sudden pull of water draws me closer as a cry rips through the air. Thunder rumbles, followed by lightning that fractures the sky, ripping through the clouds to strike just left of the vessel. The wind brings more shouts as I am caught by another current. I fight it, pulling away from the tug of the deep, staying on the surface, eyes on the ship. There are movements on board, but

I am still too far away to see properly. I hesitate, wanting to be closer, wanting to see. But I know it's too risky so I swim down, just beneath the waves, in reach of the hull.

As muffled shouts filter through the top of the sea, I glide underneath the wooden bottom of the ship. Peppered with barnacles and algae, its length spans only a fraction of the whales I am used to. I plan to surface on the other side of the vessel, but pause when the darkness shifts. The clouds must have parted momentarily, because a large shaft of light splits the water. I start toward it just as the depths are filled with a great crash, bubbles rising and bursting. As the small pockets of air dissipate, I see it.

A body.

Dark brown skin gleaming as it cleaves the layers of the sea.

A boy, a man . . . no, somewhere in between.

I reach out at the same time as he shoots through the water, the ship already speeding on, jettisoned cargo far beneath the waves. Black chains hang from bloodied skin, dragging him down as bubbles continue to pop and rise. I swim up as he sinks, my gaze locked on the pale soles of his feet and then the spread of his fingers. There is pain in every line of his body and I feel it in my heart. I push it aside and focus on him, on honoring his life.

Gently, I cradle a foot, pulling him to me. The chains knock against my side as I curl my arms around the muscles of his stomach. His skin is hot in the cool of the water, and the sea turns pink from his blood.

So much blood.

My heart thuds as our chests press together. His skin matches mine in heat and I know that life must have only just left him. I place my lips next to the shell of his ear, the coils of my black hair brushing against our skin. His body speaks of the sun and of giant mahogany trees, their flesh a delicate brown beneath the bark. I turn him to face me, my fingers slipping down his ribs as I open my mouth to speak Yemoja's words. But before I can begin, his eyes open, black pupils swallowing the white.

In shock, I shove the boy away from me. He floats backward and into the dark of the sea, clawing at the water.

I was not expecting to find someone alive. I have never found someone alive.

The boy looks at me, his eyes large.

Wide-set brown eyes.

The shade speaks to me. A rich color that reminds me of something . . . of someone. The water surges around me, plucking at the memories, but for once, I yank back.

A midnight-blue wrapper. Stars picked out in rich fabric. The memory is still there. I tease at it as the sea embraces us. A voice as smooth as silk.

Here is a story. Story it is.

The same brown eyes flecked with dark amber and the dot of a beauty mark, too, this one just above a left eyebrow rather than close to lips.

My mother.

Tears escape, instantly joining the sea as a shark glides closer. Instinctively, I reach for the boy's wrists and pull him back to me. Eyes that were open begin to flicker as the last of the air flows from his mouth. He will die if I don't do something. Panic ripples through me and I tighten my grip on him. With a push, I propel us toward the sun that is glittering through the water, wavy with ripples.

A wide smile. Full of joy, of love. I hold on to the recollection, letting it fill me as I swim harder and faster.

As we break the surface, I'm still holding him, cradling his head against my chest. The water is choppy and we bob together as he sucks in a deep breath.

He's alive.

The air is still thick with the weight and sting of thunder, but the clouds are scudding toward the thin red line of the horizon. The boy's skin is chilled now, his chest hitching intermittently. I look down at the tight curls on his head as his hands hold my waist loosely.

He's alive.

It's all I can think as I lift my face to the sky. Praise Yemoja.

The sea grows colder as I swim through the waves, my arms full of the heavy weight of the boy. He's still breathing but not for long, not if I can't get him out of the water. *Think,* I tell myself as I look down again at his thick black hair.

And then I see the fin that slits the waves.

The shark dips back down, but I have already seen it. And now that I study the rain-slashed water, I can see more, at least three.

No, I tell them. *Go.*

One peels away but the other two remain. I swim faster and pull the boy closer. His blood seeps onto my desperate hands as a dark shape cuts through the ocean toward us. I clutch the boy's warm body to my chest, trying to look under the waves.

The sharks are not listening.

CHAPTER FOUR

I SWIM AWAY from dark fins and seething water. The rain is no longer pummeling the surface, but the boy in my arms is cold now, his warmth stolen by the sea. We ride the tall heights of waves, and I do my best to keep his head above the swells.

If I don't get him somewhere safe, he will die. I think of the only land nearby, Yemoja's island, just as the blade of a fin cuts through the water. Another does the same and I force myself to take a moment, to think. Holding the boy as high as I can with one arm, I dip my face under the sea and peer down into the depths. I make out the blue-gray backs of two sharks as they circle below. *No,* I tell them. *Leave. Not this one.* I watch as one of the creatures heeds my warning and sinks farther, but the other, the largest, remains.

Pulling the boy's arms up and over my shoulders, I swim faster, dragging him, barely breathing now, through the water. I can make it, I think, as I see the rocks of Yemoja's cove. The water churns and the boy cries out, but I dare not stop to look. I push all my will into my next command.

Go. Now! I don't wait to see if my order has worked. I fix my gaze on the slice of sand just beyond the rocks. Knifing through the calm waters of the cove, it is only as I drag him closer to the shore that I really think about what I have done. I take in a ragged breath and blink.

I've taken the boy from the sea.

Saved him.

My stomach twists as I think back to what Yemoja told me just days ago. *All that you need to do, all that you must do, is to gather any souls of those who pass in the sea, and we will say a prayer to ease them on their inevitable journey back to Olodumare. This is your purpose. Nothing more, nothing less.*

I was supposed to glean the boy's soul, not his body. This was impressed upon me and I agreed. But he was alive. Should I have waited until he passed? Swum in the trails of his blood while his lungs filled with water? I shake my head, a thought, no, a memory, surfacing in my mind.

Pain as angry as red fire and bands of iron around my ribs. The tightness of my chest made worse as the water presses down on me and I sink, hands clawing at the dark shades of blue even though I am glad to be in the sea, away from the òyìnbó. A snatched look above. The ship, its hull black and large, skimming along the surface, leaving me behind. The feeling of peace at this as my vision flickers even while my chest spasms, my eyes widen, and my legs kick against the blackness of the depths.

A remembered burst of death that winds its way around and through me. With the boy's limp body cradled in my arms, I think of his brown eyes, the shade vivid, even that deep in the sea, and I know that I couldn't watch him die. Surely Yemoja wouldn't expect that of me. Of any Mami Wata.

I swim toward the land, eager to get him to the shore and safety. But as I pull him through the shallows, his long body scraping on the banks of sand skimming just beneath the clear water, I wonder what to do with him now.

The boy has lost consciousness during the journey, limbs and mouth slack, lashes black spikes against his skin. A dark blue wrapper is tied at his waist, covering his thighs. I drape him over the white sand as water laps at his feet and lean down to examine his face. With full lips and sharp cheekbones, his features resemble a regal terra-cotta sculpture. I reach for him and then stop myself from brushing the sand from his short coils when I realize his chest is still.

Quickly, I heave him onto his side so salty water dribbles from his mouth. My relief at the gasp he takes disappears when I look down at his back. Strips of skin peel away to reveal the fatty white of muscle. I freeze. Bile burns my throat as I swallow it back down, unable to turn away. I can see now why the sharks were so keen. It is far worse than the wound above his eye, which still oozes blood. Anger pulses as I contemplate the wreck of his back, seeing the wounds for the lash marks that they are, knowing what was inflicted upon him. My fingers hover over the damaged skin as the boy coughs. I want to tell him to be careful of his wounds, but before I can, he turns and fixes his gaze on me.

His brown eyes remind me again of my mother, of metallic stars on an indigo wrapper, and I slither from the last of the shallows without thinking, the sun pouring onto my tail. As the golden-pink scales turn to brown skin and a wrapper, smooth against the sand, I watch the boy stare as legs, knees, and feet form. It's too late to push myself back into the sea. His eyes widen as he takes in the length of my body, the wrapper that has formed and is tucked tightly around me, the tangle of my hair. Yemoja warned against revealing ourselves to humankind, but is this not different? He hasn't hunted or discovered me. I don't think he could harm me even if he wanted to. Besides, I think as the boy continues to stare, he's already seen me as Mami Wata.

I haven't been this close to someone since I was remade, and I can't stop myself from moving nearer, taking in the small knots in his hair, the dry gray skin around his elbows. He is weak, I can tell from the way he holds himself, one shoulder crooked. The boy watches me as I look down at his feet, so much larger than mine, and then back up at his face. The cut above his eye is open and raw. I reach out a hand, not even sure why. He pulls back, raising his fists, knuckles already scraped and swollen, the links of the iron manacles clanking as he straightens, leftover violence in his stare. Flinching, I step backward, my own fingers curling. We're both breathing hard, eyeing each other warily. I think of the pain he's feeling, what was done to him on the ship and before. Blinking back tears, I want to tell him that I understand, that I wouldn't hurt him, but I don't. I move away to give him space, and the boy lowers his hands, shoulders slumping from the effort.

"What are you?" His words are ragged, slipping out from between crusted lips, white from the salt of the sea.

He speaks Yoruba, I think. Mami Wata, Yemoja incarnate, mermaid, I want to say. But instead I answer, "My name is Simidele. Please, rest."

He crawls into the shade of a large banana tree, as far from me as he can, before he loses consciousness once again.

• • •

Walking back up the strip of beach, I am still shaky, the joints of my legs and ankles popping as they adjust to the slide of the ground. I stagger, almost falling, unused to taking more than a few steps. The sand, white-hot with the heat of the day, burns my toes, slipping between them to scald the rest of my feet.

I reach the shallow waves and dip between the sea's folds, letting my tail form, relishing the weightlessness that the water affords me. I look back at the shore, at the dark slump of the boy's body. I'm not sure how long he will sleep or if he will even wake up. Yemoja will only appear when summoned, but still an uneasiness threads through me.

I've never found someone alive before.

Perhaps I should have left him in the sea. And then I think about his torn body, and my resolve hardens a little more. There has been too much dying. More souls in the last few weeks. His life is a gift, I tell myself, but what I should do next, I don't know.

The sea carries me, the currents strong, pulling at my body. I let it. I could swim now and keep swimming until the island is a speck on the horizon. He's alive. I could leave him there and have no more to do with it.

As I dive down in the clear water of the cove, I let myself remember the brown of the boy's eyes, the beauty mark just above his eyebrow. He will die if left on his own, and then my saving him will have been for nothing. But what else can I do? I graze a coral reef, my sudden flare of anger and frustration matching its redness. I think of the boy's flayed back, his wide eyes and ruined skin. I could take him to the mainland, but it's too far. He wouldn't survive the tides and the cold for long. If I hid him on the island until he was strong enough to travel, I'd have to make sure none of the other Mami Wata would see him if they summoned Yemoja tomorrow.

I sigh into the water. Despite my growing misgivings, I know that I can't abandon him.

Somersaulting in the sea, I turn back to the island, the decision made. I'll help him heal and then take him to the mainland. He will need water and food, and I'll be careful to make sure he's not seen. I call to the fish that swim foolishly near me, darting out to grab a few from a school of sardinella. Dragging myself from the shallows, I clean and gut them with a sharpened rock before setting their carcasses near the boy so that he will have food when he wakes. The rock, I keep, its serrated edge giving me comfort.

I watch the boy as he sleeps, weaving a basket from leaves, leaving him only to collect some water from a small pool just inside the tree line. His skin is a reddish dark brown that almost glows. With broad shoulders and long legs, the boy looks to be roughly my age, no more than seventeen or eighteen years. I examine his large hands, and when my gaze reaches his wrists, I swallow hard. The black chains are thick links that encircle weeping skin. He must be in pain. I can't get the manacles off, but I can help with the welts.

Leaving the bowl of water and the fish wrapped in a banana leaf, I head just beyond the tree line. The wild lettuce is where I remember it, longish green leaves and some purple flowers. I pick all I can carry and head back to the beach. The boy's chest is still rising and falling as he sleeps. Legs drawn up and curled protectively, he still looks big.

Carefully, I crush the leaves and creep forward, gently folding the lettuce under the iron bands. There is just enough room and as I tuck the last shred under the manacle, the boy jerks awake, moving faster than he should be able to. Before I can move away, he grabs my wrist with his other hand, grinding the bones together in a tight grip. I cry out and try to yank myself backward, but he hauls me against him, the smell of dried salt and sweat and blood thick between us. I look for the sharpened rock, but it's next to the basket I was weaving, too far away, and I feel a panicked kick in my chest. I open my mouth to speak and his eyes fasten on me, gaining focus.

"What are you doing?" he hisses, eyes hard as he looks around him. "Where am I?"

I lift up the leaves, showing him, but it's only as he examines his other wrist, packed tight with the crushed plant, that he lets me go. I stumble backward, unable to stop myself from falling in the sand, feeling foolish and embarrassed. We stare at each other, my eyes narrowed in hurt and his shaded with regret.

"I . . ." The boy rubs both hands over his head, turning to the sea. "I'm sorry," he says to the waves. His voice is scratchy, catching in the wreck of his throat. The sound that comes from someone who has screamed themselves raw.

I sit in the sand for a moment more as my heart calms, his apology sinking in. Getting to my feet again, I pick up the leaves. "It will help. With the pain and the healing."

The boy looks up at me and we let the silence stretch between us as we weigh each other up. And then he nods. I move toward him slowly, trying to ignore the uncomfortable feeling in the soles of my feet. He offers his wrist, letting me pack the last of the plant under his restraints.

"Let me see your back," I demand, using his apology as an opportunity to get him to let me treat his wounds.

The boy rotates stiffly, and I stifle another gasp when I examine his shoulder blades and the stretch of flesh down his spine. There are three deep gouges. I frown, my anger blazing again, before applying the rest of the crushed plant to the wounds. He doesn't move or make a sound, but I can see the side of his clenched jaw. When I am finished, he doesn't say thank you and I can't help but grit my teeth.

He's in pain, I tell myself. *Be patient.* I push the basket of water and wrapped fish toward the boy. He slides his gaze from the sea, snatching a look at me.

"It's for you," I say simply, nudging the food and holding the water out to him.

He accepts the basket, not taking his eyes from me as he drinks greedily, water spilling down his chin. When he unwraps the fish, he fumbles, nearly dropping it in the sand. Catching it in his large hands, he eats carefully and slowly, chewing each mouthful properly. When he is done, leaving only the fish head, he picks the flesh from his teeth, wiping at his mouth.

"It was you who took me from the water, wasn't it?" A gleam of curiosity illuminates his eyes as he shifts positions. "Where is your tail . . . ?" I say nothing as he casts his gaze over the shine of my wrapper, down to my knees. "Into skin and legs?"

I consider not answering, but I know he saw me change earlier. "Yes." As the word leaves my mouth, I think again about what Yemoja would say about showing myself to a human. Another rush of guilt floods through me.

He opens his mouth to ask more questions and then stops. We watch each other, this boy and I, both fresh from the sea. His shoulders are still hunched, a frown rippling over his face, but he relaxes enough to take another sip of water. When he pokes at the leaves wrapped around his wrist and looks up at me, his face is alight with surprise. "It feels better already."

"Don't touch it," I say, turning away from him. He still hasn't said thank you. Did he believe I was that monstrous? And then I think about how he saw me, a shadow in the sea among the sharks, dragging him through the waves, and I turn back to him.

"There's more," I say, holding up another sardinella. The quicker he heals, the sooner I can get him off the island.

The boy nods, his eyes moving over the vacant beach. I lift another fish from beside me, tearing it apart with my fingers, pulling its innards free. The food looks good, but I won't keep any for myself. He needs it more than me. And if he can heal faster, perhaps I can take him to the mainland in the evening.

"We should clean your wounds properly."

The boy shakes his head and waits as I gut the fish with the sharp rock. I lean forward to hand it to him, but when he edges away, I wrap it in another leaf and place it in the sand. It is only after I retreat that the boy grabs the sardinella, cramming the white shreds of flesh into his mouth.

"You don't want me to be near you," I say, twisting my damp hair around my fingers, stretching out the ringlets, keeping the rock close by.

"I could say the same about you," he says, and then stops, picking at the bones of the fish. The food seems to have given him the courage to speak as well as much-needed strength. "It's not that, though."

But it is that, I think, turning to scan the horizon, trying to ignore the way it makes me feel. As if I am something to be feared. Is he not, too? With his fists and the anger I can still sense in him? I rub at my wrist, small bruises circling it.

"Where are we?" This time the boy stays conscious enough for my answer. "How far from the Oyo Kingdom?"

"This is a . . . small island. We're just over a day from the mainland."

"Why were you there? In the sea . . ." The boy coughs, voice still rough.

I turn back to look at him, seeing that his face is smoother now, the anxiety still there but not as fresh. He grimaces and shifts in the sand, his lips tilted up on one side with discomfort.

"I was there to help." I lay my hair on one shoulder and comb through the tangled ends with my fingers.

"Help?"

I pause, twists of black curls in my hands, thinking of what to say. But he has already seen so much, and so I don't see much harm in saying some truths. "To bless the journey of those who pass in the sea."

"To collect the dead?"

A mango-orange wrapper, bruised brown skin and hair loosened from braids. "If you wish to describe it that way."

"Yemoja," he whispers through cracked lips, eyes on me.

"What did you say?" I ask, my voice rising in surprise. "What do you know of Yemoja?"

"I know she is mother of all orisas." He is sitting up now, fingers wet from the fish, sprinkled with sand. I am struck by the stark planes of his face, the edges of his cheekbones, and the curiosity in his gaze. "I know that she is protective and . . . fierce." The boy is studying me again, eyes brighter now but with a calculating gleam. "I've heard stories of Mami Wata. Did Yemoja make you into this?" He straightens his back but still keeps his distance. "Who were you . . . before?"

His words feed my annoyance, and as my fingers catch on a knot in my hair, I tut angrily. Why must he ask so many questions? I focus on undoing the tangle and do not meet his eyes. I don't tell him that I can't quite remember, that part of assuming this form is the dissolving of who and what I was before. That more of my memories come back when I have legs instead of a tail, and that that is why, unlike the other Mami Wata, I change even when I don't need to. Because I want to remember who I was.

"That doesn't matter," I answer, deciding to keep it simple. "What does is helping souls return to Olodumare."

"Then I'm thankful that you found me," says the boy in the last light of the day, leaning forward. "I don't need returning just yet, but I do need something else." He lifts his hand and I shift away, thinking of his hard grip before. Seeing my movement, the boy stops, catching sight of the sliver of my frown, and then composes himself, drawing backward. "What I mean is, will you help me?"

"I have already." I stop for a moment, thinking of the shock of his eyes opening, of finding him alive in the water and dragging him here to Yemoja's island.

The boy inches closer once again, the manacles on his wrists rattling. While he still takes care to keep his distance, his eyes are lit with a yearning that can only mean he wants something more.

"Simidele, please. I need to get home." It is the first time he has used my name, the first time a human has said it in months. The sound of it cracks open an ache inside me and I find myself wanting to hear him say it again. "Take me to Yemoja." His voice snakes around me like smoke, a thread of fear and longing twisted through it.

My eyes widen in shock, my spine straightening. "Why?" I'm trying to keep him *away* from Yemoja, not bring him to her.

"She is a powerful orisa?"

"Yes," I answer uneasily, sliding a glance at the calm bay, half expecting the waters to part, ebony skin and a gold crown splitting the surface.

"Then she will surely take pity on me and help me get home," he says, voice low and eyes glittering in the bright sun. "I'm begging you. Please." The boy blinks and a solitary tear courses down the slope of his cheek before he wipes it away roughly. "I need to get back to my family. If I don't, you may as well have left me in the sea to die."

CHAPTER FIVE

I'VE ALREADY SAVED him and now he asks more of me? I stand up, stumbling, my chest tight at the thought of helping this boy summon Yemoja. I dig my toes into the sand. *You don't know how Yemoja will react,* I tell myself, even though uncertainty weaves through me. *Perhaps she will be proud of you for saving a life.* And then I remember the way the orisa embraced me when we spoke of my task, the strict crush of her arms and my lack of breath as she squeezed me tighter. It would be better to take my chances in hiding him on the island until he's ready to leave. The boy shifts nearer to me, the closest he's ever been, need traced in the lines of his upraised eyebrows.

"What's your name?" I ask, looking down at him. The echoes of his desperate words lodge themselves further under my skin, fighting with my panic.

The boy frowns, mouth in an unsettled line. "Adekola. Kola."

"Kola," I say, rolling his name in my mouth as I look out to the darkening sea. I ache for its cold waves and their simple depths rather than the thought of metallic eyes and the stern curve of the orisa's mouth. "I can't help you summon Yemoja. But when you've healed a bit more, I will take you to the mainland."

"No." Kola raises his wrists, wincing as the skin draws tight over his back. "That isn't good enough. It'll take too much time. I need to be there soon, I—" He hisses, mouth quivering, and then shakes his head. Curling his fingers into fists, he slams them down onto the ground.

I manage not to flinch, but I make sure that I'm not within Kola's reach. With his chest heaving and knuckles buried in the sand, I study the boy who seemed so helpless only a short while ago. His pain wraps around him in the set of his shoulders and the angle of his head.

"What happened to you?" I ask quietly. "Why do you need to get home so quickly?"

Kola is silent for a moment and then he exhales, rubbing a large palm over his hair, sliding it over his face. "I was taken and . . . traded. Put on the òyìnbó's ship a few weeks ago. That's the ship I was thrown from when you found me."

His words loosen something within me. A memory of shouts and ropes and pale faces. I reach for it, but it snakes out of my grasp and all I'm left with is a stomach twisted up in knots.

I turn back to Kola and see the same shade of suffering on his face as he yanks his wrists apart, straining against the chains. I want to tell him to stop, that he'll make the wounds worse, but I don't speak.

"If I don't get home soon . . . worse could happen." His words are tightly spun with an ache that mirrors the one buried inside me.

Kola closes his mouth on the last words, jaw clenched, but I see his lips trembling, can feel the anxiousness that rolls from him in almost perceptible waves. There is more, I think, but I don't push him to tell me. It wouldn't change the way he feels, the risk he is willing to take.

I try to think of what Yemoja will say, what she will do if I bring him to her. Will she punish me? Or him? I imagine trying to keep him hidden and Yemoja finding out anyway. Surely she will know if anyone apart from Mami Wata is on her sacred land. It feels as though either way, the orisa will find out that Kola is there, what I have done.

I touch the sapphire at my throat, thinking of the woman who sank beneath the waves and the glimpses of her life. I was able to bless her soul, but that was all. With Kola, I have a chance to do more.

"It is a risk for us both." I take a deep breath and release it, letting the words stream past my lips before I can think about it any more. "But I'll help you summon Yemoja."

Kola raises his gaze, the last of the sun's rays illuminating the spark of joy in his eyes. "Now?"

I shake my head, glancing at the sea. "We need to wait for tomorrow." At least I'll have more time to think of what I'll say to Yemoja. Kola gets up in awkward jerks, eyes hooded.

"Why?" he asks, tone sullen and spiked with anger.

I purse my lips, sucking my teeth at his question. Not only has he still not been very thankful, but he also doesn't seem to have any patience. I wonder how he will speak to Yemoja and feel another jolt of doubt at what I've promised. "We must wait for the seventh day or she won't come."

Kola plucks a pebble from the beach and throws it, even though the movement will cause him pain. "I can't afford to wait!" he says.

"You have been away from your home for weeks," I state firmly, annoyance increasing the volume of my words. "One night won't make a difference."

"It will!" Kola's chest heaves as he tries to calm himself. "It will," he tries again, quieter this time.

I turn away, kicking at the sand. Kola's tone is similar to that of a spoiled child, and his demands are wearing down what little patience I have left. When I walk stiffly over, the boy allows me to get close enough to see the grooves of his frown.

"Tomorrow is the orisa's day, the only one she can be summoned on," I say, vexation sharpening my words. "One night. I don't control it. It's that or nothing."

Kola doesn't reply, but I notice the flare of his nostrils, the chunk of his fists. I step away from his anger, nursing my own, leaving an expanse of sand and cool air between us. The boy finally nods before stalking over to the rocks that rise, splintered and charcoal gray. He climbs the dark mass, perching above the beach as the waves crash against the shore.

Kola's frustration is palpable, but I still flinch when he brings his bound fists down on a rock again and again, smashing the black iron of the manacles against the sharpness of the stone. It must hurt him. But he doesn't stop, letting his anger spur him on, swinging his hands down one last time before he holds the broken irons up. Kola's outline and the manacles are silhouetted against the moon behind him, and then he casts them into the sea with a strangled shout of rage.

Afterward, his shoulders slump, slack from the exertion. I don't hold his anger against him. The manacles are a reminder of what he has gone through, and I'm glad to see them cast into the sea. The blackest part of the night sky presses against us when the boy returns to the beach. He sprawls in the sand next to me, chest still heaving, staring at the dark sea.

"So . . . tomorrow?" he asks, and I take his words, his softened tone, as an act of appeasement.

"Yes."

Kola does not speak for a moment, and we listen to the sound of the waves crashing against the rocks. "I didn't think I would ever meet any Mami Wata." He swivels to look at me, face full of shadows.

I don't say anything for a moment, tugging a curl. "Get some rest. It will help you to heal."

Kola watches me for a moment more before he moves away, doubling the space between us, making a pillow from the crook of his arm and a bed of the sand. It is not long before the hunch of his shoulders relaxes. I watch him breathe and remember the hitch of his chest when I pressed my palm against it, the warmth of blood pumping beneath skin. Then I settle in the cooling sand, trying to stop my eyes from closing until I can't anymore.

The ship creaks around me, waves rocking a violent and unnatural cradle. It is dark and the stench matches the grief and terror thick in the fetid air. A burning-hot fear has worked its way inside every part of me. I can't tell where it begins and I end. I open my mouth to scream, lips pulled back, hands in claws, and—

"Simidele. Simi! Wake up."

I force my eyes open to a black sky sprinkled with stars. Kola is leaning over me, his hand shaking my arm. I sit up, hands checking my legs, curling my knees up so that I can wrap my arms around them.

"I'm fine."

"You were screaming," Kola says as I shrug him off.

The memories that come back to me are not always the type I want. Some I will gladly let the sea take. We sit in the velvet darkness, listening to the waves crash against the shore. I remain silent, letting the night breeze wash over me, breathing deeply, clasping my hands around my knees so that I can't feel my hands shake. Kola does not touch me again, but I can still feel the press of his fingers on my skin.

"What is it?" He is close enough that I can hear the catch in his voice.

"You were on a ship," I say, raking my fingers through the sand. "You know."

CHAPTER SIX

KOLA DOZES AS the sun rises in shades of peach and carmine, transforming the sea from a deep violet to a steel blue. I didn't fall back to sleep. I couldn't. Instead, I used the chill of the night to stay awake and focused on the crash of the waves until the shredded recollections faded.

Next to me, Kola stirs. He sits up and then winces, looking down at his wrists. The poultice has dried and only clings to his skin in flakes.

"I'll get you some more," I say, pushing myself up before he can protest. "Wait here."

When I return Kola watches me warily. I slow my steps, holding out the dark green leaves almost like an offering, wondering if he'll let me apply them.

"Shall I . . . ?"

He watches me as I stop in front of him, kneeling down so that we are eye to eye. I lift my hands and then stop, waiting. Kola looks down at the wild lettuce in my grip and then back at me. I try a small smile and slowly reach for his wrists. When he doesn't pull away, I let out a breath.

"How did you know what to use?"

I pause. I can't remember, and it weighs me down with a crushing force that makes me feel suddenly exhausted. But none of this has anything to do with Kola, so I shrug and continue to squeeze the leaves until they are soft and malleable before I wrap them in strips around the open sores on his skin.

"Thank you." Kola's words are quiet but firm and lodge inside me. "I'm sorry again. For . . . grabbing you. For—"

"You nearly drowned." I cut him off and begin to apply the wild lettuce to his skin. But his apology shifts something inside me as I do my best to be gentle. When both wrists are done, I layer the leaves on the wounds on his back, which are struggling to knit together, before I sit in the sand, still apart from him.

"Simidele, will we be able to summon Yemoja now?"

My eyes widen. I remind myself that there's no other option, but the thought of what the orisa may say or do creates knots of apprehension that twist and tangle in my stomach.

"She may not grant you what you want," I warn, fingers in my hair, plaiting loose strands within my reach. My voice wavers slightly. "I've never brought more than souls for her."

Kola turns to look at me and again I am struck by his eyes, brown but shot through with ocher. His face is open but watchful, and even though his height means that he towers over me, the sparse hair on his chin and his smooth cheeks give his age away.

"Will you be in trouble?"

The care in Kola's tone unsettles me. A reminder of his almost-tenderness when he woke me from my nightmare. His fingertips against my skin. It doesn't matter, I want to say. It's too late now.

Turning my back on the sea, I point to where the trees crowd against the beach, bushes with flowers dripping onto the shore.

"You'll need to pick seven of those. Take only Yemoja's colors, the white and blue ones."

Nodding, Kola heads in the direction I point in. He takes his time choosing the flowers, and when he's satisfied with his selection, he turns back, cradling them in the cage of his hands. I like the way he holds them, delicately so as not to crush any of the blooms.

"You must offer them to the sea," I say, fingers twisted as I think of how Yemoja will react when she sees this boy I have brought to her.

Kola steps into the shallows, walking in up to his knees before he lets the flowers fall, one by one. They float on the clear water, cresting each small wave, before sinking.

"Use this prayer," I call, trying to keep my voice calm. "You need to say it seven times. Yemoja, mo bu ọlá fún ọ pẹlú àwọn òdòdó wọnyí. Jọwọ bùkún ùn mi pẹlú wíwáà rẹ. Fi ore-ọfẹ fún mi pẹlú ìfẹ tí o ní fún gbogbo àwọn ọmọọ rẹ. Ẹ tẹ s'íwájú."

He nods and repeats what I've said. "Yemoja, I honor you with these blooms. Please bless me with your presence. Grace me with the love you have for all your children. Come forth."

Kola plants his legs firmly in the seabed, water lapping at the bottom of his wrapper, as his words ring out across the sea. Six more times he repeats the incantation, his tone unwavering. There is courage, I think, in standing in the water summoning a goddess of the sea.

When the cove remains calm, a semicircle of blue, Kola wades back to the beach to stand by my side. "Did I speak the words in the right way?" he asks.

And then the waves draw back, a sudden recession that startles a flock of birds from the tops of the trees, sending them soaring into the air, their caws loud in the stillness. The shallows retreat into the bay, the wind pushing the twists of my hair across my face. I wait, coils obscuring my view of the beach until the breeze cuts off, leaving a silence that is thick with expectation. I force myself to stand straight, to stop my legs from shaking, but my heart still pounds, a roaring pulse in my ears.

Kola stares ahead of him, the only hint of his fear showing in the defensive set of his shoulders, as a wave that gains height and momentum swells at the mouth of the cove. The waters rush back in and the boy flinches. We watch together as the wave smashes against the shore with a power that I feel in my bones.

"Stay calm," I whisper shakily as Kola takes a small step back, though I find myself wanting to do the same.

A figure emerges from the sea. Yemoja pauses, her hair a black cloak around her shoulders, coils glistening underneath her crown, sharp and gold and shining in the sun. She steps onto the beach, her wrapper forming in perfect white and indigo folds, each sinuous movement bringing her closer to us.

"Do as I do," I whisper as I bend my knees, lowering my gaze and all but pressing my forehead into the hot sand. I try to swallow, but my mouth is dry. There is movement next to me as Kola folds his height into a bow.

"Don't speak unless Yemoja demands it or I ask you."

Dark brown toes reach the white sand in front of me as the scents of violets and coconut almost overwhelm me. I lift my gaze, skimming past muscular legs, past the bright white of the wrapper, edged in indigo and shot through with delicate gold threads, up to a thick necklace of bulbous pearls.

"Simidele?"

Just the lowness of her tone makes me not want to raise my

head to face the orisa. But I do. Her veil sways, mouth a slice of full lips, pursed into a line. I lift my gaze higher to the flash of her eyes, which sparkle in a hard shade of silver.

"What is the meaning of this, daughter?" asks Yemoja, swiveling her head to look at Kola.

Beside me, the boy stands, wiping sand from his palms on the ragged wrapper tied around his waist. He looks at me and I clear my throat, pressing my shaking fingers to my sides. At least he's not opening his mouth to make demands already.

"Mother Yemoja," I begin, keeping my tone respectful. "Adekola would like to request your help. He—"

The orisa holds a hand up, stopping me. Gold rings set with unpolished diamonds and emeralds glitter from her fingers. She tips her head to one side. "How did he come to be here, summoning me?"

"I saved him." I lick my lips, tasting salt. "I pulled him from the sea."

Yemoja snaps her head toward me, the pearls of her veil clicking loudly. "You did what?"

"I was about to gather his soul, but . . . he hadn't yet passed."

The orisa swivels to face me fully. "Did you fail to remember your task?" Her words are quiet but needle-sharp.

Shaking my head, I form my next sentence carefully, trying to keep the rising confusion that mixes with anger out of my voice. I saved a life rather than a soul. Surely saving someone is a good thing? "I didn't forget, but I couldn't let the sea and the sharks claim him. You speak of my purpose, but he was *alive*. To leave him would have meant his death."

Yemoja looks down at my legs and the shine of my wrapper. "And so you've shown yourself to him and brought him here?"

The hiss of her voice makes me wince. I look back at Kola and think of his face when he saw the flick of my tail, the scales that melted into skin. At the time I wasn't thinking, flustered by the effort of dragging him to some kind of safety. Shame and heat rise and spread across my chest and up my neck. But then I think of Kola slumped in the sand, the food he ate, and some of the guilt seeps away.

The sudden roar that the orisa releases causes me to stumble backward in the sand, losing my balance so that I fall hard. My heart slams against the wrapper tucked tightly against my chest as I cower before her. Yemoja raises her hands to the heavens, fingernails like talons as she screams again. Kola clutches his ears as the cry grows louder, piercing the air. I hear the waves smash against the rocks of the cove, and when I dare to look up at her, Yemoja stares down at me, a wall of water behind her. The blue mass shimmers, its weight held back by the orisa. For a moment, I think she will release it, battering the beach and us. I snatch a look at Kola, willing him to move closer to me. He would never survive.

"Mother Yemoja," I say, raising a hand, palm up. "Please. When he's healed, I can take him to the mainland and then no one else will need to know."

The orisa quivers, obsidian hair cascading over her shoulders in a heaving mass as she regards me. Yemoja wavers, the corded muscles in her arms tight as she holds her fists high above her head. She glares at me, lips twisted into a snarl, but in her eyes, there is a gleam of fear.

"Please." I stand and place a hand over my heart. "I thought I was doing what was right."

The orisa regards me in silence for seconds that spread

longer than I thought possible. And then she lowers her hands and behind her, the water drops, drawing back into the bay. I inhale deeply, checking that Kola is still close by. His shoulders are hunched, but his eyes are sharp and watchful. Yemoja's fingers twitch and the sea grows placid once again. Her shoulders drop as she turns away from us.

"You don't . . ." But the orisa does not finish before she staggers and then crumples to the ground.

Yemoja sits in the white sand, her wrapper spread around her like the petals of the flowers that we pick to summon her. Her face is angled toward her lap, curls a dark shroud that shield her from my gaze.

"Simidele," she says softly, looking up at me through her hair. Her veil shines, iridescent strands of pearls that are tightly drawn across her nose and cheeks. A tear slides from underneath the milky orbs. "What you have done will mean our deaths."

CHAPTER SEVEN

"WHAT DO YOU mean?" I ask Yemoja, my voice cracking.

She doesn't answer me. The curve of the orisa's spine, draped with black curls, shudders once more as she remains bent over. I move closer, but the only thing I can see clearly is Yemoja's shaking hands, long slender fingers adorned with jeweled rings that catch the sunlight. They are hooked into the sand, nails slicing through the white as the orisa begins to wail. The sudden cry builds, drenched in grief and anger and fear, her body trembling as it pours from her hunched form.

Can Yemoja be killed? Does *our* mean all Mami Wata? I know we are strong in the sea and mortal as humans, but I hadn't thought about what could unmake us. Terror winds its way around me, pulling tight against my core. What could be so bad that Yemoja is reacting like this? I look over at Kola, but he is frowning and rubbing the back of his neck. The orisa's cry peaks in a drawn-out sob that slowly quiets as I drop into a crouch beside her, so close that I can feel the heat of her skin.

"Mother Yemoja?"

The orisa's spine straightens as I hear her suck a breath in, and she turns to face me, smoothing away the tears that escape her pearls. "Help me," she says simply. Her eyes are glistening, but she lifts her head and holds out a hand that still shakes.

As I rise to my feet, I see Kola on the other side of the orisa. Our gazes lock for a second and then we both bend down, taking Yemoja's hands and lifting her so that she can stand.

"I have spoken of my pain at what is happening, but what you must understand is the order of things. Olodumare's will and the decree that must be adhered to." Yemoja adjusts the twists of gold on her arms before continuing, her voice like black satin. "To fail to follow this edict would be a great risk. A price I have paid in part already."

"I don't understand."

Yemoja sighs and turns to face me, her lips pressed together. "Let me try to explain. In Ile-Ife, the first city on earth, all men were created equal, but they craved difference and begged the Supreme God for it. In the end Olodumare gave them what they wanted; separate clothes, languages, and lands." The orisa stops to look directly at me. "Can you guess what happened?"

"Chaos." I answer simply, the word springing into my mind.

"Exactly. War and inequality followed and still do. Mankind fight over the very differences they once begged Olodumare to give them." Yemoja pauses and jerks her hand upward. A wave just beyond the shallows curls in response. "And so Olodumare decided that humans would need to make their own way, learn their own lessons, and decreed that their destinies would be their own. Even orisas were bound not to directly intervene in the lives or deaths of man. This was made clear to all deities. Have you never wondered why you are only tasked to gather souls?"

"We bless them on their journey," I say, my voice small when I think of those discarded in the sea.

"And why do you think I have never wrecked the ships? Or commanded all the seven Mami Wata I created to do so?"

I say nothing. I think about her sorrow, the same emotion I feel every time we bless a soul. The thought of her torment burns within me, similar to the pain that tightens my chest in the sea.

"Creating seven Mami Wata was . . . risky. Olodumare saw it as a fracture of the decree. It did not go unnoticed, and once again I was reminded of the decision for mankind to have free will." Yemoja sighs, her hands going to the whiteness of her veil. "Olodumare saw your creation as a . . . blurring of the line. A disrespect of the rules that were set out."

"What does that mean?" I ask. A cold trepidation catches at my breath, spreading through my veins and making my heart beat faster. "What happened?"

"Perhaps it would be easier to show you."

Yemoja's fingers caress the golden clips at either side of her veil. She unfastens the jeweled grips, her silvered eyes on mine. There is a moment when she hesitates and I feel a rush of apprehension. I have a feeling that I won't want to see what lies beneath, but I know I don't have a choice. I watch as Yemoja holds both sides of the mask of pearls and lowers them.

The cry that escapes me is sharp, and I can't stop it. Yemoja tilts her chin, and the sunlight caresses her skin in soft golden tones that decorate the horror of her once-hidden face. I breathe out and force myself to look, not to turn away. The slopes of Yemoja's cheeks are scored with deep vertical gouges, three on each side of her face. The ragged grooves pull and drag at her skin, beginning under her eyes and ending just before her mouth. I hold my chest, pressing against the hard beat of my heart.

"It is not so bad," says Yemoja softly, taking a step closer to me. "Please do not be upset, Simidele. This was my punishment and I took it gladly. In return, Olodumare allowed the existence of Mami Wata and the task I have set you. But that is all you are allowed to do."

I feel a touch on my arm, and without looking up, I know it is Kola. He leaves his hand there for a moment, but I don't let myself take any comfort from the roughness of his palm. I shrug him off.

"Did Olodumare do this?" I ask the orisa, my voice cracking. I can't think of the Supreme Creator treating humans or orisas like this. Distant but loving, all Olodumare has done is create and bless both. This doesn't make sense.

Yemoja shakes her head, her curls swinging. "No, I have only unbound love for the Supreme Creator," the orisa says, a smile on her lips. "Although I know Olodumare would be furious if I defied them again, my gratitude is eternal."

"So who did that to you?" I demand, fury bubbling up in me.

Yemoja's eyes darken as she frowns, silver flashing across them. "It was Esu."

Esu. Messenger to Olodumare. Said to have over two hundred names, which show his many sides, his ability to change form and master any language. I shudder when I think of his role as kinsman to the ajogun, the eight malevolent warlords intent on the ruination of life on earth. Only Esu can keep them at bay. For these reasons alone, Esu holds power unlike any other orisa's.

"It was he who told Olodumare of my creation of Mami Wata." Yemoja grips her veil, watching the pearls shimmer as she speaks. "Although I am sure that if it were something he could have done, his view would be different."

"He was jealous?"

Yemoja laughs suddenly, a harsh bark that splits the air. "Esu covets what others have. His quest for power is insidious and constant. From stealing the loved ones of kings and queens to using other orisas for their powers in the hopes of gaining more himself."

"And so he used Olodumare's decree to hurt you?"

"All I know is that Esu was jealous that I was able to create you. After telling Olodumare what I had done, he came to give voice to the Supreme God. To deliver the message of displeasure and consequences." She pauses, touching one of the scars with a tapered fingernail. "And to mete out the punishment."

I watch as she clips her veil back into place, but the jagged scars have imprinted themselves on my mind. Realization settles in me like stone. "So, taking Kola from the sea . . ."

Yemoja frowns and brings her hands together, interlacing her fingers. "It contravenes what Olodumare set out. Your actions have broken the decree I am bound by. The decree *we* are bound by. And one that Esu will only be too eager to enforce again. Especially if it means the end of Mami Wata."

I look over at Kola, who stares back at me. My throat is dry and each swallow is an uncomfortable click as I think of how he grabbed me and the way he demanded to see Yemoja. For him I have risked so much. As if he can hear my thoughts, Kola lowers his gaze, shoulders set in awkward lines.

"But why would you not tell me?" I ask, my voice rising higher with a frustration that is tinged with anger.

"I should not have needed to!" Yemoja hisses, hands in rigid claws, her talon-like nails glinting. "You forget your place and your proper tone, Simidele. You are my creation, my daughter. All you had to do was listen to me and complete your task!"

I stay silent, words building, despair forming an unleashed

wave inside me. Yemoja should have told me about the decree. How can I do the right thing if I don't fully know what it is? Shallow breaths match the rapid beat of my heart as I struggle to hold it all in.

"The other Mami Wata do what is asked of them, nothing more. They do not prance around my island in human form, *pretending*. They do not question me. And I did not think it was necessary—"

Her words release the tide of my anger and I interrupt, my voice barbed with ire. "You should have told me!"

Yemoja glowers at me, her eyes bright with silver and rage. "I created you and gave you your task." She steps closer to me. "The task that you agreed to do just a few days ago."

"Simi—" Kola starts.

"Be quiet," I hiss at him. If he weren't here, if I hadn't dragged him from the sea and brought him to the island, then none of this would be happening.

But then I think of him in the dark water. Of the whites of his eyes when he opened them, of my first instinct to reach out and snatch him to me.

He would have drowned.

I unclench my fists slowly. Even if Yemoja had told me never to meddle in a person's life, I know I couldn't have left him in the sea. My anger is layered with guilt, but none of my thoughts are stained with true regret. I cling to the rage instead, trying to take solace in its burn.

"Mother Yemoja, should I have let him die?" I ask, turning back to face the orisa.

Moments pass as Yemoja glares at me but does not answer.

Kola swallows and shows courage by stepping between us, uneasy in his stance. "What now? What can we do, to make this right?"

"Perhaps I should have told you." Yemoja's shoulders slump, but she holds a hand out to me. "We need to set aside our anger. Now is not the time for us to be divided, daughter."

Her rings glitter on each finger, her palm a lighter brown, held up in the sun. I know that what she did, what she does, is all to help. Yemoja, mother of all orisas. She is resplendent and magnificent, willing to risk everything to ease the pain of those enslaved, and her compassion is all-encompassing. I recall her wide scars, and my rage dulls to a pulse as shame settles inside me.

I may have saved Kola, but in doing so, I failed her.

"Mother Yemoja," I whisper, taking the hand extended to me. "I'm sorry. What can I do?"

Yemoja pulls me into the heat and strength of her embrace, and it is like hugging both the sun and the moon, like fire and ice. When she releases me, she takes a moment to collect herself, standing tall, rearranging the curls of her black hair.

"Olodumare will find out eventually. Since your creation and my punishment, Esu has watched me even more closely. We will need to inform Olodumare ourselves and ask for absolution." The orisa holds my gaze. "After Mami Wata's inception, I fear I do not have much of the Supreme God's grace for me left." She brushes her fingers against the clips of her veil. "Since it was not I who broke the decree, Simidele, it is you who will have to ask for forgiveness."

I look at Kola and back at Yemoja, thinking of the other Mami Wata. If there's a way to save them all, I will take it.

"What do I have to do?"

...

The need to make everything better thrums within me. I think of Folasade and the others, of Mother Yemoja and the wrath she risked to make us. I have endangered them all.

I watch the orisa walk toward the sea, her back as sculpted as the nighttime desert. "We need clemency," says Yemoja as she regards the shifting waves.

"But will Olodumare forgive so easily?" I say, moving to her side.

"I do not know. Remember, it is not that Olodumare does not care about humankind," says Yemoja, a line forming between the slash of her eyebrows. The sea whispers at the orisa, but she ignores it. "Olodumare's past interactions have colored how they see the world they created."

I frown, twisting my fingers together. "Is there any way that we could still use Esu to gain an audience? Without telling him exactly," I hasten to add. "As Olodumare's messenger, he could pass on our words."

"Esu is not to be trusted! Not at all!" Yemoja barks, and I flinch. She lifts a hand and a wave twitches, responding in a swell. "As I told you, he thinks of himself and his own thirst for power. Nothing more. You cannot hope to trick the trickster." The image of the scars scored into the orisa's cheeks pushes that thought out of my mind. "You will need to summon Olodumare in a different way."

"Does such a way exist?"

"I was told that it does. By the babalawo who fashioned the sapphires into necklaces."

I shift my weight from one foot to the next, feeling a dull ache in my soles. "So the high priest will be able to help me?"

"Better, the babalawo has two rings in his possession. Made from obsidian mined from Ile-Ife. These are powerful. Very powerful. When they are worn together you can recite a prayer that will initiate an audience with Olodumare." Yemoja adjusts a golden bangle on her wrist, pursing her lips. "They are also another reason that Esu does not favor me. I would never tell him where they were."

But why would he need them? Since he is Olodumare's messenger, he doesn't have to conjure an audience. And then I think of Yemoja's earlier words, of Esu's craving for power. He must hate it if anyone can bypass him and speak to Olodumare.

"Where can I find him?" Breathing in deeply, I let hope bubble up within me. Gaining Olodumare's forgiveness will be our salvation. I just have to make sure Esu doesn't get the rings. "The babalawo? Is he close?"

The orisa turns to the sea and is silent, contemplating its tranquil surface. The pearls of her veil catch the sun, an iridescence that casts a glow on her neck and chest. "I am not entirely sure. I last heard he was on the northern coast, but he is not there anymore."

I rub my hands on the sides of my thighs. "And so . . ."

"You will have to find him."

I can feel my face fall at her words and the thought of having to search on my own.

"I don't think the babalawo will have gone far." Yemoja walks back to the soft sand, leaving me to follow her. "He will be close to both the sea and a large river. The power of those two bodies of water converging is one he will always seek and settle by."

I think of how many rivers meet the sea. Kola coughs and then stops when Yemoja swivels her head in his direction.

"The river Ogun is powerful," he says quietly. "My village is close to it. As well as . . . a babalawo who we consult."

"Speak up," Yemoja hisses as she drifts closer to Kola. I see his eyes go to the points of her teeth, just visible beneath her white pearls. "What else?"

"He has . . . images . . . of you."

I see Yemoja's features shift. Could this be the babalawo she speaks of? A hint of relief shimmers in the silver and black of her eyes, the twitch of her shoulders.

The sun spears through a cloud as Kola places a hand on his chest and bows. "If Simidele will take me home, I will show her where the babalawo is."

"What's the name of your village?"

"I won't say." Kola swallows, his Adam's apple bobbing as he tries to stand taller and mask his nerves. "If I told you now, there would be nothing stopping you from sending Simidele and leaving me behind." He fights it, but he can't keep the desperation out of his words. "But I can promise that I will take her to him."

My eyes widen and I suck in a breath at his words. No one should show such audacity when speaking to an orisa. Yemoja looms over the boy, but he doesn't flinch. She reaches out a hand, nails sliding down Kola's cheekbones and cupping his chin.

"What kinds of effigies did the babalawo have?"

"They show you in the mountain streams, giving birth to all the waters of the earth." Kola's voice grows louder, the bass in it deeper. "They show your tears at enslavement and your journey to follow those sold and taken across the different seas."

"Is that all?"

"No," Kola answers. "They show you and seven others. All with tails and sapphires, like the one that Simi wears now."

Yemoja snatches her fingers from his skin but doesn't take her eyes from his. A moment of silence stretches out as none of us moves or speaks. "Simidele. You will accompany Adekola home." Her words are quiet but firm. "And he will show you the babalawo."

Without giving him another chance to speak, the orisa whirls away, her steps giant as she seeks the comfort of the sea. Kola looks over at me, eyebrows raised, but I ignore him and follow Yemoja as she plays with the waves, pulling and pushing them against the shore.

"Is he right? I didn't tell him any of that!"

"I believe you. The details he described are not common." The orisa stares at the expanse of blue before us. "Take him. I will teach you the prayer to summon Olodumare once you have the rings."

The sea sighs again while I hold my breath. I think of the journey to the village and glance back at Kola, on the beach behind us, respectfully giving us distance.

"I don't think he trusts me." I touch the bruises on my wrist. I don't tell her that I don't entirely trust him, either.

"No matter. We don't have a choice and neither does he." Yemoja lets the sea rest and places her hands on my shoulders. "You must be particularly wary of Esu." I picture the scars beneath her veil and shiver. "You will do better to travel mostly in human form. This will limit rumors, and I would not see you hurt."

Yemoja's words don't frighten me. I'm more worried about anything else happening to her. Despite my yearnings, if it weren't for her, my bones would be deep beneath the sea.

"Is there any way he would know now?" I glance around me,

thinking of how fearful Yemoja was earlier. A sliver of panic slices through me at the thought of my actions bringing harm to her. "Could he be close?"

The orisa shakes her head, pearls clicking gently and the gold in her crown flashing in the sun. "Although he receives much information through the prayers and messages of humankind, he is not near. I would feel it. Orisas are . . . connected."

I touch the sapphire at my throat and think about how it pulses when any of my kind are close. "Like Mami Wata?"

"Similar, but with no reliance on jewels or talismans. If one of us is close, the other can sense it." Yemoja pauses again, running her eyes over me. "You are safe, for now." But despite her words, the orisa's brow is knitted.

"What is it?" I ask, worry settling deep inside me.

"You are vulnerable like this. Here." The orisa raises a hand to her crown, fingers scraping against the large emerald embedded in her coils. She uses her nails to tease it from her hair and reveals a slim tapered column of solid gold. I watch as the orisa snaps her wrist and a razor-sharp blade shoots out from the width of metal. "Press the emerald to retract the blade. Keep it with you at all times. It is strong and true and will cut through almost anything."

I take the dagger gingerly, pressing the gem on the end. The blade slots back inside, and I copy Yemoja by sliding the weapon between the braids that curve from my forehead to the crown of my head. I give a small bow of thanks and pat the dagger to make sure it's secure.

"Remember, also, that it is not just Esu you must be aware of." She holds my face, forcing my gaze to hers while she speaks.

"This is another reason to keep this body. Humans can often be cruel in their curiosity about the unknown. Do not trust them."

I know the truth the orisa speaks of, remembering the look from a fisherman who caught a glimpse of me. Disbelief, fear, and then the greed that slid across his face like a dark cloud over the sun.

"One more thing," Yemoja says, drawing me closer so that only I can hear her. She takes her time, picking her words carefully. "I know you sometimes remember parts of your life before, but I worry that it has clouded your actions. Keep the goal of this journey firmly in mind and do not let yourself . . . *feel* too much. Not for any human. You are of the sea now. It is forbidden."

I think of the way Kola is using me to get home and I nod, annoyance settling in among the worry. "You don't need to be concerned about that."

"That is good," says Yemoja as her eyes deepen to the dark silver of the sky on a stormy day. She blinks, hesitating before continuing. "Because if you act on loving a human, your form will be revoked and you will be nothing but foam upon the sea."

CHAPTER EIGHT

I DISMISS THE last of Yemoja's warnings. I know what I am. And what I am not. Instead, I focus on Esu. Messenger and guardian of the crossroads of life, a trickster who enjoys deceiving and creating division for enjoyment and his own gain. Still, I didn't think he was capable of the violence hidden behind Yemoja's veil. I touch a fingertip to the emerald in my hair, taking comfort in the blade it conceals.

The heat of the day grows as the sun blazes down on us. Small clouds float high above, marring the perfect ultramarine sky. Kola drags out the boat that Yemoja tells him is hidden in her cove. Obscured by the hanging branches and leaves of an old banana tree, the vessel has a peeling wooden hull, silver from the sun. He stalks around the boat, energized by the thought of going home. A short but sturdy mainmast is intact, and from inside, Kola pulls out a folded sail, dusted with leaves but usable. The boat will just about fit us both. I eye it uneasily. At least I can escape into the sea if the close quarters become too much.

While Yemoja teaches me the prayer to summon Olodumare, Kola inspects the boat, placing green bananas and more of the wild lettuce inside. He finds an old waterskin, which he rinses and fills with water from the bowl I made.

Once Yemoja has made me repeat the prayer enough times to commit it to memory, we watch as Kola shoves the boat into the clear shallows. He leaps inside, and I run my hands down the blush-and-gold folds of my wrapper.

"We should head east?" I ask.

I feel a tremor of nerves, and as I look up at Yemoja, I know the creases of my face show it. The orisa smiles down at me.

"Follow the main current east for a day and it will take you to the shore of the land you seek. The river Ogun is two days' walk if you head through the forest." She leans toward me, the cloud of her hair tickling my face, and places a kiss on my forehead. I close my eyes at the warmth of her lips and open them to her wide smile. "You will do well, in this I have faith."

"Mother Yemoja, I'm—"

"Simidele." I open my mouth to speak again, but the orisa stops me. "Simidele. Listen to me. I know you will make things right. What is done is done. We cannot change the past, only learn from it. What happens next is up to you."

• • •

The sun tightens my salt-soaked skin, and as I sit in the prow of the boat, it feels strange to be above the ocean and not below it. Yemoja returned to the sea before we set off, making me repeat the summoning prayer to her one last time. *Mo pe ẹ, Olodumare . . .* The words swirl in my mind as I let my hand dip into the waves, closing my eyes and remembering the slip of the water.

"Simi? How do we know we're traveling the right way?"

"We're sailing east, the way Yemoja told me to. But it's also the direction that the òyìnbó ships come from." I sit up, ignoring the scrape on my soles as I pull my knees to my chest.

Kola holds his hand up to his eyes, squinting into the sun, which is slipping into the ocean. He unfurls the ropes with ease and my interest is piqued.

"You're used to boats?" I ask.

"My friends . . . we sailed a lot." Kola's voice falters and he keeps his back to me as he adjusts the sail and secures the rope in a complicated-looking knot. "I didn't lie. To Yemoja, I mean. My village is next to the sea and near the river Ogun."

"And the babalawo?"

Kola pauses briefly, but he doesn't turn around. "Exactly as I said." The waves roll our boat from side to side but he moves with it, sure on the sea in a way I didn't expect.

I can't stop thinking of how he all but demanded I summon the orisa and the way he cajoled her into getting what he wanted. Eventually, Kola can find nothing more to fuss with, and he sits down opposite me.

"You took a chance. With Yemoja. Bargaining with her the way you did, I mean."

"I had to."

"Why?"

He coils some spare rope around his wrist and forearm, muscles flexing. "I told you, I need to get home."

"And you didn't think I would take you?" I say, fingers skimming over the small bracelet of bruises on my wrist as Kola looks at me. If I had been in the sea, they would have healed by now. He sees what I am doing and sighs.

"I know I haven't shown you . . . the best of me." Kola grimaces, his guilt plain in the way he hunches forward, eyes fastened on the marks on my skin. "But I couldn't take the chance that you would be content with just taking me from the water, as grateful as I was. As I am." He looks up at me, his eyes glowing. "I'm not explaining this very well, am I?"

I shake my head, but I think of how I found him. Of what had been done to him.

"I need to get back to my village. Not just because it's home but . . ." Kola hesitates for a split second. "Because of my family."

"And what else?" I ask, remembering the fear and desperation in his words when he demanded I help him summon Yemoja.

"My brother and sister need me." Kola looks away from me, picking up the rope again, uncoiling it. "I should be there, looking after them. I thought I was when I . . ." Kola shakes his head and stops talking, taking the rope in both hands this time, twisting it slowly around his left forearm. "They're . . . special." He faces me. "And I'm worried that what I did has put them in even more danger, now I'm no longer there to protect them."

There is a rawness to his voice. It fills his words with an urgency I can hear. "You'll get home."

"Thank you," says Kola. He shifts in the boat, and our knees almost touch no matter how I angle them. "For saving me." He puts the rope down and gives me his full attention. "For showing me how to summon Yemoja."

"You are welcome," I answer softly.

I begin to untangle the coils of my hair, loosely plaiting the ends. The boat feels too small. I think of slipping over the side, of diving down into the coolness. Instead, I slide the dagger from the braids at my crown, turning it over in the palm of my hand before I flick my wrist, freeing the blade, its sharpness bright in the sun.

"Did Yemoja give you that?"

"Yes," I say, tilting the weapon, admiring the way it gleams.

"And I don't get a dagger?" Kola asks, his voice light, teasing.

"What would you need one for? I'm the one taking you home."

"Hmm." His eyes follow the blade, yearning plain in his expression.

"Are you jealous?" I ask.

Kola stares at me for a moment too long before he shrugs. "Do you really know what to do with it?"

I don't try to hide the small grin that forms. As Kola continues to watch, I snap my wrist, spinning the dagger in the air. The golden weapon glints as it somersaults between us. Snatching it by the hilt, I lunge toward Kola, holding the blade lightly against his throat. He swallows, Adam's apple touching the dagger.

"Ah, you do."

But his response is blurred by the image of a man, much older than me, standing before me, showing me his stance. His short wiry hair is shot through with gray, and a large scar runs from his hairline to the top of his left cheek.

"Not like that, Simidele. Like this." And he grips the dagger he's holding in such a way that his wrist is straight and locked in position. "See?"

The man then flips the dagger, spinning it before reaching up and snatching it from the air.

"Practice. So that you can protect yourself, and others if and when they need it." He gestures to the smaller weapon in my hands. "Now you."

I copy the hold he showed me, the late-afternoon breeze cool on the bare skin of my arms. My chest tightens momentarily as I squeeze the hilt. I don't want to disappoint him.

"Breathe, ọmọbìnrin ìn mi. Breathe."

I suck in a deep breath and then throw the blade into the air, my eyes on the weapon as it tumbles through sunlight. And then, just as I was shown, I reach for the dagger. My fingers grasp the leather hilt but slip slightly as an errant curl falls into my face. I breathe out slowly, the weapon clutched in my hand triumphantly but my knees shaking from what was a near miss.

"How many times have I told you, ọmọbìnrin ìn mi? Braid your hair so that it does not distract you." And with the last of his words he leans forward and starts to loosely gather my curls. Despite his admonishment, he is smiling. I close my eyes and breathe in the smell of him. The faint tang of sweat and mangoes and hot earth in the rain.

"We will practice until it is too dark to see."

Daughter.

He called me daughter.

I sit back in the boat, gently twirling the knife between both of my hands, fingers flying on the sharp gold weapon. With a click of the emerald, I push the blade back into my braids.

"We should rest," I say, cutting off any more conversation. Curling up on my side of the boat, I stare at the horizon, my chin propped up on the knot of my arms.

My father. I hold the gray coils of his hair and his scent, which is still fresh, in my mind. Closing my eyes, I go over the memory, again and again. If I concentrate, I can almost feel the calluses on his fingers as he parts my hair, the deftness of his touch as he weaves the strands in and out, creating a simple plait.

"Simi?"

I don't open my eyes. Instead I recall the smells of mangoes and earth. A pleased grin when I block his parry.

"Simi!"

"What?" I all but explode, sitting up suddenly, causing the boat to rock violently beneath us.

"Look." Kola is pointing to the horizon, where the sun is heading in a fiery trail.

I squint, holding one hand to my brow. Already I can feel the sound of my father's voice slipping away, and then I see what Kola is showing me. I lower my hand, clutching the wood of the boat, its worn grain like satin beneath my panicked grip.

A ship.

Black masts that look like spines and a curved hull that plows through the peaks and troughs of the sea.

A ship that looks just like the one Kola was thrown from.

CHAPTER NINE

"GET THE SAIL down," I hiss, but I know that we are most likely too late. The sea is a flat calm, docile after the storm when I found Kola, so we are very easy to spot.

The ship seems to teeter in the distance, but it is moving fast, nearly as quick as the pulse of my heart. Behind the three giant masts, the sun lurks, blurs of orange and red that smudge the sky like dried blood.

Kola's fingers fly over the knots as he works quickly to bring down our sail. His jerky movements cause the boat to rock, and even as I'm thinking about turning us around, the ship alters its course, the bow pointed straight at us. Kola has seen this, too, and he sits down in the cramped stern. It would take too long to try to swim back to Yemoja's island and I'm not sure Kola would make it so far, even with my help.

"Go," he says, wrapping the ropes around his fists. He looks at a sea that imitates the sky in a vivid azure, his mouth set in a hard line.

I could.

I could slip underneath its surface, dive down to the dark cool parts. My skin is already feeling tight under the sun, and my bones feel as if they are in unnatural formations. It would be so easy.

Protect yourself . . . and others if and when they need it.

"No." I grope for the emerald in my hair, extracting the dagger from my braids. "I'm not leaving."

Kola's eyes burn as he regards me for stretched-out seconds. The muscle in his jaw ticks, but I don't change my mind. He lifts the small anchor, testing its heft, and as the ship draws closer, I flick the blade of my dagger free.

We will fight.

I will fight.

Weaving my way through the dense forest, I lead my friend to the grove of pear trees. The feast after my father's Ceremony of Knowledge would only be complete with some of the wild fruit that grows in the woods.

"Not long," I say, smiling at Ara. I'm grateful to have her with me, especially since the shadows are deepening. She plods along beside me, always happy to escape the chores of looking after her smaller cousins.

Ara is the first to see them.

Her nails dig into my arm, and I turn to see the òyìnbó slip between the trees.

We freeze. My heartbeat spikes, and for a moment, all I can hear is the thump of it. They must be spirits, with their white skin. One of them, much taller than the others, reaches us first and I am startled by the pink slash of his mouth and the hank of brown hair that sweeps back into a straight tail. His smile is full of yellow teeth as he pulls a dagger from the leather sheath at his waist. The òyìnbó be-

70

hind copy him. As the blades catch the waning daylight, my mouth goes dry. I try to stop my legs from trembling.

"Simi," says Ara, a plea in her voice.

I've heard a few tales of the òyìnbó from a traveling storyteller who had journeyed the length of the coast. He spoke of the cloth and new metal weapons the men trade with villagers in return for spices, gold . . . people. The storyteller said they were kidnappers, too. Attacking people collecting water or herding their animals. By the light and warmth of the fire, with a belly full of chicken stew, the stories had seemed unreal.

Now, fear crawls inside me, slithering through my veins.

"Stay to the side of me," I hiss as the òyìnbó move toward us.

My voice sounds far away as blood thuds in my ears. I don't have my knife. I am scanning the ground, looking for something to wield, when the tall man lunges for me. I stumble backward, pushing Ara out of the way as he snatches my arm. I think of the moves my father taught me last summer. Twisting, I kick out, my foot connecting with the man's abdomen. The òyìnbó makes a small surprised grunt, his grip loosening.

I rip myself free and drag Ara with me, scanning the forest desperately for a weapon. A dead tree lies near, its trunk shining bone white. Grabbing one of its thick branches, I swing it like a staff at the men. Ara rips off a branch of her own.

I don't understand what the òyìnbó says, but I can see that his eyes are hard, his dagger pointed in the gloom. My hands shake, but I don't let my staff slip.

The other men fan out, creating a loose circle around us. They smirk, and I swallow my tears, snarling instead, not wanting them to see how scared I am. What will our mothers think if we don't return?

The òyìnbó rush forward and I spin, whirling the branch, trying to create space for Ara to run.

"Go, Ara!" I say.

I'm breathing hard now, chest hitching. My fault, I think as I turn away from the terror that gleams in Ara's gaze. This is all my fault. If I hadn't insisted on getting the pears.

"No." Ara frowns and adjusts her stance, bare feet shuffling in the dirt of the forest floor. "I won't leave you."

"Go!" I scream, and I know that I am crying now but I don't care.

The òyìnbó circle us. I manage to hit one of them on the shoulder, but another man wrenches the branch from my grip. Backed against a large tree, I push the fear away, embracing the fury rising within me.

"Come!" I shout as they move closer. "What will you do?"

I clutch my dagger as the memories rip through me, sucking the air from my lungs. I stumble and bend over, as if punched. Kola stands before me, looking up at the hull of the ship.

I was taken.

This I knew, but it's one thing to know that it must have happened and another to remember it, to have the images in my mind, to remember that fear. I shake, my legs bending as I fight to stand upright. I think of the same kind of men on the ship before us and let the burn in my chest spread through me, straightening my back until I can see the dark wet wood of the hull looming ahead.

The waves before us double, growing in size and violence because of the approaching vessel. Kola has edged me behind him. His back is a knot of scabs, some still raw and others closing slowly. Lashes he suffered from the òyìnbó on a ship like that.

I hold my dagger with intent, wanting to see how it slices, wanting the chance to use it. "What do you see?" I hiss from behind Kola as he tips his head back, looking high up at the ship's railing.

The boy doesn't reply, but the rope slips from his hand, thudding quietly into the bottom of the boat. I move, shifting so that I can look past him. The side of the ship is peppered with barnacles, the wood glistening with sea spray. I squint upward, past the figurehead of an intricately carved woman with long flowing hair, and up to the sharp point of the bow. The triangular sails of the ship crackle in the wind, framing the forecastle. Several men holding guns and swords whose blades flash in the sun look down on us.

The grip on my dagger falters as I scan their faces. The tallest peers down, a grin spreading across his face, his skin as brown as ours.

"Greetings, brother and sister. Will you board?"

● ● ●

Kola turns around and I see the relief in the sag of his shoulders, but his hands are still clenched, knuckles tight. The creak of the hull breaks the silence.

"What do you think?" he asks in a low voice. "Why would they be sailing such a ship?"

I'm quiet for a moment, watching as the men unfurl a rope ladder, its woven rungs cascading down the side of the ship. I think of the òyìnbó who sail such vessels. The deaths they cause as if we are nothing, our bodies that they discard.

"We'll have to see. I think we should be careful, as Yemoja

73

told us to. But it looks like we're going to find out what they have to say. Besides, we don't have much choice." I pick up the rope and begin to tie it around the bottom of the ladder, anchoring the boat. "If we need to, we can leave quickly."

Kola looks at me and then up at the ship before nodding. "I'll go first."

The coarse threads of the rope, frayed and rough, are tight in my grip as I hold the bottom of the ladder. Kola climbs steadily up and I follow closely behind him, my mind whirling as I try to think about what a ship crewed by men from our lands might mean. In the time since Yemoja made me, I have never seen such a vessel or such a group of men sailing it. Despite my caution, I want to know more.

When I reach the ship's railing, Kola is there, holding a hand out to help me. I'm glad he does because as soon as my feet touch the deck, I stumble, pain shooting up from my soles. I'm still not used to being in this form for so long. Among the rigging, gathered around the three masts and standing before us, are a crew of men and women who are all the same but different. The same in that they are all from our lands, in shades of brown from tan to dark brown and onyx, but different in the people they belong to. Some have the simple vertical scar of the Ondo on each cheek, while a few wear the vibrant cloth of the Aja from Allada. Four men even wear the red headwraps of the Songhai Empire, their hands on swords tied around plain white agbadas. It's clear that there are no òyìnbó, and the crew's presence takes away some of my apprehension.

As we are led across the deck, I watch my step, careful to place one foot in front of the other. The ship rocks from side to side and I am continually adjusting my gait, sliding my feet across the wooden planks cautiously until I come to the groove of the door for the hold below. I stop, my toes just touching the black outline of the hatchway.

The space in the belly of the ship is dark, with only weak sunlight filtering through the wooden deck above. I don't lift my head from the hot press of my knees, slick with sweat and the salt of my tears. The air is humid, an almost-solid beast that squats above us, and my lungs are tight from the heat and the stench of misery.

I hold on to the memory of my last glimpse of land, its brown slice dotted with trees, framed by the churn of the sea. More water than I had ever seen before. With the waves up to my thighs, and a scream rising in my throat, I had gasped prayers to Yemoja before the wind snatched them from me and the òyìnbó forced me into a small boat.

One man had been shouting on the journey to the large ship, hitting out at the òyìnbó. Despite his manacles, matched with a ring of black iron around his neck, he struck two before they shot him once, his body tossed into the sea, where it lay floating in a cloud of blood that colored the waves in shades of red and pale burgundy. I shudder at the remembered sight, pushing my face harder against the skin and bones of my legs.

The scrape of chains against the wooden planks is accompanied by cries and shouts in Yoruba and Twi. I keep my eyes closed tight, not wanting to see the crush of bodies, limbs heavy with the weight of chains. But I can't block out the sound of the sea, the clank of manacles and the incessant groans of despair that float on the filthy air. Instead, I swallow my own cries, throat dry and raw, and I know that even if I wanted to scream, I couldn't.

Two more have died today, and even now I can feel the sickness.

It slides under my hot skin, flowing through my blood and mingling with my fear. The only thing I'm more afraid of than dying in the dark, no breath or anyone to say my final prayers, is when the hold opens. A bright rectangle of white light that blinds us. A sign that some of the òyìnbó are coming. Coming to—

"Simidele?"

My name pulls me from the recollection. I can taste it still, the terror. It's sharp on my tongue, coating my throat, slipping down deep inside me where it has nested before. I place a hand on my chest as if trying to push the beat of my heart back down to normal, taking deep breaths and focusing on the wind that stings my cheeks.

I'm not in the hold anymore.

I'm not.

"Simidele?" says Kola, and I realize he has been talking to the man who appears to be the captain. The tallest of them all. "This is Abayomi. The captain of this ship."

I force myself to open my eyes. Nearly twice my size, Abayomi steps back so as not to crowd me. His head is shaved but for a thick braid at the back, which runs down to the nape of his neck, and he wears a wrapper as black as ink with tiny bursts of gold stars.

"Welcome, Simidele." The man presses his broad chest with one huge fist and nods in greeting, his voice a deep rumble that is as soothing as it is powerful. The richness of his tone makes me think of my father. I still can't speak, not trusting my voice, so I nod instead, fluttering an unsteady hand to my chest in greeting.

"Abayomi was saying that they took this ship from a port."

"That is right. We are a crew assembled by the àwọn olórí

abúlé." Abayomi adjusts strings of red coral beads that decorate his wrist, complemented by a heavier set hanging from his neck. "Our leaders were . . . shamed. At the lies we believed and the discord sowed by the òyìnbó. Some of us were selected to work as one in order to take back those stolen from us."

"Lies?" I ask, my voice softer than normal. I concentrate on standing, willing the muscles of my legs to hold me upright.

"Yes, lies spread by the òyìnbó to incite violence among different cities and villages. It benefits them when there are more prisoners of war to be bought." Abayomi looks directly at me and I hold his gaze. "We patrol the waters of our lands, attacking any slave ships."

Fighting back. "You said some of you. What about the rest of these people?"

Abayomi nods at my perception. "Yes, the rest were liberated from such ships."

"Have you destroyed or taken many vessels so far?" Kola asks, his voice colored with hope.

"Four so far, in as many months. They are sailing northeast, back to their lands."

The thought of those ships being destroyed brings me a joy I see mirrored in Kola. He looks over at me and smiles, his eyes bright.

"I know of another, just a few days away." Kola turns back to Abayomi, stops and swallows. He looks down at the raw scars on his wrists. "Do you think you could catch up to it?"

Abayomi takes Kola's hands in his, holding the backs lightly. He frowns, eyes hardening. "I am sorry that this happened to you." He pulls Kola in closer for a brief moment, his arm around the boy, squeezing. When Abayomi releases him, Kola wipes his eyes.

"If you can, I would like you to describe the route to my navigator. If we can locate it, that ship will be next." Abayomi surveys the ship before gesturing down the stairs. "Come, join me for some food and we can talk more."

We follow Abayomi down to the main deck, and I marvel at how they have adapted the ship. Despite its use before, the aura now is one of calm and quiet focus, everyone working together. We move past chicken coops and even a pen holding a goat at the sides of the deck, before we come to the captain's cabin. It is cramped but draped with woven blankets in shades of orange, red, and yellow, the walls adorned with several depictions of Ogun rendered in small sculptures and paintings. Two tall swords shine from a corner, their hilts carved from bone-white ivory.

Abayomi ducks inside, holding the door and gesturing to the blankets that cover a sleep mat. "Please, sit. There is water in the jug. I'll get the cook to bring some food."

The captain disappears toward the galley and I move toward Kola, tripping slightly on the thick edge of a blanket. He steadies me with a hand as I lower myself next to him.

"What do you think?" I say, my voice low.

"I never thought I would see such a thing." Kola's voice is full of awe. I think the same, but I also recall Yemoja and the caution she urged.

"Let's see what he has to say and then move on."

"Agreed," says Kola, but I can see the admiration and joy emanating from him as he pours water into a wooden cup and hands it to me. By the time I have finished drinking, Abayomi returns with a man half his size but just as wide. With hair that grows in black, white, and gray tufts, the man has a face that is open, with a huge smile.

"You are lucky. You boarded just as Musa has cooked some pepper soup."

The cook proffers bowls of food. "Rice as well as spice," he says, showing a large gap between his teeth as he lets out a booming laugh, grinning down at us.

Kola's stomach growls in reply and the men chuckle. We thank Musa and he dips his head in acknowledgment before waddling off. Abayomi folds himself next to Kola and smiles as the boy eats. I cradle the bowl in my hands, letting the spice of the pepper mingle with the steam from the soup. And breathe in deeply. It has been so long since I've had such food. Slowly, taking my time, I scoop up balls of salty rice, pushing them between my lips while I let the soup cool. When I can wait no longer, I take a small sip and have to stop myself from guzzling the whole bowl. The flavor bursts on my tongue like no other, hot and fiery with a powerful kick. I drink the rest, savoring each mouthful.

Abayomi listens as Kola describes the slave ship he was on, detailing the weapons and the number of òyìnbó on board, and I feel a sense of peace that Kola will not be the only one saved. Abayomi explains how he was the one to attack the ship he now commands, taking it while it was docked.

"It is not something I ever agreed with. This trade with the òyìnbó. Of any kind." He sighs, sitting up straighter and glancing at a brass sculpture of Ogun, the orisa of iron and one who despises injustice. "At least this way, I can do something about it."

We are silent a moment before Abayomi clears his throat and splits his gaze between us both. "So, will you tell me how you both came to be in the middle of the sea in such a small boat?"

I have just pushed the last of the rice into my mouth and am chewing as he asks this question. Darting a glance at Kola, I hope he will remember the caution Yemoja pressed upon us. And then a sudden worry courses through me. What if Kola decides to join them or asks Abayomi to take him home? I don't even know where the babalawo is. The rice sticks in my throat, forcing me to take a gulp of water to swallow it down.

"Simi came across me while she was on the sea fishing. Just after I had been thrown overboard. The storm was bad, but it meant no one saw her."

I put the bowl down in relief, its hard bottom cracking on the wooden planks of the floor. It is not entirely a lie, but I wonder what he will say next.

"We were pushed farther out by the strong winds." Kola gestures around. "And then luckily, we came across you. How far until we reach land? One day?"

Abayomi slides his gaze from Kola and contemplates my silence. I can tell that he doesn't fully believe what the boy is saying, but he's also seen the wounds on his wrists. Those welts are not something that can be made up.

"Where did you sail from, Simidele?"

"A village on the coast," I answer, keeping my words simple.

"A fishing village?"

"You know of many?" asks Kola, pulling the conversation back to him. He tells Abayomi of the coves and rock formations on the western shore. The way the jagged coastline makes entering and leaving almost a complicated dance between the shallows and boats.

"It is not far. Not even a day," Abayomi says, spreading his palms wide in the small space. "The wind must not have blown you as far away as you thought."

"This is excellent news," says Kola. "Should I speak with your navigator before we leave? Or do you have all you need to track the ship I was on?"

Abayomi gets to his feet, and we copy him. The cabin feels much smaller when we are all standing. "I have enough. Let me furnish you with some supplies before you go. Just in case you are blown off course again."

I snatch a look at Kola and he raises his eyebrows. "We would be very grateful," he answers.

"Thank you," I add.

Abayomi smiles, and I know he senses we haven't told him everything. But he's willing to help us anyway. I send a grateful prayer to Olodumare and step out of the door the captain holds open for me.

As we head back to the forecastle, I glance around at the crew as they scurry across the rigging and swarm about the ship, each doing their part to keep such a large vessel going. Abayomi asks a boy who looks to be the same age as Kola to get some food and fresh water and we wait, a growing breeze ruffling our wrappers. I still can't believe so many have come together in alliance; I run my gaze over them, trying to count the different types of people on board, and then I see them. Two older men linger near the mainmast. Wearing dyed indigo wrappers, covered with white concentric circles and slung low around their waists, they speak together, but their words are taken by the wind.

We wind our way through the market, passing stalls selling everything from leopard skins and mangoes to small silver daggers with prayers to Ogun carved into their simple wooden handles. It's busy today and the air is full of the smells of turmeric, nutmeg, and black pepper and the spiced aroma of cooked goat. Calls and greetings mingle with varying levels of haggling and even a full-blown argument between a large round woman and a wiry man. An elder soothes them as they argue over the price of a bulbous terra-cotta pot, its painting and gloss making it more expensive than the man wants to pay.

If I were on my own, I would weave through it all, straight to my favorite fruit stall. It's run by an aunty who always wears a grass-green wrapper. She sells the freshest papaya in all of Oyo-Ile and always puts aside the ripest for me. I would gorge myself on the sweet bursts of the fruit, wiping the juice away before I fetched everything my mother had sent me for. But today, we are all together as a family to buy something special, and we head for the stall closest to the palace compound entrance.

Fabrics hang in folds of color, from rich burgundy to gauzy swathes of light violet. With the soft curve of her back and her white hair in neat braids, Mobolaji sits to the side of the stall, smiling as my mother approaches. The old woman is well known for the highest level of quality cloth in all of Oyo-Ile.

"A new wrapper for one of the chosen scholars?" Mobolaji asks. "I heard the news this morning."

My mother's face almost splits with the size of her smile. "That is right, aunty. Only one of a dozen announced each year. Please tell me you have some of the official cloth left."

"Of course I do. I set some aside for you specially."

I watch as my mother bows, clasping Mobolaji's hands and cooing over the fabric she pulls out from underneath a pile of plain cotton. The thick waxed cloth is a deep indigo, decorated with interlocking white circles. Made only for the Aláàfin's scholars, it is one of the rarest designs.

I edge away from their chatter and run my hands over a fabric

I covet every time we visit the stall. A pale and delicate yellow shot through with gold, the diaphanous material feels the way I imagine a wisp of cloud would. I run a finger over a section edged in bright gold and try to tamp down my desire as it nearly swallows me whole.

"I will buy this one day for you, Simidele." My father is next to me. "You deserve a wrapper as beautiful as you are."

I let go of the material and lean over to kiss him before my mother pulls him to her and holds the indigo cloth against him. He runs his fingers over the raised circles of the waxed surface.

"You've earned this, bàbá," I say as he grins at my mother.

I stand back, admiring both of my parents as they clutch the deep blue cloth, faces filled with broad smiles. When my father wears the new wrapper for the Ceremony of Knowledge, along with all the other newly appointed officials, I know that my heart will burst with pride.

The men are from Oyo-Ile. They must be. And that is where I am from. I sag against the railings, wanting to sink to the deck and go over and over all that is coming back to me, but I don't get the chance.

The sky swirls, whipping to a smear of charcoal gray with slashes of pale blue. I grip the wooden rail as a sudden wind stirs, wrapping itself around the ship, pulling at the rigging and the lateen sails. I press a hand to the fabric of my wrapper. Something doesn't feel quite right.

I glance around, scanning the deck. Women and men shout, calling to one another as they scurry about, securing ropes and trying to get to the sails. All looks normal, but my stomach lurches in a way it does when there's danger in the sea. I drop my gaze to the water, examining its surface for anything unusual, but the blues and grays shift and heave in their usual waves. For a moment, a large swell rises and I think of Olokun deep beneath us, but then I remember how the orisa is chained to the bottom of the sea, destined never to see the sun or moonlight again after trying to flood the earth.

Breathing in deeply, I feel a small relief when Kola returns; I am already used to his lithe movements and the greetings he has for all on deck. He stops to help a man finish securing a barrel with large tight knots, and as he heads toward me, I see light in his eyes and a small smile on his lips. He opens his mouth to call to me just as a crack of thunder rends the air.

Kola flinches, arms raised to his head automatically. I start toward him, the feeling of wrongness strong and acute, as a burst of lightning tears through the clouds, missing the ship by mere feet. I cringe, dropping into a crouch as Kola skids down beside me.

Above us, the clouds are being torn apart. My heart stutters, starting again as another bolt is thrown from the sky. There is only one orisa who can control lightning.

"Sango," I whisper, panic coiling deep within me.

I'm not sure Kola hears my words, snatched by the unnatural wind, so I point up at the orisa, who looks as if he is tearing a hole in the very fabric of the sky.

CHAPTER TEN

THE ORISA AIMS another bolt of pure energy at the sea. It's closer to the ship this time, and Kola holds his arm over us as a shower of sparks rains down. Sango rips through the last of the clouds, fully materializing among the shreds, eyes shot through with silver and slabs of muscles gleaming. Legs like baobab tree trunks emerge from a red-and-white wrapper heavily edged in thread that matches the metallic glint in his gaze. The orisa is twice the size of Yemoja, with coils of fire around both ankles and white forked energy twining around his wrists. Sango opens his mouth to roar, the long twists of his hair standing on end as he glares down at the ship. In one hand he wields a giant double-headed axe, its edges crackling with blue lightning.

I cross my arms over my head, cowering against the side of the ship. Why is he showing himself to humans unsummoned? And why is he attacking us? There's a small moment of calm, the air singed and close, when I dare to sneak a look up at the sky, only to see another orisa.

Oya.

"She who tore," an orisa who can command winds and storms and one of the fiercest warriors ever known. She floats next to her husband, hair a mass of black that almost eclipses the last of the sun. I see her lips moving as her arms wheel gracefully, drawing the energy of the wind and sky to her. If Sango releases what Oya has harnessed, the ship will be destroyed.

"Is he aiming at us?" shouts Kola next to me, eyes narrowed.

I can't answer. I'm not sure what's going on, but as Oya raises the tips of her fingers to the top of the clouds, I brace myself. When the orisa lowers her arms, it feels as if she has taken the pressure from the air and crushed it down on the sea. My ears crackle, popping as the compression increases. I drop my head, and all around me, I hear men and women moan as they cover their ears.

Sango hovers next to his wife, a sphere of lightning gathered in his large hand. He moves his open palm, massaging the crackling energy so that it grows until it has doubled in size. Sango brings one hand behind him, the lightning gathered in it, brilliant against the blue of the sky, and then catapults it down at us. As the bolt soars through the clouds, the ship fills with fresh gasps of fear. The scent of burning is overwhelming as Sango's lightning smashes into the bow, ripping away part of the ship's rail.

A large woman leaps up, muscles flexing as she grabs a bucket of sand and throws it on the flaming timber. Despite the screams as Sango gathers another ball of energy, the woman is joined by two others, smaller and wearing red wrappers, who beat the last of the smoldering wood into submission. The shortest woman looks up into the sky and places a hand on her broad chest, screaming up into the wind and clouds Oya has created. Whatever the rest of her prayer, her fierce words seem to have been heard, and Oya swoops to Sango's side, stilling his fists, which are wreathed with blue-and-white snakes of lightning. The orisa descends, her hair a crown of tight spirals. As her feet touch the deck of the ship, the air on board stills and all is quiet. Around the vessel, the wind continues to screech and whirl, sucking waves up into gigantic summits and throwing needle-thin spikes of rain horizontally.

Peering up at Oya, I forget the pain in my ears for a moment, struck by her beauty. With a high forehead framed by tight curls, her nostrils flare as she surveys us all. Twists of gold are spun around every elongated limb, and a wrapper of deep purple flutters in the wind. Oya tilts her head to one side at the sight of the people writhing in pain at her feet, large opals glimmering from the depths of her hair. With a flick of her wrist, the pressure is lifted. I sit up, shaking my head slightly, but freeze when I see that Oya is looking straight at me.

I try to scramble backward as the orisa stalks the deck in my direction, but I am already pressed against the railing.

"Be calm," says Oya. She stops, not coming any closer. "Who is in charge of this ship?"

I open my mouth to speak but don't have the chance to answer. Sango lands on the deck with a crashing thud. Metallic blue sparks still fly from the tips of his fingers as he swings his large head around, twists of black writhing in the breeze.

"Where are they, Oya?" His voice is loud and raw and his eyes flash, the whites making his pupils look like tiny silver specks.

Oya lifts a hand, not looking back at Sango, who stomps toward her. The ship shakes with each one of his footsteps, and a few of the wooden planks of the deck splinter beneath his gigantic tread.

"All is not what it seems, husband. See for yourself." Oya smiles, revealing the whiteness of her teeth. "This ship is not crewed by the òyìnbó."

Sango pauses, looking down at those around him as they

press their foreheads to the deck beneath them, showing their supplication and honor of the orisas and this unexpected appearance. This is a tale the storytellers will tell for generations, such is its rarity. Oya takes a step closer to me and I force myself to bow before meeting her gaze, trying to stop myself from shaking. The orisa peers down at me; her eyes are large and rimmed with short but thick lashes, the silver of her eyes flashing in the meager light.

"You." She gestures for me to stand and I do, wincing as the bones in my feet and legs click from squatting. "Tell me what is going on. This ship is one that carries people sold as goods."

"It was," I say, raising my voice so that it can be heard over the wind. "But it was taken by a man named Abayomi and is now crewed by the men put together to fight against the òyìnbó."

Sango draws level with Oya in time to hear my last sentence. His thick eyebrows draw low over his eyes. He's still on edge, fingers flexing around the handle of his axe, but Oya places a hand on his arm.

"Look around you properly, husband," she urges.

The orisa scans the men on the ship, his gaze roaming over each one before he turns back to face his wife.

Oya is quiet a moment before she speaks to me again. "Where is this Abayomi?"

"I am here," comes the reply from the forecastle deck. Abayomi picks his way past the small davit where the ship's boat is stored, and as he walks, the crew rise tentatively behind him.

Sango turns to the captain and I am struck by the fact that, as tall as Abayomi is, he is dwarfed by the orisa. Abayomi bows respectfully, eyes on Sango's axe, and I can't tell if his gaze shows fear or envy as it slides over the weapon. While the captain explains how he took the ship, and their task, I use the time to watch the orisas. Like Yemoja, Oya and Sango have black eyes with hints of silver, but these gods are larger, gripping weapons that could destroy the whole ship in a moment.

After Abayomi has finished explaining, I force myself to step forward, curiosity fighting with my fear-tinged respect. "Oya," I say, lowering my head as I bow before the orisa, "if you would permit me to ask you something." The orisa faces me but does not speak. I take her silence to mean she agrees. "You came to attack this ship?"

Oya steps closer to me, her gaze as keen as the blade in her large hand. The orisa dips her head near to mine and the scent of mint and the tang of ice-cold water roll over me. "We are destroying as many of the vessels that carry the enslaved as we come across."

"We will not sit back and watch. We will not leave the pleas of our people unanswered," adds Sango, his rumbling voice as deep as the ocean beneath us.

"Even if it means Olodumare's wrath?" I ask, my curiosity uncontainable, apprehension wrapping around it like a paper-thin shroud.

The orisa turns to me, eyes matching the intensity of the storm still whirling around the ship.

"We will not stand by!" bellows Sango, only calming when Oya places her hand on his arm.

"Even if it means we have to face Olodumare," the orisa adds, courage in the angle of her raised chin. "Besides, Esu is not relaying all that he should to the Supreme God, only that which serves his favor or gives him more power. It is in his interest to have us on his side." The orisa tips her head. "I know Esu and his tricks. We will take our chances."

"Abayomi, you and the others on this ship show great courage and integrity," declares Sango as he faces the captain and the crew behind him, planting each foot with a loud crack. "We will come with you." The orisa runs a thick finger over the edge of his axe blade, triggering white sparks of energy that crackle in the still air. "And together we will destroy as many ships as we can find."

Abayomi grins, nodding at Sango as the crew murmur and smile. While Sango asks questions in a booming voice, Oya moves even closer to me, and I resist the urge to take a step backward, overpowered by the scent of mint and the thickness of the air. I lower my face in deference, a sliver of panic kicking in as her fingers reach for me, pointed nails painted the same purple as her wrapper.

"May I?" asks Oya, her voice deep and smooth.

I wait for the heat of her skin on mine, but her hands don't touch me. They stop at the sapphire of my necklace. I freeze. How could I have been so silly as to leave it out in plain view? But Oya lifts the jewel gently so that it glistens in her palm, and when I look up at her I see both questions and understanding in her eyes.

"You are of Yemoja?"

My tongue stills and I wonder what to say. Oya tugs the sapphire gently, her purple nails sharp on its blue surface.

"I would know one of Yemoja's sapphires anywhere. What are you doing on top of the sea with legs and not scales?" The rings fill my mind but I don't say a thing. Oya studies me, her eyes bright and quick. "Esu has told us he will not tell Olodumare of our actions, but we had to pledge our allegiance to him." She glances behind her at Sango, who has his large back to us. "We are to remain vigilant for something he is trying to find. Something Yemoja told me long ago that she knew about but would never tell him. He told us to see if we could learn what he could not. But I will never betray her," says the orisa, her voice deep and low. "And now you are here, where you should not be."

I open my mouth and then shut it, worry coursing through me. If I tell Oya, will she let Esu know?

Oya sees me hesitate and snatches another look at her husband. Sango is speaking with Abayomi, gesturing with large hands that still crackle and glow with white energy. The orisa stoops down so that she is closer to me and speaks even more softly. "Perhaps I can help, but only if you tell me why you are above the sea." Oya smiles, a gentle twist of her mouth that seems almost out of place. "I know of her love for humankind and you, her creations. And I know the price she paid." The orisa's lips flatten into a line as her silvered eyes gleam. "I would not see Yemoja hurt again."

The emotion in Oya's tone coaxes some of the truth from me, and perhaps she can help. "I'm looking for the rings of Ile-Ife. I need them to seek Olodumare's . . . forgiveness."

"What did you do?"

My face burns and I snatch a look at Kola. "I broke a decree. If I can't summon the Supreme God, Yemoja and the other Mami Wata will . . ." I stop, inhaling deeply before I can go on. "I want to keep them safe, and the only way to do that is to find the rings."

"The care in your words shines through." Oya releases my hand, though she still towers over me. "I do not know where they are, but I can tell you this: Be wary."

Curiosity catches me as I squint upward at the orisa, the setting sun behind her giving her a flaming halo. I open my mouth to ask more, but Sango has his eyes on us now. Before I have a chance to say anything else, the orisa draws back, her manner becoming more detached.

"Esu will want to know how many ships we find, husband," Oya says loudly, feeling his gaze even though her eyes are still on me. "Remember we promised we would tell him all of our encounters."

The storm swirls just beyond us, the air licking close, a crackling energy that I can feel in my very bones as I shiver. I understand what she's trying to say, that Esu has them helping him, keeping a lookout, while they track ships. Sango turns away as Abayomi asks him a question.

Checking that her husband is not watching, the orisa darts forward once more, bending down to whisper in my ear, her breath as cold as a winter storm. "You seek the very same rings as Esu, so you will need to be careful. The rings of Ile-Ife are powerful in many ways. He has told us he is closer than ever before to obtaining them."

Oya turns back to Sango before I can say anything else. Unease builds as I slip the sapphire into the top fold of my wrapper. Oya's words repeat in my mind as I edge my way back to Kola. I think of Yemoja and the other Mami Wata.

Esu wants the rings.

But I need them.

• • •

While Oya and Sango roam the decks, some of the crew trail after them, offering prayers. Abayomi approaches us, gripping a large sack.

"Supplies. As promised," he says. "I had a feeling you would want to be on your way."

"This will help us," Kola says, taking the food. "Thank you." He clasps the older man in a half hug and I know he's thanking him for what is to come. For the hunting down of the ship he was on. For revenge and liberation using orisa magic and the rage of people who are always willing to fight for freedom.

"May Yemoja protect you on the sea," offers Abayomi.

"And the same to you," I answer as I follow Kola to the rope ladder that slaps gently against the side of the ship.

"Abayomi said it'll take half a day to get to land." Kola slings the sack across his back, tying the ends so that it's secure for the short climb down. The wind still buffets the ship, the ladder swaying. "Which means we should be there just before sunrise."

"I thought perhaps . . . that you might have asked him to take you back home." Even as I ask Kola the question, I realize that I could be putting the idea into his head. My breath shortens at the thought of searching for the babalawo without him.

"Why would I?" Kola glances at me over his shoulder, eyebrows raised. "I told you I'd take you to the babalawo. I wouldn't break my word."

I nod at his response, feeling a warmth that turns into a smile, facing the sea to hide my expression. As Kola grasps the rope, his foot on the first rung, I look back, trying to see if I can spot the Oyo-Ile cloth. I can't see the men, but my eyes rest on Oya just as she turns to me. She smiles again, until her expression freezes. In two steps, she is next to me, the sheer fabric of her gown whispering around my legs, her fingernails digging into my arm.

"You must leave!" she hisses. With a shove she propels me closer to the side and I stumble against the smooth rail, only to be hauled quickly to my feet by Oya. "Esu is coming! I can feel him. Sango may have summoned him, or one of the crew could have prayed to him, showing you in their pleas. Go! Now!"

The orisa's eyes hold me, the dread in them sharpening the silver. I spin away and scramble down the ladder, wondering how far away Esu is. Kola stands, feet wide apart in the boat as he reaches up for me. My foot catches on a rung and my left hand slips.

"Careful!" Kola steadies me with a hand to my waist.

My heart is beating so fast that I'm not even annoyed at Kola for scolding me. I hook my foot back on the rung and hold tight to the sides of the ladder, the muscles in my arms and legs pulling uncomfortably. When I take the last step to reach the boat, Kola releases me.

"I'm beginning to think you like me catching you," he says with a grin, untying the rope.

"We need to go now," I say, my voice tight. "Oya said Esu is coming."

Kola sees my face and his expression hardens. Spinning away from me, he grabs at the knots, unfurling the sail as the wind plucks at it. Purpling clouds are gathering, thick and fast in the direction we need to travel in, and the smell of rain is heavy in the air.

"We're behind the storm Oya created." He slides closer to me, pointing east. "It's headed out faster than we can sail, but it'll give us enough wind power to get some distance between us and the ship."

"Quickly," I say, crouched in the middle of the boat as it pitches us from side to side.

Our small vessel skims the tops of the waves, moving away

from the ship. The clouds are racing now, but their denseness still makes me nervous. I say nothing, eyes on the larger vessel, willing the distance between us to increase as the last of the day departs in swathes of orange and red. Soon the colors are swallowed by the darkness that begins to unfold across the sky. The ship disappears, too, taking with it some of my tension. If Esu is on board, at least they are heading away from us.

Kola struggles with the sail, constantly adjusting it as he tries to keep the boat from spinning and tipping us into the waves. When the sun slips fully behind the horizon, the sea loses some of its wildness, flattening into a deep dark blue. I lean against the side of the boat as Kola finishes tying complicated-looking knots in the rope.

Finally he sits down, rolling his shoulders, glancing between the sea and me. Kola's large hands rest on his knees and I remember the way he held my waist when I slipped down the ladder. The palms, both soft and rough, and his warm grip. I shiver.

"Are you cold?" he asks.

I shake my head and force my gaze away from Kola. I think of the crew united in their mission to save more than themselves. Their courage reminding me of what Kola has also shown.

"Can I ask you something?" I tuck my feet underneath me, holding on to their new soles.

"You can," Kola says, his voice even.

"How did you end up on the ship you were thrown from?" I think of his words with Abayomi and my own memory of the hold.

Kola's hands twist into fists, mouth pulling down in a gleam of fresh moonlight. For a moment I think he won't answer, and then he begins to speak, his brows knitted tightly. "The Tapa from upriver waged war against us after we refused a trade. I wanted to prove myself to my father. I thought that if I could broker a peace between us, it would save many lives."

"And then?"

"They killed some of the guards I was with and sold the rest. Including me." Kola's eyes flash in the gloom. "I was traded to another village before being bought by the òyìnbó."

His words loosen something within me, but when I reach for it, it snakes out of my grasp.

"And that is the ship I was thrown from when you found me. I'm glad that Abayomi, Sango, and Oya will find it. Destroy it." Shadows wreathe Kola's face as the boat crests each night-darkened wave. I let the silence stretch, snatching looks at the boy, who stares out at the rolls of water.

"This is part of the reason I need to get back home," he says finally. "To see if my actions brought more than my own capture. What if the Tapa used me as leverage? What if my father has given in to their demands with me in mind? What if the òyìnbó . . . ?" Kola's face is wet. He can't finish, and his words are tightly spun with a pain that reflects the one buried inside me. He adjusts the knots of the ropes even though they don't need it, and I see him wipe his cheeks. "I saw your face on deck when we first boarded. What happened to you? How did you . . . ?"

I cast my mind back to when Yemoja had first given me purpose just months before, the seventh and last of the girls she remade in her image.

"I know I was on a ship like yours." The memory brought on by the sight of the hold courses through me once again and I am silent for a moment before continuing, swallowing the pain and fear down for the moment. "Mother Yemoja followed the òyìnbó ships when the first people of our lands were taken a little while ago, mourning their loss. Some say she swam alongside, offering comfort, while others say she wrecked the vessels, freeing us all in one way or another." I run a hand down my leg, massaging the softness of my soles; the dull ache that has been spreading eases momentarily. "But she did more than this for seven of us."

"She created you."

I nod. "The rest you know. Yemoja always impressed the importance of our task on us. I was the only one who didn't listen."

"No," says Kola, leaning forward out of the shadows at the same moment that a cloud shifts, showing the earnestness of his expression. "You were the one to find someone alive. To save them. Save me. And now, because of that, you're doing even more."

I think of what Kola has said, letting his words sink in. He smiles down at me, cheekbones sharp over his full lips, and I feel caught in his gaze. I look at our legs, so close that if I were to move even an inch, they would be touching. Kola watches me, and for a moment, it feels as if he's thinking the same, shifting his knee so that it briefly grazes mine. I freeze, my chest tightening as I hold my breath, my skin crackling at the barest brush of flesh.

Keep the goal of this journey firmly in mind and do not let yourself . . . feel too much. Not for any human.

Inhaling deeply, I draw back, pressing my spine against the wooden side of the boat and twisting away. I pretend to study the surface of the sea as moonlight splashes on the tallest waves before I sneak another look at Kola. The boy has his arm stretched along the rim of the vessel, looking relaxed, but he turns his gaze away from me, and for one silly moment, I feel a flood of disappointment. Don't start overthinking, I tell myself. It clearly doesn't mean anything to him.

You are of the sea now. It is forbidden.

And it can't mean anything to me, either. I sigh and turn away from Kola, studying the rise and fall of the waves.

The rings. They are what matter, I tell myself. Not this feeling that doesn't make sense, that can't make sense. I draw in a deep breath and turn back to Kola.

"Your family is clearly very important to you. For you to take such risks to get home . . ."

Kola doesn't reply straightaway. He leans back, features dipping back into the shadows thrown by the sail.

"They are special," Kola answers in a low voice. "My brother and sister doubly so."

I can't help the smile that appears, mirroring the one that blooms on his face. "Tell me about them."

"Twins." Kola exhales, lips still curved. "Taiwo and Kehinde. Loud and kind and . . ." The love in his tone softens the words, but then his face falls. "They are unique in another way, too. I'm supposed to be there for their ceremony performed by the babalawo—"

The sea cuts him off suddenly before he can finish. A heaving mass of waves snatches at our boat, tossing us toward the sky in an angry crush of water. Clouds swerve unnaturally, rushing on a vicious wind and accompanied with a crash of thunder that shakes the very air. We cling on as the storm surges back, folding in on itself, and aims for us, straight in its path. Kola looks at me, confusion on his face.

"It was pulling away!" he shouts above the wind that howls around us, reaching a feverish scream.

Holding on to the boat, I flinch as spikes of lightning stab through the mass of clouds. Silver and blue, they dazzle against the dark sky. This storm is not natural, I think, remembering

Oya's words. If Esu has commanded her to direct this at us, it means that he knows of me, perhaps even suspects that I'm looking for the same rings he is. I think of Oya, my certainty of her loyalty wavering, but I don't see why she would have warned me only to attack me. Maybe all it took was for one of the crew to describe me in their prayers, or maybe Sango saw my necklace before I hid it.

Regardless, it's clear that this sudden storm is meant for us.

Clinging to the side of the boat, I want to tell Kola that we need to change direction, that the storm won't ease, not if Esu is behind it, but it's too loud to make myself heard—the wind only snatches the words and eats them whole. The water roars as thunder booms, and then the sky is filled with shards of white light. Kola is thrown backward into the boat as I squeeze my eyes shut. I could dive under the water, but Kola wouldn't survive. The storm batters us with giant waves and blistering winds. The next peal of thunder seems even louder and forces us both to clap our hands over our ears as a large fork of glowing lightning hits the water next to us.

"Hold on!" I scream as winds tear at us, rocking the little boat violently. Another crack and even the air feels as if it's on fire.

"Simi!" shouts Kola, grabbing me, his voice piercing the night as we tumble backward.

We land in a pile of sea-slicked limbs as our mast, splintered and smoking, breaks free. I lean against the boy, my breath caught, chest hitching as the hot smell of fire permeates the air. Smoke and ashes slide over my teeth and onto my tongue as I try not to swallow. The mast has smashed right through the hull, leaving us perched precariously on what is left of the boat.

And then the lightning splits the sky open once again, blue

and brilliant white energy that zigzags toward us, and I fall back onto Kola, sending us crashing into the waves. I keep hold of him as my tail forms, seeking the surface, dragging him with me. We gasp into a burning sea and sky, the water foaming around us.

Our splintered boat careens on another wave, and as I hold Kola against me, we stare up while clouds are tossed about among the stars, revealing the rind of a thin moon. The sea heaves again, picking up the shards of our boat, breaking them apart and showering the remnants down on our heads.

CHAPTER ELEVEN

I OPEN MY mouth to scream and wake up to a swollen sky and knots of seaweed. My ears are ringing and there is sand in my mouth.

A flash of silver that ripped through the night. Thunder that made the whole world shake.

The sea laps at my side, rushing over the scales of my tail as I blink my eyes open on a new day. All I can see is water and clouds. The brightness sharpens the pain in my head and I close my eyes again, waiting until the worst passes.

A burning sail and Kola's screams.

Kola. Where is he?

Panic spikes in me when I think of him hurt, imagining his lifeless body sucked down into the deep or pushed against the beach. The sun is white-hot and relentless as I scrabble in the sand, trying to haul myself out of the incoming tide. My head rings from the effort and I lift an unsteady hand to my temple. I can't leave the water just yet. I'm not strong enough. I think of trying to find the babalawo on my own and doubt courses through me. I can't do this without Kola.

Brown eyes wide in shock as the night was lit by the energy of the storm. The mast crashing down on our heads.

The violence of the sea storm has shocked me, but really it's how vulnerable I was, only changing as the boat was smashed around us. Slow waves push me back and forth against the sand as I force the images from my mind and examine the shore. From the shallows, I can see that the beach is deserted, its bone-white sand stretching into the distance. The sea shows no hint of the viciousness it held last night. We've arrived at land, just not in the way we had planned.

"Kola?" I croak, scanning the sliver of beach all the way to the tree line. There's an opening where a river feeds into the bay and, bobbing just to the side, charred splinters of wood. "Kola!"

I push myself back into deeper water and swim toward the tributary, hating the sluggishness I feel. The ringing in my ears is gone, but I'm still weak enough that I must struggle with the surge of the current from the river. I swim until I get to what looks like part of the mast from our boat. Its edges are burned black, and shredded splinters show the force of the lightning that struck it.

"Kola!" Concern taints my voice with a shrillness I'm unused to.

I scan the beach and the narrow strip of earth that lines the river. And then I see it. A small scrap of blue farther up, half in the water. I swim deeper into the mouth of the river, eyes fixed on what looks like a torn part of Kola's wrapper. I pick it up, my hands shaking. It's definitely his, the same faded blue. Kola must have gotten this far. He could have decided to use the water to navigate inland.

I think of the wounds on his back and the way the storm battered even me. What will it have done to him?

I need to find him.

As I swim upriver, trees press in on either side, green and raw and alive. Flocks of birds, whose caws are as loud and bright as their fluorescent feathers, take flight from the tops of trees that seem as tall as the sky. The tributary shifts to brown, growing warmer as the bank turns to earth and grass. A movement below startles me, and I tense as a large catfish darts beneath my tail.

While it is still water, the river is different than the sea, and I try to relax the tension that knots my muscles together. It's easier than land, I tell myself as the current tugs at me. Cautious, I scan the forest as I go, hoping to see more signs of Kola but wary of Esu and any òyìnbó. The bank is full of low bushes with budding flowers that are just beginning to unfurl. There is still room for a person to walk next to the river, so I continue until I hear a sudden rustle. Leaves shake as something moves through the bushes. I place wet fingertips on the emerald of my dagger. Just as I'm about to slide it free from my braids, I freeze, staring open-mouthed at the creature standing on the narrow bank.

Silver-gray hooves paw nervously at the earth, and two long pearlescent horns spiral backward from its head. With its squat donkey-sized body, it does not, at first, resemble the magical creature storytellers describe to children, but as I glide closer, it turns to look at me with turquoise eyes.

An abada.

It is said to be a harbinger of the lost; I don't doubt that it is showing itself to me for a reason.

Kola.

I try to swim even closer but stop when the abada prances backward, eyes rolling.

"It is fine, little one. I won't hurt you," I murmur, my heart beating wildly.

If the creature bolts, I doubt I'll be able to find it again. Abadas are only found when they want to be. I am about to emerge from the river when the animal snorts and trots down the bank a little. Its neigh is soft, almost like a sigh. The creature turns its head to look at me and I slip back into the river and begin to swim alongside it.

As the abada canters beside the water, I'm careful not to lose sight of it, especially when the creature is forced to weave in and out of the trees where the bank of the river is too narrow. Every so often, it pauses, checking to make sure I'm still following.

We are deeper inland now and the trees bend toward one another, stretching over the water, nearly blocking the sky and providing a cool relief from the midafternoon sun. The forest is louder. Looking up into the canopy, I catch sight of tiny birds that hover high above, their red-and-yellow faces peeping at me from behind the large leaves of banana trees.

When the heat of the day grows to nearly oppressive levels, the abada stops at a split in the river where a smaller stream bends to the left. It paws at the ground in agitation.

"What is it?" I whisper, sweat trickling from my brow. I want to duck underneath to cool myself, but I don't want to risk losing the abada.

The creature neighs again.

"Kola?" I call softly, hope coloring my words as I turn in a slow circle, looking around.

No answer. The abada neighs again, more loudly this time, before it treads carefully around the bushes and trots along the smaller waterway.

"Wait!" I call, diving to catch up.

Mud scrapes at my tail as the stream, just deep enough for me to swim, leads us farther into the forest. The quiet and gloom are disconcerting after the wider river, and I glance about uneasily. Even the bank is narrower, forcing the abada to prance in and out of the stony shallows. As we work our way down the stream, the trees cover the sun almost entirely, making shadows on the brown water and darkening the green of leaves. The bank is a sliver of black earth and stones, and I frown at the thought of Kola trying to navigate this part of the tributary. The abada ambles ahead of me, nimble even on the rocky ground. I start to have second thoughts about whether I should have followed it this far, and then I see the stream open out into a large pond. The abada emits another neigh, louder this time, as it heads toward the bushes that line the water.

There are no birdcalls or hoots now. I peer around as the silence grows. *Keep moving,* I think as I heave myself from the water. My wrapper forms as I hunch over at the side of the pond, wet hair and skin glistening in the muted light.

"Please wait," I call to the abada as it moves between the bushes. And it does, not flinching when I reach for it. "Thank you for bringing me this far," I murmur as I stroke its silken mane.

The creature can't be taller than my shoulders, but its horns are almost twice its height, curving backward, glowing in a shaft of sunlight that pierces the canopy. It is said that an abada's horns have the power to cure disease or counteract any poison. The creature turns to me with its turquoise eyes, silvered around the edges, and I feel a sense of calm flooding through my mind. I run a hand down its withers and the abada tosses its head in pleasure, allowing me a moment more of its attention before it presses forward through overgrown bushes. I follow, the shadows deepening as we move farther inland.

This part of the forest is humid, the heat trapped beneath the canopy above. The ground is damp beneath my feet, deep with decomposing leaves and soft black earth. A large gray spider with a yellow stripe down its back and red eyes scuttles past, and I take even more care where I'm treading, measuring my steps and getting used to the rhythm of walking again. As the abada pushes past a bush with oversized purple flowers and a scent that reminds me of honey, I hear a sound that makes me stop.

A faint pounding of drums. As thick and fast as my pulse, the sound grows louder until the ground feels as if it is shaking beneath the soft soles of my bare feet. The abada comes back to stand beside me and then nudges me forward, its muzzle and breath warm on my back, until I stumble through the bushes and find myself looking out onto a large glade.

The hot curve of the sun slides behind the tree line, and in the middle of the wide-open space people are dancing, weaving between grasses almost as tall as they are small.

Tiny people.

With silver hair braided into long plaits, they whirl almost frantically to the beat of a dozen gangan drums. Small hands beat sticks against the taut skin, a blur that produces a rhythm I've never heard before. And there, in the middle of the clearing, laid on a bed of dried grass and draped in white cloth, is Kola.

The beat of the drums covers my gasp of surprise. His eyes are closed and his arms are folded over his chest. His feet stick out from the end of the cloth, and I remember the paleness of his soles when I first found him in the water.

Lifeless, he is laid out as if ready for his last prayers, and something inside me shatters.

I swallow hard and creep forward, trying to get a better look. The abada snorts suddenly behind me and I jump, tripping over a rotting tree trunk, and stagger into the clearing.

The drums stop. The dancers freeze, their plaits cascading down narrow backs. Turning almost as one, they regard me with pale golden eyes.

"Yumboes," I whisper.

CHAPTER TWELVE

I SCRAMBLE BACKWARD to stand at the edge of the glade as the yumboes stare at me. No higher than my hip, with gleaming ebony skin encased in ivory wrappers and silver hair in skinny plaits, the fairies number at least a hundred. Backing away, I press against the abada, trying to remember what I know about yumboes. Also known as the Bakhna Rakhna, Good People, the fairies live underground in secret hills, fishing and stealing corn from humans. They are not a threat, I remember that much, especially if they show themselves to you, which is very rare.

"Kola?" I call as I edge closer.

The abada is warm behind me, its hide prickly against my skin. If it's not scared, then I shouldn't be, I tell myself, and I take another step forward.

Kola does not stir, and I hold my breath as I scan his chest, looking for movement. The yumboes don't try to stop me as I wind my way through the throng. A small boy, with tiny plaits twisted with silver, bows as he moves from my path, and I feel my nerves ease slightly.

"He is not dead," says the yumbo, his golden eyes crinkling as he grins at me.

His words offer me a brief respite from worry until I see again how still Kola appears. "Are you sure?" I ask, pressing forward.

The boy follows me, skipping to catch up as I reach the bed of grass. "I found him after the storm. In the sea. I persuaded my grandfather to bring the rest of the boats to help and we pulled him from the bay."

As I get closer to Kola, I start to see the rise and fall of his chest; relief weakens my legs and I stumble again, this time barely catching myself. "Why is he laid out like this? I thought . . ."

"We are singing and dancing for his health." The yumbo boy is at my side still. He leans over and pokes Kola's stomach lightly. "He ate and then lost consciousness again, but he should wake up soon."

The beat of the drums begins and the yumboes start to dance around the abada. The creature prances among them, tossing its mane. I sit by Kola, watching as small feet produce complicated rhythms and silvered plaits glitter in the sunlight. It is when they begin to sing that I start to smile. Almost as one, their voices blend together, high and sweet, a prayer of good health and luck, their blessing filling the clearing and my heart with joy.

The yumboes continue to dance, small hands thrown to the sky as they stamp their feet to the beat of the gangan drums.

"Simi?" Kola's eyes open as he shifts, and the cloth slips from his chest. He tries to sit up and I hear the hiss that escapes his lips, see the way he holds his left side. A large bump has formed on his forehead, but other than that he is uninjured. "How did you get here?" he asks, eyes flitting over me. "Are you hurt?"

"I am well," I answer. I'm so grateful that Kola is alive that I almost reach out to smooth his hair and feel the warmth of his skin for myself. "I woke up on the shore. All that was left of the boat was splinters. I thought . . ." I slide my gaze away.

"I was worried about you, too," says Kola. At his words I feel a warmth bloom inside me. "The yumboes saved me. I saw them in the water. Simi, I swear I thought they were sent by one of the ajogun before they dragged me from the sea." Kola grins.

"Which warrior? Death?"

"Why not? Mami Wata, Sango and Oya. What next?"

"This is the second time you have nearly died," I say, looking down at the curve of Kola's lips. "Are you trying to make this a habit?"

"Passing in the sea?"

And with those words I'm reminded that I am not the same as him. I wouldn't die in the sea. I wouldn't drown. But Kola could.

He is human and I am not.

For a moment, this is all I can think of.

"Nearly dying," I confirm, looking away. I tell myself that I only care because Kola's death would mean that the sacrifice I made was for nothing, but the thought of it makes my heart beat hard against the cage of my chest.

"Simi—" Kola sits up as the drums build to a crescendo, the sheet falling from his body.

"You are awake!" exclaims the same yumbo boy who had told me Kola was alive earlier.

No taller than my knee, he runs over and beams at us, his face turned up at Kola as if he were the sun. Grinning widely, the yumbo comes closer, teeth shining like tiny pearls. He bows again, right leg crossed over the other as he lowers his head and places a tiny fist against his heart.

"I am Issa and I am the one who found you!" The yumbo flattens a hand on Kola's chest, pushing him back down. "You must rest. Save your strength for when it is time to eat." He fusses with the sheet around Kola, clucking like a mother hen. "Now that you are awake, I will fetch my grandfather and some food."

"Thank you, Issa," replies Kola, smiling at the boy as the yumbo finishes tugging the cloth back over his chest.

When he's satisfied that Kola is tucked up properly, Issa runs off, shouting loudly about fish and scattering other yumboes as he flaps his arms. He returns almost immediately, accompanied by an older yumbo with amber eyes and long silver-gray plaits.

"Welcome. My name is Salif." He bows, a hand splayed on his bony chest. "We are grateful and blessed to have you both as guests. Only people chosen by the yumboes can even find this clearing. Unless you are otherworldly . . . And then the abada will choose whether it leads you here. Like calls to like." Salif catches my eye before his gaze goes to my feet. "We have come across Mami Wata before in the seas. Yemoja has always blessed us with our fishing. Please thank her next time you summon her."

I nod once, scuffing my feet in the dirt as Issa looks up at me shyly.

"Join us and eat. My grandson would be most upset if you did not," continues Salif, patting Issa's shoulder. "And if we can help you in any way, we will discuss it then."

"Thank you," I answer as Kola murmurs his agreement.

Salif darts away, calling out orders, and we are left with Issa, who sits next to Kola. The smell of spiced food floats across the clearing from a bank of fires, where several yumboes oversee the preparation of an enormous catfish, baking slowly at the outer edge of the burning coals. Wooden tables are set up with small narrow benches under the largest tree that leans over the glade. Smaller yumboes flit about, decorating by adding purple flowers with golden centers. Others dig at the edge of the clearing, excavating buried flasks of palm wine. Carefully, they fill the cups set out, not spilling a drop.

As the yumboes take their places at the tables, Issa leads us to a bigger log that has been set out for us to sit on. Kola's side seems not to be paining him as much, and even the lump on his head has subsided somewhat. He catches me examining him and I look away quickly.

Salif remains standing. He claps his hands together three times and the yumboes look up from their seats, eyes glowing the color of dark honey.

"We are honored today to have not one but two special guests." Salif remains standing, smiling at us. "As you all know, we rescued one from the sea and its black rocks, and the other was brought to us by the sacred abada. Let us all eat and drink together!" He raises his glass and takes a large gulp of palm wine. "Sí àwọn olóríire! To the lucky ones!"

"Sí àwọn olóríire!" The yumboes hold their wooden cups up and Kola nudges me to do the same. I do, until I see the food arrive and nearly spill my drink.

"What is *that*?" I ask as steaming dishes of fish that seem to float along head our way.

"Food," Issa answers brightly, giggling at my shock. "We have helpers, but ones which you will never see. Well, not all of them, anyway."

The silver platters bob in the air, weaving round tree roots as they make their way to the tables. Deep brown hands hold the trays of food with thick fingers, but I can't see anything else of the strange creatures.

"Who's holding it?"

Issa grins and points at a matching set of brown feet, which pick their way across the forest floor. "They are invisible apart from their hands and feet. We call them olùrànlọ́wọ́. Helper."

Altogether, I count ten helpers who lay more platters of corn and peppered catfish on the long table. Two others come with smaller calabashes of water to wash our fingers, and more flasks of palm wine. I can't take my eyes off the bobbing hands and am relieved when they have served the food and disappear.

"Don't worry, the olùrànlọ́wọ́ are conjured beings. Summoned only when the yumboes find certain tasks difficult or need help." Kola grins at my face, nudging his cup against mine with its smooth wooden side. "Drink your wine. It will make Salif happy. Bakhna Rakhna consider one guest to be a gift, but two is a veritable blessing."

I take a sip and my mouth puckers as my eyes water, its sourness too much for me.

"Strong?"

"I'm glad the cups are small," I say, and Kola bursts into laughter. His laugh is loud and sweet, and I realize it's the first time I've heard it. I take another cautious sip, but this time I don't wince.

Around us, the yumboes strip the fish with their fingers, placing white fillets in tiny mouths. Issa sits beside Salif and chatters away, bits of corn smeared around his mouth.

"How do you know all this?" I ask. "The helpers, the customs?"

Kola looks slightly sheepish. "I loved the tales of the elders. I always listened, and then I would tell them to Taiwo and Kehinde. A story always helped them sleep." His small smile contains so much love that I feel my mouth forming one, too. "Never did I think they were real or that I'd be sharing food with them." He takes another sip of his drink. "But then I didn't think other things were real and . . ."

"Here I am," I finish. "So, tell me," I say, folding the nervous quiver of my hands in my lap. "What were your favorite stories? Of the ones you used to listen to? Pretending you were only there for the twins?" I nudge him with my shoulder. "Which ones did you beg for?"

Kola pushes the bones of his fish to the side and lifts the golden corn, biting some off and chewing. I can tell he's taking the time to think carefully.

When he is done, he lifts his head and looks straight at me. "Tales of orisa, of course."

"There are over four hundred Yoruba gods . . . be more specific," I tease, finishing the last of my wine. I set the cup down, vowing never to drink something as foul again. From the other end of the table, Salif sees me and lifts his glass, grinning. At least he's enjoying it, I think.

"Which orisa's story do you think I asked for the most?"

"How about Osun?"

"There is no one more loving or beautiful," Kola says. "But not her."

"Osanyin, god of plants and healing."

Kola shakes his head. "I'll give you one last guess."

I turn to watch some of the yumboes who have left their seats and have begun to dance again, most with wooden cups of wine still clutched in their hands. The humidity of the forest seems not to affect them as they spin and turn, sunlight skittering from their skin and the precious metal in their hair.

"What about Ori?" I say finally. Truth be told, Kola's favorite story could be one of dozens, especially since the power and origins of orisa are changeable depending on whom you speak to.

"Ogun. He is my ancestral orisa." Kola takes another sip of

his drink and grins, his lips wet with wine. "And my favorite. In my village the elders used to tell the story of Ogun before anyone went out to hunt." Kola leans toward me, elbows on his knees, his leg brushing against mine. "I love his strength."

"And his weapons, no doubt," I say. The orisa is famous for his blacksmithing skills.

"Well, yes, but it is more than that. He is honorable. Ogun deals with justice and oaths." Kola shifts next to me, placing his cup on the table. "I swore to the twins and to the rest of my family that I would always protect them."

We are silent a moment. His hand is next to mine on the table and my fingers twitch, wanting to touch his. To comfort. We both have responsibilities, those we want to protect. I think of the scars on Yemoja's face, my shoulders slumping at the thought of anything else happening. I won't fail her.

"And you will," I say. "We'll leave after we have eaten. In fact, I'm sure Salif can tell us the fastest way to get to your village. What's the name?"

Kola pauses and I don't take my eyes from him. Will he keep this from me, even now? "Oko," he answers. "My village is called Oko."

I nod, rolling the name in my mind, more pleased than I can admit that he has told me, has trusted me. "Let's see if the yumboes can direct us."

Salif sees me craning my neck, looking for him. He pushes the last of the peppered catfish into his mouth and then jumps up and makes his way over to us, followed by Issa. Salif motions, one small hand chopping the air, and a large flask of wine hovers over to us, carried by strong brown hands.

"No!" I clap my hand hastily over the rim of my cup and try to soften the move with a smile. "Thank you."

The elder yumbo bows to us. "As you wish."

"Salif, do you know of a village called Oko, near to the mouth of the river Ogun?"

Kola leans forward, eager. "They mainly trade in fish, with some corn in the later summer."

"Yes, yes, I know of it." Salif tips his head back, finishing his drink. "A bountiful village. Is this where you are headed?"

"We are," I answer. "How far would you say it is?"

"If you left now, you would reach it by morning."

I rotate my ankle, pointing my toes to stretch my thigh muscles. I'm not sure how well my legs will serve me on an entire nighttime's worth of walking.

"Have you or any of the others been there recently?" asks Kola.

The yumbo sets his empty cup on the table. "We have not heard anything about Oko, no. Although—"

Salif doesn't finish his sentence, his voice cut off along with the other yumboes'. They freeze as one and even Issa, tucked next to Kola, stops chewing his food, his mouth hanging open, a solitary piece of corn clinging to his bottom lip.

I look around us and Kola does too, the same confusion I feel rippling across his face. Gently, he shakes Issa, who doesn't respond, his amber gaze remaining unfocused. Salif shudders once, his whole body quivering before he folds over, a loud keening noise coming from his open mouth. The rest of the yumboes do the same, eyes closing as they cry out. Those who have been twirling to the beat of the drum fall to the ground, tiny bodies and silver plaits scattered in small mounds across the glade.

"What is it?" asks Kola, his voice rough as he peers down at Issa. "Are they all right?"

"I don't know," I answer. There is a small, unsettling tug in my stomach, but it's nowhere near as strong as what is happening to the yumboes. I bend down to touch a hand to Issa, but he doesn't respond, eyelashes metallic bright against the brown of his cheeks.

I walk into the center of the clearing, bending down to check each yumbo that I can, the unease in my stomach growing, tightening. "They're all breathing," I say, straightening up to turn back to Kola, but he's not there.

I am surrounded by a forest of black trees, their gnarled branches clawing at a sky the color of fresh bruises. A thick, unnatural silence blankets everything and the stench of rot and death hangs in the air, catching in the back of my throat and making me retch. Spinning, I stagger, crying out with pain as I look down at the dark earth. I am standing on shards of tiny fairy bones, splintered in the gloom of the dead forest. A tide of sorrow grabs at me and I bend over, clutching at my stomach.

"Kola!" I scream, inching backward, hands at my mouth.

But there is no one to answer me. Only desiccated plants and the remains of the yumboes in bleached white fragments that litter the ground. I am running then, tearing past charcoal trees, slipping on the remains that I don't want to see. The forest opens up, sloping down rolling hills that join fields dotted black with the stiff stalks of dead crops. The corpses of cows and goats decompose gently in the sun, its heat and light the only vibrant thing in this landscape. Spotting a wall that surrounds multiple compounds, I head toward the village, my heart beating faster. Slowing down, I pass through flung-open gates carved with images of the sea and lush crops. When I see them I stop, breath burning in my chest. The dead. The villagers lie on the red earth, mouths open in final screams, hands in claws, skin hanging in dark folds. Sores and bones and ribs poke through wrappers. I squeeze my eyes shut and open my mouth, screaming until my throat is scraped dry.

"Simi, Simi!"

I open my eyes to Kola's, his thick eyebrows drawn together in a frown of concern. Sobbing, I push my face against his chest as he holds me until I stop gasping and crying.

"What is it? What happened?"

"I saw—" But I don't have a chance to finish. A loud collective gasp fills the air and, as one, the yumboes sit up, faces blank, nectar-colored eyes blinking, their gazes soft and unfocused. Issa begins to cry and Kola releases me to wrap an arm tight around the yumbo.

"Salif," Kola murmurs. "What was that? What just happened?"

The elder yumbo takes in deep breaths, smoothing his plaits back, gold and silver twined around each braid. "We are connected to the earth." Salif fills his cup with unsteady hands. "Anything that upsets the balance of it? We feel." He drains the palm wine and swallows.

"Did you . . . see anything?" I ask, gulping in air, heavy with the despair of my vision. I force in a deep breath, calming the tremble of my legs.

"Something has happened," states Salif, filling his cup again, his hands shaking enough for him to spill some of the palm wine.

"What do you think it could be?" I ask, thinking of when the storms at sea form, the feeling I get, the scent in the air. The feeling of something coming. I think of the bones I stood on in my vision. The dead crops and the twisted corpses in the village.

Kola's face is ashen as he looks at me. "I think I know." He turns to Salif, his words slow and heavy. "The twins, Taiwo and Kehinde."

"What do you mean?" I ask, frowning now. None of this is making much sense.

Kola shifts on the bench and places his hands flat on the table in front of him. He takes a deep breath. "They are Ibeji."

"Orisa?" I ask, the word rising with my surprise. I think of what I know of the twin gods, one soul in both bodies, orisas of glee and mischief as well as abundance. Their presence brings happiness and health to people and life to the lands they live in.

"Close enough. The Ibeji have manifested in Taiwo and Kehinde. The babalawo prophesied it." Kola brings his hands together, squeezing a fist with the long fingers of his other hand. "With their birth came a time when Oko truly flourished, as well as the land all around it."

"This is why we settled here," adds Salif, his hands gesturing around him. "We had heard that there was Ibeji power within these grounds. And when we arrived here, we felt it."

"My family kept this quiet, not even the villagers knew. There is to be a ceremony. To confirm and protect them. I was supposed to be there, to make sure they were safe until it was done." Kola turns to Salif, bending down so he can look him in the eye. "Could that be what you have sensed?"

I hear the hope in his voice, but Salif shakes his head. "Such a ceremony would only confirm and establish their power. What I felt, what we all felt, was a . . . severing of some kind."

"What if something has happened to Taiwo and Kehinde? What if I'm too late?" Kola runs both hands over his face, fingers snagging on his lower lip. "What if they're dead?"

CHAPTER THIRTEEN

"WE DON'T KNOW anything for sure yet," I say to Kola, trying to keep my tone calm. But why didn't he tell me about the twins before? Is it just that he doesn't trust me? He acted as if summoning Yemoja was his first time meeting an orisa, and now this. And then I think of his need to protect the children, and not mentioning their power makes more sense.

At the thought of kept secrets, I think of my vision. Perhaps I should say something. About the death. The yumboes and the village. Shuddering, I push thoughts of it away. I try to tell myself that what I saw doesn't mean anything, but even as I think this, I know it's not true. But I do know that I can't tell anyone else about it until I understand what it means myself. Both Kola and Salif are worried enough. Before I can give it more thought, the older yumbo claps his hands together.

"I hope all of you are well. Do not worry, we will work on finding out what this means. All signs need to be understood, not feared just because they are unknown. So, in the interim, let us finish the feast." The yumboes nod at Salif's instruction. The olùrànlọ́wọ́ flit about, clearing the silver platters and banking the fire as the sun dips behind the tree line. Yumboes, the energy seemingly drawn out of them, are dotted in groups around the glade, speaking quietly.

"There is one more thing that adds to what has happened. I am not sure if this is connected, and I do not wish to worry the others, so I will say this only to you two." Salif turns to us with a solemn face, his hands clasped in front of him. "Some of the yumboes have been out gathering, and our brothers have only just returned." Salif pauses before picking up the wooden cup again and then putting it down. "They overheard the men talk of . . . Esu on the borders of our lands."

"Esu?" I ask uneasily. "Why would his name be mentioned?"

"It is not the first time we have heard it lately," says Salif. "There are . . . rumors."

"Go on," says Kola, his face drawn as he swallows carefully.

I see worry and concern in the molten amber of Salif's eyes, and I think I know what he's going to say. "Rumors that he is searching for something."

Oya said the same. If the babalawo has the rings and Taiwo and Kehinde are in Oko . . . I look over at Kola, the worry I feel matching the expression on his face.

"We need to leave," I say quietly, my words taut with apprehension. First Esu arrives on Abayomi's ship and now his presence is being spoken about closer to Oko. Kola nods, his expression as grim as mine as he gets to his feet.

"Allow us to present you with supplies," says Salif, tasking his grandson with the responsibility.

Issa, the job giving him some energy, orders the other yumboes around, changing the waterskins they have for bigger ones and inspecting all the fish wrapped in banana leaves.

"You have to fold them tight! Or they will spoil!" he admonishes a boy larger than him. The yumbo huffs but begins to wrap the food again.

Issa nods in satisfaction and then darts over to Kola. "I want to help," he says.

"Come now, Issa, let them prepare," says Salif, tucking the boy under his arm.

"But I can help!" The yumbo darts from under his grandfather's grip and runs over to us, his eyes never leaving Kola.

He snatches the sack from a yumbo heading toward us. Dragging it quickly along, he drops it at our feet and looks up at us, golden eyes shining. "I can guide you to Oko. That's where you are heading, no?"

At this, Kola bends down, a slight smile on his lips. "We appreciate your hospitality, but you are very young. Your place is here."

"Please!" Issa cries, and turns to Salif. "Grandfather, they might get lost! Or, or . . . they'll take a long way and not get there for days! We all felt . . . whatever that was earlier. They need to get to Oko fast, and I can help them do that."

Kola stills at the mention of time, and I know he is wavering.

"Grandfather, I have scouted before. Please let me! I know all the paths and tracks to take. The routes to avoid." Issa puffs his narrow chest out. "They *need* me."

I consider the yumbo with his tiny sticklike arms and his pointed chin. He flips his head, pushing plaits from his eyes and watching Kola, who looks down at him with a tenderness that makes me uneasy. We don't need someone else to look after.

"Kola, I don't think that's a good idea."

"It could take you days if you don't go the right way," says Issa, offering Kola a grin. "I can get you there in half the time."

"It would help," says Kola softly.

Issa beams at him and then turns his honey gaze on me. "I can do it, Simi. I can."

Kola places a hand on his shoulder and looks at me, too. "If he can guide us there, we need him. Besides"—he pats Issa on his head—"you'll be good company."

"I will be, ẹ̀gbọ́n ọkùnrin." The yumbo grins up at Kola, jiggling from foot to foot.

I frown. What does Issa think he's doing, already calling Kola big brother? But his smile is sweet, and we really can't afford to waste any more time getting to the village. I nod. If Esu does know the rings are in Oko, we need to get there first.

"Grandfather?" asks Issa.

Salif takes a moment to think before answering the yumbo. "I give you my permission, little one. But only as a guide." He holds a finger up. "Nothing else."

Issa scrambles around the sack, tripping. "I will get my things!"

"You will need to come straight back after they reach Oko," calls Salif. "Straight back!"

"I will!" Issa throws over his shoulder as he scurries off.

"I'll look after him as if he were my little brother," says Kola, pressing his open palm to his heart. "I promise."

"Make sure that you do." Salif bows, mirroring Kola's action. "I would like to know what caused the feeling that affected us. We need to know if we are still safe here."

He waits as Kola checks the bag, extracting a short sword that he slips into the tight folds of his wrapper. "We are grateful, Salif. To have saved me and now to allow us a guide? We are blessed. You have my thanks. And as much corn as you wish to take once I get back to Oko."

"I will collect on that promise," answers Salif, managing to crack a small smile as Issa runs back, giving him a quick hug before he comes to stand by our sides. "One more thing we can give you." Salif holds out a tiny bag. "The abada allows us to harvest part of her horns every few years. There is a small amount in there. It can be mixed with water to drink or used to make a poultice. Either way, it will cure almost anything." Salif nods solemnly. "We will bless your journey with dance and prayer."

While Issa tucks the powder into the sack with our supplies, Kola nods, returning the gesture. "And I thank you for rescuing me and making both of us welcome."

"I will be back," says the small yumbo, throwing a grin at his grandfather. "Do not worry."

Salif reaches down and kisses Issa on both of his cheeks, taking a moment to stare into his eyes. "Remember, stay safe and return once you have guided them."

The yumbo nods eagerly, spinning away to grab at the sack, but Kola plucks it from Issa's grip, ignoring the boy's protests. The rest of the yumboes begin to sing softly as the gangan drums begin again, beats that reverberate all around, bidding us goodbye as we head toward the sunset-soaked tree line. Issa skips ahead, moving fast as he chatters to Kola, taking pride in leading us through the easiest paths.

"And what is this plant, àbùrò ọkùnrin?" Kola points to a large bush, its leaves spiny and dark green.

Little brother. Issa lifts his face to Kola, as he talks about the Nganda coffee plant, plucking some of the ripened cherries that produce beans. "My grandfather loves the bitter drink they make and so I collect lots for him." Issa tucks the cherries into the bag and skips ahead, looking back over his shoulder at us. "Come on, this way!"

We follow the yumbo through the forest, moving quickly through the crash of olive and lime foliage. Issa selects pathways that skirt white mahogany and pear trees, leading us deeper where the air is more humid and the smell of the rich earth rises to greet us with every footstep. He talks nonstop, making Kola laugh at one point.

I drop back a little, my feet aching already. Flexing my toes, I take a moment to stretch the arches, taking a sip of water. Kola and Issa continue walking, the setting sun blazing through the canopy. The yumbo reaches up and takes Kola's hand, hopping and jumping to keep up with the boy's stride. I hear another giggle and feel a shade of envy at how easy they are together already.

Worse, I still can't push away the mention of Esu. That he has been rumored to be nearby only makes my stomach twist even tighter into knots.

I force myself to quicken my pace as Kola turns around, looking back for me.

"How much farther, Issa?" I wipe my face, feeling sweat trickle into the folds of my wrapper. It is an uncomfortable feeling and one I haven't experienced for a while.

"We'll reach the river soon," says Issa as he pushes a large leaf out of his way. "And then Oko is a few hours' walk from there. We should—"

The rest of the yumbo's words are swallowed by the cracking sounds that echo around the forest. We freeze. An owl calls out in the distance as the night claws more light from the day, and then the noise is there again. Louder this time and coming nearer. Trees shake and it sounds as if thunder is striking the ground.

"Kola?"

He doesn't answer but lifts Issa and backs up, standing slightly in front of me.

My breath comes in panicked exhalations as the first creature bursts out of the trees directly in front of us. White tusks flash in the gloom along with ears that hang down in great loops of tough gray skin. The large elephant sweeps a sapling out of her path, trumpeting loudly. Lifting her thick gray legs, she barrels toward us, her eyes shining and rolling with fear.

I drag Kola to the side as the elephant sweeps toward us, trampling bushes in her path, making way for the rest of the herd behind her. With our backs pressed against the rough bark of a white mahogany tree, I hold my breath as she stampedes past us, four smaller cows following with two calves that they shove along between them. One falls to the ground and cries out, but its mother nudges and pulls, dragging her baby up before it can be crushed. None look at us or take any notice of our presence. They move fast, running hard and leaving a ruined path of forest behind them.

"They can sense something, too," Issa says from the safety of Kola's arms. He wriggles free and takes a tentative step in the direction the elephants came from. "This is the way we need to head."

Of course it is. Peering ahead as the shadows creep through the trees, I swallow and take two steps forward. "Then let's go."

I walk as fast as the ache in my feet will allow me, pushing the growing pain to the back of my mind. The elephants have cleared a path, but I can't stop thinking about the fear in their eyes and the way the young calf was nearly stamped on in their haste to get away. From what? Salif said that the yumboes had felt a disconnection from the land. Was that enough to scare the animals?

I think of my vision and the rumors of Esu as another trickle of sweat runs down my back. I slip my fingers into the tight braids that crown my hair and pull out the dagger, flicking its blade free. The weapon makes me feel better, but not by much.

We pick our way through the destruction of the forest until my soles feel as if they are on fire with raw pain. I fight the urge to limp, relieved when I feel a tug deep in my stomach and my skin crackles as if the scales are trying to slice their way through. Water. It's close by, I can feel it. Hobbling a little faster, I'm rewarded with the rushing sounds of a river. If I can soak in the water for a bit, I know I'll feel better. The sound is clear now and growing louder, permeating the still night air that wraps around us. Issa scampers next to me and points to a bend.

"There. A river," he announces as the muted sound grows louder. He speeds ahead of me, little legs pumping as he vaults a fallen tree before spinning to face me. "One we need to cross."

We follow the yumbo as he pushes through the undergrowth until the flowing water is revealed. I gaze around warily, trying to find a clue to what the elephants were running from, but there's nothing apart from the scent of stones and mud with an underlying rot. I push the unusual smell out of my mind and place the dagger back among my braids. Rivers are different from seas, that's all.

Twilight shades the rocks that line the banks, and trees loom over the fast-running current. The eddying water calls to me and I slink forward, eager to feel its coolness.

I bend down, dipping a hand into the river, exhaling as I feel the silky slip of it, the thought of submerging myself in it all-encompassing.

"It looks deep," says Kola, peering over my shoulder. "Will it help?"

Startled, I pause in reaching down before nodding. He noticed, I think, feeling a warmth spread across my chest and up my neck. I thought I had hidden the pain well.

"Good," Kola adds softly, his eyes lingering on me for a moment before he pads after the yumbo.

"Ẹ̀gbọ́n ọkùnrin, we can cross just over here." Issa parts a large leaf to reveal the first slats of a wooden bridge held together with thick rope.

"Are you sure this will take my weight?" Kola eyes it critically. "I'm definitely not as light as a yumbo."

"Yes, yes, it can hold many people," answers Issa, scampering ahead to the bridge. He jumps a few times to show us how sturdy it is. "See?"

I watch them from the bank, feet already eased into the water, the scales developing quickly, the pain in my soles disappearing as my fin forms. Issa is already across the bridge, waving at Kola happily, the silver in his hair glittering in the moonlight. I submerge more of my legs until they fuse, gold and pink scales glinting. It feels so good that my eyelids flutter with pleasure and relief. I let the river swallow me, dipping underneath its surface and spinning in the chilled water.

When I head back to the humid air, Kola is halfway across the bridge and Issa is jumping about on the other side of the bank, clapping his hands. I smooth the curls from my shoulders and smile.

"I told you it was safe!" the yumbo crows.

Kola looks up and waves, and it is at this moment that the

wooden slats beneath his feet crack loudly, giving way and sending him plunging into the river below. When he surfaces, spluttering, I laugh and twirl in the water, letting the fan of my tail split the river's surface.

"Shall I come and help you?" I cup my hands and shout, not bothering to hide my smirk.

Drops of water sparkle in midair as Kola shakes his head. "I'm fine."

"Oh, ẹ̀gbọ́n ọkùnrin, I am sorry!" calls Issa, almost in tears. "The wood must have rotted since we last crossed. Here, come to me and I will pull you out!"

"I'm all right, little one," says Kola as he begins to swim to the bank. "There's no need to get upset."

As he cuts through the water with powerful strokes, I notice large bubbles and a ripple from upstream. The smell of rot from earlier grows stronger and I swim closer, examining the water, the hair on my arms rising when I see it surge. The river begins to churn and then Kola is gone before I can speak, snatched beneath the surface.

• • •

I dive under, but I can't see through all the mud in the river. Swimming back up, I gasp in the still air. "Issa! Did you see where he went?" I yell. I scan the river wildly, but it's calm now, small eddies the only disturbance.

The yumbo shakes his head, his mouth pulled down, eyes wide. He crawls forward to the grassy lip of the bank.

"Kola!" I call again, my hands making small circles as I hover just above the surface, half expecting him to appear, splash water at us, and laugh. But the river is smooth, flowing quickly downstream. "Adekola!"

There's a whorl in the middle, and the river starts to froth as if beginning to boil. I pull my dagger free just as Kola bursts through the surface, clutched in the jaws of something both serpentine and strangely equine.

Kola reaches out a hand to me as the creature rears up, his side clamped in its mouth. The rotten scent I caught earlier increases as the breath of the creature reaches me. Three horns jut from the large head as yellow eyes roll from river to sky and then back to water. With a thick sinuous body and a long neck, the creature looks just like its name, devil-dragon.

"Ninki Nanka! Ninki Nanka!" shouts Issa from the opposite bank, his voice high-pitched with panic.

Kola struggles in the enormous jaws as the serpent uncoils in the river, throwing waves of water over the banks. Horror snatches at my breath and I am caught in the roll of the river as I fight to keep upright. Kola beats at the slick fur around the creature's face with his fists, gasping and gulping in air.

"Hold on, Kola!" I shout, pulling my dagger free. "Issa, what should I do? What's its weakness?"

"The Ninki Nanka will not eat him alive, it will drown him first like a crocodile," Issa shrieks, tears streaming down his pointed chin. "You must stop it before it submerges."

I nod and tighten my hold on the weapon. As the creature draws in a deep breath, coils tightening around the boy, I dive again. My scales flash in the murky water as the Ninki Nanka sinks, dragging Kola with him. I swim down, heading to the center

129

of the river and the coiling mass I can just barely see. Clouds of brown burst and bloom in the water as the creature writhes in the mud, Kola a thrashing blur. When I get closer I see that his arms are sinking by his side, bubbles leaving his mouth. *Don't give up,* I think desperately, slashing at the Ninki Nanka's scales, dragging the dagger down through the beast's side.

I am rewarded with a large bellow as it thrashes its giant head. The water is a mixture of silt and screams trapped in bubbles as Kola is dropped, sinking to the riverbed. I swim to him as moonlight brightens the depths, pushing him behind me as the creature dips down to us, baring its fangs. Coiling and uncoiling, stirring the silt at the bottom of the river, it lunges forward as I strike again. With a twist of its brown furred head, the Ninki Nanka knocks the weapon from my hand and rears back. Behind me, Kola is running out of air. He scrabbles at my back as the Ninki Nanka swims toward us, opening the black maw of its mouth.

I search for the gleam of gold or the glitter of an emerald in the riverbed. I see the dagger, half hidden in the mud as the monster draws closer, gnashing teeth as large as Issa. I snatch up my weapon and spin, trying to hold it steady in the churning current as the creature hurtles toward us. We are thrown about by the motion in the water, the Ninki Nanka almost upon us, before I think to try something else.

Stop! I command in the way I have always spoken to the sharks. *Leave him.*

Kola's fingers clutch at me from behind, pulling me against his chest as the creature snaps its jaws shut and halts, retreating into the gloom of the river. I can still see its great head and the shimmer of its scales, but it is not attacking.

I take a gamble, pushing Kola toward the surface before he drowns. He shakes his head at me, but I shove him up. I hold my dagger point out, but the Ninki Nanka only glares at me, and I realize I am right. The creature has to do as I say.

Wait. I swim closer, nerves coiled, blade ready.

The Ninki Nanka opens its mouth in a gurgling hiss. I snatch a look above me, relieved to see Kola swimming to the bank. Looking back down, I see that the creature still has not moved. Snaking through the water, I approach the Ninki Nanka as it opens its mouth, several rows of teeth glinting from within.

Why were you attacking us? I am close enough now to touch one of the three horns if I wanted, though I keep an arm's length away. *We didn't attack you.*

The Ninki Nanka snorts and roars. The water pulses with the sound, but I do not move, do not show the fear that is still wound around my spine, cold and tight.

We know you did not, but you are here and so are we and we are so hungry. We had to.

Had to?

There is no choice. The creature looks up at the moon wavering through the water. *Already things are changing.*

What is changing?

We cannot say.

Curls float across my face. I push my hair away and hold the dagger toward a yellow eye, the emerald digging into my palm. The Ninki Nanka opens its mouth, but I force my fear away, swimming forward and pushing the blade against the fur of the creature's face.

Tell me.

It watches me with a baleful gaze, teeth flashing. Its jaws quiver, and I know it would like nothing better than to close them around my flesh.

The land.

What about it?

It is changing. Can you not feel it? Or do you feel only water?

The creature wriggles slowly. I press the tapered blade tighter among the fur, sliding it down the skin of the Ninki Nanka's cheek. *Feel what?* But I'm already remembering the stampede of elephants.

The balance is gone. The land and all on it will slowly rot. It's happening already. The creature grins. *And soon you will die with it.* The Ninki Nanka licks its gray-stained teeth. *I will still eat you, even if your limbs are blackened with disease and death.* It looks up at me, tongue retreating. *All will die, but I will still need to eat.*

Before I can think anymore, the creature opens its mouth wide and bellows, and I'm not sure how long my commands will work on it. I act fast, pressing the dagger into the creature's neck, forcing it deeper as a loud squeal spreads throughout the water. The Ninki Nanka snaps its jaws, trying to bite me, but each time I twist just enough to stay out of its reach. When the creature stops roaring, I yank the golden blade free, swimming to the surface as it retreats.

"Simi! Over here." Issa leans from the bough of a tree bending down toward the river.

"Are you hurt?" Kola lies next to the boy; one hand reaches for me, while the other is clamped to his side. Issa helps me from the water and I feel Kola's gaze on me.

I flop onto my back, squinting against the sun as it warms my skin, my tail splitting into legs. I want to go to Kola, but I have to wait for the bones to split and join, for skin to grow over retreating scales. For the first time, I look down at myself in frustration and annoyance, wishing I didn't have to change. Wishing I were still human.

Kola frowns, his chest heaving as he catches his breath. "What was that thing?"

"Didn't you know the Ninki Nanka was in the river?" I ask Issa, finally able to get to my feet, my voice growing shrill. "You said you scouted before."

The yumbo stares at me, eyes as round as small golden suns as he sniffs away tears. "I am sorry, Simi. You are right, it is my fault." Issa takes a step away from us, tiny shoulders slumped in dejection. "There is only one Ninki Nanka in these waters, but it traverses the river as it sees fit, eating mainly fish."

"So you did know?" I ask, my eyes narrowing as I walk unsteadily to Kola. "And you still took us this way? How could you be so foolish? Kola could have been killed!"

The yumbo hangs his head, plaits spilling over his eyes. "This is the quickest route. I didn't think any of us would be in the river. If the bridge hadn't broken . . ." He presses the heels of his hands against his face. "The Ninki Nanka is usually in the mountain streams in the summer months. Where it is cooler."

Kola's wounds look mainly like severe bruising but with a few puncture marks. I think of the Ninki Nanka's teeth and shudder.

"I knew we shouldn't have taken you," I all but spit. I can't stop thinking about Kola in the mouth of the Ninki Nanka. Anger pulses at the thought.

"We're alive, no harm done," says Kola as he rolls onto his knees, unable to get up but crouching to face the yumbo. "I know you're trying to get us to Oko as fast as possible."

"That's not the point, Kola," I continue, unable to stop myself, moving around him, checking his body for more wounds. "It was irresponsible."

"Simi, you'll get the rings. Now, just stop . . . being so hard." Kola shakes his head and winces, rocking back on his knees. Holding his side, he beckons to Issa, who shuffles closer. "Whether the bridge broke or not, the Ninki Nanka might still have attacked." He lays a hand on the yumbo's thin arm and tries to smile. "You are an excellent guide, little one."

Issa sniffs and moves toward Kola tentatively. "You are not angry with me?"

"No. And we would still have had to cross this river at some point," Kola says, still slightly out of breath. The Ninki Nanka's teeth pierced his skin in several places, and the lacerations still ooze blood. I watch as he tests the wounds with gentle presses of his hand, trying to pretend that it doesn't hurt. "Besides, I was extremely lucky—look! Only a few scratches!" Kola murmurs to Issa, who is still looking up at him, his honey-colored eyes full of worry.

"For such a lucky person, you've needed rescuing quite a few times," I snap. What if I hadn't been able to command the Ninki Nanka and then overpower it? I wipe the creature's blood from my dagger on the grass. How did I miss its approach in the water? Annoyance and guilt wash over me. "Perhaps you need to start thinking about being more careful, or you'll never make it home at this rate."

As soon as the words leave my mouth, I regret them. I know that Kola is only trying to make Issa feel better. That the Ninki Nanka was an accident, and something I should have sensed. But

I'm angry, and I know it's because I'm scared. Scared not only of failing Yemoja but now also of losing Kola.

Kola.

I want to go to him and examine his wounds properly. Run my fingers over the creases of his ribs, to see for myself that his injuries are not serious. Instead, I watch as he holds his side, anger in his eyes as he turns away from me, back to Issa, taking the yumbo's hand. Kola's irritation at me cuts through my outrage, but I straighten up, scuffing my foot in the dirt. I won't feel bad about trying to keep them all safe.

I think about what the Ninki Nanka said, about the land losing its balance and everyone dying along with it. I think of the vision I had, how it matched what the devil-dragon said, and my fingers curl around the hilt of my dagger so tightly that my nails dig into the flesh of my palms.

I force myself to relax. Kola is right, it might still have attacked us. The main thing is that we're alive.

"Let's go," I murmur, sliding the dagger back into my hair, trying to stop my hands from shaking. "The sooner we reach your village, the better."

CHAPTER FOURTEEN

WE WALK FOR half an hour in the growing twilight before we leave the sound of the river behind. Refreshed by the water, my feet are only slightly tender now, the bones of my ankles and knees moving with ease. The blackest part of the night has fully claimed the forest, creating shadows as dark as ink. Kola holds his hands to his side, and although the bite marks have stopped bleeding, they are an angry red, the skin puffy. Some of the wounds on his back have opened up, too, edges yellowing in a way that makes me anxious about infection.

And worried about Kola.

"Issa," I call, "how much farther? Can we stop for a moment?"

The yumbo runs back. "Of course. Do you need water? Some food?"

Kola slumps beside a tree and I sigh, annoyed at myself for not thinking about this earlier. He clasps his left side, the same one that troubled him from the wreck.

"We need some of the abada powder your grandfather gave us," I say to Issa. "Kola's hurt."

Issa's eyes fill with concern. "I'll mix some together right away."

As the yumbo hurries off to rummage in the sack, I extract the waterskin and hold it out to Kola.

"Drink."

He takes it from me without meeting my gaze, removing the hand from his side and sitting fully on the ground. One large swig and he slumps back in relief.

"Eat." I unwrap a parcel of fish and pass him half.

Kola lets out a short, exhausted laugh at my tone and I smile a little. The shade from the tree darkens his face, but I can still see the lines of exhaustion that run between his eyes, highlighted by the moon.

Issa returns with a wooden cup full of a thick gray, citrus-smelling paste. "This will need to go on the wounds. Save a little at the end, mix it with more water, and then he will need to drink it."

"Thank you, little one." I bend down to make eye contact. He really is still a child, and I know he cares about Kola. Everything he has done has been to help us. Guilt wells as I think of the way I behaved after the Ninki Nanka. "You're appreciated. Greatly."

The yumbo smiles shyly, a large dimple appearing in his right cheek.

"I'm going to put some of this on your wounds." I say to Kola. I scoop out the mixture and it tingles on my fingertips, glittering in the moonlight. He hisses as the medicine touches his skin. "Tell me about your home," I say, hoping to distract him as I begin to pat the paste onto the puncture marks. "About your brother and sister."

"It is like most large villages. But mine is different." Kola turns to face me, the faint outline of a smile growing. "It's . . . special."

"How?"

Holding his shoulder carefully, I slide my fingers across the silk of his skin, examining the bite marks and the wounds that have reopened. Kola winces again and irritation rises in me as I think about him trying to walk on like this. He must have been in agony.

"My great-grandfather founded our village on the edge of the Oyo Kingdom, close to the river Ogun. We had the benefit of the sea as well as the river, and the land was so fertile that he named it after the orisa of farming. My father is the head of the village." The son of a village leader. I can understand a lot of his behavior now, his sureness. I ease Kola sideways and he twists his body for me, allowing me access to the rest of his wounds. "The Aláàfin of Oyo at the time of my grandfather was Onigbogi. Impressed by our wealth, he gave us a bronze plaque that told the story of Oko's prosperity. My father still has it hanging from our compound wall. It's magnificent." He smiles. "In the midafternoon sun, the carved figures and crops shine in a blaze of golden fire."

"Tell me more," I murmur. He looks over his shoulder at me. I swallow and force my gaze away from his mouth, shifting my body away from his.

"My mother used to sing her prayer to Olodumare when she prepared our food. She sang anytime she had the chance. Her voice was low, and sweet like fried coconut." He grins and turns back to face the forest. "She would always make that for me if I was feeling sad."

I imagine a woman with welcoming smile and a voice that fills the village and the hearts of anyone listening.

"My brother and sister would wedge their sleeping mats next to mine, but I liked to know they were next to me. It always helped me to sleep better." He looks at me again; this time shyness hoods his eyes. "I was allowed to choose their names. Taiwo came first but Kehinde is wiser. It makes sense that she sent him out first in the world to scout ahead. She always waits before reacting, whereas Taiwo?" Kola raises an eyebrow. "He's always charging into things. Like the time they both decided they couldn't wait for me to take them out on my boat. Kehinde convinced him to sneak and hide, reasoning that once I had set off, I couldn't say no to them. Taiwo couldn't help himself, though. He popped up from their hiding place under the seats before I'd even pushed the boat from the shallows. Kehinde was furious with him for giving them away."

I imagine a smaller version of Kola, hopping from foot to foot in excitement. "What did you do?"

"I ended up sailing just out to the bluff, letting them have a little taste. Really, they were too young, but I wouldn't have let anything happen to them." Kola pauses, his voice dropping lower. "I would never let anything happen to them."

I move in front of him to cover the scratches on his chest and shoulders. Sweat glistens on his face as his smile wanes. My heart sinks at the expression that slips across his features. Longing, fear.

The wounds are covered and I push backward, reaching for the waterskin. The paste in the bottom of the wooden cup mixes well with the water and I offer it to Kola, holding my breath when the tips of our fingers touch. He grasps the cup in his hand, watching as I put more distance between us. Kola's expression is a careful blank, as if he doesn't care, but I catch the tightening of his mouth before he raises the cup to his lips. He downs the concoction in one long swallow, eyes still on mine. Setting the empty cup next to him, he clears his throat, leaning against the tree.

"What about you? What about your home?"

The question catches me off guard. What can I tell him? Of a mother with eyes the same shade as his? Of a father who taught me to wield a dagger? Of the glimpses of a city I can't fully remember, the comforting scent of fried plantain and hot rice? Of a past that the sea has swallowed?

"I . . . I can't remember most of it," I answer, my voice low, staring down at the tops of my feet. "Not since I've become Mami Wata. Only . . . parts." And if I were in the water, this wouldn't matter to me. I wouldn't feel this straining, this wanting to be someone else. Something else.

I can feel Kola watching me. "You will. It's still all there, deep inside you."

His simple words make my eyes burn with tears that I try to blink away. While the remembering can bring me comfort, it's always a reminder of a life I lost. Even the need to change, the draw of water, is another sign that I am different from Kola.

"We should rest now," he says quietly.

"You should rest, you mean," I whisper. Kola smiles, brown eyes crinkling, and shifts again, closer to me. He still smells of the sea mixed with the delicate fiery spice of the fish we've eaten. For moments, we watch each other. Slowly, Kola's eyes begin to close and his head droops so that it rests on my shoulder.

I freeze, feeling the softness of his exhalations, regular and deep. His lips brush the slope of my upper arm and my skin tingles at the contact. I can't remember anyone being this close to me before. Maybe my reaction is just that, a craving of human contact.

And then I look down at Kola, the lines of his body against mine. I think of the love in his voice when he told me about his family, the earnestness of his words, and of what I'm allowing right now. I am doing exactly what Yemoja told me not to, getting close to Kola in ways I didn't think possible.

Sighing, I lift my eyes to the sky, searching for the Ìràwọ̀ Ìrọ̀lẹ́. It is known as the Courting Star; lovers would use its nightly emergence to arrange secret trysts. Something I will never be able to do with Kola.

I want to place a hand on the boy's head, let myself stroke his black curls. Instead, I form a fist to stop myself. I mustn't allow myself to forget that I am of the sea and he is not.

An hour passes, and the forest grows full of the low calls of owls and the occasional grunts of baboons. I watch Kola rest, drinking in the pinkish-brown fullness of his bottom lip and the crescents of his thick eyelashes. He sleeps peacefully, mouth slightly open now, his hand warm against mine.

"Simi?" whispers Issa, who has been dozing fitfully. "We need to go if we are to get there before morning."

"Of course," I answer, shifting, feeling the knots in my muscles. I don't want to move, to disturb Kola, but the yumbo is right.

Issa climbs over tree roots and crouches in front of the boy, his eyes glowing in splashes of moonlight. "Ẹ̀gbọ́n ọkùnrin, how are you feeling?"

Kola sits up slowly, twisting to look at his side while I scan his back. All that is left of the bite marks and other wounds are faint lines in his skin. He runs a hand over them, fingers tracing the puckered marks.

"How do you feel?" I ask.

Kola nods and straightens his back, grinning at us both. "Well enough for us to keep going."

Issa claps his delicate hands and does his best to tug Kola to his feet. He leans on me and I shift my weight, helping him up with a push from behind. Once he's standing, I brush twigs from my wrapper, looking anywhere but at him.

"Thank you. For the medicine." I hear the smile in his voice. "And for being a very warm pillow."

I can't hide the twitch of my lips as I gather our bag of supplies, nodding once at him as Issa capers before us. It's as if I can still feel the heat of him against me. I push the thought out of my head and take a deep breath, gripping the bag tighter, stretching my legs.

"Come, Oko is this way," declares the yumbo as he takes Kola's hand, pulling him east through the trees.

We walk through the rest of the night, our path lit by the low bright moon. The air is still warm but more comfortable now, the humidity swallowed by the dark. Giant moths swoop down and Issa shoos them away, his face creased in annoyance. Screeches and calls of nighttime creatures have Kola's hand permanently on the hilt of his dagger, but nothing attacks us. As the sky begins to lighten, Issa slows his steps.

Kola turns slowly, his brows furrowed. "Oko is just beyond the next set of trees, after the hill." He twists and points in the other direction. "The river runs back that way, opening out to the sea."

"This is good, yes?"

Kola doesn't reply, pausing in the spreading dawn. "What if . . . what if I'm too late? What if the ceremony didn't happen because of me?"

I allow myself to touch his arm, waiting until his eyes are on mine. "You'll be home soon. Let's focus on that."

Kola nods, although his frown remains. Reluctantly, I release his arm and sweep my gaze around the trees and ground, the blush of the sun lightening it all. Soon it will give way to fields and people and compounds.

Oko.

Where I will leave Kola and journey on to the babalawo. I have kept my promise to take Kola back to his village, and now it's time to keep the one I made to Yemoja. A burst of melancholy seeps in at the thought of leaving him, and I force myself to think of the chance I have to make things right with the orisa and all Mami Wata.

It's only as we draw closer to the outskirts of the forest that I notice the thinning trees and the plants that surround them. A few are still green, vibrant even in the cloak of early dawn, but the rest are brown, with a few twisted branches. We stop and my body goes rigid as I survey the land.

Blackened with disease and death.

I think of the Ninki Nanka and wipe at my mouth, a feeling of disquiet burrowing deeper inside me as I take in the dying earth. And dying it is. Even the flowers on the twisted limbs are desiccated husks, their brittle petals succumbing to the wind. Grass still reaches up to our knees, but it is dry, the edges like blades, quick to slice our skin.

Kola turns in a half circle, lips thinned in anxiousness. "It wasn't like this a few weeks ago."

"Perhaps it's something in this part of the forest," I say. "Come, let's keep moving. We're practically there."

The sun breaks free from the distant tree line as we crest the hill, spilling its pale cherry glow onto the village below. Cows are huddled together under a few dead and wizened trees, and the corn is a dark brown. A sense of familiarity slows my steps, my brain whirring as I take in the hills that roll into fields. Blackened branches grasp at the skies, dying trees hanging over heaps of crops, ruined and rotting.

My vision.

The land ahead of us is identical to what I saw. Bile rises and I swallow it down. We're still too far away to see properly, but already it looks as if the vegetation of the village is suffering the same fate as that of the forest. Beyond the corn, tan walls and thatched roofs make up many compounds that circle around one another, and Kola walks faster toward them.

"It's still standing!" he says, joy flooding his tone.

"Perhaps we should be cautious," I say. A few figures stand spaced evenly outside the village walls, and something about them makes me feel uneasy. They hold themselves stiffly; I see the occasional glint of sunlight on the bright metal of blades. These are not just any villagers; they are on guard.

"Issa, let me carry you." Kola picks up the yumbo, who climbs into the sack. He smiles down at the boy as Issa nods, folding his knees and arms. "Yumboes are tales of the storyteller to the people in Oko."

"I do not mind, see?" Issa snuggles down, looking about the size of a large yam. Kola holds the sack loosely so that plenty of air can get in and heads off toward the outer fields of Oko.

Dread snakes through my blood with every quickened beat of my heart. Our path takes us through the crops of corn, plantain, and cassava. Although they are still alive, the stems and leaves are wilted, with patches of brown and black among the plants. We draw closer, our feet kicking up small puffs of red earth from the path as I scan the village walls. No greetings are called out, no children run to welcome us, just darting figures that are blurs in the early light.

My throat tightens and I reach out, snagging Kola by his hand. He slows, scanning the perimeter just as an arrow lands in the earth in front of us. Kola staggers, almost falling until I catch him, pushing him back upright with a strength that surprises me in my present form.

"What is this? They're shooting at me?" Kola is incredulous, but I scramble farther back, trying to drag him with me. He cradles the sack and follows, but he eyes the village walls angrily, his other hand on the sword.

"They haven't seen you in a long time," I say, checking on Issa. The yumbo has curled himself into a ball, eyes tightly shut. I reach inside and give his hand a quick squeeze. "Wouldn't you be cautious, too?"

Kola takes a deep breath, his chest heaving as he calms himself. He eases backward slowly and makes a show of placing his weapon on the floor before straightening up fully, watching the guards who gather in front of the tall wooden gates. I go with him, careful not to make any sudden movements.

Two people peel away from the rest, loping down the main path, gaits long and easy. The guard on the left is almost twice the size of the one on the right and carries a sword almost half the length of my body. In the other's grip I can make out the flash of two blades. Axes. My fingers twitch, wanting to go to the emerald hilt tight against my braids.

Kola focuses on the guards and suddenly breaks into a sprint, arms held open.

"What are you doing?" I say, lurching forward in panic. I pull at my hair, fumbling with the dagger, but by the time I manage to yank it free, they are upon him.

. . .

"Adekola!" cries the huge guard, grasping Kola with both arms.

"Bem! So this is how you welcome me home? By shooting at me?"

With his wrapper of onyx black and burnished straps of leather to hold his weapons crisscrossed over his chest, the smile that splits the face of the imposing giant guard looks out of place. Holding Kola away from him, Bem lifts his head and releases a deep laugh into the sky.

"We are blessed! We are blessed! Yinka? Did I not tell you that he would come back to us?"

The guard's bald head gleams in the sun, matched by the head of the girl standing next to him. Tall, with long limbs that move with the grace of a leopard, she regards me with wide-set eyes. The lack of hair only accentuates high cheekbones and the arc of her neck. Yinka's wrapper is the same black as Bem's but cinched tight around her chest and waist. The same polished leather straps wrap around her shoulders, tight against skin that shines like the midnight sky. She keeps her eyes on me and a firm grip on the golden axes in each hand as she squeezes Kola to her.

"You did, Bem," she answers, her voice light and even.

There is a cool assessment in the gaze she turns on me that makes me want to shrink back. I lift my chin instead.

Kola puts his arms around them both. Their heads come together, Bem bending low, and for a moment, there is silence as they grip one another's shoulders. When they pull away, Kola looks from one to the other. "Is Oko well? The Tapa didn't attack again?"

"They didn't. But after you were taken, your father ordered us to launch an assault upon them anyway." Bem pauses, brows low over his eyes.

Yinka opens her mouth to speak, but Bem cuts her off, wrapping his arm around Kola's shoulder and steering him toward the village gates. "Come," he says gently. "It's a long story best told by your father."

Kola nods and then turns to me, motioning me forward. I walk over to him, and Yinka's face shimmers with something else I don't quite understand.

"Bem, Yinka, this is Simidele. Without her I wouldn't be here now."

As they exclaim in blessings to Olodumare and Ogun, I don't take my eyes off Kola. There is still a glaze of anxiety over my thoughts. While this is what I wanted, the thought of going any farther without him makes me feel somehow off-balance. Besides, seeing him with Yinka and Bem, how close they are, makes it even more obvious how much I don't belong. I think of the press of Kola next to me when he was resting and then of Yemoja's words, of her warning not to get too close to humans. I'm beginning to understand what she was trying to tell me. How it hurts to feel, knowing that you will have to leave them.

I stop and raise my voice, cutting through their chatter. "Now that you're here, I'll be on my way. If you'll just point me in the babalawo's direction, I'll find him."

Kola lets Bem's arm fall from his shoulder and crosses the short distance between us. His eyes are on mine, flicking over my face and down to my feet. "I said I'd take you. And I will." Kola moves closer, and I fight the urge to back up. His hand encircles the top of my arm gently, and I feel the burn of heat across my chest again. "I'll keep my promise, if it's all the same to you."

I turn away and stare in the direction of the sea, and then back at the walls of Oko. Anywhere but at Kola's face.

"Simi." He says my name softly, and I can't help but snatch another look at him. "You've done so much for me that I can't even begin to know how to pay you back. Taking you to the babalawo is at least a start." His fingers slide down my arm as he releases me, and I fight not to shiver at his touch. "Please?"

I look at his mouth as he says my name and nod, unable to trust my voice. Kola waits until I move to his side before he starts off down the path to the walls of his village.

As we draw closer, the dark wooden gates of Oko seem to ripple with images, and when we reach them, my legs weaken with a rush of foreboding. The door on the left side depicts the sea, with fish, sharks, and whales, each scale and tooth and eye scored delicately into the surface. The right side shows the produce of Oko's lands, with unending fields of corn, plantain, and cassava, leaves and stems and flowers looking as real as the vegetation behind us.

The gates are the ones in my vision.

Was I wrong earlier to hope that the hills and the failing crops I saw were different from those in my mind? The carved sides of the gate stretch from one smooth tan wall to another, but Bem is large enough to reach both, muscles bulging. Will he throw them wide upon the corpses of Oko's villagers?

"Simi, are you all right?" Kola asks me, his hand hovering near my elbow. I manage to nod, wiping at the beads of cold sweat that drip down my forehead. "Don't be nervous. We'll stop and then be on our way to the babalawo."

I can't speak. I hold my breath as the gates swing smoothly open onto the main thoroughfare, lit by the early-morning sunlight. The villagers of Oko are stirring and the streets are full of women with calabashes of water and freshly harvested crops. Gathering together, they make their way to the market that is being set up at the square in the center. I release the breath I have been holding, letting the hand clasped to my chest fall back to my side.

Alive.

The people are alive.

A few brown crops doesn't necessarily mean anything. I try to relax as we make our way down the wide main path. The polished walls of compounds spiral away, each an exact replica of the others. Decorated with horizontal ridge designs as well as images of the warriors of Oko and tales of their fishing prowess, the walls tell stories of success and power.

As we walk down the main road, heading to Kola's family compound, women and men bow, lowering their goods and calabashes, touching the ground near his feet. Children call out their pleasure, bending into respectful poses when reminded.

We join the flow of people who head toward the market space, goods in hand and woven baskets on heads. Carts are full of corn, yams, freshly slaughtered carcasses of goats, and cages of chickens. Although the market should soon be open, I see that a few sellers are grouped together at the corner of the stalls, not bothering to set up yet. As we walk past, they don't look up, preoccupied with their frowns and with the goods they poke around on a trestle table. Craning my neck around Yinka, I see that the corn they have is brown, with a gentle rot that can be smelled from where I am. A fisherman approaches them and holds up a tiny catch, dull scales that fail to sparkle in the morning light.

My mood dips again, apprehension threading through it. Yinka looks in the direction I am staring in and narrows her eyes, faltering for a moment before carrying on behind Kola.

As we walk around the market, we pass an old man sitting in the entranceway of a house, his faded green wrapper tucked around skin folded with age and sprinkled with dark spots from the sun. Chickens cluck from the hutch next to him, their brown feathers drifting in the growing heat of the morning. The elder sucks on an ivory pipe that resembles a tiny leopard, releasing a thin trail of smoke before glancing up at Kola and nearly dropping it.

"Praise Ogun!" he exclaims, shock and pleasure twisting his wrinkled face into a smile. "Look who has been returned to us."

Kola nods and grins in his direction, lifting a fist to his heart. "Yes, uncle."

"It is good to see you back." The old man collects his composure and a shadow slides across his expression. "Go straight to your parents! Go now!" he calls again as Kola hurries his steps and I rush to keep up.

People continue to dip and bow to Kola as he rushes to his family compound, flanked by Bem and Yinka. I quicken my steps as I follow them.

The red clay walls of Kola's home gleam from the pathway as he passes me the sack containing Issa. I set the bag on the floor against one of the outer arches. "You can come out soon, little one," I whisper.

Kola passes by the bronze panels depicting Ogun, their surfaces shining. On them, the orisa is shown with glowing swords and scales to represent the justice he oversees. An altar is arranged beneath the panels, with offerings set on it of palm wine, kola nuts, one large rooster, and two yams. We follow closely behind Kola, pausing as he steps into the central courtyard. He spins slowly to face each of the four walls of his family quarters, arms hanging down at his sides as if he can't believe he's actually home. Just as he turns back to smile at us, a loud wail rends the air.

A woman, her plumpness straining at the complicated folds and knots of her white wrapper, rushes into the courtyard, a matching pristine headwrap framing her oval face. She raises her hands to cup her nose and mouth, but the gesture does nothing to temper the sound of her cry or the tears that run down her cheeks. Kola rushes to her side as the woman staggers, falling to her knees, sobbing. He skids when he reaches her, sinking to the ground as her arms stretch partway around his back.

"Ìyá," I hear him gasp as the woman pulls him down against her, sobbing into his neck.

"Adekola! You are alive!" she cries, her fingers fluttering against his tearstained cheeks as he kisses her forehead. "Praise Ogun. I have prayed for this for weeks and here you are." She holds him away from her so she can look at him, her eyes still glazed with tears as she smiles through them. "Here you are."

"Ìyá, why are you wearing white?" Kola pulls away from her grip and looks around the courtyard. His voice grows thinner with concern. "What's happened? Who has passed?"

Kola's mother doesn't answer. She gets to her feet, pulling her son with her and smoothing her wrapper, trying to brush off some loose dirt that clings to the fabric.

"Where's bàbá? And Taiwo and Kehinde?"

I see Bem and Yinka look at each other as they stand next to me, before both look down at the tightly packed earth. Fear draws an icy veil over me that is at odds with the growing heat of the morning, and I rub my palms on my wrapper.

"I am here," answers Kola's father, stepping into the courtyard from his quarters opposite. "And glad to see you home, ọmọ mi." Nearly as tall as his son, and with the same shade of dark reddish-brown skin, he doesn't smile. His white wrapper is stark, immaculate, and tied crisply, a matching fila atop his head. Thick gold rings shine on every one of his fingers. Kola's father gathers his son to him, pressing his forehead against his, blinking rapidly. "We thought we had lost you."

Kola clasps his father by the shoulders, his fingers digging deep as he holds back more tears. He nods instead and I see his hands shake as he releases the older man.

"Ìyá, where are Taiwo and Kehinde?" Kola's mother turns her face away, her sobs growing as she clutches at herself. "Bàbá, where are they?"

There is silence in the courtyard as the rising sun sears the compound, flashing upon glazed eyes and teeth that are bared in both grief and fear.

Kola balls his hands into fists, his mouth pressed into sudden flat lines. "Will somebody tell me where my brother and sister are?"

"Gone," says Kola's father, his voice low and hoarse. "Taken last night."

CHAPTER FIFTEEN

I REMEMBER SALIF'S face, the vacant look in his amber eyes and the ragged cry that he was unable to stop. The yumboes felt it when the twins were taken, I'm sure of it now.

Kola looks from his mother to his father, shaking his head, a minute expression of his confusion. "No, no. They can't be."

His father reaches for him, clasping Kola to him as the boy's legs give way. Together they crouch on the ground as Kola's mother goes to them, her hands on their backs and her tears flowing as fast as theirs. They remain entwined for some moments before Kola rises from the huddle, helping his parents up, watching as his father leads his mother inside to rest. He promises to join them soon, and once they are out of view, he strides toward Bem and Yinka, his head held high. His cheeks are lined with dried tears and his eyes burn with a fury matched only in the fists he swings by his sides.

"Why didn't you tell me?"

Bem lowers his head, but Yinka reaches out a hand to Kola, her fingers grazing his shoulder before he jerks away. A shadow passes across her face at his reaction.

"It wasn't our place," says Bem quietly. "There has been no

sign of them since. We've been out looking the entire night, the whole guard."

Kola glares at them both, his eyes shining with more unshed tears. "They're not . . . dead. I know it." He takes a deep breath, exhaling it slowly, letting his fists unfurl. "Who took them?"

Bem looks at Yinka, his eyes dark, thick wrinkles of a frown marring his forehead.

"Esu," she answers quietly, and then clears her throat. "Several guards were killed. The ones who weren't described the orisa."

The silence is tight. A brittle absence of sound until Bem sighs, his eyes filling as he blinks slowly. He opens his mouth to speak but is cut off.

"And where were you?" hisses Kola. "You know that the twins are Ibeji embodied, that they are important. Where were the rest of my family's guards?"

"You don't need to make us feel even guiltier," says Yinka, stepping up to Kola. Her head only reaches his shoulders, but it feels as if she towers over him with just the curl of her lip. "In fact, we weren't here, that's right. But why? Because we were out looking for *you*." She bares her teeth, anger contorting her face. "The son who decided to ignore his father and take matters into his own hands. Leaving without permission, trying to make a deal with the Tapa."

I shrink back against the passageway wall at the anger in their voices. Not to mention Yinka's fingers on the bone handles of her golden axes.

"Every day, Bem and I search, visiting different villages, asking questions." Yinka is not giving up, incandescent with anger. "Trying to find *you*."

"I was attempting to make sure the Tapa didn't attack!" snarls

Kola, but even I can see the conflicted guilt in his face. "I was try-ing to make sure Taiwo and Kehinde were safe." His voice cracks on the last word.

Bem looms above them both. He lifts a large muscled arm and edges them apart. "Now is not the time to be divided. Your feel-ings are because of your concern for each other. Both of you." He stands between them now, gaze fixed on neither, voice melodious and calm. "Let's think of a solution, not the problem. None of us prosper when we're divided."

Kola breathes hard before whirling away, opening his hands, pressing his palms against the wall, his shoulders tensed. Yinka paces away toward the well at the back of the courtyard.

"What about the confirmation ceremony?" I ask quietly. "Did the babalawo perform it?"

"Yes, and one for protection," says Bem as Kola makes his way back to us. "Just a few days ago. I think that's part of the reason their father is furious. He's talking about punishing the babalawo because it clearly didn't work."

"It can't have, if they were taken." Kola has reached us now, his shoulders taut. "I'm going to take Simi to him and see for myself what he has to say."

"We'll go with you," says Bem as Yinka returns. She's let go of her axes but still frowns.

"It's only a few hours," says Kola.

"We're part of the guard, it's our duty to protect you," she adds, nostrils flaring. "We're coming with you."

Kola and Yinka face each other and I brace myself, but the girl cocks her head and lifts a hand to pinch her nose closed. "But first you need to bathe and change your wrapper. You stink of the sea and sweat."

I don't move, holding my breath and flicking my gaze between them as Bem suddenly splutters with a laugh that booms around the courtyard. "This is true, Kola. Clean up and then we'll head to the babalawo." He claps a hand on Kola's shoulder and squeezes. "Together."

Kola stares at Yinka as she tries a small smile for him. He nods, eyes clearer. "All right, all right." He walks up to me with concern on his face. "Do you need anything? Food?"

"We will take care of her," says Bem, releasing him and standing beside me.

"Is that all right with you?" asks Kola quietly, and I nod. I've already adjusted to being around so many other humans. "I won't be long."

Kola walks into the quarters directly on our right, head swiveling as he continues to drink in the sight of his home.

"I'm going to check the guards on rotation today," says Yinka, and she starts across the courtyard without another look at me, disappearing into the corridor at the end.

I crouch beside the sack and draw down its sides, checking on the yumbo. Issa sleeps at the bottom, curled around a large yam, his mouth open slightly. I close the sack and stand to face Bem as he returns from the well with a shining copper pail. He reaches down, unhooking a matching cup from its side, dipping it into the water and handing it to me. I accept with a nod of thanks.

"We haven't been properly introduced," says Bem, holding a hand twice the size as mine to the slab of his chest. "Bem."

"Simidele," I say, mirroring him. "Simi."

"Have you come far? Where are your people, Simidele?"

The question is asked in a soft voice, but it still surprises me.

I take a moment, fiddling with the emerald in my hair. I think about the market, the Aláàfin's palace, my parents.

"Oyo-Ile."

"The capital?" Bem looks up at me, surprise in his open expression. "That's a long way."

I shrug. He looks at me quizzically, eyebrows raised, as if trying to work me out.

"What about you?" I ask, trying to deflect the attention. My tone feels awkward. I'm not used to this anymore. "Have you always lived in Oko?"

"Oko is the only home I know, but my parents weren't born here." He pauses, adjusting the sword buckled onto his back. "My mother and father fled a war far away in the north. I was a baby. It's why they chose the name they gave me."

"It means . . . ?"

"Peace." He picks up the other cup and fills it, taking a delicate sip. "We settled in Oko because they welcomed my father's skills. He was a fisherman, an expert in rivers, but he quickly adapted to the sea. He taught me a lot. Ropes, knots. He used to take me out when the sky was still dark. My father taught me how to use the stars to navigate." Bem pauses, his eyes glazed as he remembers. "We'd eat the breakfast my mother would pack, usually plantain and some boiled eggs if we were lucky."

"He sounds very clever."

Bem grins widely, and his openness puts me at ease. "He would have loved to hear you say that."

"What about Kola? Have you known each other for a long time?"

"Since we were very young. He never minded that I wasn't

born in the village. And once he accepted me, so did everyone else. We always wanted . . . Never mind." He shakes his head, a shy smile on his lips.

"No, go on."

Bem leans toward me eagerly and he looks younger, his height and size falling away for a moment. "We both talked about sailing as far as we could go, visiting as many new lands as possible."

"A new world," I say, remembering how I felt when I was beneath the sea and all that it contained. A whole other universe.

Bem nods his head vigorously. "Exactly! But to explore . . . not take. What about Kola?" His voice is quieter now. "How did you meet?"

"I . . ." I stop, wondering how much to say. "I found him after he had been thrown overboard from a ship belonging to the òyìnbó." The ugliness of Kola's other fate sits between us a moment as Bem thinks on what I've said.

"Then I owe you a debt, Simidele." He's not smiling this time, and his bow catches me unawares. "Thank you. For saving him."

I open my mouth to answer, but as Yinka reappears, striding toward us, I close it. She's a touch taller than me, with a leanness that explains why she has been accepted into the Oko guard. Even though she is slimmer, muscles bunch under her skin as she shifts her stance, moving, always moving. I detect resentment as she deliberately avoids my gaze. Her large eyes are fixed on Bem, but I have a feeling that if I were to move even an inch now, she would sense it.

Yinka glances at me and then swiftly away, her gaze alighting on the sack next to me. "What's in there?" she asks.

"Supplies," I answer. I should keep my answers to a minimum from now on. It's safer.

I am rescued from more questions as Kola emerges from his father's quarters and heads straight for me. His skin shines in the sunlight, and with a fresh wrapper slung around his waist, hanging in clean folds, he looks exactly like the leader of a village's son.

"Simi," he says, coming close to me, smelling of black soap, shea butter, and the coconut oil that has made his clean curls tighter. "If Esu took the twins, do you think the babalawo might be able to tell me where he is?"

I look up at his face, my eyes trailing down to the pinkish-brown tone of his bottom lip. I turn away, my heart thumping in a way that usually happens only when something is wrong.

"Perhaps." I manage to force out the word, unable to look at him directly. "If he's the one Yemoja described, his knowledge will be infinite."

"Good." Kola spins away from me, allowing my pulse to even out. "Bem, Yinka? I'll say good-bye to my parents and then we'll leave."

Neither questions him. It's easy to see their loyalty and trust in him, and I wonder if he will ever feel that way about me.

Kola straps his sword back on, tightening the leather around his waist just as his mother arrives, her face as ominous as the thunder Sango conjured. His father follows close behind, trailing half a dozen guards, who bristle with swords, axes, and spears.

"Where do you think you are going?" Kola's mother rushes up to him and grabs his hand. "You have only just returned!"

"I know, ìyá. But we're going to the babalawo. Simidele has to see him, and I want to find out if he knows where Esu is."

"Simidele? Who is this Simidele?" Kola's mother peers around him to examine me and I dip my eyes in deference, wondering if I should touch the floor before her feet. Before I can do so, she jerks back to her son, anger and fear contorting the lines of her face. "No, Adekola. I want you here, safe with me, behind Oko's walls and with the might of the guards to defend us."

"But Taiwo and Kehinde—"

"We have sent people out to search for them and will continue to do so." Kola's father cuts him off, glowering, fierceness crackling in his gaze. "I will not have you rushing foolishly off again."

Kola squares his shoulders and takes a moment before speaking, measuring out each word. "I was wrong to go to the Tapa without you, bàbá, no matter what my intentions were." He holds a hand to his heart, keeping his tone even. "And for that I apologize. But ever since then, my family and my home have been constantly on my mind. I stopped at nothing trying to get back here. Taiwo and Kehinde are not dead, and I will find them." He pauses a moment as his voice cracks, and I take a step toward him without realizing it. "I will find them and bring them back to Oko, to our lands. Back to you, back to us, where they belong. But in order to do this, I need to speak to the babalawo and see if he knows where Esu is."

"It is not safe!" Kola's mother bursts out, her face creasing with grief.

"We will look after him," says Yinka, her tone firm as she glances from Kola to his mother.

Bem steps forward and bows. "You know that I would give my life for him."

Silence stretches as Kola's father glowers at us all. And then he nods, shoulders slumping. "You will go to the high priest," he says, his voice more resolute than the expression on his face. "And if he tells you where Esu is, I give you my permission and blessing to go in search of him. But—" Kola's father holds a hand up. "You will come back for sufficient supplies and you will take Ifedayo with you."

The tallest guard behind him shifts so that he faces us fully, skinny plaits and a long face at odds with the other older-looking sentries.

"A new guard, bàbá?"

"One who has come from Oyo-Ile to assist with the Tapa threat."

Kola hesitates a moment before nodding and taking his mother's hand, pressing it against his cheek. "I'll be back before sunset, ìyá."

She stares up at his face and nods instead of speaking. She seems to have swallowed her worry as she realizes she can't change Kola's mind. "First, you will eat." She holds up a dimpled hand, fingers sparkling with polished chunks of diamonds set in thick gold bands.

"Ìyá—"

"No. You will eat before anything else." Kola's mother places her other hand on his cheek, cradling his face, bringing his gaze down to hers. "You will allow me that at least."

Kola goes with his mother as she starts across the courtyard, his arm tight around her shoulders. They spend several moments speaking before she disappears into the corridor and Kola walks back, his eyes on me. I open my mouth to speak and am interrupted by Yinka's shout. She's next to our bag, drawing her axes as the sides ripple.

"There's something in there!"

I run to jump between her blades and the sack. The woven

side is pulled down and Issa peeps over the side. Yinka draws back with a gasp. I look over helplessly at Kola, who scoops the tiny boy up.

"A yumbo!" exclaims Yinka as she leans down, trying to get a closer look. Issa grins at her from the safety of Kola's arms.

Bem approaches, too, his face open in growing awe. "I didn't think the tales of the Bakhna Rakhna were real."

"I never had a doubt," says Kola defensively as he lets Issa climb down. The yumbo bows to Yinka and Kola. "They saved me when our boat was wrecked. Just be careful with him. He's small."

Issa looks up at Kola and frowns. "I am tiny, but I am strong. You know this, ẹgbọ́n ọkùnrin."

"Come, sit with me so that the servants do not see you," says Yinka as Issa skips over to her side, holding the hand she offers him. "Do you like corn? The storyteller said all yumboes like corn."

"Mm-hm." Issa nods happily as he follows Yinka. "Very much so."

Kola trails them as Bem holds his arm. "Are you sure you're not going to spring something else on us?" He laughs, and I see Kola force himself to smile, but he looks at me very briefly. My knees tremble slightly and I can't help but look down at my feet, still brown and ordinary-looking.

"Let's get ready to eat, shall we? The sooner we finish the food my mother will force on us, the quicker we can leave."

Issa slots himself between Yinka and Bem when we sit on the mats laid out for us, and he's so small that the folds of their wrappers all but hide him. When Kola's mother returns, she is followed by servants who bring out a low mahogany table. Another group of servants make their way over with several dishes on gleaming platters. The scent of the roasted goat makes my mouth water.

"My son has told me just a little bit about you, but it is enough to know that I owe you my thanks." She smiles at me, her round cheeks shining. "Please, eat."

She passes me a bowl of ẹ̀gúsí and a separate plate of iyán as I sit down opposite Kola. My mouth waters at the scent of the soup and pounded yam, and the courtyard blurs around me.

"Like this, Simidele," says my mother, peeling the brown outer layer of the vegetable. She slices the white part and washes it in a calabash of clean water. "Now add it to the pot. It needs to boil for around ten minutes."

I am just tall enough to be able to see into the cooking pot. Carefully, I add the sliced yam to the boiling water and then help to clear the peelings away. I check on the chicken that is stewing separately and pick up another red pepper, ready to add it.

"Not too much, Simi. All we will taste is heat."

I roll my eyes and slip half in when her back is turned.

"When your father is choking and gasping for water, I will tell him who to blame."

I push my tongue against my teeth and fish the pepper out with a spoon. The compound is rich with the smell of cooking, and my stomach rumbles when I think of the meal we will be sharing. It is the Aláàfin's birthday and a great celebration is being held in the main square.

"Test it," my mother says, peering into the pot and moving aside to make room for me. "Make sure it is soft enough."

I lean into the steam, piercing a piece of yam with a small knife. "It's ready, ìyá."

"All right, now be sure that the water is not completely dried, because you will need it while pounding the yam. We can always add some, but it is better to use the water it cooked in." She places a mortar and pestle beside the pot. "Now use the pestle to pound."

"Like this?" I ask, grinding the pestle against the stone mortar.

"Yes, like that," answers my mother, smiling. She wipes a shred of yam from her wrapper and places her hands on her hips as she watches me. "You are doing a wonderful job, Simidele. Well done, little one."

"What is this?" asks my father as he enters, drawn by the smell of food. He breathes in deeply, hands on his stomach. "Who is cooking all this delicious food? The Aláàfin will smell this and demand it all!"

"Me, bàbá!" I crow. "It was me!"

He looks down, feigning shock. "No, how can this be? You are not big enough, surely?"

"I am!" I say, laughing as he picks me up and kisses my cheek, once, twice, three times. "Not only are you growing as clever and beautiful as your mother, but now you are cooking like her?"

I glance over at my mother, at her round smiling face and even teeth. She adjusts her wrapper. Even her simple movements are graceful.

To be like her? My heart swells. I grin and kiss my father back.

I blink, the memory of my mother teaching me how to make iyán strong in my mind. Her strong hands, the way she taught me just the right amount of spice for pepper soup. The compliments her food would receive before she told her stories. How everyone would watch the beauty of her shining face, as mesmerizing as the fire that they gathered around.

In front of me the ẹ̀gúsí steams, a reminder that I will never

164

teach my own daughter how to make food. I will never have a family like Kola, Yinka, and Bem. I'll never feel love or be loved. A wave of melancholy tugs at me, but I refuse to be sucked under. I knew this, I tell myself. Being here, with Kola, remembering what my life was like before, changes nothing.

I am not the same, but I won't let it stop me from doing what I need to.

"Eat," repeats Kola's mother, holding the bowl out to me.

Thanking her, I force myself to pinch some of the iyán and mold it in my hands before dipping it into the ègúsí, trying not to make too much of a mess. Bem and Kola choose the roasted goat and spinach, eating more meat than I think two people possibly could.

Kola's mother watches us all, a faint smile at her son's face as she orders the last dish to be brought out. Shredded fried coconut fills the air with its sweet tang as Kola's eyes widen. I eat a little, urged on by him, and as the warm white meat of the coconut melts on my tongue I stifle a groan of appreciation.

When the food is finished, servants with solemn faces clear the platters as we get to our feet. Kola draws his mother in for a tight embrace, her head only reaching his chest.

"We'll be back later today," he murmurs.

When he releases her, she holds him at arm's length, drinking him in.

"You are not wearing white?" Kola's mother asks as she examines his wrapper, a small line between her eyes.

"No, ìyá." Kola shakes his head. "And neither will you. I'm not going to mourn Taiwo and Kehinde. I'm going to bring them home."

CHAPTER SIXTEEN

KOLA PLANS ON sailing down the river Ogun to where the babalawo lives. Three skinny rafts are moored at the side of the bank. Wood has been lashed together to make buoyant platforms and a larger pole is attached to the ends to steer, but they look as if they could barely hold Issa, let alone someone like Bem.

"It's quicker if we take this route," Kola says as I eye the vessels. "Trust me."

They look even more insubstantial than the boat we had taken from Yemoja's island. But at least it'll just be the river we're dealing with.

The river. A wide ribbon that snakes through the forest. Mud mixes with the scent of fresh water filtered through stones, and the burble of the water seems almost to be calling my name. I wish I could just dive in. My skin feels tight, the bones awkwardly arranged. Despite all the times I lay on Yemoja's island, letting memories of my human life come back to me, all I can think about now is being underneath the water's surface. Tail flexing. Scales flashing. Free from worry, free from care. But I remember the fear on Kola's face when he first saw me, and the wrath on Yemoja's at the fact that I had revealed myself to a human.

Kola's hand hovers at my elbow as we climb onto the raft. "Careful," he says, and I recall the times I stumbled in front of him. Not now, I think, concentrating on where I place my feet until I can sit down at the front of the raft, far away from the water lest the change begin. Although my legs are dry, the scales feel as if they are there, nudging at the surface of my skin. I rub at them, sliding fingers to my toes, squeezing them until they are numb.

Yinka takes Issa on her raft, the yumbo waving at me from his perch at the front. He twists around to grin up at the girl, and I see her struggle not to respond to the blatant adoration on his face. Bem laughs at the tiny boy, feet wide apart as he pushes his raft off from the bank, and I wonder how it can even stay afloat with such a giant on it.

The river meanders, calm but fast-flowing, and I see why Kola chose to take this route. I stroke my soles in gratitude, watching the land as it passes us, alive with the screams of the white-throated monkeys and the trills of the rhinoceros hornbills, their red-orange beaks flashing in the sunlight.

"Thank you."

Kola's words are quiet, caught up in the swish of the water as he pushes the pole to steer us.

I lift a hand to shade my eyes from the sun, buying time for a response that I'm not sure how to deliver.

"I know you need to get to the babalawo. I know you need to get the rings." Kola pauses and I hear him haul on the pole; the scent of shea butter laced with sweat washes over me. "I'm grateful for you for seeing me to Oko. You didn't have to."

I choose not to uncover my eyes. "You're repaying me by taking me to the babalawo now." I don't add that I am grateful, too, glad that he's still with me. "I'm sorry," I say, guilt deepening my tone. "About Taiwo and Kehinde."

"Don't be." Kola pushes down hard on the pole, grunting. He doesn't look at me. "I'll get them back."

I don't say anything else and neither does he. The rest of the journey is filled with the stirred-up silt of the river, its rotting moss and ripples of epuya, their tail fins just visible at times. Issa chatters away, Yinka's answers intermittent, her voice lighter than I've heard it. Bem remains behind us, scanning the land, one sword free of its straps. When the river begins to widen out, Kola pulls to the side, wedging the raft against the soft dark mud of the bank.

"Let's leave these here before the coastal current becomes too strong."

Yinka and Bem follow suit, winding rope around the rafts, securing them together using a large ube tree, its purple yams hanging in small bunches. The forest is thick here and Bem leads the way, using his sword to hack at the underbrush and the snaking vines that wind around red mangrove trees. No one else seems to find the ground hard to walk on, but my feet soon begin to hurt. I slow down, trying to pick the route that has the most earth.

"It's not far," says Kola softly as he falls back next to me. "Just through the next grove and the forest gives way to the sea."

He runs his gaze over my legs, resting on my feet. The pain is back, and while it's dull at the moment, I know that I've already begun to limp slightly. I push ahead of him, determined not to hold us back.

The trees begin to thin, and I breathe a prayer of relief to Yemoja as the sound of the sea winds its way through a copse of banana trees. A rolling shush of water that sounds like home. The ground becomes sandier, and we soon leave the forest behind for a beach that sweeps ahead of us. Bleached white, the sand glitters, stretching into waves that reach toward the land, their brown-and-white water fingers grasping for more. A small dwelling squats close to the tree line, just where the sea and the shore curve away together.

"The babalawo has been our high priest and the one we consult for as long as I can remember," says Kola as he trudges across the sand. "Did you bring him the wine?"

"I did," answers Bem, patting the bag he has strung across his back. "The babalawo would never speak to us without it." He chuckles. "This I know as surely as the sky is blue."

The air fills with a tinkling that changes with the breeze, and as we get closer, I see the shells that are strung around the small circular building. Dangling from a roof made of large banana leaves, they knock against one another, creating a delicate melody that blends in with the sounds of the sea. The dwelling is simple, with walls made of tan clay and a plain woven fabric hanging from the arched entranceway. I think of Yemoja's assurances that the babalawo will give me the rings and I inhale deeply. The twins' disappearance has sowed seeds of worry, and now that I am finally here, I am fearful that I'm about to reap them.

"Kola, if it's all right, I'll go first," I say, my voice carrying over the others.

Yinka glowers at me, but I ignore her. It is not just the twins at stake.

"Here, take this and let me know when you are ready for me to come in," says Kola, passing me the palm wine.

I nod at his understanding as I take the flask. I think of the scars on Yemoja's cheeks and then I am pushing aside the fabric, entering the cool darkness all in one movement.

My eyes take a moment to adjust to the gloom before I see the man sitting in the center of the room. Swaddled in a fine wrapper so yellow that it almost appears gold, the babalawo is smaller than I expected. He is bald apart from one tuft of curling white hair at the back of his head, which matches a thick beard the same color. Tiny black eyes fix on me from the folds of skin that are spotted with age and the sun.

"Greetings, child."

I bend down, touching the floor before his feet and placing the wine on the swept hard floor. The dwelling is spacious, with a cooking pot neatly stored to the side and a red-and-orange sleeping mat on the other. The sea can still be heard, a constant rush of water that sounds like slow whispers. Dried bitter leaves hang from hooks, and bark and berries are piled neatly on a low table underneath. Their sharp smells are comforting, reminding me of the medicines used by the babalawo in Oyo-Ile, but it is not the scents that hold my attention. Carved into the clay are the swirls of a sea that wraps around the inner walls. Curlicues and waves wind their way around seven girls with tails, their hair tight coils adorned with pearls and shark's teeth.

Mami Wata.

Kola was right when he spoke of the priest to Yemoja.

"Is Mother Yemoja well? Or is she the reason you are here?"

Relief fills me as I straighten up, swinging my gaze back to the babalawo. I'm confronted with a gap-toothed smile that pulls the loose skin of his face into even more complicated wrinkles. The babalawo beckons me closer, thick gold bracelets on both wrists clinking together softly. Shafts of sunlight pierce the roof and shine onto the old man so that he sparkles.

"How did you know?"

"I can sense the orisa magic on you," he answers, his lilting voice rising at the end, as if his words are a song. "Even the scent of your blood is of salt and sea. Not to mention the jewel at your throat."

My fingers go to the sapphire, sliding over the facets.

"I carved seven of them, sanctified them all. I would know one anywhere." The babalawo pats the floor. "Sit, child of the sea. And tell me why you have come this far."

Unnerved, I settle on the packed-down earth, crossing my legs underneath me in a way that I know I used to do with ease. Now I have to think of every move, every bone and muscle, to make sure I'm doing it right.

"Yemoja sent me. I . . . I did something, and now I must make it right." My chest feels tight as I think of the covenant between Yemoja and Olodumare. The one I broke. I hold a hand to my face and wipe at my cheeks, as if I can stave off the tears I feel coming.

"What, child?" The babalawo's voice is deep and soft, suffusing his words with warm concern. "What did you do?"

"I took someone. From the sea."

"You saved a life?"

I nod. "But I didn't know of Olodumare's decree. Of the punishment Yemoja and all Mami Wata will face." My voice lowers to a whisper as tears slip down my cheeks. "The death. The . . . unmaking."

The babalawo leans back, sucking at his bottom lip. He places his hands in his lap and looks down at me. "You have come for the rings of Ile-Ife."

I sniff, wiping at my face and sitting up straighter. "Yes. Yemoja said it's the only way I can summon Olodumare so I can ask for forgiveness."

The babalawo rocks backward slowly. "My child, I am sorry." His smile dissolves. "But I do not have them anymore."

His words settle like stones in my stomach. "You don't have the rings?"

"No." The old man shakes his head. "I did until a week ago, and then they were claimed."

I sit for a moment, unable to move as my reality crashes down upon me. What will I do now? A sickness churns through me and I bend over, wrapping my arms around my abdomen. I stare at the packed-down earth of the floor, my vision wavering with the gathering of tears. How can I go back to Yemoja and tell her this?

The babalawo holds out a hand to me; his fingers are bent, knuckles swollen. "Come here, child. Please."

There is no way to make amends for what I have done, and now Yemoja and the other Mami Wata will suffer for it. When I still can't move, when the tears come and I hear myself sob, the babalawo eases himself from his low stool and enfolds me in his thin arms. I clutch at his wrapper, the scent of musk and bitter leaf strong. I can still hear the sea outside, and it speaks to me more powerfully than ever, the waves breaking loudly now, a crashing call that I can't answer.

"There is still a way," says the babalawo, crooked fingers patting my back.

I don't look up. I can tell that my face is swollen and wet, and the shame I feel goes deep. Deeper than crying and being comforted by such a babalawo. What have I done? In saving Kola, I have condemned my own kind.

I hear someone enter, but I still don't look up. "Simi." Hands take hold of my shoulders, pulling me back against hot skin. "It's all right."

Kola.

I turn in his arms and press my face against his chest, and even in that choice I hate myself. Because I have a feeling that I might still have saved him even if I had known the consequences. How could I have let anyone die in the sea?

"I heard what the babalawo said. But did you really listen to him? There's another way." His lips are by my ear, voice as comforting as faded cotton. "Don't give up now. I won't let you."

I don't answer. I let the salt of my tears mix with the scent of sweat and black soap that is Kola. I keep my face pressed against his skin and breathe him in, until I am partly calmed.

"What other way is there?" I ask, my voice scratchy. Despair sticks in my throat like a crooked fish bone.

I turn to see the babalawo sit back on his stool, arranging the folds of his wrapper. A long thick gold chain hangs outside it, set with an emerald the size of a bird's egg. "The twins are unique."

"It was confirmed in the ceremony?" asks Kola, his voice rising with hope.

"Yes. After you were taken, your parents brought them to me on the allotted day." The babalawo turns his small eyes on Kola, lips pursed thoughtfully. "We already suspected their rareness, but while initiating the ceremony, the truth of it was fully confirmed."

"They are orisa incarnate," I say quietly, unwinding myself from Kola's arms to hold the priest's gaze.

"Yes. The Ibeji have indeed manifested in them. Two with one soul. Rainmakers, bringers of prosperity and health." He raises a hand covered in darker brown patches and touches a finger to the jewel at his own throat. "And the reason Oko and the surrounding lands thrive."

Two rings, both with immense power. The realization is enough to make me sit up straight. "You gave them to the twins. The rings, I mean. One each."

The babalawo exhales and then nods. "I did. Just as I gave the sapphires to Yemoja. The stones speak for themselves, and they chose the Ibeji. But there is more. As well as holding great potency, they are amplifiers." The elder stops, his face bathed in light. "Whichever orisa has them, their power is strengthened."

"How much?" asks Kola.

"The true extent is not known, but it is of unimaginable magnitude. When the twins were born they connected with the earth, and Oko and the surrounding lands have flourished. But with the twins in possession of the rings? All lands will thrive." The babalawo's eyes light up, his wrinkled mouth unfolding into a smile. "*All* of them. And with that, perhaps a way to peace. Enough food for everyone, health, more trade. A chance of unity not seen before."

I am silent a moment. It makes perfect sense, and I see why he would have given the rings to the twins. But if I can't use the rings, it means the death of Yemoja and our kind.

"Simidele," murmurs the babalawo, seeing my face fall. "Do not despair. I wasn't able to protect the twins from Esu, but I was able to bind them to the rings, in life and death. None can remove or use them unless they permit it. They can also still be used to summon Olodumare. But first you will need to find them."

"So Esu really did take them?" asks Kola, standing, his head nearly scraping against the leaves of the roof.

"He did."

"What of the protection you promised my parents?" Kola's words are threaded with frustration.

"My ceremony was strong enough against the Tapa. But an orisa as powerful as Esu? No."

Kola moves closer to the babalawo, his hands twitching. The old man does not move, just watches as Kola's hands graze the sword at his side. I know Kola wants a reason to be angry with someone, but this is not right. Just as I am about to pull him back to me, Kola kneels before the old man, touching the ground near the toes of the babalawo.

"My apologies. For being disrespectful." Kola lifts his head, tears shimmering in his gaze. "Please. Tell us how to get them back." He glances at me and then back at the babalawo. "The twins and the rings."

I creep forward so that I am next to Kola. "Where has Esu taken them?"

The elder places both swollen hands on his knees and stares past us at the murals on the walls. The only sound is the sea, which has died down to a low swish and hush. "I understand your pain. Both of you." He lifts a hand and twirls a gnarled index finger in the air, gesturing to the images behind us. "Esu has taken them to his island."

"Why?" asks Kola.

I think of Esu, of his discontent and his hunger for more, of his search, which Oya and the yumboes have both described.

Power amplified.

Dread shoots through me, slithering down my spine. "He wants the rings of Ile-Ife," I say quietly.

"He does. But since the twins are bonded to them, he will have to try to persuade them to offer them up to him."

"What would he want with them?" I ask, twisting my fingers nervously. "What about his duty to Olodumare?"

"With the rings would come the amplification of all of Esu's powers." The babalawo twists a heavy golden bracelet behind the bones of his wrist, swollen knuckles quivering. "And he would not have a duty to Olodumare. Instead, he would be able to rival the Supreme God. He would not have to pass on any messages. Would not have to listen to Olodumare or any of their decrees."

"He could do whatever he wanted?" I whisper, my voice shaking with horror at the babalawo's words. I think of what Yemoja said about the orisa's greed and jealousy.

"Yes," answers the babalawo, his voice cracking. "Esu has long been tired of being Olodumare's messenger. He craves more than he already has, more than passing on the prayers of mankind." The old priest sucks air through the gap in his teeth. "If he obtains the rings, his power will be such that he will be worshipped with as much reverence as the Supreme God, have as much influence over humankind and orisas. With no one to answer to, he'll be free to do anything he wants."

"Perhaps he would . . . do good?" I ask, hope lifting my voice. "He's not evil. He keeps the balance between the ajogun and orisas. This brings a level of peace to the world."

"He does. But what if he decided not to do this anymore? On a whim or just for his own entertainment? There is no telling. That is the gamble. We've all heard the stories of the arguments started by Esu between brothers, neighbors, kings, and queens. But think on this . . ." The babalawo leans toward us, his gaze piercing as his voice grows lower still. "Olodumare has always been the greater force . . . there to keep him in check. With the power the rings give? Esu could bring chaos to the whole world and no one would be able to stop him."

I shiver at the babalawo's words, at the thought of the world at Esu's mercy.

"What will happen to the twins after Esu takes the rings?" Kola's shoulders hunch slightly, as if his body already knows the answer.

"He won't stop until he possesses them. Afterward? I can't be sure, but they would no longer . . . be needed." The babalawo turns to Kola. "Their lives as your brother and sister are important, but so are their ties to the land."

"What do you mean?" I ask, but already my mind is whirring, thinking of my vision and what he'd told us earlier.

"Do not forget the twins' connection to the earth. They are the reason our lands are bountiful. The reason it is so *alive*."

"And so without them . . ." I remember the fear of the elephants as they fled, the twisted black branches of the trees at the edge of the forest. The brown rot already beginning to infect the plants around Kola's village.

My vision.

The bones and their bleached sharpness. Yumboes and humans.

"Without the Ibeji the crops will die, as will animals and people. There will be famine of a proportion we have not seen in a thousand years. And Oko . . ." The babalawo strokes his chin, hand shaking. "Oko will be unable to exist, and the chance of health for the rest of the land will be lost."

CHAPTER SEVENTEEN

SILENCE SITS BETWEEN us. Obtaining the rings was something I had to do for Yemoja and all Mami Wata, but now it is much more. The pressure constricts my words, and all I can think of is what needs to be done.

"How do we get to Esu's island?" I ask.

The babalawo pauses before he opens his arms and nods toward the curved walls. "If you look behind you, then you will see."

I spin slowly. What I noticed before, the carvings in the clay of the dwelling, depict more than just Mami Wata. They are a record of the entire world. I examine seas split around islands and bigger masses of lands, complete with volcanoes and the etchings of forests, grassy plains, mountains, cities, and villages. The beauty of the carvings stretches around all of the walls, encompassing us in our lands and those of our ancestors.

"This is amazing. And we are . . ." Kola's eyes are wide with passion as he runs his hands over a large bay, stopping when he reaches a forest that leads to the sea. "Here?"

"That is correct," answers the babalawo. He gets up from his stool and shuffles to the far side of his dwelling. With an arthritic finger he traces a lick of the sea and stops at a small mass, alone in an ocean of wild curlicues. "This is Esu's island, covered in forest, with only occasional grass plains and a live volcano. His palace is surrounded by water."

When I lean forward, I see that the speck of land is not entirely on its own. Small monstrous shapes are etched into its surroundings, some feline and others with wings. All have fangs. I shudder and look at the old man.

"You did not expect it to be unprotected, did you?" He makes his way back to the shaft of sunlight and sits down. "Do not worry, I will explain as much as I know while you copy the map."

I look from the images to Kola. "How will we do that?"

"Wait for one moment," he says simply, and ducks out of the entranceway.

He returns minutes later with Yinka, who slips into the babalawo's dwelling and immediately bends to touch the floor at the elder's feet. She murmurs a prayer that elicits a smile and a nod from the old man. He leans forward, touches a hand lightly to the girl's bare head.

Yinka rises, taking in the map, her eyes wide in reverence. Kola reaches for Esu's island, pointing out the small speck of land. I see her blanch slightly at the figures carved alongside it.

"Yinka will create a map for us," says Kola, looking at me. "But we'll need you, too, Simi."

I am opening my mouth to ask why when I see Yinka unbuckle both of her axes and place them by the doorway, within her reach. She sits on a small stool collected from beside the table and beckons to me impatiently. She's not smiling, but she's not glaring either, and I take that as a positive sign.

"You will help me collect some more bitter leaf and bark," announces the babalawo to Kola, nodding as he passes me. "And

I will do my best to describe the island and all you should look out for." He waits while Kola pushes the entranceway fabric aside. "But remember, much of this is myth. No one has ever been there and returned to speak of it properly."

"Trust her as I do," murmurs Kola to me as he turns to leave with the old man. "She can create patterns in hair that are maps. It's how the Oko guard has outlined new areas surrounding our village. Once the guards have returned, the maps are transferred onto scrolls and, if they are very important, into carvings using stone or metal."

I look up at the perfect smoothness of Yinka's head, and then drop my gaze when I see her watching me.

"Just because I choose to shave my hair doesn't mean I don't know what I'm doing," says Yinka, an edge to her tone as Kola and the babalawo leave. "Come."

I lower myself onto the floor between Yinka's legs, thinking about the ingenuity of their cartography. Living maps. The skill needed to braid them must be great, I think, as I remove the dagger from my plaits. Yinka's fingers scrape on my scalp as she pulls apart the braids already at the crown of my hair. She is gentle, but sometimes her fingers get caught on the knots and I wince. I pull apart the ones I can reach, letting her move my head into the positions she wants, not complaining when the muscles in my neck spasm. When my hair is loose, Yinka takes a moment to stroke and rub my scalp with some coconut oil left by the babalawo, running her hands to the ends of my curls.

"Do you think you'll be able to fit it all on?" I ask, hands on my knees.

"I think so. Your head is quite big." I am silent for a moment before I realize she has made a joke. Smiling, I lean back and close my eyes. Yinka's fingers slide through my hair, tugging and twisting the dark strands. Every so often, she pauses, glancing at the carved map, pulling my head with her.

It feels wrong not to speak, sitting so close to Yinka, but I open my mouth to talk several times and then shut it, unsure of what to say.

"Oko is a unique place," I offer.

"It is." Yinka says nothing more for a while, and I curse my choice of words. They sound plain and silly even to me.

"You and Bem and Kola are very close," I try again.

"We are." Yinka's voice is low and almost rough. "Everything they did, I did, too. Including the sea. Most of Oko are taught to sail as soon as they can walk, but Kola's father took him to the waters as soon as he could crawl. He gave him a small boat for his sixth birthday with strict instructions to stay in the shallows, but we didn't listen."

Yinka laughs quietly. I stay very still in case any movement might make her change her mind about speaking to me.

"The fishermen had to save us when we were pulled out to sea by the currents. I was petrified. Bem was shaking, but Kola was grinning. Exhilarated. He always wanted to go as far as he could. His father thought it was to escape his responsibilities, but I knew it was because his spirit is restless, always wanting to explore new things." She is silent a moment, hooking errant hairs back into place with a nail. "Kola's father gave him his larger boat when he was twelve. Sometimes we would spend the whole day out at sea."

As she tugs my hair to the side, I catch the change of tone when she mentions Kola. "Yinka, can I ask you something?"

The girl's fingers pause. "The answer is no." Her tone is icy, at odds with the heat of the dwelling and the sweat that slides down our collarbones and backs.

Yinka's abrupt answer makes me twist my fingers together in my lap. There's a long moment of silence before she carries on, her knees gripping my shoulders just a little bit tighter.

"I know what you're going to ask." She sucks in a deep breath and lets it go slowly. "Kola's family wanted us to marry eventually, and for a time, I thought maybe I did, too."

My heart sinks as I hold my breath. "What happened?"

"He was never mine, and he certainly isn't now." Yinka smiles and I hear it in her voice. "He is a brother to me, and one I will always protect."

I think of the cutting looks she gave me at first; now they make more sense. Yinka's fingers move faster as they finish the end of a braid. "I would always want the best for him. Nothing less."

And I am less. The thought is sharp and sudden. Less than human. I don't know how I even let myself entertain thoughts of Kola, even if I were allowed to be with him. Her words stay with me as several hours pass; the sunlight moves through the holes in the roof, providing light for Yinka to see. My legs go numb as she folds and tucks the braids tightly against my scalp. Even though she has quick and nimble fingers, by the time she has finished the hut is humid with the thick heat of late afternoon.

When she taps my shoulder to let me know she is done, my hair snakes down over my shoulders, falling to the middle of my back in slender plaits. I pat my head, fingertips skimming over the patterns in my hair, which show the expanse of seas and the bumps that mark islands, both large and small. It feels as if Yinka has left nothing of our route out, her deft fingers including every-thing carved into the walls.

"Thank you," I say quietly as I ease myself up from the floor, kicking some life back into my muscles.

"You are welcome," answers Yinka. She doesn't smile, but her expression is softer.

"Can I see?" Kola steps into the dwelling with a calabash full of fresh water and a small sack of bitter leaf. He places them on the low table and approaches me.

"Yes," I say shyly as I angle my head.

Kola puts his hands on either side of my face, examining the coils and patterns of the braids that curve from my forehead to my crown. I hold my breath as his hand slides across my cheeks, moving my head gently.

"Perfect," he says, his voice low and gruff. I think he means my hair until I look up to see his eyes on my face.

"Thank you," I manage. "Yinka is very talented." I sneak a look at her and she turns away, but not before I catch a small nod.

The babalawo insists on serving us some ẹ̀fọ́ rírò as Bem and Issa crowd inside. The spinach stew is fresh from the pot, gently spiced and warm, and it fills my stomach in a way I had forgotten.

"As I told Kola earlier, you will need to be careful of the creatures Esu uses to protect his island and palace."

"What will we be dealing with?" asks Bem, slurping the spinach and receiving a cross look from Yinka.

"Stories differ," answers the babalawo. He holds his arms open wide, skin sagging from his biceps. "From creatures like lions to giant bats. While I cannot be sure what you will face, just know that Esu's land will be guarded by something. Do not trust what you see or hear."

The stew is finished, and all eyes are fastened on the babalawo as he sweeps his gaze over us. "Remember who Esu is."

"The trickster," says Kola.

"The guardian of the crossroads of life," adds Yinka.

"Master of language and messenger to Olodumare," finishes Bem.

"Hmm, yes." The babalawo leans back, his eyes crinkled with worry. "Do not forget any of this." His hands rest on his knees. "Do not underestimate him. Not at any cost."

· · ·

The sun burns above us, the sky a baked crystalline blue that hurts to look at. As we trek back to the rafts, my breath is ragged in the heat and I'm sweating again. Even the leaves seem spikier, scratching at my arms and legs. I think of the cool water of the river and swipe at a cloud of flies angrily. Yinka falls back next to me, eyeing my displeasure with a quirk of her lips.

"Here," she says, plucking a leaf from a plant that has tiny purple flowers. She crushes it between her fingers and daubs it on her neck. "It keeps most of them away."

She passes me some of the leaves and I copy her, smearing the juice against the sweat-soaked skin of my neck.

"Thank you."

Yinka nods and strides ahead, her axes shining on her back. I try to quicken my pace to match hers, but the shooting pains are back in my soles; I stumble and Kola lunges to catch me before I fall to my knees. Behind, always behind, or falling over. My face burns and I pull away as quickly as I can, ignoring the hurt in his expression.

The babalawo was earnest in his warnings, and while I know how to handle my dagger in a fight, how can I keep up when my legs are this weak? What if I fail them all? I hurry along behind them, pushing myself to go faster, even when it feels as if needles are being stuck into both feet with every step I take. My braids are heavy on my neck, wet with sweat, and even my arms ache from pushing bushes out of the way.

I feel the tug of the river before we reach it, and when it winds into view, I all but lower myself onto the bank. Kola stops for water, but I know he's done it on purpose to give me time to gather myself.

After sipping from the drink Issa offers me, I stare back at the river. The surface ripples, light bouncing from it in sharp rays as I draw up my legs. My bones feel softer and my skin harder. I can feel the scales trying to form, and for a moment, I consider just slipping in. Issa sees me looking at the surface longingly and moves to my side.

"Bem or Yinka wouldn't think of you any differently," whispers the yumbo. "They like me."

His words bring me back, and I think of them seeing me in my true form. I shiver but force a smile for Issa, thinking of Yemoja's words. "Thank you, little one, but I don't think it's wise."

I massage my feet. Yinka springs onto her raft, balancing perfectly as the others untie the ropes and check that they are secure. Envy stirs in me as I watch her jump back onto the bank to gather up Issa. With the yumbo clinging to her neck, she makes the leap again, flawlessly.

Kola holds the raft steady as I clamber on, warning me that it may be slightly harder since we will be going against the current. "There's a smaller tributary that will be easier, so we'll take that route."

I nod, but I'm closing my eyes already, grateful for the breeze on the river and for finally being off my feet. Breathing in the damp wet scent, I try to take some calm from the swathes of late-afternoon sun that cause the surface to sparkle. The river's sound is more mellow than that of the sea, a lighter rush of water that nudges gently at my mind.

It is my tenth birthday and my mother is taking me to the Ogun river, as she does every year. The walk there is long, winding through the edges of the forest, but I skip for most of it, earth rising in little clouds of reddish dirt.

When we reach the grassy banks, my mother lifts the folds of her yellow wrapper, and together, we wade into the shallows.

"Oof, it is cold, Simidele!"

I smile and plunge my own hands into the currents, watching small fish dart out of our way.

"Can you feel it, ọmọbìnrin ìn mi?" She laughs, touching her fingertips to the surface of the river and flicking the water at me. "Can you feel the power of the river?"

"Yes, ìyá," I answer, feeling the water tug at me.

She slips her wet hand into mine. "Let us pray to Yemoja. Say the words with me."

Our voices swirl with the current, rising with each word. When we finish, my mother pulls me to her, tipping the water over my head, blessing me in Yemoja's name. I gasp and grin, blinking through the veil of sparkling water.

We climb out and sit on the grassy bank, letting the sun dry us. Later, we will share a meal with my father and the other people of our compound. But this afternoon? It is just for us.

After we eat, I am allowed to play and swim while my mother

bathes her feet in the river. I keep my legs together, pretending they are a tail and I am Yemoja. When I dive down, the mud from the bottom clears and I watch the fish that swim away from me, heading to the reeds. My mother's legs disappear, and when I surface I find her lying in the sun.

"Simidele! Come and rest." She pats the grass. "Sit next to me."

I swim back to the bank and climb out, tying my wrapper and sinking down beside my mother. She picks at my hair, unraveling one of my braids, taking the chance to plait it while I am still. I lean into her, her skin warm against mine. "Do you remember the reason we come to this river every year?"

"To celebrate the day I was born?"

"That's right. But did you know that it's also because you were born right here, in this very river?" She lets go of the finished plait and pats my hair.

I shake my head and she smiles. "I will tell you how it came to pass."

"Yes, ìyá," I say, closing my eyes and waiting for her to begin.

"Here is a story. Story it is . . . When you were in my stomach I would often come to the river. Sitting on the banks here, I would feel you move. Tumbling and twisting inside me."

I crack open an eye. She has never told me this before. I don't say anything, not wanting to interrupt.

"The last time I visited was a week after you were due to join this world, worried that you were not moving as you should be. I came to the river for peace and guidance from Mother Yemoja. I was very large and it took me twice as long as usual to get here." My mother places a hand on my shoulders, squeezing and rubbing gently. "As I cooled my feet in the water, I prayed to Yemoja for your safety. After a while, I felt you moving. Just a shift and a wiggle, but it was enough. I was blessed, but as I was about to head home, I felt the first great pain. I couldn't return to Oyo-Ile and had no one with me, but I wasn't worried. I knew Yemoja would take care of me. She called me to the river."

"You saw her?" This time I can't help but interrupt. I open my eyes and sit up. "You saw Yemoja?"

My mother nods and pats her lap. She will not continue until I lie back down.

"She called me into the waters. I anchored my feet in the mud of the riverbed and clung to the banks, letting the current carry away some of the pain. Yemoja stroked my back as I labored, and she took away the rest. When you were born, she fished you from the river and passed you to me, blessing you as she did so."

I open my eyes and stare up at my mother's face. She bends down and plants a kiss on my forehead. "Just remember that you have Yemoja's blessing. She is always with you. You don't need to just pray to her here. Whenever you need her strength, say the prayers I have taught you."

Yemoja is our ancestral orisa, I feel it. And with that knowledge comes peace.

And strength.

I flex my feet, twisting my ankles. The memory reminds me of my mother's tenacity. Of her love for me and of Yemoja's blessing even before I was re-created. Of the orisa's courage in creating more Mami Wata. It reminds me of my own determination.

My choice.

My decision to have the fortitude to make things right. To get the twins and the rings.

Reaching up, I run my hands over the map plaited in my hair.

My fingertips touch whorls of the sea and bumps that demarcate islands until I reach the small braided knot of hair at the back of my skull.

Esu's island.

I pause, moving back over the plaits, index finger resting on the emerald of the dagger. Whatever it takes, I tell myself.

CHAPTER EIGHTEEN

THE FISH BOB on the water of the river, bloated pale bellies offered up to the sun. Dull flesh stretches far enough away to make the river look as if it is lined with carcasses. We remain silent as our rafts head toward the bank, the wooden platforms cutting through the dead fish as my unease returns.

Yinka bends down and scoops one up, examining it before looking over at Kola. "Not a mark on it," she says, eyes narrowed as she tosses it back into the river. She wipes her hand on her wrapper, mouth twisted with disgust.

"I don't like this," says Bem, his huge shoulders hunched as he bends closer to the mass of bodies.

Kola looks away from the dead fish and glances at me briefly. "Neither do I." I can see the worry in the grooves of his forehead. "We should get back as quickly as we can."

Bem and Kola tether the rafts and we scramble onto land, holding tree trunks that are now covered in brown-and-black patches of rot, their leaves wilting. Silence greets us, blanketing the forest, heavy enough to smother our words if we found the right ones to speak. But we don't talk, and as we pick our way along the path back to Oko, the trees become more afflicted, some with their branches entirely blackened, stripped of leaves and any greenness.

The babalawo's prophecy of famine and death at the loss of the Ibeji fills my mind, and I shudder at the land that is already beginning to prove him right.

"Kola—" I begin, but I am stopped by a sudden scream that cuts through the thick heat.

Bem and Yinka sprint through the thinning trees, and Kola pauses only to scoop up Issa, heading after them. I follow, feet skimming the earth as blood thunders in my ears. We reach the path to Oko, which is now framed with obsidian trees and piles of rotting crops. The smell of death fills the air. Bem and Yinka cut through the carefully plowed land, their bare feet crushing the dead corn as another cry rips through the air. I lower my head and pump my arms harder, skidding to a stop behind Kola. Edging around him, I see Yinka bent over a girl who can be no more than ten years old, squatting between the ravaged plants. She rocks back and forth, her hands on the wrapper of an old woman collapsed on the ground. White puffs of hair escape thick plaits wound in red thread.

"Please, ìyá àgbà fell and now she . . ." The girl dissolves into more tears before she can finish. Yinka draws her away gently and leans down to check the old woman's pulse.

"She's alive," Yinka offers, "but we'll need to get her inside Oko's walls now. She needs a healer."

Bem scoops the old woman up carefully while Yinka helps the girl to her feet. "What happened?" she asks as we double back to the path.

The small girl tries to lick her cracked lips, but her mouth is too dry. I pull out my waterskin, holding it out to her, watching as she drinks.

"Our cow was sickly last night," the girl rasps. "Ìyá àgbà thought she could help her this morning, but when we arrived she was already dead."

"What happened to your grandmother?"

"I'm not sure. This morning she woke up and her breathing was difficult." Her voice weakens, falling to a whisper. "I tried to persuade her not to walk all the way out here—I said I could go on my own, but she wouldn't let me."

Bem cradles the old woman. Her head lolls on the boy's chest and she draws in breath with small jerks of effort. I draw level with them and see the sores on her thin legs.

"Are these new?" I ask, gesturing to the elder's skin.

The girl nods, scratching lightly at her own arm. "They appeared last night."

I try to smile, hoping reassurance shows in my features. "I'm sure a healer will know what to do."

The gates of Oko are still open, and I see Yinka and Bem exchange an uneasy look at the lack of guards. When we enter, it is to the press of humidity and the scent of rot mixed with sickness.

"I'll take them to their home and we can summon a healer," says Bem as the girl murmurs directions to their compound.

"We'll wait here for you," answers Yinka, fingers on the handle of one of her axes.

Kola nods and sets Issa on the ground. "Where is everyone?"

"Exactly what I was wondering," says Yinka. She unsheathes her axes now, eyes darting around the empty thoroughfare.

The sun produces a blistering heat, and I can feel it burning the pale parts of my scalp that the braids expose. Sweat beads along my hairline, slipping down the planes of my face, and I touch my fingertips to my dagger. There is something ominous about the silence, not even the cluck of a chicken or the shout of a child. Kola starts along the path to his family compound, peering ahead, just as Bem returns.

Kola picks up Issa and we move without noise, our feet kicking up small puffs of dust as we pass closed doors and an empty market. We hear the people before we see them: shouts of rage paired with anguish. We run toward the cries, and when the path turns, we see why the other parts of Oko are empty.

Almost all of the villagers are gathered around the gates to Kola's family compound. The street is filled with the low rumbling of complaints tinged with fear, and a few of the men have gone as far as the steps, held back only by Oko's guards. The armed soldiers gesture to the people to keep their distance, and it's as we draw closer that I hear what they are so enraged about.

"Our crops are dead!" shouts one woman, her voice high with despair. In her hands she clutches some blackened corn.

"Overnight. How can this be?" another calls.

"What will you do? Before we all starve!"

More of the villagers join in, their calls rising to a crescendo that splits the air. The doors of the compound are flung open and Kola's father appears.

His white wrapper reflects the sunlight as he steps forward, flanked by more guards. "I am aware of what is going on." The people quiet as the leader of Oko holds his hands out. "And I ask for your patience."

"Patience won't feed us!" shouts one woman, clutching the baby bound to her chest. "Tell us what's going on."

Kola begins to push his way through the crowds, helped by Bem and Yinka. Issa ducks down into the sack, a slash of worry on his face before he disappears. Kola's father is silent until his son reaches him. There are gasps and praises to Ogun and Olodumare, as if Kola has been resurrected from the dead. And to them, he has. He nods, accepting the prayers and touches of a few of the village people. But I can see the tightness around his eyes, the thinning of his lips. The scent of palm wine is strong, and when I look down at the offerings to Ogun, I see that someone has spilled the drink.

"It's true, bàbá," I hear Kola murmur. "Something is happening. Even the fish in the river are dying." Their faces, shielded from the people by the guards, mirror each other in contained panic.

The older man grips his son's arms and then steps around him, standing above the people of Oko. "Go back to your homes!" he calls. "I will find the cause of this sickness, and together we will overcome it."

"But what is going on?" asks a rotund man, his big belly hanging low over the folds of a scarlet wrapper.

"We are not sure yet, Adewale, but I will find out."

"How? And when?" calls the same man, his eyes bulging. Gold glints on his fingers and around his wrists. "Will people have to die like the crops before you take action?"

"It has been a day, Adewale." Kola's father's voice is thin with exhaustion, and I think of the weight he must carry. First with the twins missing, and now this. "Expect more from Olodumare, but I am just a man. Now go back to your homes, take stock of the food you already have, and come for a meeting tomorrow evening."

"You heard what was said! Go home, people!" The guards begin to move down the steps, dispersing the last of the lingering villagers.

Adewale is the last to leave, giving the guards a look of disgust before he waddles away.

Kola turns to us, a muscle ticking on the left side of his tight jaw. "While I explain to my parents what the babalawo said, can you all prepare what we need in order to leave?" I feel the urgency in his voice. We don't have much time. "Take Simi and Issa to the boat," he says to Bem. "Collect all the food and water we'll need. And Yinka?" Kola nods at her, his eyes cold. "Gather as many weapons as you can."

As Kola passes Issa to me, the heat between us shimmers.

"I'll be there soon," he says.

I look up at him and try to smile in reassurance, but knowing that so much rides on our obtaining the rings makes me feel nauseated. Kola nods at me once and then slips through the compound doors.

"This way," urges Bem. We thread our way through the empty streets of Oko, heading to the sound of the sea and the encroaching sand that parts tufts of grass and hard-packed earth.

I force myself to move faster, to match Bem's long stride. We pass compound gates and doors that are sealed, as if wood and stone could keep out the pestilence. I say a prayer to Yemoja as we pass each one, the fear of the villagers almost palpable, a tightness spreading across my chest.

I straighten my back. I will not see anyone else harmed because of Esu. Whatever I need to do, I think as my hand goes to the emerald in my hair, I will do it.

Yinka peels off, heading to a compact fortress on the bluff, while Bem points to a vessel, moored just beyond the shallows. We traipse across the shifting sand, its heat adding to the ever-present pain in my soles.

"Welcome to my ship," Bem says, but I look past the boat to the swell of the ocean, its flex of dark and light blue. "Well, Kola's ship, really, but I've put just as much love and work into it."

I step past him, his words seeping away as I listen to the waves. They roll onto the land in blended browns and blues, and I feel the power of the water. Seaweed is draped across the wet sand as the shallows throw their salty frills onto the shore. I continue walking toward the waves, their wild crashing matching the pulse of my heart.

Come, says the sea, white-tipped water from afar catching my eye. *Return home, where you belong.* I take another step, my feet sinking into the hot sand that gives way to the hardness of the wet ground.

"Simidele?"

I don't hear my name, not really. All I can think of is the sea and its call. Its power. My feet move me forward. The water rolls closer to me, and I can feel the spikes of the scales that begin to push through my skin. They glimmer, a golden pink just visible among the veins of my feet and legs. It would be easy to return.

"Simi!" says Bem, examining me closely. "Are you all right, Simidele?"

Bem's question frees me from the overwhelming urge and I stagger backward, nearly falling in the sand. I blink at the sea. I can't go back yet. "I'm fine."

Yinka returns, sprinting to the beach carrying a cache of weapons: a sack bristling full of daggers, two swords, the tips of several arrows, and the lean supple wood of bows.

"Kola is on his way, and so is Ifedayo."

"Ifedayo?" I ask.

"The guard from Oyo-Ile. The one his father said he wanted to send with him. It's still the only way he'd let him go." Yinka dumps the weapons on the floor in front of her and straightens up, hands on her hips. She faces the sea, squinting against the breeze and muttering so that I almost can't hear her. "As if Bem and I can't be trusted anymore."

Bem lays a hand on her shoulder briefly and she relaxes into it, throwing him a grateful look.

Kola turns and makes his way down to the beach. Next to him is Ifedayo, and immediately I recognize him from Kola's compound. As tall as Bem, but not as broad, almost skinny, Ifedayo has a headful of slim plaits that grace a pointed jawline, skimming his thin lips as he tosses the braids out of his face. His eyes are so dark that they look black, and a sense of strength crouches in the way he holds himself, posture loose but muscles coiled tight.

"Simidele, Issa. This is Ifedayo." Kola strides ahead as the young man nods at us once before walking to Yinka. A slight limp interrupts his steps as he speaks with her, peering at the collection of weapons. He must approve of what he sees, because he smiles, although it doesn't quite reach the ink black of his eyes. I search his face, wondering if I have seen him before in Oyo-Ile, but no feature looks familiar.

"We'll set sail straightaway." Kola turns his light brown gaze on me. He's so close that I can smell a hint of familiar black soap. I feel the flush of heat as he comes closer still, until I realize he's looking at the map of my hair. "If we leave now we should arrive by late afternoon, early evening tomorrow."

I have opened my mouth to answer when I see his troubled expression. "What is it?"

"I don't think we should take Issa." Kola sighs and runs a hand over his curls and down the side of his face. "He's too young. And . . ."

"You don't want him to get hurt."

Kola nods and we watch as Issa stands next to Yinka, his hand curling into hers. The girl glares at Ifedayo, who merely flashes an easy grin at her, seemingly not bothered by the sight of a yumbo. Issa pulls the girl by her hand and turns her attention to him, choosing a small dagger that he wields as if it were a sword.

"He won't leave easily."

Kola breathes out hard. "I know."

Issa capers around Yinka as she pretend-spars with him, an axe held loosely, a mock frown on her face. They kick up sprays of hot sand as they circle each other, shielded from the rest of the beach by a strip of coconut trees.

"So ferocious," she growls, pretending that he has struck a fatal blow.

"And so obviously skilled with a sword," calls Kola, smiling as he jogs over, grasping the yumbo by the waist.

"Adekola! You are ruining my attack!"

"I'm sorry." Kola sets Issa down and turns the tiny boy to face him. "I was just speaking with Simi, and . . ." He pauses, ordering his thoughts, wanting to get his words right. "We think it's about time for you to go home, little one. After all, you showed us the way to Oko."

Issa looks up at me. "But ègbón okùnrin, you need me." The yumbo scurries over to the sack of supplies and grabs hold of a corner of the bag. "I am fine," Issa declares. "Besides, who will help with all of this?"

Bem, seeing Kola's face, removes the sack from the yumbo's grasp and throws it over his shoulder. I see Yinka's eyes glisten, but she takes the dagger Issa has been sparring with and places it back with the other weapons.

"He's right," she says, her expression sliding back to neutral. "It will be too much for you."

"No! It won't!" Issa spins, looking at each one of us in turn, his body ramrod-straight and his hands clenched. The yumbo's bottom lip wobbles and I suck in a deep breath. "Please. Is it because of the Ninki Nanka?"

"No, it is none of that and all about my promise to Salif." Kola places his hand on the boy's shoulder, his bones almost as fragile as a blue-naped mousebird. "You were an excellent guide—we would never have gotten to Oko so quickly without you. But now it is time for you to go home. I don't want to put you in any more danger."

"But you are not! Please," pleads Issa, grabbing Kola's hand. "I want to help you and Simi."

"You will help us," I add, trying to smile. "By going home. That way we will know you're safe."

Kola takes a breath and then pushes the yumbo gently. "Go. Go on. We don't need your help anymore. *I* don't need your help anymore."

Issa stands apart from us, molten eyes hot with tears. "But ègbón okùnrin . . ."

"I'm not your big brother. I never was." Kola's voice is sharp and loud enough to make the yumbo boy flinch. "Now go! Before you get us killed by something else."

Issa looks at me, his cheeks stained with silvery tears, and then at Kola's balled fists before he runs. When the yumbo reaches the beginning of the forest, he stops and allows himself one last look before disappearing between the bushes.

"It's for the best," I say quietly. Kola is frowning at the tree line now, his eyes shining. I think of reaching for him, but he turns quickly away, beckoning to the others to collect what we need.

"Come, we're wasting time."

• • •

Kola is quiet as we are taken to the ship by boat, his gaze in the direction that Issa disappeared in. Another vessel, manned by two villagers, bobs alongside, with food and weapons in sacks and barrels that are passed up the rope ladder to Ifedayo. Kola inspects the ship to see that all is in order as Bem reefs the sails and Yinka hoists the anchor.

Bem consults the map in my hair, deciding on the best route to take. The day is drained of the sun, and we quickly lose sight of Oko. Watches are divided among us all, with Yinka taking the first. I listen to Kola's murmurs as Bem asks him questions about the weeks he was gone from Oko. Most words are snatched by the wind, so I only catch the tones of his pain and anguish.

When I feel Kola look my way, I feign sleep, arms pulling my legs to my chest. Cheek on the bones of my knees, lashes spiky against the smoothness of my skin. My blinks stretch out until I fall into an inevitable doze.

We are on an island filled with black and red, dying and blood, pain and death. Kola, Bem, and Yinka are there as we climb peaks, the scent of rot and bones picked clean of flesh in the air, clinging to our skin and coating our throats as we breathe. I see Esu, larger than I thought possible, grasping at the others, not giving them a chance to fight but pulling them limb from limb, their bodies scattered in the dark earth of a barren island. Blood seeps into the ground, its sharp copper scent fresh as my wails rend the air and sorrow pierces my soul. It winds its way to my core, filling me with a blackness only matched by the deepest part of the night, and whirling around me are the deaths of all those I have come to care about. And then Esu turns to me and I—

With a sudden gasp, I wake up to a moon that hangs low above the sails, its yellow glow coating the deck as the ship rocks on night-splashed waves. Someone has placed a woven blanket over my legs, but I can still feel the chill of the evening. Stretching, I bend my neck to either side, rolling my shoulders as my gaze spreads to the sea, the blue-black waves shifting like molten glass.

I look back over the deck, the screams and broken bodies of my dream fresh in my mind. Everyone is sleeping still; even Ifedayo, whose watch it is, appears to be dozing. My heart splinters at the thought of anything happening to them. Both of my hands go to the map in my hair, fingertips and nails moving over the whorls of islands and sea. It's the only way to find Esu's island apart from the walls of the babalawo's dwelling.

What if I did this on my own? If I left now, they wouldn't know how to get to Esu's palace. They'd be safe. The thought slips inside, growing until I stand under the moonlight, casting my gaze over them all. I could face Esu and rescue the twins. Ask their permission for the rings.

Kola twitches in his sleep, cheek balanced on the cradle of his hand. I pad over to him, crouch down, running my gaze over his face. Holding out a hand, I nearly cup his chin but stop myself.

Kola.

I sigh. I want him and the others to be safe, but I know that if I left, he would not stop until he found me. He would not give up, I feel that in my bones. Even if it means going back to the babalawo to copy the map again and then going to Esu's island, he would find me.

There's only one thing to do. I stand, my knees clicking, glancing at the sea. We're roughly six hours away from the shore, which means we should be close to the destination I have in mind. Heading to the rail, I think of the sea below me, its depths and its darkness and all that it holds, monstrous and wonderful, dead and alive. Shuddering, I know I have no choice. It will have to be this, I tell myself. Seeking this help is the only way I can guarantee the lives of everyone. Of Yemoja, Mami Wata, the twins, and the people of Oko.

Checking that no one is watching, I unfurl the rope ladder and slip my legs over the side of the ship. My skin tingles, so tight that I feel my bones crackling beneath it. I take a breath, knowing I can't hold back any longer.

Noiselessly, I dive into the ocean, feeling the split of my thighs joining and the tail that forms in a large fan. I lean back in the sea, wrapped in its deep folds, buoyed by the waves that carry me away from the ship. Above, the night is rich with stars that rip through the sky, stretching into infinity with their dying bursts of light. Suspended between the sea and the glittering expanse of sky, I feel unimportant. Tiny. And then I think of Yemoja under the same blanket of stars, of the twins and the fear they must feel, and I am filled with a purpose that spreads to every part of me.

Sitting in the babalawo's dwelling for hours while Yinka

braided my hair meant that I scanned the map over and over again. A tail and a cape of pearls had become clear toward the end, depicting an orisa that humankind often fears but sometimes forgets, and a kingdom that spans the entire deep of the sea with a palace that grazes the route we would take to Esu's island.

Olokun.

Orisa of the deep and keeper of the Land of the Dead. Imprisoned beneath the sea, Olokun has not seen the sun for a thousand years. Furious that humanity did not offer him homage, the orisa sent gigantic swells of water to batter and bury the land. Upon seeing the mountainous waves that invaded the earth, the people beseeched Obatala, the father of all humanity, to help. He intercepted Olokun and put himself between his beloved mortals and the fury of the great waves. Fearful of the danger his creations were in, Obatala chained the orisa to the deepest seabed, banishing him to the Land of the Dead, where he still resides now.

My resolve strengthens and I flip away from the moonlight, diving down. The water slides over me like satin as I swim underneath the ship, knifing between the waves. A shoal of mackerel spiral in the sea. Swimming left and then down, I avoid them, wanting only the blackness of the tides that sweep the deeper part of the ocean. It gets colder, but I do not stop, only doing so when I see the white gleam of bone.

Sometimes I come across more than souls. Sometimes I see the cages of bodies that once held a human's essence. They will whiten in the years to come, scattered by currents and scavengers. Mouthing a prayer for the goodness of their lives and their journey home to Olodumare, I push the sand back over the remains, hoping that they looked up at the light of the sun above before passing to Olodumare. Dark water swirls around me as fish, both gray and monstrous, glide by. With bulbous eyes and stunted fins, they are whispers and shreds of nightmares.

"Why do you come so deep?" The voice echoes in the water, sending ripples along the seabed.

I snatch my hands back, feeling the sudden, intense coldness in my core. "Olokun." I can't see the orisa yet, but I lower myself into the silt, stomach scraping the rocks as I wait for him to appear. The deep is illuminated by the lights of gnarled anglerfish and the blue glow of firefly squid that cling to reefs. In the distant water I can just make out the outline of his coral palace, walls sharp and jagged.

I hear Olokun approaching before I see him. The golden chain that encircles his waist rattles as I sway in the water, my heart pulsing in a near panic.

Olokun glides from behind the black rocks on the seabed. "Your place is not down here." His tone is acidic, vexation edging his words. Twice the size of Yemoja, Olokun has scales that are a deep purple with shimmers of silver that match the chill of his eyes. Suspended in the depths, he lets the cold current pull him closer to me, revealing a generous mouth and a long nose set in a face that could be carved from stone, so stark are its peaks and lines. He lifts his cleft jaw and speaks again. "Are you well, Mami Wata?" A cascade of grape-sized black pearls spills over his shoulders, forming a dark cape that shifts and clinks gently in the water.

"I'm as well as can be." I have always had a sympathy for this orisa. Punished without recompense or chance for redemption. Free to roam the darker layers of the sea but chained just deep enough never to be able to go to the surface, never to be able to see the sun again. Rising from my bow, I watch as the orisa approaches me. "I came to ask you for your guidance. For your wisdom and knowledge."

"You should not be this deep." Olokun rears over me, tail corkscrewed beneath him in hulking iridescent coils. "But I will hear you speak."

I nod, the ends of my braids snaking in the water as I place a cool hand on the ice of my chest in greeting. "I'm on my way to Esu's island."

"Esu!" Olokun spits the name and circles me, his skin gleaming in the anglerfish's pale light. "He ignores my pleas to take messages to Olodumare to petition my cause. Why would you pursue him?" He tips his colossal head to one side, watching me.

"He's taken two children."

"Ibeji incarnate."

"How do you know?"

The orisa swims around me, churning the silt up in brown sprays that rise and settle in gentle arcs. "There have been rumors. I hear things, but others never listen to me."

Following his movements, I spin delicately in the water. "What kind of rumors?"

"Of a wish for more power." Olokun stops, his back to me, black pearls thick on his neck and shoulders. "Of rings and twins."

I wait, twisting to keep Olokun in view. He surges toward me. I do not flinch, but it takes every nerve I have. The orisa reaches out and catches a hank of my braids, winding it around his fist, bringing my face closer to his. "What is it you want of me, Mami Wata?" Olokun grunts softly, golden chain clanking in the water, its broad links as solid as the bedrock.

I swallow, preparing my words. "Help with Esu. I need the

twins and the rings. He has them both," I call as Olokun releases me, watching the slablike muscles of his back as he swims away and then dips, turning toward me again.

"Help you when no one has ever helped me!" Olokun gathers up a length of his chain and tugs the links, dark muscles corded tight. "I have borne my punishment, yet I am forgotten down here!" His words are serrated with anger, face twisted in outrage and desperation. "I have been alone for a millennium. No one but the remains of bones to keep me company." Olokun comes closer, wrapping the chain around his great fists. I don't let this shake me, holding his gaze until he drops back and smashes the chain on a rock in the seabed. The links do not break, will never break unless Olodumare or Obatala releases him. "People tell stories about me now, but I am more than a myth! I am more than a tale to be told by storytellers!"

I flinch from the pain and torture in his voice. "If you help me, I will do my best to do the same for you. Just tell me how."

"You would aid me, Mami Wata?" Olokun's voice is soft and slippery now. "No matter what I ask of you?"

I think for a moment, wondering what he could demand. Anything would be worth it, I think, if Yemoja and the twins are safe. "I would if you would do the same for me. As long as Esu is defeated."

Olokun's face shifts, his eyes narrow with a slyness that makes me feel like swimming back to the surface and never looking back. The orisa must sense this, because he leans forward, gathering me up in his arms as he holds me close and murmurs in my ear, my hair wound around the chain that hangs from his wrists. Olokun's words drip with venom and revenge, and when the orisa is done, he releases me.

Olokun floats in the sea before me, his muscles rippling and tail so long that it coils beneath him like a gigantic sea snake. He watches me, waiting for an answer.

My throat feels as if it has closed up at the bargain he has offered, at what he expects of me in return for his help. I think of the sun and the air above. Of Kola. And then I remember the fear on Yemoja's face and the thought of the punishment of all Mami Wata, the grief of Kola and his family. I try to summon words that won't come. Lifting my gaze to Olokun's, I swallow hard and nod, the ends of my braids floating around my head.

"So be it," says Olokun. He smiles, smacking his teeth and his lips together in satisfaction, before he spins back into the blackness, his chain dragging against the seabed.

I wait some moments, letting myself sag, resting in the silt that looks soft but is only a thin sheen between my scales and the rock beneath. *You have agreed,* I think, *and now it is time to carry on.*

I propel myself back up to the ship as the first of the day's light begins to brighten the way above. Trepidation and hope make a nest in the spaces of my heart now free from rage, and at the sight of the curved hull, I swim faster, dragging myself clear of the sea when I reach it. The night is just ending, the moon fainter now, and I realize that I've spent more time in the sea than I had planned. My wet hands claw at the rope ladder, leg bones forming and cracking as I haul myself up, arms shaking from the effort.

Just as I am about to reach the ship's rail, Yinka appears, the planes of her cheekbones luminous in the early sunlight. Her face is pulled tight as she reaches down and takes my hand, helping me over.

CHAPTER NINETEEN

SHE SAW ME in the sea.

Dawn drapes the sky in rose gold and gray as I freeze, staring up at her wide eyes. Yinka helps me up the last part of the ladder and lets go of my hand, stepping backward. She watches as the last of my scales fade to skin and then hurries away. I swing my legs over the railings, landing on both feet, feeling unsteady with the rough deck beneath me and the lurch of the sea. Yemoja advised me to stay in human form because of the greed and violence appearing as Mami Wata can bring, but I also followed her edict because of the other reactions. The ones I caught on Kola's face just after I had saved him. The ones I am frightened of seeing on Bem's and Yinka's.

Fear.

Revulsion.

A shard of shame lingers within my heart. At being the creature that doesn't remember who I was. At how people might see me now, not an orisa but something else.

Inhuman.

I look up from my feet, wondering which response will be

spread across Yinka's face, only to see her back as she heads down the deck.

"It's Simi," she calls, leaping over ropes thick with knots.

I follow cautiously. Kola straightens up from the boom and watches as I lurch toward him, tripping on the same rope Yinka skipped over. My face must be an open question because he lunges forward, one hand on my waist to steady me on my freshly formed feet.

"Don't worry," he says in a low voice tinged with apology. "But I had to say something. They woke up and you were gone."

"You told them?" Even as the words leave my mouth I think of Yemoja's warning about humans and trust. Kola has just proved her right.

I sneak a glance at Bem and Ifedayo. Ifedayo's expression is quizzical as he examines me, stopping when his gaze rests on my feet. Bem winds a twist of rope around his arm, mouth straight. I will him to smile, but then Yinka draws closer to him and whispers into his ear. Neither looks at me, and the heat of shame crawls up my neck to my face.

"They understand," Kola says, but I can't tell if the uncertainty I hear in his voice is real or imagined.

"It doesn't look that way." I jerk away from him, whirling back to the railing.

After facing Olokun, must I come back to the people I was trying to protect, only to find them snatching looks at me as if I am the monster? I bite the inside of my mouth, using the pain to ignore the urge to dive back into the sea.

"You shouldn't have said anything to them," I manage to say. Hurt tightens my throat, strangling the words. "It wasn't yours to tell."

"Simi, I didn't have a choice. You just disappeared, and at some point, I knew you'd come back." Kola sighs and moves to stand beside me. "Well, I hoped you'd come back. Would you have wanted to explain then? Answer their questions?" He rests his hands on my waist again and I find that I can't breathe, focusing on the grip of his fingers. "Besides, they were worried. And so was I."

When I turn to him, I see that his eyes are filled with nothing but concern.

"They were worried?" I whisper.

"Yes." His hands are still on me and I don't move away. "You can trust them. You can trust me. None of them would be on this ship right now if I didn't have faith in them entirely."

"What about Ifedayo?" I ask, catching sight of the swing of the young man's plaits as he checks the knots of the jib sheets. At least his curiosity is better than disgust.

"If my father trusts him, so do I."

"And Bem?" My voice is small now when I remember my conversation with the giant boy back in Oko. His thirst for adventure and his kindness. I liked him, and I wanted him to like me, too.

"He is overwhelmed. You'll see." I suck in a deep breath and let Kola turn me to face him. "Give them a chance, Simidele." He smiles at me, and despite my annoyance, my stomach flips at the sight of his curved mouth. "Let them have time to think on it. To absorb the fact that they are in the company of a daughter of Yemoja."

I pause for a moment, but the anger is already fading. Nodding, I push his chest gently, using it as an excuse to feel the slide of his skin. He lets out a small laugh colored with relief, and when he releases me, I find that I want to step back into his arms, to have his hands on me still, but then Bem calls to him and Kola steps away.

Keeping busy by checking the stores, I tell myself that it's good Kola told them. I can't keep pretending that I'm human. This is what I am and there is no hiding, should be no hiding. Not even from myself.

When Yinka calls us for some dried papaya, I join them on deck. We sit down, and as Bem passes me some fruit, he nods at me, pressing blunt fingers to his heart.

"You see?" Kola whispers. "He just needed a moment."

"And Yinka?" I ask.

Kola stoops closer to me so he can peer in the same direction, our cheeks nearly touching. "It might not look like it, but she is in awe."

I snort. "Really? I can practically smell the contempt rolling off her."

"She can be . . . overprotective. Give her a chance, Simi. I know she might seem difficult, but it's because she cares, and she knows that you saved me. When I was taken, she and Bem were blamed. Not officially, but I know they held themselves at fault." Kola sighs. "I didn't want to take them because I didn't want Oko to lose them if anything went wrong."

"Yet you were willing to sacrifice yourself?"

"It's what you're doing right now. What I'm doing again. For the good of the ones I care about, I would risk myself over and over."

He's right, I think. As he begins to move away, I catch his wrist, fingers around the healing scabs. "Sorry," I blurt as I hastily let go. "I went down into the sea to find Olokun. I thought maybe he could help."

"Olokun?" Kola stills and then turns back to face me. "I thought he was banished. Somewhere no one would find him."

I think of the strange fish and the blue glow from the squid. "In the water there are many things that mankind doesn't know about." The image of the bones resting quietly beneath the weight of the water comes back to me, of Olokun's black pearls and the chains that lace his body. "When you peel back the skin of the sea, you never know what you will find."

"Did you see him? What did he say?"

I force myself not to shudder, but when I recall the words Olokun whispered to me in the darkness, I feel a coldness that I have only ever felt down in the deep. I can't tell Kola. I look away from him and back at the waves.

"No, I didn't see him." The wind picks up, blowing the ends of my braids across my face. I shiver and flick them behind me.

"Just as well. There's a reason some things are hidden," says Kola.

"Do you really think that they'll . . . accept me? Accept what I am?" I ask, changing the subject. My promise to Olokun is not one I have to worry about, for now.

"Why don't you see?"

When Yinka finally meets my gaze I attempt a smile, sliding the dagger from my hair. I will try, I think, and what better way than with something the girl seems to thrive on?

"Will you spar with me?" My question is met with raised eyebrows and a twitch of her lips.

Kola chuckles as I step back into the small clear space on deck, planting my feet wide apart and throwing the weapon from hand to hand. Yinka unsheathes both axes and grins, showing the sharpness of her canines. I flick the dagger once, watching her surprise when the wicked blade is released.

"Go easy on her, Simidele," calls Kola, and Yinka almost hisses in annoyance as she dances forward, bringing one axe down in a golden arc. I block it with my dagger, pushing back against her so that I have room to slash down. I knock her other hand with my free one, unsettling the grip on her left axe.

Yinka tightens her fingers around both handles, lowering herself into a supple crouch, the sinews of her limbs shifting in graceful lines. *Don't trip,* I tell myself as I slash forward, aiming at Yinka's stomach. She whirls away, hitting me on my shoulder with the handle of an axe. I stumble and regain my footing, spinning back to face her. I'm breathing heavily and am happy when I see that Yinka is, too. She grins at me, crosses the blades together, and then pulls them apart with a satisfying *ching*.

"Come on, Mami Wata, let's see how good you are out of the sea!"

I smirk in response, my muscles warmed now, the dagger blurring in my hands as I swipe and jab, parrying multiple blows and managing to land a few of my own. Yinka spins around me, her axes flashing and her grin lighting up her face. I block another attack before I manage to find an opening, lunging at her unprotected right side. Yinka twists away at the last moment, rolling on the deck and rising several feet away from me, her laugh caught and tossed by the wind.

It's only when Bem approaches us with some much-needed water that we stop, our bodies coated in sweat, legs and arms trembling with exertion. Sitting down with the starboard rail at our backs, we take turns gulping from the waterskin, allowing our burning muscles to rest.

"Kola told us how you saved him." Yinka sloshes water over her face, letting it run in rivulets down her neck. "And what you do with the souls of those you find."

I am quiet. Her tone is one of respect. "My task was to save souls, but I could never have left Kola in the sea." I squeeze the back of my neck, grimacing. "And now it's why I face Esu. Well, one of the reasons."

Yinka watches as I wipe the moisture from my face with the inside of my elbow. "We are blessed to have you."

I let her words sink in, savoring her acceptance.

"Yinka, how did you learn to fight the way you do?" I ask.

She pauses, sipping some water. "My mother. She wasn't from the Oyo Kingdom."

The questions about where she was from are on my tongue, but I hold them, sensing Yinka needs no coaxing, just listening.

"Her name was Nawi." Yinka pauses and tightens her wrapper, fiddling with the folds before continuing. "She lived with the Fon. She was taken from the kingdom of Bornu for her beauty and strength. Initiated and trained to be one of the Ahosi."

"Protectors of the king?"

"Yes. All women warriors," says Yinka, her tone full of pride.

"I've heard stories of them," I say, draining my waterskin. "They're ferocious. Better fighters than the Fon men."

"My mother said the same to me when I was a little girl. She taught me to fight. To never submit." Yinka smiles, her eyes shining. "She used to sing me a song before I went to sleep each night . . . about being better than men in every respect. She said that when she left the palace, a servant always went with her, ringing a bell to warn men to move out of her path and look the other way."

"I think you could do the same," I say. I grin at the thought of the young men of Oko and the awe on their faces whenever Yinka passes. "Although from what I've seen, you don't need a bell for that to happen."

Yinka laughs, a soft sound that I haven't heard before now. She leans forward, elbows on her knees. "The Ahosi training is like no other. Jumping over walls of thorns to learn how to endure pain, wrestling, and endless drills with spears. It is said that the Ahosi can cut a man in half with one stroke." She slices the air with a grin again. "They swear an oath to always be victorious or die in front of the enemy."

There is a small moment of silence before Yinka stares straight into my eyes, her pupils almost as dark as the irises. "I want to be that strong, that ruthless, that *relentless*."

"You are," I say, truth ringing clear in my words.

Yinka looks down at me, her eyes clear. "Thank you, Simi."

"How did she end up in the Oyo Kingdom?" I ask.

"I don't know the whole story," says Yinka, her tone changing. "Just that she washed up on the beach, half dead. My father found her. She chose to stay." Yinka looks up at me. "There were rumors of her being banished, but I never asked her and she never told me. They both died last year when sickness swept through Oko. Disease is not something that can be defeated with axes."

"May Olodumare bless their journeys," I say quietly.

"She could have chosen to go anywhere, but she chose Oko." Yinka finishes the last of her water and looks at Bem and Kola. "And that's my choice, too."

• • •

The day speeds past in a blur of sails and winds that push us faster than I thought possible. By late afternoon Bem has checked the map in my hair multiple times, making sure we're on course. Finally he tells us that we'll arrive at Esu's island in a few hours, and the mood changes. Expectation turns to foreboding and a sense of purpose as everyone gathers together, peering at the horizon, gripping the rail.

"What about when we get there?" asks Yinka. "Is there anything specific that we should be looking out for?"

"I think it's best to assume it's dangerous," says Ifedayo. "We should be prepared for that. Esu's not just going to let us stroll in and say 'Greetings, powerful one, give us the twins and the rings.'" He raises his eyebrows at Yinka's scowl and tightens his weapons belt.

Maybe Ifedayo's flippancy is just the way he hides his nerves, but I don't like it, either. "Kola, what did the babalawo say to you?"

"He could only retell the stories he's heard." Kola hesitates. "Of giant winged bats that circle the castle and the volcano." He stops and fiddles with the hilt of his sword. "And creatures he thinks may be some kind of big cat."

I picture the images I saw on the babalawo's walls, and I shudder.

"Well, whatever is there, we'll meet it head-on," says Bem, and then he smacks his hands together loudly, making me jump. "And so that we're prepared for all to come, let's eat and rest while we can." He turns to grin at us. "My cooking is legendary in Oko, so you are all in luck."

Yinka guffaws. "Do we need to remind you of the time you made pepper soup? You nearly burned a hole in our stomachs."

"That was pretty bad," agrees Kola.

I try to smile along with them, but I can't. Ifedayo catches my eye and I see that he's not at ease, either. As Bem takes over the cookbox, checking the layer of sand in its base that keeps the deck safe from the fire, I follow Ifedayo to the stern.

"Are you worried?" I ask Ifedayo as I stand next to him. "Or are you used to such things? Not that Oyo-Ile has giant bat creatures." I watch his expression as he faces the water.

"No," he says simply, his plaits swaying in the breeze. He draws out a small throwing knife from his leather strap of knives, flipping the blade between his long fingers.

We stand together in silence, watching the sun smear the horizon, until he turns to me, tucking the knife away. "I've been told much about Esu," he says. "Is there anything else you could add?"

I search his narrow face. "What have you heard?" There are so many stories of Esu that mistakenly focus on him as a trickster rather than on his vast knowledge. I'm keen to hear which side Ifedayo will lean to.

"He is Lord of the Crossroads . . . master of the opening and closing of doors and paths in life. Powerful, he represents the routes we take, the beginning and end of life."

"Yes, he is," I say.

Ifedayo's eyes flash as he continues. "And he'll trick humans and orisas for his own entertainment. Sounds like he could be a lot of fun in other circumstances."

I wait for Ifedayo to laugh, but he doesn't. "Stories," I say with a sigh. "A lot of them exaggerated."

"So you're saying he's misunderstood?"

"That's not what I meant," I say, and cross my arms. "I'm not saying he doesn't . . . trick people and orisas, but he is the most important link between heaven and earth, between humans and Olodumare. He even keeps the ajogun from destroying both mankind and orisas. It is a shame that he would ruin all that in his need for more." I pause as the familiar worry rises. "Esu is a powerful being. One that will be hard to best."

"Ah, so you think we have a chance, then?"

"Of course." But I can feel myself frowning, nails digging into the flesh of my arms. "Like Esu and his crossroads . . . it's up to the person which path they choose to take. And we've all made this choice."

"I agree." Ifedayo turns back to the sea and I study his profile. His thin black plaits frame a high nose and wide mouth.

"Will your family be missing you, Ifedayo?" I ask, taking in his dark gray wrapper. Although the fabric is plain in color, the weave is fine. "What part of Oyo-Ile did you say you were from, again?"

"I didn't." Ifedayo stays facing the churning waves. "But my family compound is near the tenth gate."

I trawl through the memories that have come back to me, but only the seventeenth gate sticks, and I know it was the closest one to where my family lived. "Oko is far to come," I say lightly.

Ifedayo takes out the knife he has just put away and begins to flip it in the air again; his eyes stay fixed on me rather than its blurring spin. "I could say the same to you."

"Mm," I say, turning my back to him. All of a sudden, I don't like the turn this conversation is taking. "I'm going to ask Bem when we'll arrive."

I don't wait for an answer but stalk off along the deck. Something needles me, another thing that I can't recall about Oyo-Ile and my life before. It will come, I tell myself, just as the other memories have been flowing faster the longer I stay in this form. I just have to be patient. Frowning still, I'm stepping over the hatch to the small hold when I hear a sound from below.

A thump.

And then another.

I stop, crouching lower and sliding the dagger from my hair.

Another noise, a scrabbling one this time, and I creep toward the rope handle, flicking the blade free. If it's a rat, it would have to be a pretty big one.

Just as I'm standing with my toes at the edge of the hatch, there's a flurry of bangs from within. I jerk away, sucking in a breath, my heart spitting a wild rhythm. Scrambling backward, I run to the bow. Kola sees me coming and rushes to meet me, grabbing my elbows, his eyes raking over the panic in mine.

"There's something in the hold," I hiss.

CHAPTER TWENTY

WE GATHER AROUND the grooves of the hatchway, waiting.

"Are you sure, Simi?" asks Ifedayo, making his way over, his slight limp rolling his gait. "It's most likely a rat."

I hold in a sigh. I'm sure I heard something, but now there's not even a whisper.

"There's only one way to find out," says Yinka, bending down and wrapping her hands around the rope handle. "Be ready."

My hands shake as I adjust my stance, blade held out. Bem and Kola have drawn their weapons, too, and Ifedayo holds the knife he was spinning, matching it with an identical one.

The wood creaks as Yinka heaves the hatch open, grunting as she props it wide. The hold is a black square against the white-yellow sunlight, swallowing part of the day. We stashed the larger sacks of rice and vegetables down there in case we were thrown off course. As my eyes adjust, all I can make out are three of the sacks. And another one that begins to shake.

"There!" I point my dagger toward the movement.

"If that's a rat, I'm the queen of the Mali Empire," murmurs Yinka.

We wait, watching as the sack ripples more, its end unraveling as a yam falls free.

And something else.

A flash of silver thread. A gleam of gold the exact shade of honey.

"Steady, steady," says Kola as he holds an arm in front of me. I push it away and lean down.

"Wait."

The sack splits down its entire length, spilling the rest of the yams and a small yumbo onto the rough wood of the hold.

"Issa!" I cry out, my heart stuttering, the blood pumping in my ears lessening. My legs shake with relief. "What are you doing? Have you been hiding down there all this time?"

The yumbo nods, squinting in the light. "Are we far from land?" Issa climbs to his feet and looks up at us.

"The yumbo? What next?" drawls Ifedayo. He examines the boy and then stands up. "In answer to your question, we are already nearly a day from Oko."

"Good. There's no way you can send me back now!" Issa crows and does a little dance before staggering. "It is very hot down here. Can I have some water, please?"

Yinka reaches down for him, lifting him easily in her arms as Bem gets the waterskin. Both are trying to look cross but can't seem to manage it. When I sweep a look over Issa, the smile on his face makes it hard to be angry.

"He should be at home," Kola says, sighing as the yumbo sneaks a glance at him. "Where it's safer."

"But what is safe?" Issa says, his voice rising in indignation. "I don't want to sit and wait, I want to fight!" He pushes a silver-threaded plait from his sweaty forehead and blows air from his lips, trying to fan his face. "I want to help you both."

His words are cut off when Bem helps him drink from a waterskin. When he finishes, the yumbo smacks his lips loudly and climbs from Yinka's arms. "Will we be there soon?" he asks, walking to the side of the ship so he can peer at the horizon. "Look! I can see land!"

"Don't try to distract us from what you've done, little one," reprimands Kola. "Sneaking on board is a serious thing. I told you to go home!"

Issa does his best to look contrite, lacing his fingers together and looking up at Kola through the silver of his eyelashes.

"Issa, you can't—"

"Land! The yumbo is right!" calls Bem. We rush to the starboard side, silent as we watch the black rocks and green slice of land grow larger. Ifedayo sits on the rail, the wind lifting his plaits, his dagger still in his hand.

"It will be night soon. Not the best time to land," remarks Bem, worry lowering his voice.

"I think the dark will give us some cover." Yinka rolls her shoulders backward, rotating her neck. "We've got enough fish oil to make torches."

"Simi? Do you know any more about Esu?" asks Issa, eyes round with wonder and flecked with cunning. He is trying to distract us from talking about him, but Kola continues to glare at Issa before stalking to the starboard side.

"Yes, tell us a story about Esu while we approach," says Ifedayo, a shade of sarcasm staining his voice. "Since his island is right there, it seems fitting."

222

"Knowing more can only help," adds Yinka with a scowl at Ifedayo.

I see Kola watching him and I wonder if he's thinking the same as me. That perhaps Ifedayo was not the best person to bring along. But if Kola's father trusted him, his skill must be worth the burden of his personality.

"All right," I say. There are lessons to be learned in every tale, and talk of Esu has brought one to mind. Pleased at more memories, I take a deep breath and then begin. "Here is a story. Story it is . . ." I let my mother's words roll from my tongue. "This is one I was told about a caravan of nomads. They were seasoned travelers who were used to traversing the oceans of sands that stretch from one end of the land to the other, carrying goods to trade. One day, as the sun burned high overhead, they became lost in a vast desert.

"The nomads stopped to rest and then used the setting sun to tell them that they were heading west. They decided to wait for evening, when they could check their position with the night sky. When the moon shone, the nomads confirmed their location.

"Morning came and they set off in the direction they thought the town would be in, but the entire day went past and *still* they were lost. None of the nomads could work out why using the sun and moon were not helping them find the right route.

"Days went past and their supplies began to run low, and some of the animals were slaughtered. First as a tribute to Olodumare, and then to keep everyone alive as their rations ran out."

I shiver at the thought of death in the sands.

"What happened then?" asks Issa, his eyes large, the same molten shade of the slowly setting sun behind him.

I rub my arms before continuing. "The nomads consulted their elders, who said they had been tricked."

"By Esu," squeaks the yumbo.

"Yes, by Esu. The nomads had not given tribute to him. They had forgotten, and as punishment, he lured the sun and the moon into changing places, wrecking their forms of navigation."

"They didn't die, though," states Ifedayo, his voice quiet.

"No," I say, turning to him. "They apologized and offered Esu coffee and the last of their honeycomb. He returned the sun and moon and stars to their correct places, and the nomads were able to navigate to the town they had set off for. Esu is not inherently evil. He showed them mercy when they showed him respect."

"If you're expecting Esu to show us mercy if we just show him respect, I think you must be as delirious as the yumbo," scoffs Ifedayo, shrugging when I cut my eyes at him. He slouches against the mast and surveys us all. "I'm not trying to worry you." He holds his hands up, large pale palms. "We just need to be prepared, that's all. According to Kola, the babalawo said that all the lands surrounding Oko will die. And if that happens? So will its people. So tell me, what else do you have planned?"

We fall silent at Ifedayo's simple truth. If we fail, it's not just Mami Wata and the twins in danger. I lift my chin and force more confidence than I feel into my voice. "First we need to get through the forest to Esu's palace. We'll need to be careful in navigating, be alert, trust our instincts," I say, looking out at the black mass of rock as it moves ever closer. "We'll need to find out where he's keeping the twins."

"I can sneak in," suggests Issa.

"And then we'll . . . free them." Even I'm not impressed with my tenuous plan. "Listen, until we get there, we just don't know where or how. But I know I'm going to do everything I can to make sure that when we leave, it's with Taiwo and Kehinde."

"And the rings," adds Kola, nodding in encouragement. "Simi is right. The babalawo said to beware the plains and the grounds directly around the palace. That is where he thinks the . . . creatures will be."

"No matter what, I'm with you," says Bem, adjusting the leather straps holding his sword.

"And me." Yinka scowls at Ifedayo. "And if you're going to be picking holes in everything we do, perhaps it's better that you stay on the ship."

"I am only trying to ensure we are prepared." Ifedayo opens his mouth to speak again and then seems to think better of it, busying himself with checking that his weapons are all secured. "I promised Adekola's parents I would return with their son." He looks up at me. "I would not swear an oath that I can't keep."

His words are better than nothing, I think, as I whisper a prayer to Yemoja. For our strength and protection.

• • •

We sail as close as we can get to the shore, and now I can clearly see the giant spears of rock and charcoal sand that seem to leach the light from the sky. As we prepare to take the small rowboat to the shallows, I think of swimming, but instead I squeeze in with the others, not yet wanting them to see me change. Bem rows us closer, his swords shining, crisscrossed on the broadness of his back. When our boat nudges the gray sand, the others leap out into the shallows, but Kola sees me hesitate.

"Shall I . . . ?" he asks, holding his arms out to me.

I nod before I can change my mind. Kola grasps my waist and lifts me, pulling me against him. The quickened beat of his heart thuds against mine as he holds me tight, and for the space of a few seconds, I forget where we are. All I can think is that if I tilted my head, our lips would touch.

Your form will be revoked and you will be nothing but foam upon the sea.

Yemoja's words cut into my mind, and I lean away as Kola swings me through the air, setting me on the sand. As I pull back, I pretend that I don't see the confusion in his eyes.

The others are silent, and as I reach them I realize why. Together we face a forest that crowds the beach, raven sand sucking at our feet as a sky the color of slate presses down on us.

"Have you ever seen anything like this?" asks Bem.

No one answers him as we take in the stark and solid tree line. Wide black trunks stretch up, crouching over the sand of the beach, and behind them all, wreathed in low clouds, juts the peak of a volcano. The forest looks like an extension of the mound: gnarled, misshapen trees that appear to have been burned and re-formed somehow. I think of my dream, of a land of red and black, and I shudder.

"Northeast," says Kola, his hand on the hilt of his sword, scanning the beach ahead of us. "The babalawo told me that Esu's palace is northeast. Just beyond the volcano."

"Then that's the way we go," I answer, finding the words and forcing a confidence into them that I don't fully feel. I step toward the tree line, pushing my shoulders back and trusting the others to follow behind me. The hot sand is rough beneath my feet, but I don't wince, taking one step at a time until grass begins to sprout in coarse spikes.

Ifedayo is the first to draw level with me, his limp not slowing his pace. He has one of his knives out and has adjusted his belt so that the rest are within easy reach. He spins what I'm learning is his favorite dagger; the carved ebony handle is a blur as he flicks it up in the air and catches it. Over and over he does this, but even he falters when we reach the edge of the forest. Wild undergrowth frames trees, flanking them with spiny bushes and thorns the size of fingers. On several of the plants, bulbous fruit hangs in gleaming shades of garnet and ruby. Ifedayo reaches for one but recoils when he sees the raised veins that cover the large berries. With a quick chop, he slices the flesh of the fruit, releasing a viscous juice that oozes down the stem, scorching through the dark green leaves.

"No snacks here, then," he says lightly, stepping carefully back from the plant.

"We'll need to forge a path." Kola stands next to us as we survey the edge of the forest. "Keep your eyes open and be ready."

Bem joins him as they use their swords to hack at the bushes and brambles until we can enter the forest. The undergrowth gives way once we are past the tree line and we are able to pick our way past the massive trunks, the canopy arching above, the wizened branches curved together like hands clutching at one another. I gaze upward, the hairs on my arms rising as I realize that the trees give the illusion of being in a cage.

Kola stops now and again to check that we're heading in the right direction. The story I told about Esu won't leave my mind, and I'm constantly worried that we're going the wrong way, especially since the fading sun keeps disappearing behind the dense clouds. With those thoughts in my head, navigating the forest becomes even more disconcerting. The screaming calls of monkeys shatter the quiet, making me jump, their red eyes and white faces flitting between the branches they swing from. Birds screech from the tops of trees that we can't see, their caws stretched out and human-like.

"Have your weapons ready," I say, unease making my voice higher than normal. I wipe a moist hand on my wrapper and tighten my hold on my dagger.

We continue through the forest, the supple creep of our feet sinking in a ground rich with rotting foliage, a pungent smell rising with every footstep. Despite the soft earth, my feet soon begin to grow sore again. When I pull back, Kola slows with me.

"Is it too much for you?" He glances at my feet with concern. "Should I ask the others to stop so you can rest?"

I shake my head, trying to increase my pace. The thought of slowing any of them down makes me feel hot with shame.

"I'm fine," I say, wiping sweat from my neck and forcing myself to take normal steps, even though it feels as if needles are being pressed into the soles of my feet.

"Simi—"

Walking on, I lift my hand and shake my head. I don't want him to feel as if he has to look after me.

We only go a few more steps before we see the others motionless ahead of us. They stand at a bend in the land, and Bem turns slowly to us and raises his index finger to his lips. For moments we are frozen, and then I feel the familiar tug. The others keep listening until it becomes clear what the sound that has rattled them is. A low constant roar of water.

Kola moves around Bem and steps past the trees that curve to the left. He's only out of sight for a few seconds, but my heart clenches until he steps back into view.

"A river." He gestures with his sword. "Let's fill up and rest before it becomes dark and then keep moving," he says, his voice low, his eyes scanning the bushes and trees. "It feels as if it's all been too simple so far."

"As if we're just waiting for something to happen?" I ask.

"A little bit." He runs a hand over his face, sighing into his palm.

"We'll find them," I say quietly, stepping closer to him. He drops his hand and slumps, head close to mine. "We will find them," I repeat.

The river is surprisingly clear, skimming over the dark pebbles that make up the bottom. Since the trees end at the verge of the grass banks, the water is free from the leaning blackened branches. Pale light dapples the surface, a silver glittering that is inviting. I dip my hand in the river and close my eyes. The current kisses the tips of my fingers with a slight chill as I feel the urge to be in the water.

Beside me, Issa cups a small handful, drinking delicately, and when he smiles at me, I think of Bem and Yinka's reaction to him, and the way they were on the ship after I returned from the sea.

"If it helps you, you should get in," the yumbo says, gesturing to the river with wet hands. "Do not be ashamed of who you are."

I smile at the young fairy's wise words as the water calls to me. The others know what I am, I think. Besides, if I soothe my feet now, I'll be stronger later.

I nearly weep with relief when I finally lower my body into the river. The fire in the soles of my feet disappears as the fan of my tail forms, a shimmer of gilded pink that flashes in the sun. I sigh and close my eyes in contentment as I dip my head back, plunging my scalp into the welcome coolness. The rest of my scales form as the wrapper molds to my body, covering my chest and then extending below my waist in scales that are golden-flecked shades of blush and rose pink. When I lift my head and open my eyes, it is to the looks of everyone else. Kola blinks before dragging his gaze away, and Bem and Issa have stopped filling skins, checking weapons, snatching glances. Ifedayo turns away and continues to throw his daggers, aiming for a tree at the edge of the grass. I lower my head, shame eating away at the pleasure I feel in the river.

"They are staring because you are magnificent." Yinka is the first to move, slipping between Kola and Bem. The boys look away now, busying themselves with checking their weapons. "Kola in a different way from the others." Her voice is light and teasing, but her words weigh heavy on me.

I don't look at Kola, even though I want to. Submerging myself, I let the water calm me, pushing out all thoughts, rising only after I can feel myself begin to relax. Yinka sits on the bank as I emerge, plunging her long legs into the river. She kicks one leg, making a ripple.

"I have to admit, that feels good." Yinka dunks her wrists under the water and rubs the water up her forearms. "Can I ask you something?"

I finally look up at her as she rubs her wet hands over the back of her neck, lacing her fingers and squeezing. This time it is Yinka who sighs in contentment. I nod.

"What's it like?" I see her looking into the river at the brilliance of my tail. "Because when I am fighting, it's as if . . ." Yinka pauses. She pulls her legs out of the water to let them dry and tugs the leather harness that fits flush against her shoulder. "As if I change. Almost as if I am out of my body."

"As if you are something else?"

"Mm-hm." Yinka scoops up a handful of water, letting it run between her fingers.

I watch her, this girl my own age who fights like a lion. "It is getting . . . easier. To change and to . . . be, in front of you all."

"But I don't physically transform." Yinka turns to face me. "How does it feel?"

Swimming backward, I let the fan of my tail spray water in the air, the arc of droplets sparkling in the sun. I take my time to think before replying. "It feels as if . . . I belong. To the water. That I'm a part of it and it's a part of me." My brows knit together. "Although for that to happen, it also feels like an abandoning of what I was. Most of my memories are lost, although some come back to me when I'm in human form. My thoughts are mainly of the sea, the other creatures in it." I swim back toward the bank, twirling in the gentle current, careful not to catch myself on the rocks. "Sometimes I feel as if I'm lost. As if, when I can't recall who I was, did I even exist?" I feel heat in my cheeks and dunk my head under the water. Maybe I've said too much. I graze the riverbed for a while, settling on the bottom and looking up at the light that spears the water's surface. The blurred figure of Yinka remains, and I know that she won't leave until I reappear. When I rise, Yinka places a hand on my shoulder, her gaze softened but fierce.

"You are *you*, Simidele. Nothing has changed that and nothing will. You haven't lost yourself. You're right here." She leans closer to me, bright eyes locked onto mine as she offers me a smile, the first she has aimed directly at me. "And I see you."

• • •

When we have left the river behind, the sun sets, a final blaze of red behind the black trees. Hours later, we are all struggling, our torches burning low. The heat has left the forest and now chilled sweat plucks at our wrappers and coats our skin as we hack at the foliage. When we come to a part of the forest that begins to thin, everyone's relief is palpable.

"How are your feet?" asks Kola.

I know I'm limping again, but I hoped no one would notice. The river only soothed my body for a while. "I can walk," I say. "We need to keep on. The sooner we find the twins, the better."

Slices of a dark blue sky flash through the gaps in the canopy as I pick up my pace. Kola moves quickly to stand in front of me, barring my way. "Let's have a short rest," he calls to the others.

"Finally," groans Yinka, sinking to the ground. Issa copies her, mimicking her relieved expression. She pulls out her waterskin and drinks deeply.

Bem and Ifedayo sink into squats, checking weapons and sipping their water. I stand for a moment more until Kola pulls me to a fallen tree and sits on the rotting bough. He pats the space next to him, and I hesitate only a moment before sitting down. I lift my feet, closing my eyes, releasing a small groan of pleasure at the relief.

"Wait here." Kola hurries to a light green bush, bending down to pick something near the earth. When he returns, it is with a handful of leaves. "When you need to rest, you should say so."

I can feel myself scowling as I continue to massage the sole of one foot. Resting means stopping, which takes up time we don't have.

"Let me see." Kola takes my foot from me. I try to pull it back, but he sucks his teeth. "Be still for a moment. If you're injured, we all have to go slower."

I huff but don't move as Kola cradles my foot gently, and I hold my breath as my heart beats just a little bit faster. He runs a thumb over the sole and I wince.

"Sorry," he says softly. He crushes the leaves in his other hand, releasing some of their juice, and wraps them gently around the sole of my foot.

"You need a proper poultice, but it's better than nothing."

"Lettuce? I haven't heard of that before," I say, trying to keep my tone light as he does the same with my right foot. Kola smiles but doesn't look up at me, concentrating on applying the leaves to my soles.

"A little bird said it helps with pain. It's worth a try."

I swallow and sneak a look at his face. Sweat beads along his hairline, and his lips are pursed, a slight line between his eyebrows as he concentrates on applying the leaves.

"Simi, I . . ." Something in the softness of Kola's tone makes my heart trip. I think of his worry for me when I went in search of Olokun, of the way he looked at me when he lifted me from the boat and onto the beach. I swallow, eyes skimming the wideness of his shoulders. "I wanted to tell you how thankful I am for all your help. And that I . . ." Kola pauses, and the light in his eyes makes me panic even more. If he tells me he feels the same as I do, I will have to explain why nothing could ever happen between us. I will have to explain Yemoja's warning.

A yearning rushes through me.

If only I were human.

The thought crashes in, and I snatch my foot from his grip and stand up, ignoring the jagged pain in my soles. If he tells me he feels something for me, it will be harder. So much harder than this already is.

"We should keep moving," I say. I look away from the confusion and hurt on Kola's face. "Let's get ready to go."

I lead the way as the moon finally makes its dim appearance, just as our torches die.

"We must be close to the volcano. The babalawo said there's a passage through it that will take us to Esu's palace," explains Kola. "Let's push on."

The forest is even darker now that night has surged in, and we move more slowly, wary of the shadows that flicker alongside us. When the trees begin to thin and we can see more than a few feet ahead of us, I start to feel a little bolder. Until a howl splits the air.

CHAPTER TWENTY-ONE

I SLIDE THE dagger from my hair, golden blade glinting in the silver light. "What was that?" I whisper.

Kola scans the trees as Yinka gathers Issa to her, axes held up. Even with the moon there are deep pockets of darkness that anything could be hidden in. Another howl shatters the night air and I shiver, slowly turning in a circle. There's something strange about the growls that follow. The echoing calls creating thoughts of teeth and blood.

The hairs on my arm stand on end. "We have to keep going," I say, my voice low, my blade held out in front of me.

I lead the others through the last of the trees until we come to a clearing full of tall grass. We creep forward as a swirling fog winds its way around our legs and a yip cuts through the night.

"Jackals?" asks Yinka as Issa stands close to her, clasping his small knife.

Kola shakes his head. "Jackals don't sound like that."

"It's a howl, what's the difference?" asks Yinka, eyes gleaming in the dark.

In this clearing, we are completely exposed. We strain, listening carefully, until another howl pierces the air, followed by an almost imperceptible chitter.

"Hyenas, maybe," says Bem, his face aimed at dense foliage on the edge of the clearing. "Can you hear it? It's almost like a shout at the end."

"Hyenas?" asks Kola. "But—" And then he stops. "The babalawo said something similar to that."

I peer into the growing gloom, anxious when the underbrush rustles in the night breeze. "It could be any creature if it's something to do with Esu."

"We need to light a fire," says Bem. "Fire will scare them."

"We don't have time," barks Ifedayo, inching into the glade. "We should attack before they can. Whatever they are."

"Stay together," I urge as fear threads its way through my veins.

I force myself to keep moving, Kola by my side and the others just behind me. When a dark shadow peels away from a tree, I hold my arm out, making everyone stop. Ifedayo draws level with us, knives in both hands.

"What is it?" hisses Yinka. "Can you see?"

I hold a finger to my lips and motion for them to get down in the grass. When I turn back, a shaft of moonlight picks out the glow of eyes low to the ground.

One of the creatures slinks out of the forest.

A hyena, much larger than any I've ever seen. With an enormous gray body and black spots scattered over its coarse fur, it sniffs at the ground and then toward the high grass. Lifting its heavy head, the animal emits a high-pitched cackle. Beside me, Kola and Bem stiffen as they spot it, too. My mind whirs through our options.

"Get ready," says Kola, his eyes large in the dark. "It's heading this way."

"I've never seen a hyena that big," says Bem, hefting his sword.

I exchange a quick look with Kola. "I know."

"When I tell you to, I want you all to run back to the trees," I say as I eye the grass that stretches away into the darkness of the forest. If there's one, there will definitely be more. "Climb."

"No," Yinka says, moving to stand next to me. "No one is leaving anyone."

And then there is no time to argue. The shadows split as several hyenas join the first. I try to slow my breathing, sweat running down my chest. The bushes shake. Eyes flashing in the gloom, pinpricks of amber in the dead light.

"There!" I whisper, readjusting my grip on my weapon. More eyes appear, piercing through the fog, revealing themselves.

"One, two, three . . ." Ifedayo stops counting as more slink through the edges of the grass, shadows with eyes and teeth.

The hyenas prowl closer until their large bodies part the mist, ragged spots dotting their muscular torsos. I stop counting after ten. The howls of the beasts are loud, their heads bowed as they sniff at the ground, jaws hanging below thick shoulders.

"Make a circle. Tight!" calls Kola, his arms held out wide.

I turn to close the gap between me and Issa. I controlled the Ninki Nanka; I was able to talk to it. Perhaps the sapphire will work for any animal. Wrapping my fingers around the blue stone of my necklace, I collect my thoughts and push all my energy into my voice. *Stop.*

The hyenas' ears prick up, but they still move across the meadow.

Go. I hold my breath, watching to see if they will do as I say.

The optimism in Kola's eyes pushes me on.

I said stop. I pull the words from deep inside me, much the same as when I pray to Yemoja, forcing strength and belief into my tone, curling my fingers to stop them from shaking.

For a moment the hyenas pause, and my heart feels as if it's pulsing in my throat. The largest animal tilts back its head, drool hanging from black lips, and lets forth a loud howl.

Hope burns in my chest.

Then the hyena lets out a snickering sound and continues toward us. The rest surge after their leader.

No! Frustration mixes with dread as we stand shoulder to shoulder.

The leader reaches us first. It lunges, jaws snapping for Kola's throat, but Bem swings his sword, nearly catching the creature's muzzle. It retreats, fur standing in stiff tufts along a curved spine as it crouches before us. The rest run to catch up, weaving in and out of the grass, flickers of glowing eyes the only sign of their movements. They spread out, calling to one another to coordinate.

We are surrounded.

Once they are in position, the lead hyena opens its black muzzle to emit a low growl that turns my stomach. It circles our group, teeth bared.

"Will they kill us?" asks Issa, his voice small.

"We won't let them," I say. The pack leader stares at me, eyes luminous in the near dark.

The hyenas chitter, jaws snapping in the night air as they call to one another in their high-pitched yelps. They dart, slinking around us, jumping forward and biting at the air as we strike back with our weapons. Yinka lashes out, slicing the flank of one of the hyenas that has dared to come too close.

It yowls before another takes its place. They circle, trying to separate us, but we stay in our formation, backs close and weapons bristling. I slash out at a hyena that prances forward, its breath reeking of rot and old blood, and I'm rewarded with a yip as my blade cuts into its thick shoulder. Ifedayo throws his knives, causing one creature to fall back, but another takes its place, and I wonder why none have gone for the kill yet. Perhaps they're trying to wear us down.

"Stay strong," urges Ifedayo as more hyenas slink into the clearing. Slowly he draws two more daggers from his belt.

The animals circle us; the sound of snapping jaws fills the air, but the hyenas do not rush for us straightaway. They spread out, barks and growls used to coordinate their approach. Exhausted, we keep up our defensive positions until one of the creatures sinks its teeth into Bem's upper arm.

The flare of blood makes me scream. Ifedayo releases a spinning dagger, smiling at the hyena's yelp as his blade finds its target, scattering the rest of the creatures, forcing them to back away from Bem.

Blood spills on the moonlit earth and the hyenas howl in elation.

"No!" A fiery rage flows through my veins.

Yelling, Bem raises his sword, blade flashing, his face twisted in pain. The copper scent of blood lends the air an iron tang as the wound on his arm flows freely. He steps forward, bringing his blade down in an arc, as the same hyena lunges at his leg. The creature dodges Bem's weapon and buries its teeth in his thigh, dragging him to his knees. Before he can stand, another hyena lopes closer, goading him with snapping teeth.

"Bem!" screams Yinka. She swings her axes at two of the creatures that lunge toward her at once.

The boy tries to stand, but the hyena yanks him down again, joined by another that latches onto his shoulder. The ragged bite on his biceps continues to pour blood, but he still attempts to lift his sword, managing to wound the creature, which finally releases his leg.

"There are too many!" shouts Kola, hacking at the spine of a hyena that's turning, going for Yinka. Two more of the creatures launch themselves toward us, but he slashes at them, catching one just above its eye and the other on its foreleg. "Stay close!"

Bem attempts to drive his blade into the hyena that locks its jaws onto his shoulder, mouth twisted as he shouts in pain. Kola runs to join him, trying to deliver a blow that will pry the creature from Bem, leaving his back exposed. A hyena leaps, crashing into him and pushing him to the ground.

I run forward, shouting as another hyena bites into the flesh of Kola's thigh, pinning him in the dirt. As the first leans down, teeth white in the gloom, I slice at its face, triumphant when it yowls and spins away.

Behind me, Yinka roars, and I spin to see her axes wheeling in the dark, barely keeping two hyenas away; the leader launches itself through the air at her. It catches her with a swipe of its claws, knocking her down. Yinka screams into the darkness of the night.

I tuck Issa in front of me as he holds his knife in a shaky hand, tears on his cheeks. "What do we do, Simi?"

I open my mouth, but nothing comes out—and then something heavy smashes into my side, knocking me to my knees. My dagger spins from my hand, falling among the long grass. I can feel the heat of the hyena's breath. There is a sudden weight on my shoulders as the creature pushes me down, its warm drool pooling on the back of my neck. I close my eyes, shaking as Issa cries out beneath me, waiting for teeth to tear into my skin.

CHAPTER TWENTY-TWO

BUT IT DOESN'T come.

I lie splayed beneath the hyena, its claws sharp against the muscles of my back. Howls and screams accompany the sound of bones cracking. The pressure on my spine and shoulders disappears, allowing me to scramble toward my dagger, snatching it up before I push myself up onto my knees. Issa crawls from the dirt, pressing himself against me as I drop an arm around his thin shoulders.

"Kola? Bem?" I ask, my breath ragged, fear scraping my voice almost hollow as I look around me. "Yinka?"

I feel a slow trickle of blood between my shoulder blades as the others rise to their feet. In front of us, the hyenas arrange themselves in a loose semicircle, their bodies contorting. My mouth goes dry when I see Kola hold his hands against the wound on his thigh, trails of red running down to his ankle. Bem has multiple bites. Ifedayo and Yinka look shaken but have only a few gouges from claws. If the hyenas are playing with us, the game is not far from being over.

The largest hyena stands before the others, jaws opening and snapping shut again, teeth protruding over black lips. The creature lowers its head, its gleaming eyes on Yinka as it shudders, body writhing, skin stretching. A loud yowl tears free as it arches its head toward the star-filled sky. Yips echo wildly as fur is absorbed into obsidian skin, as legs lengthen and claws retract into nails. Luminescent eyes strain and close momentarily with the pain of the change. It is when the howl becomes a scream that I see what is emerging.

The young woman stands before us, a sheen of sweat coating limbs that shake with the effort of transformation. She wipes her forehead, hands quivering, nails still pointed and curved. Black hair is arranged in two large coils on either side of her head, giving the semblance of ears even in human form, and some fur remains on her lean body, creating a kind of wrapper in light gray. Faltering, I gather myself as I look up at the woman who, only minutes before, was a hyena.

With long thighs and bunched muscles beneath smooth skin, she stands up straighter, rotating her neck. I flinch as her bones click, loud in the silence of the clearing. Taller than even Bem, her small eyes look us over before settling on Yinka. Taking a step toward her, the young woman smiles, lips spread around her still-sharp teeth.

"Are you kin?" she asks, voice melodious and deep, her eyes still on Yinka. "We will not harm those like us. That cannot be commanded."

Behind her, the other hyenas yowl, their limbs lengthening, features shimmering in the twilight. One by one, they change, bones snapping and crackling. Muzzles shorten and gray spotted fur gives way to skin in dark shades of brown. The boys wear their hair shaved on the sides with two braids on top that hang down on either side of their heads, and the girls all have the same coils that wind around their ears.

"Bultungin," says Ifedayo, fascination drawing him closer. The semicircle of people, all with wrappers that look as if they are made of short gray fur, focus on Yinka, eyes glowing imperceptibly in the dark. "Those who can transform into hyenas," offers Ifedayo when he sees the confusion on our faces.

We raise our weapons as the people before us, all with long limbs and sharp teeth encased in soft smiles, watch us. The young woman who transformed first walks toward Yinka, while the others keep their distance.

"I am Aissa," she says, her eyes on Yinka still. The leader holds a hand to her chest, fingers elongated, with pointed nails. "Are you kin?" Aissa repeats. "I think I can smell it on your blood, on your flesh. But I cannot fully tell. . . ."

"What?" Yinka grips her axes, raising the blades higher. "What do you mean?"

Issa lifts his face to mine and frowns, his golden eyes flashing. "They are her family?"

"I . . . I'm not sure." I think about Yinka's mother, how she came to be in Oko. Could she have been bultungin somehow?

The leader leans forward slowly and reaches for Yinka's arm. She doesn't move, but she darts nervous looks at the crowd before her. With a hand outstretched, the young woman doesn't take her eyes from Yinka.

"We would not harm you," she says.

"You think Yinka is bultungin?" snaps Kola as he hobbles to her side. "She's been in our village her entire life." He reaches out to pull her to him, away from Aissa. "She'd know if she were such a thing."

There is a growl of annoyance from a short boy with thick plaits. "We are not 'things,' but a people that have been scattered

243

because of the fears of others." His features are twisted with anger, his fingers curling and then shortening. As he raises his head, neck cracking, his body shimmers and lengthens.

"Umar, easy." Aissa's words are quiet but firm, and the boy nods, body changing once again back to skin and taut limbs.

I run my gaze over the rest of the pack, and notice the same thing happening. Legs lengthen and then snap back. The bultungin are fighting to keep their human forms.

"Esu has bound us to protect the island," says Aissa. Once again she looks back at her people, and I see the worry in the folds of her grimace, which spreads to me. "But those like us? We cannot kill."

I swallow hard, looking around warily as I lift my dagger, ready.

"You smell as if you might be kin." Aissa swivels to gesture at the rest of us. "But they do not."

A howl erupts from the middle of the group and Aissa moves back, searching for those who can't keep their human appearance any longer. "You need to go, before we lose control of our change."

A girl, almost as tall as Aissa, fixes her hard gaze on Kola. She opens her mouth and screams, nose and mouth elongating, teeth growing until they curve past her lips. Two boys near her try to calm her, but she can't stop herself. Gray fur sprouts along every limb as she falls to the ground, a snarl ripping its way past her blackened lips.

"You must go now. Quickly," hisses Aissa as she surveys the pack and then turns back to Yinka. Behind her, more of the bultungin are changing, as growls escape from contorted lips and brown skin disappears beneath fur. Aissa opens her mouth to speak again, but only manages to moan, her lips stretched wide, long teeth bared as a muzzle forms. She twists her neck, dropping to the ground as her haunches thicken, hands and feet changing into claws and pads. Behind her, the hyenas whoop, jaws raised to the low moon as the last traces of humanity leave them.

. . .

"Yinka, come on," I urge, running to grab her as she walks backward slowly, her eyes still on Aissa.

The pack leader is on all fours now, head hanging down as she opens her mouth to growl. With her long back arched, gray fur lining the ridges of her spine, she is not a woman anymore, but I wonder if there is still a human consciousness there. One that hates what Esu has compelled them to do.

Yinka stops, her eyes flickering uncertainly over the creature that was Aissa. I pull on her arm just as the hyena lets loose a shattering howl and leaps forward, the pack close behind her, surging through the grass with steaming breath and bared teeth.

"This way!" shouts Ifedayo as he scoops up Issa and sprints toward the looming volcano.

My limbs are heavy from the fighting, every step a flash of pain, but when I glance at Kola and Bem I feel even more worried. Both are staggering, blood running down their legs from ragged bites, and I can clearly see that Bem is finding it hard to hold his sword.

"Hurry!" I scream. I pray I don't trip as the meadow gives way to cooled swirls of hardened lava and the trees of the forest are left behind. Blood thumps in my ears, along with our desperate gasps and the yips of the hyenas.

Ifedayo reaches the rock face and hovers in front of a crooked fissure. As we reach him, I see that it's actually a small entrance flanked by slim ornate columns that have openmouthed monsters with long teeth carved into them. He slips into the stark blackness of a tunnel with Kola and Bem close behind him.

I snatch a look behind me and see the bultungin streaming toward us. My throat closes up as I struggle to draw in a breath.

"Come on, Simi!" yells Yinka as she pushes me into the tunnel ahead of her.

It's hot in the passage, and I let my fingertips graze the roughness of the wall as I run forward, the way ahead lit by red light. It's not long before my lungs feel as if they've been seared by the arid air, and when I try to swallow, my tongue clicks, the taste of sulfur in the back of my throat. As the tunnel opens out, I spot the others just ahead, moving along a narrow path. Beside it, a river of lava moves sluggishly, cracks of red, gold, and black threaded through its thickness. I keep close to the wall as we hurry to catch up.

"Are you both all right?" Kola turns to me, holding my arms lightly as he examines me for injuries.

Yinka nods as I look up into his frown. "We're not hurt. What about you? And Bem?" I peer around him. "How is he?"

Kola releases me, and I feel the absence of his touch immediately. "He's bleeding badly, worse than me."

"We keep going, Simi," calls Bem as he ignores Kola and limps on ahead behind Ifedayo. Issa is perched on the young man's shoulders, but he turns to peer at us and I see the worry in the pinch of his mouth.

"We're all right, little one!" calls Yinka as she follows my line of sight. "Keep going!"

I can sense the urgency in her voice just before I hear claws on the hard ripples of old lava behind us. A soft yip is followed by low barks and whoops amplified in the confined space, and we move as fast as the narrow trail will allow, Ifedayo still leading us. It's hot and I'm constantly blinking the sweat from my eyes as we move along the path that runs parallel to the lava, cutting upward through the rock itself, until Ifedayo stops.

"What is it?" I whisper, swaying from the heat. I can't see much farther behind us, but I can see the pinpricks of glowing eyes.

"The passage is . . . blocked." Ifedayo raises a hand to his neck, squeezing the back of it, his mouth set in a line of annoyance.

"Blocked?"

"Yes, we won't be able to get out this way." In front of us is a cascade of stones, spilling onto the path. I walk toward it slowly and clamber over the lowest ones, ignoring the pain in my feet. A thin, slightly cooler breeze whistles through the small gaps.

"Is there any other way around? Another passage?" I turn back to face them, my voice tight.

Ifedayo shakes his head. "This is the only route."

"There must be a way through," says Yinka as she peers ahead, sweat glistening on her forehead.

A howl echoes in the stale humid air, and when we look down we can see the line of hyenas making their way toward us. I turn back to look at the main rock blocking the entrance. It's big, but not monstrous.

"We can move this." I reach down as Bem and Kola step together, fingers grasping at the rock, trying to find purchase. Bem places his back against the boulder and squats, palms finding a crevice behind him, while Ifedayo and Kola push at the sides.

A louder snarl reverberates around the tunnel. Yinka raises her axes instinctively, looking at me before edging back along the path.

"A bit more," grunts Kola, and they heave again, muscles straining and glistening in the muted light.

Bem rams his back and shoulders against the boulder, shaking with the effort. With the other two pushing hard, the rock shifts upward so that fresh night air streams into the passageway. Fragments of stars glitter in the jagged gap, framed by rock.

The lead hyena has reached Yinka now as she plants herself in the middle of the tunnel, between the encroaching bultungin and us. As the hyena growls, Yinka swings her axes in warning arcs, the glow from the lava transforming her blades from gold to a gleaming blood-red.

"There should be just enough room," says Ifedayo. He lowers Issa and pushes him through the gap, flicking a glance at the hyenas. "Quickly."

More howls fill the sulfur-riddled air, but this time they're accompanied by a cascade of stones falling, and a quivering rumble fills the cavern. The path underneath us trembles, shaking rocks and stones until more fall into the river of lava. Yinka shouts as the lead hyena darts for her, using the butts of her weapons to strike at the creature's shoulders and head, but the bultungin is faster. With a snap, it bites at Yinka's hand, knocking one of her axes free from her grip, where it clatters to the rock floor. I watch in dismay as it skitters over the edge, disappearing into the thick ribbon of lava.

"Yinka!" I shriek.

She turns to me, her face calm. "They're trying to get to you. You need to go. Now."

"I'm not leaving you," I call back, my voice cracking with the heat and exhaustion. "You're coming with us."

"I can hold them off. If I don't, you won't stand a chance." Yinka shakes the blood from her bitten hand and readjusts her grip on her remaining axe. "Besides, if I really am kin, then I won't come to any harm, right?" She fixes her gaze on me and tries out a half smile. "Look after them."

I turn back to Kola and Bem, pushing my dagger into the folds of my hair. Ifedayo has squeezed through and has wedged a large bough in the opening from outside, keeping the boulder from dropping back into place. I watch as Kola eases his wounded friend through and then turns back for me. Taking a last look at Yinka, I run toward him, grasping his fingers as he drags me toward the gap.

"Where's Yinka?"

I shake my head and feel the grief twist in my guts as Kola's eyes dim with understanding. I let him pull me through the space, the bark of the bough scraping my side. From behind I hear a yelp, and then the distinct snapping of jaws and a cry. Growls emanate from the tunnel, and just as I am clear of the gap, I look down to see luminous eyes and fangs layered over peeled-back lips force their way past the boulder.

"Yinka!" cries Issa, but Ifedayo is there, yanking away the bough, bringing the rock crashing down, sealing the tunnel off.

CHAPTER TWENTY-THREE

PANTING, I SIT in the cool dirt under the moon, not caring when the tears come.

Yinka.

Kola, Bem, and Issa are crouched, bent over with their own exhaustion and grief. But Ifedayo takes a few paces ahead with his limping gait, scanning the rocky path that leads away from the volcano. Aside from a few gouged claw marks, he's uninjured, and I fight the feeling of resentment that he is here and Yinka is not.

"Simi . . ." Kola reaches for me, his eyes glassy, and I go to him, letting him push his face against my shoulder as he cries.

I don't move. Not even when the muscles in my neck cramp. And definitely not when Kola takes my hand as his tears slowly stop. Something inside me unfurls at his touch and I close my eyes, trying to stop my own cries.

"If she's kin, they won't hurt her," I whisper, my hands sliding from the smoothness of his shoulders to the ridges of his back before I let him go.

If.

Bem sits on a fallen tree, his skin stained with the dark red of blood, his chest heaving with quiet tears. Issa approaches him carefully, getting him to drink from a small wooden cup. It is only when he scurries over to us that I see what it is. The last of the abada powder.

"I kept some. There's not much left," says the yumbo, his voice thin as his bottom lip trembles. "But it will help."

Kola gives Issa a small hug, wincing slightly. Issa only allows himself a short moment before he pulls back, offering us the cup.

"Drink, both of you. I wish there were more."

"Thank you," I say to him after taking a few sips. It's grainy but not unpleasant; I feel the burn as soon as it passes my lips. Kola drains the last of the liquid, then passes the cup back to Issa.

The potion does not totally heal us, but it does stop the wounds from bleeding and reduces the pain to a dull ache. After finishing the water in our skins, we get to our feet, checking our weapons and the terrain around us. There is only one way to go, so we set off on the path that wraps around the volcano, the twisted rock hard beneath our feet. None of us speaks, but Bem and Kola stay close to me, Issa stuck to Kola's side. Only Ifedayo walks alone, leading the way.

As we pick our way along the path, the true darkness of the night is kept at bay by the bloated moon, leaving the volcano looming next to us. Thinking back to the babalawo's map and the creatures depicted on Esu's island, I find myself scanning the sky in panicked bursts, searching for wings and teeth and serrated claws. My worries fade for a moment when we take the bend that curves away from the volcano.

I stumble to a halt, the pain in my feet making me sway briefly as I gape at the sight of Esu's palace filling the land and the sky ahead of us. Stone that mirrors the night's dusk rises in shards that puncture the clouds. The only windows are huge perfect ovals, so big that a hundred giant eyes seem to stare down at us. But what astonishes me is the fact that the palace sits atop a fragment of black rock, separate from the island we stand on. Below it, the crash of the sea can be heard, and I can feel the draw of the water even from here.

Finally I step forward, peering ahead uneasily. "How do we get across?"

"There's a bridge," says Ifedayo. "Look, can you see?"

A sliver of gray stone stretches from the shore, arching over the chasm. Ifedayo leads the way to its base, skirting among the few sable trees that grow here, the same as the ones in the forest. We take care not to let the fruit touch us as we ease past.

"Stay close," says Kola as he draws level with me. Issa clings to his back now, thin arms wrapped around Kola's neck, his small face solemn. Bem moves alongside him as I walk faster, keeping pace, heart pumping in time to every quick and painful footstep.

The bridge is just wide enough for three abreast. At the end is a small platform that leads to burnished bronze doors, their surface shining yellow-gold even in the moonlight. Below churns the sea, rocks ripping through some of the shallows, and then the blank darkness of the deeper water. I turn my attention back to the bridge, easing a foot forward, and it is then that I see the images carved into the stone.

"Come," says Kola, moving ahead of me. "Let's not waste any more time."

"Wait—" I say as he rushes forward, pressing a foot down on a picture of stars.

It is too late.

As he stands on it fully, both feet on the stone, the bridge shudders. The farthest slab slots back into itself with a loud grating noise, leaving a gap at the end that can just be seen.

"Don't move!" I shout, looking down at where Kola stands, Issa clinging to his neck with his eyes squeezed shut.

Standing behind him, I examine the stones around us. A man with thunder shooting from his hands, the plants of a garden, and the plaited strands of a woman's hair. I scan what else I can see. There are other images along the bridge, but I can't quite make them out.

"You stood on that one and all was well . . . and then . . . you stepped on that one and the bridge receded," I murmur.

"A trap, maybe," says Kola, looking over my shoulder at the images.

"Most definitely," I answer. "But I think it's more than that. Give me a moment. Stay where you are."

I hop onto the section behind him, gripping his arms as we balance on the stone with the hand and scattered stars. "It's as if the pictures are . . . telling a story." I peer closer at an orisa I recognize from his playful expression, and the symbol of a trident, its handles overlapping another line to form a crossroads. "There's Esu!" Once I pick him out, I can see repeated stones with his image on them. "If it's a story, it must be told in a certain way."

"So we need to step on the stones in the right order?" calls Bem, his voice low.

"Yes, exactly." I leap back to join the others. "What story would Esu choose, do you think?"

Issa opens his eyes enough to take a peek and then shuts them again while squeaking out, "I'd make it a story about me."

I think of all the images of Esu on the bridge. "You're right."

"Which one, though?" asks Ifedayo. "There are so many."

Think, I tell myself, but my heart beats so hard that for a moment I can only concentrate on the blood thundering in my ears. Sucking in a breath, I gaze at the bridge, thinking of the stars that begin the story. "The second stone. See? There's a figure, larger than the others, holding a staff with a dove atop. Obatala's symbols. I think that represents him, the father of all humanity. It looks as though Esu is starting with the world's creation."

I think of the stories of Esu's tricking and pitting friend against friend. But also tales of him defeating enemies by talking his way out of a situation. What would Esu be most proud of?

"What else can you see?" I call to Kola.

He cranes his neck while still keeping both feet firmly on the second stone. "There is something that looks like a yam . . . and flowers and trees. I can see the moon and I think . . . the sun. There are a few other symbols there, too."

Esu *would* put others in, to make it harder. It wouldn't be nearly as difficult if one had only the correct images for the story.

And then my eyes widen with recognition of the symbols, my mind filling with memories of another favorite story of my mother's. "Why not tell the story of your most important role and the way you got it? The ultimate trick you played on Olodumare."

"The story of how Esu became a messenger," says Bem quietly, nodding in encouragement.

"Exactly." I run onto the bridge and stand behind Kola. Carefully, I turn him around, easing my feet down in place of his until he is back on the first stone behind me. The bridge stretches ahead, and I notice that there are three stones with images to choose from for every few steps. The stones glitter slightly in the moonlight. If I look closely, I can see threads of silver that run through the rock.

"Let me go first, and then follow me," I say, forcing myself to slow my panicked steps. "Step only on the stones that I do, and stay close in case we have to run.

"I'm choosing the story of how Esu tricked Olodumare and became the divine messenger, responsible for carrying news between heaven and earth." I don't wait for an answer; instead I step on the image of Esu creeping among some flowers and trees.

"Here is a story. Story it is . . ." My mother's words and her tale come back to me, her voice calming me as I try to focus.

"One day Esu sneaked into Olodumare's garden."

We all stand still, eyes on the end of the bridge, which remains unmoving. I shuffle forward, edging past the few blank stones until I come to another set of three images. A bowl, a yam, and a pear.

"He stole some yams from the god's earth." I step forward onto that image, encouraged when the bridge still doesn't move. "Olodumare was furious that someone would steal from a celestial garden." I continue, moving again to stand on an image of the Supreme God, face contorted with rage. My voice grows louder with confidence. "Esu didn't want to get caught, so the next night he took Olodumare's slippers and put them on, using them to make footprints in the garden as he stole more yams. This way it would look as if the only person who had been walking around and stealing was Olodumare."

A salt-filled breeze laced with a raw chill blows my hair, the ends loose now, spiraling around my shoulders. We're halfway there. But the next three images I see make me pause.

"What is it, Simi?" asks Kola, trying to look over my shoulder. "Oh."

All three pictures show a type of slipper.

"It could be any one of them," I whisper, fighting the panic that rises. I know the story inside and out, but I don't know what type of footwear Olodumare wore. How could I know what slipper the Supreme God would choose?

Breathe, I tell myself, placing a hand on my chest. How many of us will make it back if I choose the wrong one and the bridge begins to recede again?

Etched into the stone as they are, it is not easy to make out the finer details on each shoe. I bend down, keeping my feet in place, so that I can get a closer look. The first shoe is plain with a back to it, so I discount it as not being a slipper. The second has a small heel and geometric circles, and the third has intricate patterns that give it a more luxurious air than the average slipper. Surely Olodumare's slipper would be more opulent, I think as I stand up straight. Unless the god is a less frivolous one. But then Olodumare is the Supreme Being, I think. Anything else would not befit such power. The intricate slipper must be the one.

The sea roils beneath us, reefs and crags and currents turning it into a seething thing that bares its black-rock teeth and snaps at the land. I'm not sure whether I would survive the fall before my change. The others don't stand a chance. I step forward gingerly, closing my eyes as the soles of my feet press down on the cool stone. The bridge begins to quiver, and I stumble close to the edge as another section at the end slots into itself. I'm shaking. A stupid mistake, I tell myself, you should be able to do this, you know the story.

The shriek is faint but fractures the night, loud enough for us all to hear. I freeze for a moment, jerking my head up and examining the starlit sky for movement, removing the dagger from my hair.

"Simidele," Kola murmurs in my ear. "We need to move. Now."

I bend down, examining the stone closely again. If I don't get this right, more of us will surely die. My throat feels as if it is closing up; I take another deep breath and let it out slowly. Olodumare has no need of fancy patterns or decadent designs. The plain shoe must be the one, I think, even though it has a back. I open my eyes and step forward onto the image, the stone slightly rough beneath my bare foot. The bridge remains still, and my legs almost give way as relief courses through me, until another shriek rips through the night air, accompanied this time by the beating of wings.

I look up as clouds drift across the moon, shadows sprawled across the sky, but I still can't see anything. Don't stop now, I tell myself, peering down. "Esu showed Olodumare what looked to be the Supreme God's own footprints and suggested to Olodumare that they had stolen the yams," I say, my voice quivering as I rush my words, heading for the last selection of images.

I hear the scream and beating of what sounds like giant wings just above me. Tipping my face up to the night sky, I watch as a creature dives from the cover of clouds straight toward us, its leathery wings blotting out the moon, twisted feet dangling back to front. Bem raises his sword, lunging, forcing it to swoop back up into the air, but not before I catch a glimpse of claws as long as my arm and a large body both furred and muscular. With a batlike but strangely human face, the creature is twice as large as Kola. And when it dives again, its crimson eyes burn a hole in the night before it wheels away at the last second.

"Sasabonsam!" yells Ifedayo as four more of the creatures shred through the clouds, shrieking.

Kola peers up, fear in the corners of his eyes and in the way he tightens his grip on Issa. "I should have known. Or guessed from the drawing." He sets Issa down and adjusts his grip on his sword.

"It doesn't matter, we'd still have had to face them," Bem says. "I'd say aim for the head and chest, or try injuring their wings."

Three of the creatures spiral away into the dark, their screeches echoing around us as the night conceals them.

"Annoyed and confused, Olodumare worried that they'd missed something, and so ordered Esu to visit the sky each and every night in order to tell them what had happened on earth that day." I'm gabbling now, voice high and wobbling as I step on the moon and then the sun.

The remaining sasabonsam dives, aiming straight for us. A scream blooms in my throat, but Kola drives his sword at the creature as it flexes its metallic claws. Bem turns, thrusting his blade across the sasabonsam's side as it shrieks, dark blood spraying the gray stone of the bridge as it retreats toward the volcano. The other creatures caw in the night sky, their winged bodies deeper outlines of black against the moon.

"You can do it, Simi." Issa looks up at me, his eyes round as he reaches out to hold my fingers, squeezing gently.

"And so Esu became messenger to Olodumare." With the last word, I step on the final picture of the orisa, my legs weak. In it Esu is standing, looking up at the sky, his hands cupped around his open mouth as he recites what has happened on earth that day. I hold my breath, fingers outspread. The bridge remains still. Peering ahead, I gauge the distance between the last image and the gap where the stone has receded. It's large enough to require a giant leap.

Two sasabonsam emerge from the cover of clouds. They plummet together, revealing spiked iron teeth as they scream.

Cutting through the air, they speed toward us, eyes like blazing coals.

"We'll need to jump!" I call out, and then, before I can think about it, I spring forward, landing on the platform ahead.

Turning to face the others, I see Kola lift Issa, crouching close to the gap. He soars through the air, landing safely, and I wind my arms around him briefly, letting myself breathe in the faintest hint of black soap. I stroke Issa's head as he slides from the boy's back, clutching his knife. Gently, I push them behind me on the small platform, making room for the others.

The sasabonsam descend on the bridge in a whirl of claws and teeth as Bem stands back to back with Ifedayo. They lunge and dodge the beasts while maintaining their balance, even as the bridge begins to tremble beneath them and another section recedes. As a sasabonsam screeches and soars toward them, Ifedayo spins to the side and thrusts a knife into one of the creature's eye sockets.

The injured sasabonsam wails, flying erratically in the direction of the forest as I study the bridge, wondering if only a certain number of people can cross at a time, or whether this is just another trap. But either way, the walkway is fracturing. "Come on!" I yell, beckoning with frantic hands as Kola and Issa scan the air around them, arms shaking, faces drawn and dappled with sweat. "Ifedayo!" I call, stepping back as he begins to sprint, making room on the platform. "Now!"

Hands outstretched and legs pushed forward, he lands on the rim of the platform, where Kola pulls him to safety.

Bem shouts with fury as he whirls his sword, cutting the other sasabonsam's throat as it tries to grab him. The creature plunges into the sea below, its strangled scream silenced by the waves. He turns to us, chest heaving and covered in the black blood of the creatures as well as the red of his own, and I see the recognition in his eyes as another segment of the bridge recedes.

Bem won't make it.

"Go back!" I bellow in a voice scraped up from deep inside me. If he can get to the first platform, he'll be safer.

Bem turns and heads back toward the end of the bridge, dragging his left leg, the injuries slowing him down.

"Faster!" cries Issa as we watch the segments slide under one another, the bridge growing shorter with every second. One of the two sasabonsams left shrieks again and cuts through the air, winging toward Bem as he races to the bank.

"No," I moan. I squeeze the handle of my dagger, unable to do anything but watch.

Bem tries to run faster, his sword flashing as he puts his head down, focused on getting to the end of the bridge. The sasabonsam reaches him just as he hits the ground, rolling so that the creature skims over him, thrusting his sword upward, slicing at its furred stomach. Bleeding and howling, the creature wheels away. Relief floods through me as Bem sits up, safe on the other side of the bridge, sword still in his grasp. The other sasabonsam sees this and opens its mouth to emit a cry of rage, spinning and turning, flying toward us instead.

"It's coming!" I shout, my grip sliding on my dagger as I shove at the bronze doors behind us. They don't budge and I yell in frustration, turning back to the sasabonsam as it brushes across the bridge.

"Try to injure its wings, and I'll aim for the heart," says Kola as he draws level between Ifedayo and me.

The sasabonsam opens its mouth to screech again as it flies

toward us, its heaving wings beating loudly in the night. And then it is upon us, and I am stabbing at one wing as Ifedayo attacks its other. It's hard to land a strike as it slashes with its long claws, cutting the skin of my shoulder open. Blackness spreads across my gaze at the burning sensation and I gasp, holding a hand over the gash. Kola raises his sword, but the creature darts forward and bites into the flesh of his forearm, teeth piercing muscle, clamping down on bone. Kola yells as blood spills down his hand, his sword clattering to the stone platform.

Issa's golden eyes ignite with ferocity as he leaps up, brandishing his small knife, slicing across the sasabonsam's cheek. The creature bellows, its breath a mixture of rot and the copper tang of human blood. It releases Kola's arm, but before Issa can strike again the sasabonsam lunges, seizing the yumbo's shoulder and chest with its serrated teeth.

"Kola—" Issa cries out, his voice strangled, blood dribbling from the corner of his mouth. He holds his arm out to us, but before we can take it, the creature tightens its jaws on his tiny body and his plea is cut short. The sasabonsam's teeth puncture easily through delicate yumbo ribs, the cracks sharp as the air fills with the scent of fresh blood. Almost immediately, I see the sparkle of Issa's soul, a beautiful and delicate silver that spirals from the ruin of his chest.

Despair rips through me. Roaring and filled with a desperate rage, I aim for the creature's neck, but the sasabonsam jerks backward and soars into the star-scarred night with the yumbo's lifeless body in its mouth.

CHAPTER TWENTY-FOUR

THE STONE IS rough beneath my hands and knees as the bridge and the sky spin. I retch, and bile rises until I swallow it back down. There are hands on my back, but I can't move. Not yet.

Issa.

Little Issa.

My stomach convulses, and I let it purge itself of what I ate earlier.

"Simi. Simi?" It's Ifedayo, and I wipe my mouth, swinging my head around, dizzy still. "The sasabonsam will come back. Stand up, we need to get inside."

I push myself up and into a squat as Kola picks up his sword and takes my arm. Tears stream down his cheeks, but his eyes are hard and he clenches his sword tightly.

"Kola," I begin, but he shakes his head and keeps hold of me as he turns to the bronze doors that glow softly in the moonlight.

"I'm not letting anyone else die." Kola's eyes glitter and he blinks rapidly as my own heart lurches in pain. "Ifedayo's right, we need to get inside."

"But Issa—"

"Is dead," interrupts Ifedayo. "And so will we be if we don't get off this platform."

I nod and wipe my face. With the bridge behind us, I face the burnished panels of the doors, full of effigies of Esu. In one, he is holding a slipper and smiling slyly, in another he is watching a village and pointing.

"I couldn't open it before." My words are raw. We can't have come all this way just to be kept out by a locked door.

"There must be some other way to open them," says Ifedayo, inspecting the panels, one hand on his knife and the other out-stretched, palm pressed gently against the door.

I sweep my gaze over the panels. The largest image stretches across both doors and shows Esu straddling a giant crossroads. The orisa owns all pathways, and this is represented by a depiction of him in the very center, head thrown back midlaugh. I brush my fingertips over his raised form and along the paths that run east and west, sliding each hand far apart. Unlike the rest of the bronze panels, these sections feel cooler. There must be a reason they're different. Keeping my palms on the metal ribbons of roads, I push gently, holding my breath.

Nothing happens.

"What if we try pressing every single crossroads, not just left and right?" croaks Kola, his voice shaking. I turn around and he wipes the sweat from his brow. "It's worth a try, isn't it?"

It makes sense, I think. All roads in life are options. "I'll push east and west," I say, spinning around to place my hands on the same roads. "You press north and south." Kola stands next to me as I take a deep breath. "On three. One. Two. *Three.*"

We heave together, hands against the cooler part of the bronze doors, and there's a loud snap as the panels disengage, revealing a strip of light.

I push open the doors, squinting as a white glow seeps through the widening gap. We walk into a light so intense that I am forced to stop, holding my hands up to my brow as I place a foot on a glistening floor. After the muted shades of the night, the pearlescent corridor twists away from us, undulating like a glittering snake that is almost too much for my eyes. I blink a few times, slowly becoming accustomed to the brightness as Kola heaves the doors closed behind us with a loud click. The light of the corridor shows the naked grief in the lines of Kola's face, and as I walk back toward him, his knees buckle and he slides to the floor, his sword clattering beside him.

"Kola!" I quicken my steps, crouching in front of him as he holds his head in both of his large hands, a strangled cry escaping the cradle of knuckles and palms.

"I should have done something. I should have protected him. I promised." Kola's shoulders shake as my hands hover over them. His voice is thick with tears and anguish. "I promised, Simi."

Slowly I lower my hands until they touch the skin of his shoulders. Kola's grief is silent as it wracks his body in shuddering waves. I say nothing, my fingers slipping to the curve of his neck as I bring his face to my chest. He stiffens at first before taking his hands from his face and wrapping them around my waist, holding me tight. My body shakes along with his, but I don't cry, willing some of my own strength into him.

"We will find the twins and the rings," I whisper into his ear, my voice rough and fierce. "And then we will mourn together, properly. As Issa deserves."

Kola stills at my words and nods against me. For a moment,

we remain locked together, our grief heavy between us. And then Kola is releasing me, climbing to his feet and wiping his face. With a loud sniff, he picks up his sword and rolls his shoulders. "You're right." He nods at me, eyes flashing with the same determination I feel. "Let's go."

I lead the way, letting my fingertips trail against the walls, which twinkle, layers of light reflecting on marble and white gold, while matching sconces hold unnatural ivory flames.

"Something doesn't feel right," mutters Ifedayo.

The corridor stretches before us, without windows, only an entranceway at the end. Beside me, I can hear Ifedayo ready more of his knives, the sound of blades being drawn from sheaths, a small unmistakable rasp of metal on leather.

Ifedayo is right. There's a tightness in the air that matches the feeling in my chest. Kola looks at me and I rotate my wrist, the blade of my dagger glinting in the light. I take the lead, and slowly we make our way down the hallway, feet silent on the cool marble floor. There are columns spaced equally apart, decorated with all the orisas. Sango soars at the top with Oya by his side. Farther down I can make out swirls that represent the ocean, with Yemoja floating on the waves while Olokun lurks at the bottom. I peer up at the figures of many more as we pass, running my fingers over the arm of an orisa that looks like Esu with what seems to be two faces. Something about the depiction nags at me, a feeling that grows as we near the end of the corridor.

The double doors that we come to are an orange-and-yellow citrine. Ifedayo limps forward, placing a hand on one of the crystal handles. He holds his fingers against his lips as he presses down and pulls open the door. Easing his way through the gap, he beckons us to follow him. The room that we enter must span the whole width of the palace, but it is empty save for a large throne in the center. Carved from the darkest of mahogany wood, the chair is decorated with etchings of raven wings, sinuous twines of snakes, and the jaws of a coyote. The seat and armrests are covered in a fiery silk that gleams in the light.

"Can you see anyone?" asks Kola, edging to stand partially in front of me.

"No, but that doesn't mean he isn't here." I move around him, walking toward the throne in the middle of the room.

"Simi!" hisses Kola. "What are you doing? Don't just—"

"What do you want, creation of Yemoja?"

The words come from nowhere and everywhere. Kola holds his weapon aloft, eyes darting.

"State your need."

I whip my head around, searching for Esu, but the orisa is nowhere to be seen.

"State your need," Ifedayo says again as he saunters toward the throne, his voice deeper now.

• • •

Almost as one, we turn and gape at Ifedayo, whose wrapper, cinched tight around his waist, has transformed to ruby and obsidian swirls. He looms above us now, even taller than before, his limbs thicker and longer. A necklace of bulbous rubies and black pearls hangs down to the center of his chest, and raw onyx is spun around each of his plaits, long enough to graze his now-wider shoulders. Even his face is different, no longer gaunt, his cheeks rounder, lips fuller. He turns his back on us, dark muscles flexing, and strolls to the throne, where he sits down, leaning forward and looking at me.

"Come now, Mami Wata . . . speak." Ifedayo nods smugly. "I thought you had something to say."

"Ifedayo?" Kola asks, his face creased in confusion.

Anger stretches my spine ramrod-straight as realization hits me. "Esu," I manage, my voice tight.

Ifedayo looks over at me and grins, teeth sharper now, their pointed tips catching his top lip. The curve of his smirk makes me want to slap it from his face, but I ball my hands into fists instead. I think back to when I spoke to him on the ship, his vague answers. Even his limp makes sense now, one foot in the human world and one in Olodumare's. I grind my teeth, trying to release the tightness in my chest, as he continues to study me, eyes black with fragments of silver. I should have worked it out. I should have known.

"But not one of you guessed!" Esu crows, throwing himself back against the throne in triumph.

Kola gazes at the person his father trusted to look after him, the person he has been sailing with, who now sits on a throne before him. The bewilderment and hurt on Kola's face only make me angrier.

"Why?" I snarl, my hands curling into fists. "What was the point of all this?"

Esu's laugh cuts off so abruptly that the sudden silence echoes in the chamber. "Be careful of your tone, little fish." He leans forward, the muscles in his arms bunched, his eyes shining as he glares at me. "You might think you've been clever to get this far, but I've known about your little quest since you boarded

Abayomi's ship. Sango told me of the jewel at your throat. You thought you hid it well enough, didn't you? Silly little fish." Esu laughs. "I heard rumors that you saved a human. And if you need to seek forgiveness? Well, the rings are the only way."

The storm. I was right.

"I didn't need to keep track of anything else once I found out who you were with." Esu leers at Kola. "This one was always going to do whatever he could to get back home, back to his brother and sister. But you were too late, were you not? Such a shame."

Kola moves closer to me, his hand on the hilt of his sword, his jaw clenched tightly. "Where are they?"

"What allies you have become," purrs Esu, smiling again and ignoring Kola's question, but this time his voice is full of ice. "A lot has changed since you pulled him from the sea. But is that all you are?" He slaps his thigh and brings a hand to his forehead, smoothing back his plaits. "Of course. A silly question. Because we know that is all you can be. Isn't that true, Simidele?"

I don't say anything, but I feel Kola move forward, wanting the orisa to continue. My blood runs hot, but I feel cold as I swing my gaze from the orisa to Kola's tensed back.

"After all, you're not human, no matter what you look like at the moment. Not now, anyway." Esu leans back, legs splayed beneath his opulent wrapper. "Never again. You can't even walk for a few hours before your feet betray your unnatural state. And if you're not human"—he gestures to Kola and then back to me— "you two could never be more than . . . allies. Otherwise, what is it that happens?"

I open my mouth and then close it as Kola looks back at me. Nails dig hard into my palms and tears prick at the back of my eyes. I should have told him before. Kola's shoulders bunch and I

268

want to run my hands over them, to smooth away the tension and explain what the orisa means. My hand hovers over the scars of Kola's back, but I don't touch him.

"Come on, little fish. Will you not tell Adekola what will happen?" Esu cocks his head to one side, sliding his gaze from me to Kola. "Simidele is forbidden. Since she is no longer human, if she acts on her love for a mortal, she will become nothing but foam upon the sea."

Kola remains standing in front of me, and he doesn't turn. I lean forward to finally touch his arm and he slides his hand back around, grasping my fingers briefly before letting go. Even that touch eases something inside me. Esu looks from Kola's face to mine, and I see it fall at the lack of reaction he's received. Trying to act nonchalant, he picks up his onyx dagger and begins to pick beneath his nails, head down, plaits swinging.

His words have layered more rage on top of my ever-present anger. From Yemoja's scars, Yinka . . . to Issa. And now this. Breathing heavily, I imagine using my dagger to slash at Esu's chest and face over and over. Since he loves red and black so much, I would decorate him in the crimson of his blood.

"Where are the twins?" Kola's voice is forced, his shoulders hunched.

Esu stops laughing and raises his hand, fingernails in wicked points. "Taiwo and Kehinde are safe."

"What about the rings?" I try to calm myself and focus on the children. "Where are they?"

The orisa pauses, knife held up, hands splayed. He sighs and then places the weapon in his lap. "I'll admit I underestimated the girl. She hid hers somewhere on the way here and still won't tell me. That's the reason I went to Oko, but everyone there was useless. I had hoped one of you might have an idea, but it seems not." Esu frowns. "You might think badly of me, but I didn't want to have to resort to other means. Though that's looking more likely now."

Kola lunges forward. "Where are they?"

Esu is on his feet in one fluid movement, the ebony blade in his hand. "Do not attempt to make demands of me, Adekola."

"Tell us now," snarls Kola. "Issa died for this. Yinka is . . ." He stops, breathing hard before he can continue. "For your tricks and games. You crave power, but for what? At what cost?"

"Olodumare rained powers down on earth as if they were *nothing*," spits Esu, glaring down at us. "Nothing. Letting orisas scramble about in the dirt to collect what they could. How is that fair? And those that use their powers revel in the adoration of humans, doing little more than establishing their status as orisa, bestowing favors and blessings here and there. Meanwhile I stop the ajogun from destroying humanity, and report all that happens on earth to Olodumare." His chest heaves, swelling with anger. "And while I am doing this, mankind runs amok. I will not allow it!"

Next to me, Kola adjusts his stance, muscles bunched as he squeezes the hilt of his sword. "Where are the twins?" he asks again, his voice low.

"Your getting this far is a good thing." Esu raises his eyebrows, a mocking smile on his face. "Perhaps Kehinde will be more willing to answer my questions if it means the safety of her brother."

The orisa slashes his long dagger down in a sharp arc, Kola blocks it with his blade, but the force of the blow pushes him backward.

"No!" I scream as Kola tries to attack again, swinging his sword just as Esu kicks him in the stomach. I try to thrust my blade in the direction of Esu's throat, but the orisa turns to jab his knife at me.

"This was never needed," Esu says as I dance back, away from his blade, moving with Kola so that we draw closer to the throne. "But I always welcome a little entertainment."

The orisa starts toward us, his head lowered slightly, braids swaying with every step he takes and eyes flashing with glints of silver. Kola reaches for me with his free hand. He cups the back of my head, pressing his forehead against mine for not even a second before he pulls away. When I open my eyes it is to his brown gaze, his breath soft against my lips. I can see the puckering of skin from the wound on his forehead as he tries to smile. "Find them."

Kola releases me and runs forward to meet Esu, sword held high, weapon whirling and crashing against the orisa's. Esu presses his blade down on the boy's, forcing him to his knees, but Kola rams his fist upward into the hard ridges of the orisa's stomach with his free hand and rolls sideways before springing to his feet. Esu growls, and even I am surprised at Kola's strength and speed. Moving into the center of the chamber, he wipes his face with one hand and jerks his head at me, gesturing to the door opposite the one we entered through.

"Go," Kola hisses as he thrusts his sword at Esu, spinning away before the orisa can retaliate. "Find the twins."

The orisa takes his moment of distraction to spring forward, bringing his dark blade down on Kola's side, scoring a line of blood on the ridges of the boy's ribs. I hesitate as Kola yells, but he remains standing, readying his own weapon.

"Go, Simi," Kola pleads as he grabs his side, blood seeping between his fingers. "Save them."

CHAPTER TWENTY-FIVE

I RUN ACROSS the chamber as Esu roars and the clash of blades echoes all around me. Blood pounds in my ears as I wrench open the door to a spiral staircase. Raven-black steps wind upward, but the walls are the same luminous crystal as the corridor and glow enough for me to see. Breathing hard now, I climb, not caring that every step is like walking on hot coals, the wound on my shoulder throbbing. The scent of salt soon reaches me and the air grows colder the higher I get. The twist of the stairs feels never-ending, and I have to pause, my chest on fire. Hunched over, I wrap my arms around my stomach, wheezing and crying. I think of Kola still down there, fighting Esu.

The twins.

Pushing myself up, I climb again, listening for sounds, but all I can hear is the raggedness of my own heavy breathing until I finally reach an archway that leads to the sky. Or that's what it looks like. This room is half the size of the throne chamber below, but it's open to the heavens, making it feel larger. I creep to the edge, looking down at seething waves and a stretch of rocks and sea. There's a whimper behind me and I whirl around, my dagger held out.

Behind me is a cage made from thick citrine. The yellow crystal glows, casting a pale light on the two shapes crouching against the bars. The twins have the same reddish-brown skin as Kola's and wear tattered matching royal-blue wrappers. They look so small, no more than eight or nine years old. I stagger over to them, my hands tight fists at the sight of them in a cage.

"Taiwo, Kehinde." The little girl pulls her brother behind her, scowling at me. She has a sliver of rock in her hands that she holds like a dagger. "Your brother sent me. He's downstairs."

"Kola is here?" Taiwo rushes to the bars, his eyes the same brown as Kola's, large in his heart-shaped face.

"Taiwo, get back," cautions his sister as she joins him, rock still held out toward me.

"Why isn't he with you?" asks Kehinde, her eyes darting to the doorway.

"He's down in the throne chamber." I take a breath, trying to calm my tone. "Kola sent me on ahead to help you." I slide my hands down the crystal bars, fingers fluttering.

"There's a lock," says Kehinde, pointing at the middle of the cage.

I slide my fingers down it again until I find the hidden mechanism in the crystal. I curl my fingers around the bars and pull, hissing with anger and frustration. "Do you know where the key is?"

"Esu has it," says Taiwo. "He won't let us out until Kehinde tells him where she hid her ring."

"He can't take it from me unless I give permission. The babalawo said no one can." Kehinde holds her right hand up, empty fingers bare. "And he can't ask for permission, or trick it from me, if I don't have it."

273

I smile at her cleverness and she grins back a little, her eyes shining with fierceness. Stepping away, I look around the platform. If there's no key, perhaps I can use something to smash the lock open. But the room is bare, its rock floor stretching away to the edge, where the sea crashes incessantly below.

Then I hear the scrape of a blade and leaden footsteps. My blood stills, anger spreading. I hold the dagger before me, wrapping both hands around the hilt to steady my grip, a scream building in my throat as the door is pushed open. Kola appears in the archway. He sways before us, a crown of blood dripping down his face, sliding into his eyes and coating his lips in a sticky crimson.

"Ẹ̀gbọ́n ọkùnrin!" shouts Taiwo, while Kehinde's mouth crumples at the sight of their brother.

Kola staggers forward, his sword clattering on the ground as he collapses. I rush over, the twins sobbing behind me as I cradle Kola's head, keeping it from the stone floor. There are deep gashes on his shoulders and side. His blood is warm when I try to wipe it from his face.

"He's coming," Kola whispers as he holds a fist toward me. His fingers uncurl to reveal a hefty crystal hexagon. The key. "I got this from Esu. Is it . . . ?"

"It is," I answer, trying to smile reassuringly at him through a veil of tears that threaten to spill.

"Hurry." Kola squeezes my fingers as I reach for the key. I nod and gently lower his head to the floor. He watches me, a hand coated in gore, groping for his sword.

I turn to the twins, wiping away the tears that keep falling. The key is slick with blood and sweat and I clutch it tightly; its sharp edges digging into my palm. The bars of the cage shimmer and glitter through my tears and I fumble, trying to find the lock again. Kehinde darts forward and points to it, her eyes going to Kola.

"Don't worry," I say as I push the hexagon against the lock, twisting it until it fits, engaging with the crystal spines inside the mechanism. "He's alive." But dread is winding its way through me, harder to fight when I think of Esu making his way up the stairway.

I twist the key again until a loud click sounds and the bars descend into the dark rock floor. The twins run straight to their brother, who opens his arms, blinking tears that spill down his bloodstained cheeks. Burrowing against his side, Taiwo cries as Kehinde lays a small hand on his cheek, a frown marring her brow.

"It's all right, little ones," Kola murmurs, but I can see the effort it takes to form the words, the bright vermilion at the corner of his mouth. His gaze slides to the ring on Taiwo's finger and then to Kehinde's hand. "Where's your ring?"

The little girl clutches the lighter band of brown skin, twisting her finger around the bare flesh.

"Kehinde, I said, where is your ring?" Kola sits up, his eyes flashing. Blood coats the skin of his ribs, dripping down onto the stone floor. "Tell me. Quickly, before Esu gets here."

Taiwo draws backward, flinching slightly at the cutting tone of his older brother, but his sister stands up abruptly, staring down at Kola. She opens her mouth to speak, and it is then that we hear it. The scrape of feet on the stairs and the drag of steel on stone.

I glance around the room open to the sky. There is no way out apart from the door that leads to the stairway and the sea that crashes below us. My heart constricts, chest heaving. The only option we have left is to fight. I turn to the doorway, dagger in hand, ready.

"Kehinde." Kola's voice is almost a snarl now. "Where is it? Tell me now before Esu arrives."

I spin back to see the twins cowering against the wall, eyes bright with tears, lips trembling. With their arms wrapped around each other, they look even younger.

"Kola—"

"Quiet, Simidele!" Kola climbs to his feet, his eyes cold, a darker shade of brown than I am used to. "The ring. I need to know where it is."

I move backward in shock and confusion. The footsteps in the stairway grow even closer. Fear trickles through my veins, immediate and icy. "Kola, we need to make sure the twins are safe so that . . ." But I don't finish what I am saying, because the doorway is suddenly filled with brown skin and blood and the eyes that I would know anywhere.

"Kola?" Incredulous, I take a painful step toward him.

"Simi," he answers, the familiar light in his eyes flickering in the glow of the moon as his gaze locks with mine. The real Kola rests against the entranceway, chest heaving as he pants, hand clamped on the wound in his side. "Get away from them," he hisses.

I swing my gaze back, already knowing what I'll see. Instead of small tight curls there are now long plaits, a rounder face and a hulking height. Esu stands in the middle of the chamber, his eyes glinting with anger, the rubies of his necklace matching the blood he conjured to masquerade as Kola.

Esu. Pretending again. How could I be so gullible? I swallow down my feelings of stupidity and move toward Kola. Blood is flowing down the hand he has clamped to his side, splashing onto the ground in scarlet droplets. How did he even manage to climb the stairs?

"I told you he's not to be trusted," whispers Kehinde furiously as she tugs Taiwo against her.

"Stop this foolishness and tell me where the ring is," the orisa barks at the girl, raising his obsidian blade and stepping toward the children.

Kola is almost a blur as he streaks across the chamber, planting himself between the orisa and the twins. Holding his sword steady in both hands, he curls his lip. "You won't harm them. I won't let you."

Esu pauses and cocks his head to one side, braids grazing the shimmering rubies of his necklace. "All I want is the rings."

"I can give him mine," whispers Taiwo to Kehinde. "If it means he'll let us leave."

"No! He won't stop at one." Kehinde drags her brother closer to her as Esu steps forward. "We talked about this."

"Step aside, boy."

Kola doesn't answer but lunges forward faster than I can see, slicing at Esu's chest, drawing a slash of blood bright in the light of the fat moon. The orisa bellows in surprise, and fury twists his mouth. Nostrils flaring, he brings his sword down in a hard arc at Kola's head, but the boy twists at the last moment, whirling to the side. Before he can bring his weapon up again, Esu clenches his fist, driving it into Kola's nose. Kola sinks to the floor, the scent of blood fresh in the salt air.

"This did not need to be," says the orisa, kicking the sword away from them. "But I will have what I need. What should be mine."

"No!" I scream, wheeling away from Esu to limp over to Kola. I lift his head gingerly, fingers in his curls, searching for a sign that he's at least still alive. "Kola," I whimper.

His eyes are closed, mouth slack. I place a hand on his chest, the skin hot to the touch, and I feel a barely perceptible rise and fall of his ribs. Relief courses through me.

"Come!" I shout to the twins. "Quickly!"

The orisa watches from the center of the chamber, surveying the crumpled figure of Kola and then the quiver of my hands as I crouch in front of the boy, holding out my dagger.

The children dash around the edges of the room to me, their eyes wide at the sight of their brother. I tuck them into a shallow fold of rock, my hands shaking as I snatch glances at Esu. He strolls toward us, pausing to adjust his wrapper. He knows there's nowhere for us to go. "Stay tight against the wall," I urge.

"There is no point in fighting me," he says, but I lunge anyway, slashing at the air in a hopeful swipe. Esu laughs again and grins at me.

I can feel despair trying to push its way into my mind, but I haven't come this far to give up now. I slide backward, trying to tug Kola with me. His head lolls to the side and his eyes roll, the whites bright in the chamber. Taiwo begins to cry and Kehinde murmurs to him, terror hitching her own voice. Kola coughs and winces, and I can see the russet of the dried blood on his wrapper and the sparkling red of the fresh splatters on his skin. *I won't let them die,* I think furiously. My heart thumps, and the rage that seeps in feels as if it will break the bones in my chest.

"Well done, Mami Wata. For a creature of the sea you move surprisingly well on land."

I say nothing. Esu stalks past us, moving to the edge of the platform. As he peers down into the sea, I glance at the open doorway. We could run, I think, if Kola were not injured.

Esu spins, regarding me with his black eyes. "Orisas are different, all with various forms of powers that they caught when they were rained down by Olodumare." He leans closer to me. "Do you know what I received?"

"You are Lord of the Crossroads, overseeing all paths in life." I tighten my grip on my weapon to stop my hands from trembling. "A messenger. You are humankind's way of communicating with Olodumare and should be passing on their prayers. But you're also a trickster who entertains himself by mocking people and orisas for your own amusement, no matter the cost." I swallow hard. "And you've become greedy."

"Why should I be content with being a mouthpiece? A joker? Keeping the balance between the ajogun and orisas? I need more than that. More than passing on the needs and wants of man. More than bargaining with the anti-gods. I want to be powerful, strong. Our lands will never survive without an orisa like me." Esu stalks over to where I stand, his mouth turned down into the beginnings of a snarl. "Look at what is happening on earth. Orisas have no true freedom to use what they were given, what they were created for." He looks at the twins and his lips twist back into a smile. "To rule. To be worshipped. To reward if we so chose, and to discipline those who deserve punishment."

"You still wouldn't rival Olodumare."

"You are wrong. The rings will ensure that I can fully influence humans and orisas." He spreads his arms wide, palms held to the moon. "All would have to do what I say. What could be more powerful than that?"

"What would you do with that, though?" I hiss. "What have you done with your own powers so far, Esu?" I stand upright. "What have you done apart from cause distress, pitting friend against friend, tricking others just to amuse yourself? Yemoja follows the people stolen from the land. She blesses the souls of those who die in the sea, and I saw Sango and Oya destroying òyìnbó ships that carry the enslaved away. Do you even take mankind's messages to Olodumare anymore? You say they don't listen, but do you even *speak*? You curse the Supreme God and act as if other orisas don't care, but does Olodumare even know what's happening?"

"Not all messages are worthy of being heard and relayed."

Something in his tone stops me, and I think of what Olokun said about Esu's not taking his pleas to Olodumare. "Did you even pass on Yemoja's messages of atonement?"

Esu pauses, and I know then that I'm right. He didn't. How many other bits of news and prayers did he neglect to give to the Supreme God? "Why was she able to create Mami Wata? Why should she have the sapphires and the strength to do that, and not I?" Esu spreads his hands, holding them palm up to the stars. "Besides, it was not a lie—Olodumare was not pleased at being disobeyed."

"Olodumare didn't need to hurt her." I pause, swallowing a sob, thinking of the orisa's cheeks and her fear of the Supreme God's wrath. "Scar her."

"She needed to learn her place," Esu says, his voice tight with menace. "Not that Olodumare would have said or done what was truly needed. Besides, look at her arrogance when it came to the rings. She always knew who had them and would never tell me. I have had to find them myself."

My eyes meet his cold silvered gaze full-on as he smirks crookedly. "You did that to her because you were jealous? That wasn't Olodumare's command, was it?" The revelation creeps over me. "You were never told to hurt Yemoja."

"Olodumare wanted to me to remind her of the decree but didn't detail how." Esu shrugs, plaits flying.

I clench my jaw. "It is not about power, but about protection! For orisas and humans!"

"I will protect them. When they all bow down to me instead of Olodumare. I will never forsake them."

I think of Yemoja and of Sango and Oya and their selfless acts. I think about taking Kola from the sea. "But you already have." My words are soaked in sorrow and regret. "In your jealousy and your desire for more power, you have forsaken humankind and orisas."

"You think you know the answers, but you are nothing." Esu's smile slips, jolted by his anger, but he hitches it back up, draping it over the bones of his face. "Do not keep trying to question and test me, Simidele." He lifts his chin at Kehinde. "You will tell me where the ring is and you will give them both to me."

"No." The small girl trembles but shakes her head. "I know you won't use them in the right way."

"I told you. You will never have them." Kola pushes himself into a crouch and grabs his sword. With his limbs shaking, he uncurls his body to stand next to me. Blood still wreathes his head, but he holds himself upright.

The orisa flicks a hand dismissively, gaze fixed behind us where the twins try to press themselves into a crevice of the wall.

Kola uses the last of his energy to dart forward, driving his sword at Esu's stomach. The orisa moves faster than I can blink, side-stepping the blade, knocking the weapon from Kola's grip with a fist, and hitting the boy so hard I hear his jaw crack. Kola's sword drops to the stone floor, glowing under the moonlight as Esu wraps a hand around his neck and lifts him. The orisa throws his head back, grin splitting into a laugh that cracks the air around us. With a snap of his wrist, he tosses Kola against the wall near the twins.

"No!" I scream as Kola crumples into a pile of awkward angles and new blood.

"Would you still say no now?" roars Esu at the twins. "I will cut the skin from his body, remove his bones while he is still living, if you do not give me the rings."

Taiwo comes forward, twisting an obsidian band around and around on his finger as Kehinde begins to weep, opening her mouth to speak. Esu's smile widens and I spring at him, my dagger held high. Yemoja's blade gleams as I slash down, aiming for the orisa's heart. Esu steps neatly to the left, grabbing my wrist. The orisa grinds the bones just above the joint of my wrist, making me cry out.

"Such soft skin." Esu stoops so that his face is level with mine. "I'll bet you would taste of salt." He closes his eyes and inhales, tightening his grip, trapping my hands and wrapping his arm around my waist, holding me against him. We sway on the edge of the platform, a stinging wind blowing braids and curls across our faces.

"Simidele," he croons. "Why did you fight me when you could have helped me? Did you know that I could have made you whole again? Made you *human* again?"

I stiffen as Esu presses his lips against the whorl of my ear.

"You'd like that, wouldn't you? To be with . . . him."

"Kola," I whisper, my gaze flicking to the boy unconscious on the floor.

"I saw the way you were, the way he looked at you." Esu's breath tickles the skin of my neck. "I know what you feel for him. The thirst you have for his love."

The orisa saw it all when he was Ifedayo. I cringe when I think of the way every touch from Kola sent my heart racing, the looks I allowed myself, the graze of his fingers on my jaw whenever he checked the map in my hair. Heat rises, spreading across my cheeks when I think of Esu witnessing all that.

I turn my head enough to see the smooth red-brown skin of Kola's foot, his sole pale, and I remember when I found him in the sea. I saved him and he has saved me. Esu will not sully any of that.

The orisa grins, showing all his teeth. "He lives still. But only just." Esu shifts, and I feel him lift one of the curls that has escaped my braids. "Imagine what you could have had. No more cold depths. No more black-eyed sharks, their white bellies mixing with the blood in the water. Life. Together. Forget what Yemoja told you, I could make this so."

I think of the sun's heat sinking into my bones, the earth under my feet. And Kola with me, the slip of his skin, the taste of his smile and the way his eyes crinkle when he laughs. I will not feel ashamed anymore. Not for saving him and definitely not for loving him. But is what Esu is saying possible? For a moment I hesitate. Could I be human again?

I look up at the silver-streaked black of Esu's eyes and force myself to remember what he is capable of: promising people what they most desire and twisting their wishes for his own power and pleasure. He doesn't care, not truly. If there's a way for me to be human, I will find it on my own.

"I serve Yemoja." I take a deep breath as I try to back away. "And I would never have helped you."

Esu chuckles, his throat exposed. "As you wish, Simidele." He reaches out, seizing my neck and pulling me closer to him. "The twins will tell me anything I want now that you've brought me their brother."

Sweat rolls down my face and chest, soaking my wrapper as Esu grins at me, squeezing slowly. I scrabble at his thick fingers, tight against my skin. Blackness creeps into the edges of my vision as bright stars sparkle and bloom.

"Wait!" I croak, squeezing the words out. I draw in a deep breath as the orisa loosens his grip momentarily. "What if I told you I knew where the ring is?" I drag the words up from a raw throat. "Kehinde doesn't truly know. But I do."

"What do you mean?" The moon breaks free from shifting clouds to hover over us, coating the room with eerie light. Esu's face is lit up on one side and draped in darkness on the other. He leans closer, his lips inches from mine. "Where is it?" he growls.

"Kehinde threw it into the sea. She couldn't tell you exactly where it is, no matter what you did. I know where it landed, who has it now."

Esu looks over to the girl, who has placed Kola's head on her lap. "Is this true?"

Kehinde nods, eyes flashing as she curls her arms around her brother. "I dropped it in the deepest part as you brought us here."

"I'll tell you," I say. "As long as you can solve my riddle."

I register the surprise in the orisa's eyes before he cackles loudly.

"Why would you laugh?" I ask, pulling my neck from his grip. He lets me but clamps his hand around my arm. "You want the ring and I know where it is. Or is it that you don't think you can solve my riddle? That you're scared I may be able to trick you?"

Esu draws himself up straight, brows knitted as he looks down at me. "I am Esu, trickster of all. There is no riddle beyond me." His grip on me loosens as he pauses, my body held close to the edge still. "Very well, Simidele." His mouth is a tight curve. "Come then, let us play your little game."

I knew he wouldn't be able to resist. I think of the repeating patterns that are threaded through the culture of our lands. The braided decoration of our hair, the designs on our cloth, the paths and homes in our cities. All the same but in different sizes, repeating over and over again. Licking the dryness from my lips, I tip my head to face him. "I exist to be discovered but cannot be fully explored." I suck in another ragged breath. "I am ever-changing yet born of the same. Some say that I lead only to Olodumare." I stare at Esu, feeling the strength in my words. "What am I?"

"Is this the riddle you think you can trick me with?" Esu laughs in my face, and I shrink from his fetid breath. He shifts, his feet close to the rim of the platform. "I have traveled the world, Mami Wata. I have seen the cold seas with their icy bite, the ships that shatter in the freezing depths. I have seen the canopies of forests as vast as the oceans. I have charted stars in the sky and absorbed knowledge that most men could only dream of." The orisa hauls me even closer to him, his lips nearly touching mine. "You cannot fool me."

"Then answer. Or is it that you don't know?" I say.

Esu narrows his eyes at me. "I know more than you ever could. But I will humor you. Games are what makes this fun." He smiles, tightening his grip once again. "The greatest mathematicians of this land passed all they know on to me, and in that lies your answer. Our world is full of repeating patterns that we discover in nature and that we create." The sea is a roar just behind him, and I let it spur me on. "And while the shape may change, as it repeats, it always remains the same. It's the reason our people lay out cities the way they do, the reason they use certain designs in their art, their hair. The patterns of life are everywhere and they are never-ending. And because of this, there is one true path that can only lead to Olodumare."

"And so what's your answer?" I ask, blood pumping, heart hammering once again.

"I am infinity," says Esu, a smug grin carved into his midnight skin. "And I never end." He tilts his head back, aiming his deep laugh at the night sky. And it is then that I act, throwing myself forward, winding my arms around his thick neck and pulling him over the edge of the platform and into the chasm where the sea waits below.

CHAPTER TWENTY-SIX

I AM STANDING on the outside of the rail, holding on to the ship by my fingertips, feet hanging over the curve of the vessel's side. The sun is rising in bursts of gold and pink, burning along the line of the horizon. I close my eyes briefly, feeling the chill of the morning wind as it whips my hair into black clouds that rise around my face.

The òyìnbó reach for me, but they are wary this time, marked with the bleeding red gouges I scored in their skin. I know what they've done to the others. The ill and the punished. Tossing them into the sea, where they were pulled under by currents and chains.

As if we were nothing.

I snarl, twisting away from their grip, and say a prayer to Yemoja as I open my arms to the waves below me. Light sparkles on the white foam, the sea inviting me.

They don't have the chance to throw me.

I jump.

The water crashes around me, bubbles rising as I sink beneath the ship, watching it sail on, thinking of my return to Olodumare. Water fills my mouth, my nostrils, seeping into my lungs. My legs kick into the blue-blackness of the deep. I can't help the surge of terror that once again rises, threatening to overwhelm me.

Instead, I think of Yemoja. Her love for us, her children.

There have been rumors that she follows us.

The stolen.

The sold.

The taken.

That she cries for us, her tears adding to the sea as she murmurs prayers of comfort. Some are sure she will wreck the ship and release us, while others call for her blessing.

I am not sure what to believe, but I know that being below the ship is better than being on it. As the last of the air leaves my lungs, I blink, catching a glimpse of something that glitters, even this deep in the sea. The currents shift around me as I search again, catching sight of scales that sparkle in the blue. Shimmers of turquoise and indigo. Dark skin and black curls. The milky gleam of pearls and white gold.

Yemoja.

I am too weak to do more than widen my eyes as she swims up, my vision darkening, the silver in her eyes matching the stars that flare and explode in my gaze.

My ancestral orisa. Present at my birth and now at my death.

My heart pulses weakly as Yemoja gathers me to her, whispering that she has always been there. Her skin feels hot in the cold sea as she tells me of a task, a calling, and gives me a choice. I do not need to consider it, for I would do anything for her. I nod my head, spreading blackness across my vision.

And then my chest clears. There is no need to breathe. Instead, the skin of my legs prickles as scales slice their way through, the same colors as the pink sky at dawn. Pain enfolds me, making me scream into the water, eyes rolling, fingers like claws as they clutch at Yemoja. She whispers to me of love and strength and courage and

I listen. The bones of my limbs crackle, thighs and calves fusing as the flip of my tail cuts through dark water.

When it is done, Yemoja slips a gold necklace over my head. A sapphire hangs from the chain, the color of the sea and sky on a perfect day. The orisa murmurs of a way to bless the souls of those whose murder the sea hides. Of the burden but also of the joy in blessing their journey to Olodumare.

The sea and its waves enfold and cradle me.

I am Simidele, "follow me home."

In the moments as we fall, as my fingers anchor into the flesh of Esu, who I was and who I am pulses through my mind.

I will take him home with me. Home to the sea, which will swallow him whole.

I am more than memories.

I am more.

The roar of the orisa only makes me cling on tighter. Esu's scream mingles with the whistling keen of the wind as we fall past splintered black rocks under the light of the moon.

When we crash through the waves, the coldness steals my breath until my scales form, legs fusing into a tail that is powerful, its golden fan dividing the water. My arm catches on the serrated edge of a reef, but the wound heals before I can bleed. Esu is not so lucky, and he is battered by another rock as I catch the gleam of alarm in his eyes. He fights to be free of my grip and I release him, welcoming my transformation as the sea fills me with strength.

Esu turns, trying to slash at me, but his blade is slowed by the thickness of the water and I laugh, dodging its obsidian edge easily, knocking it from his hand with my tail. He roars again and then stops, water filling his mouth, spreading to his lungs.

I lunge, grabbing his other ankle, and dive so that we leave the midnight sky behind. Esu twists and wraps his hands around my neck, squeezing my chilled flesh. Despite the tightness at my throat, I grin, dragging him farther into the darker places of the sea. The orisa frowns, his black eyes on mine as he holds on to my neck. Our bodies graze the bedrock, throwing up arcs of silt that form pale clouds around us. I raise my hands to his knuckles, but I don't try to pull them away, my fingers caressing as I see triumph alight in his eyes. The stars that sparkle across my vision bloom and fade like the dying suns in the skies far above us. I manage a tilt of my lips despite the pain and take my hands from his fists, holding them out in the water, palms up, blinking slowly.

Come. Coil around. Come.

The eels twist up from pockets of black rock, their flesh dark. Esu doesn't notice them cleave through the water until they wind their bodies around his wrists in sinuous arcs, long ribbons of fins brushing against his skin. They pull his grip from my neck.

Bite.

The orisa's mouth is a ragged maw as the eels latch onto his hands, needle-thin teeth splitting his skin like sharp knives. Released, I swim backward, watching as more eels flex in the water, wrapping their bodies around both legs and arms. Esu thrashes, a sheen of panic in his eyes.

From the tight folds of my hair, I ease out the black pearl given to me, its surface satin smooth, magic throbbing in the dark iridescence of its outer shell. Releasing it, I let it settle on the bottom of the sea and swim back to Esu. Satisfaction swells, growing more when I think of what he did to the twins, what he did to Kola.

Kola. My mind goes back to his broken body on the floor beside his brother and sister.

I know that only another orisa can fully bind Esu, but it doesn't stop me. Teeth bared, I dart forward and grab at Esu's face, holding it still as I flick the golden blade of my dagger free. I visualize the deep scars that Esu inflicted on Yemoja, using Olodumare as an excuse.

Three deep slashes on each cheek.

A physical manifestation of his greed and lust for power.

There is revenge and violence in my blood as I bring the blade down. The gold of the dagger flashes in the water and Esu screams as I slice through the apples of his cheeks, one deep cut on each side. His pain is a balm to my fury, but it is not enough. When I pull back, blood twists and knots into almost-bows between us as the orisa manages to tear the eels off his right arm. Clawing at his skin, he frees his other arm and turns not to me but toward the surface, eager for the air and moonlight. I let him kick his way upward, swimming through trails of his own blood, following until it seems as if his head will split the waves, and then I grasp an ankle, yanking with all the power I have, dragging the orisa back from the world he scrabbles toward.

Esu doesn't call out again. His chest hitches with lack of air as I pull him back down; his large hands are held out to the surface, skinny plaits floating in the water. With an inhuman surge of strength, he reaches for my neck once more, his thumbs digging into the softness of my throat. The orisa doesn't hear the rattle of chains or see the flash of gold that glints in the water as a shadow looms behind him. Only I see the gleam of black pearls, the broad links of a chain that has lasted more than a millennium. I smile through water tinged with blood.

Olokun slinks behind Esu, his tail a sinuous twist in the depths, chain bunched in his huge fists. My hair waves in the current, braids floating upward and across my vision, framing Olokun as he lifts the metal bunched high in his grip. His gaze connects with mine, and I manage a tiny nod as the orisa brings down the chain in an arc of gold, looping it around Esu's neck. With a jerk, Olokun pulls the orisa backward, wrapping more of the chain around the thickness of the body he has trapped.

"For all the times you would not pass on my messages." Olokun's rich voice pulses through the deep. Esu attempts to spin in the water, but Olokun pulls tighter, restraining the orisa where he floats. "And for all the times you tried to trick your way into gaining the powers of the sea, taunting me with my punishment when I would not fold." He loops another length around Esu's neck. "And Yemoja. When you could have pleaded on her behalf to Olodumare but instead you meted out a punishment borne of your own discontent."

Free of Esu's grip, I swim around him, elation filling my movements with grace. "You came," I say to Olokun as he hunches over Esu, twice his size, pearl cape whirling in the water.

Olokun nods and holds out one hand, holding the chain tight with the other. The black pearl I released into the water sits in his lined palm. "You summoned me." He hisses something in Esu's ear. The orisa gasps, no longer fighting for breath, able to breathe in the water, as he glares at me, his gaze filled with malevolence. "I will bind him at the bottom of the sea until Olodumare sees fit."

"And the ring?" I ask as Olokun towers over me. The orisa promised his help, as well as the band he found, but he never showed it to me, and now a slice of doubt forms.

He leans toward me, salt and silt and the chill of the depths in his breath. "Here." A dark hoop of obsidian is deposited into my waiting palm. I curl my fingers around it, trembling with relief and swimming backward as Esu kicks out at me. His eyes are wide open, incandescent with cold rage.

I propel myself farther out of reach, my heart smashing against my ribs, throbbing with the pressure of the deep and the bargain I made with Olokun. I turn to Esu now. Olokun's tail curls around Esu's legs, and their eyes glitter with silver among the black. The thick golden chain is wound around Esu's body, pinning his arms and holding him in place as Olokun grasps the links tightly. Muscles gleam, their flesh quivering with tension and power.

"I'll honor my promise." I bow to Olokun, the hand holding the ring a fist against my chest, tight against my heart.

Olokun nods and grins, his teeth great ivory spikes. "You are sure?" he asks as he prepares to haul Esu farther into the depths with him.

Sorrow threads its way through my very blood, but I keep it locked and buried within me. "Yes," I answer quietly before turning and pushing myself toward the moonlight that spreads its light on the waves. "It will be done."

...

The shore is full of rocks and sudden waves that threaten to pull me back into the sea. Shivering, I crawl up onto the land, arching my back as my body changes once again, bones resetting under the gentle light of the moon. A rough archway leads me to the bottom of black spiral stairs, an extension of the ones I took before. My feet stumble on each step as I drag in damaged breaths from the wreck of my throat. Pausing, I lift a hand to the sore flesh. I should have left more time for it to heal in the water, but all I could think of was Kola.

Kola.

The thought of his injuries pushes me onward as I hobble up the stairs, trying to ignore the ache in my feet and in my heart.

Smears of blood mark the wall as I go higher, and the sight of it makes me dizzy.

"Simi!" exclaims Kehinde as I stagger into the room. She jumps up from her brother's side and rushes to me, small hands sliding around my ribs in a hug.

My eyes go to Kola. Dark skin and smooth lips. Tight black coils of hair. His pale palms facing the sky. Blood and bruises that cover his body, a chest that rises and falls in minute movements.

"Kola," I murmur.

He manages to turn his head, only a slice of his pupils showing. Falling to my knees, I take his hand, folding both of mine around his loose grip, and my tears slide freely now. There is blood by his side. Too much. It's on the skin that stretches over his ribs and soaks through the makeshift bandage of his wrapper. I hold my hands up; they are full of blood too, dark red lines ingrained in my palms.

"Kola," I whisper again, leaning forward to breathe in the scent of him.

My saying his name does not stop the warmth from fading from his gaze. It does not stop his weak smile from slipping.

I say nothing else. I can't. Kola's face is slack and smooth. His eyes are closed, his hands open still, chest unmoving. I look at his fingers and think of the way he pressed the wild lettuce to my soles. The gentleness of his touch.

Placing Kola's head on my lap, I tip my face up to the black sky, swallowing the wail that has been building inside me. Instead, I run a hand over his curls, and with a gentle pressure, I close his eyes, feeling his lashes soft against my skin.

And then I see it. Kola's soul. A sparkle of silver shot through with pure gold. It spirals from his body, floating into the night air just above his chest.

CHAPTER TWENTY-SEVEN

"NO." I SHAKE my head, not wanting to see it even though it is pure and beautiful, just like Kola.

I lift my hands toward his soul, as if to cradle it, cradle him, but I know it can't be contained by my flesh alone. I could place his essence in the sapphire of my necklace and keep him, so that he'd be with me always. But I know I won't, that it wouldn't be right.

He will be blessed by Yemoja, and he will return home.

I take a shaky breath and wipe my tears, reaching for the glowing spiral of his soul. When the tips of my fingers touch the golden strands, I close my eyes, enveloped in images of Kola.

He sits on his father's lap at his brother and sister's naming ceremony a week after they've been born. Kola feels proud to have helped his father choose the name for the new babies—Taiwo, "having the first taste of the world," and Kehinde, "arriving after the other." And then he is on the boat given to him by his father. It's bigger than any other he's sailed, but he's not worried. His face is open, a smile cracked wide, the planes of his cheeks held up to a burning sun. Bem and Yinka are with him and they are laughing, leaning into a strong sea breeze. I smile, but then the last memory causes my breath to catch, my heart to stutter. I am standing before Kola on the deck, my brown eyes narrowed after the transformation, but to him they glow with courage. I know that, at that moment, I feared that the others would be afraid of me, my scales, my hair a wet tangle from swimming in the depths, but in his eyes I am much more than this.

More than Mami Wata.

More than just a girl.

"No," I moan, trying to hold his soul in place as the images begin to fade, feeling the love of them flood through my mind.

The sapphire at my neck glows, its light bright in the dark. I need to say the prayer to gather his soul, but I hesitate, wanting to stay in his memories, to feel his joy, to keep him with me. And then I feel the hard band of the ring in my other hand. I open my fingers. The obsidian circle is warm in my palm. The babalawo's words come back to me. Enhanced power. The twins' abundance and life that are shared with Oko, the lands and the people's health.

"Kehinde, here." I call the little girl over, taking her right hand in mine. The ring slips on, fitting perfectly. "Do you feel it? Do you know how to use it?"

As Kehinde looks up at me, I see the silver that now flecks her eyes. "I will try. We will try." She turns, and Taiwo does the same, both moving to their brother, lowering themselves at either side of him. The children place their hands on his chest, black rings shining among their fingers, and close their eyes.

Kola's soul hovers still, glittering and beautiful.

"Stay," I whisper, eyes darting between his face and his soul. "Live."

I begin to whisper parts of prayers, memories, and my own hopes.

My arms curled around his ribs in the water while the sharks circled us.

His belief in me.

The twins' lips move, but I can't hear what they are saying. Their small hands are splayed across his chest, fingertips touching, their rings shot through with a shining gold that pulses with their words.

The feeling of his fingers sliding against my cheek, tipping my face to his as he examines the map in my hair.

The soft grip of his hands when he lifts my feet.

The sapphire grows warm against my neck, and as I lean forward, its pale blue glow spreads over Kola's face. The soul ripples.

You are blessed.

Come back.

Kola's essence eases toward his body. Spinning and curling, it snakes back into his chest.

The twins stop, voices silent as Kola's body jolts once, twice beneath their touch. The brightness from the jewels disappears as I hold my breath, searching Kola's face, the line of his cheeks and parted lips. Please, I think as I bend over him.

Come back to us.

Kola does not move. His chest is still. I place my hand on his cheek, running it lightly down to his lips, blinking tears that fall onto his skin.

Come back to me.

I lean down and lay my head against his chest, feeling cold from the sea and the wind and the loss. I cry, mouth twisted, pressed against his flesh as his rib cage heaves. Once and then again. Breath sucked into lungs. Pushing myself back from him, I see Kola's fingers flex and then he gasps, his eyes flaring open.

• • •

I take a deep breath in the early-morning air, grateful for the sun that is rising, casting its blush over the sea, lightening it to a blue that will mirror a perfect cloudless sky.

We are still in the room at the top of Esu's palace. Kola rests between Kehinde and Taiwo, his strength growing. The twins each pass me a ring. No one speaks.

The journey I have made has always been leading to this moment, and now I find a small part of myself wishing it weren't here. I sneak a look back at Kola. His brown gaze meets mine, and the tilt of his head, the small smile he offers, help me to set my shoulders squarely. What I did, saving him, came from my heart, from not being able to stand by and see a person die. Olodumare will see that, will know that.

I hope.

Shaking, I slip the rings on so that they encircle the fourth finger of each of my hands. They sit below each dark brown knuckle, gleaming and absorbing the first rays of the sun. The openness of the room makes me feel closer to the heavens, a fitting place to summon Olodumare. I move to stand on the edge of the platform, the stones cold beneath my feet, feeling the rings as they spread a warmth through my body. I cast my mind back to the prayer Yemoja taught me. I lift my face to the rising sun, the words spilling from my mouth.

"Mo pè yín Olodumare. Jọwọ́, gbọ́ àdúrà mi, wo ìwúlò mi láti

298

dáhùn ìpè mi." I pause a moment, eyes squinting against the brightness of the morning, before repeating it. "I call to you, Olodumare. Please, hear my prayer, see my need, and answer my call."

The rings grow hotter. When I look down at my splayed fingers, I see that they are now circles of gold that shine, growing brighter until the light eclipses my hands, swallowing my arms and enveloping me. And then there is no up or down, left or right, nothing but dazzling white. Love floods through me, seeping into the smile I know would be there if I could see my body.

"Forgive me," I whisper. "For saving Kola. For breaking your decree." The words are simple but they are all I have, accompanied by a quiver and a tentative hope that grows with each moment.

A sudden pulse of energy that swirls around, surging through my mind and filling me with an all-consuming peace. There is no voice to answer, no words to explain, but none is needed.

I am shown it.

Images flood my mind. I am small, selecting yams at the market, helping my mother to cook them. My father sits with me, using a game of Ayòayò to help with my numbers. The story of creation told by my mother in her star-patterned wrapper. The press of their bodies on either side of me as I fall asleep listening to them talk.

Their love for me and mine for them fill me, flooding over the time I spent on the ship, chains heavy, the scent of misery and pain thick in the back of my throat. Olodumare shows me images of those returned, at home and at peace. Those who have made their way on their own and others that Mami Wata has blessed and guided. I am shown myself. Dragging Kola through the sea, eyes desperate, heart full of righteousness. Olodumare's gratitude envelops me now, folding in with the blessing and the forgiveness I seek.

For all that Yemoja and Mami Wata have done.

For all that I have done.

When the light fades I open my eyes to the fresh clean of a new day, breathing out, my chest light. The rage is gone, replaced with a comforting peace that settles within me.

"Simi?"

I turn back to Kola, a smile stretched across my lips. For a moment I'm unable to speak, but he sees the light in my eyes and matches it. Beside him, Kehinde and Taiwo grin, and when I walk back to them, I hold a hand out to each one. They slip each of their rings from my fingers and back onto theirs, where they belong.

"It is done," I whisper, awe laced with simple words.

"What happened? With Esu?" Kola asks. "He is . . . ?"

"Bound. By Olokun at the bottom of the sea."

"How? I mean, how did you manage to get him to help you?"

I think about what words I will use next. Unable or maybe just unwilling to tell him any more than I have to, I keep my voice the same, not letting my tone change. "I lied. I'm sorry," I add quickly. "I did see him when I went searching for him. At first, I thought he might be able to tell me something that would help, something that would work to our advantage." I place my hands on my knees. "Olokun was fuming. He said Esu refused to take any of his messages to Olodumare. I asked for help and he agreed."

"But what did he want in return?" Kola's forehead creases as he sits up slowly, wincing even though his body is healing faster with the aid of the twins.

"He gave me a pearl as a way to summon him, but he told me

not to tell anyone." I skate away from the question, eyes darting around the chamber instead of looking at Kola. "That I couldn't be sure of anyone."

"And he was right," Kola says as I let my gaze fall on him briefly. "Imagine if you had told us of this plan when Ifedayo was with us."

I shudder and rub at the chilled flesh of my arms. "We agreed that I would summon him once I had Esu in the sea, that he would chain and bind him. Who knows what Esu has neglected to tell Olodumare, or"—I stop and shudder, thinking of Yemoja—"what Esu has done in the Supreme Creator's name? Olokun will release him to Olodumare, who will deal with him as they see fit."

"And Olokun, what did he want in return?" presses Kola, his eyes glinting. The way he watches me fractures my heart. I want to sit down with him, to tangle my fingers in his, lean into his heat, his comfort.

But I know I can't.

"I made a vow to help him."

"What?" Kola asks, a spark of panic in his eyes. He gets to his feet, hissing in pain. "How?"

Kola stands before me and I look up into the clear brown of his gaze. The beauty spot above his eyebrow is almost lost in the folds of his frown. I reach up and touch it gently.

"Esu was right when he said we could never be together. I'm sorry, I should have told you earlier." I pause to take a deep breath. "But at least this way you're safe. And the twins and Oko."

"Simi, what have you done?" Kola slides his hands around my arms, pulling me to him when I don't answer.

I don't speak for a moment, taking in the shape of his mouth, the smoothness of his skin, committing it all to memory.

"Tell me," demands Kola, his voice breaking.

I pull away from him, his fingers tightening momentarily before he lets me go. The space between us already seems too much, but I back farther away, moving to the end of the platform, scanning the white-tipped waves. The water just below is seething against the base of black rock, but farther out it is calmer. Deceptively so. Giant swells rise and fall under the morning sun, its soft light dappling the surface. I turn to face Kola, the dawn growing behind me, spreading its new-day glow.

"I agreed to help Olokun fight the loneliness he faces, to shoulder the burdens he bears." I lock eyes with Kola, lifting my chin. "I promised to make the Land of the Dead my home."

Kola's eyes widen, and he moves toward me as I take another step back, soles burning against the cool stone.

"You're leaving," he states, pausing. Close enough to touch.

It's not a question, but I know he expects me to answer. "I am of the sea. You know this." I want to soften my voice, but I don't. "And this is the only way. Without Olokun, we wouldn't have been able to bind Esu."

"We could have tried—"

I shake my head. "Don't." It was hard enough to make the sacrifice I did. "There wasn't a choice."

We are silent a moment. A muscle ticks in Kola's jaw and I want to touch it, to smooth his anger away, but I force myself not to. He runs a hand over his face and then breathes out heavily, his shoulders sagging.

"Serving Olokun will be an honor," I say, but the words sound hollow even to my own ears.

When Kola looks at me, it is through a glaze of tears. Twisting back to the angry waves, I don't blink, not wanting to cry. He reaches for me as I turn, but I glare at him, fists clenched, and he stops, leaving his hands hovering between us. I want to tell Kola not to make it any harder. That I would love nothing more than to stay with him.

But we are not the same.

We can never be.

The words stay stuck in my throat, and so I shake my head, facing the morning sun. Hoping that Kola doesn't touch me, because if he does, I may not be able to leave. I focus on the water, the waves tipped with foam as they surge against the shore. A tear escapes as I teeter on the edge of the platform.

"Simi, wait—"

I close my eyes as Kola's fingers graze the small of my back, and then I let myself tip forward into a dive. As I soar through the salt-filled air, I let the rest of my tears fall, and when I open my eyes, it is to a cold sea, washing them away.

AUTHOR'S NOTE

When I was six years old, my favorite book was *The Little Mermaid* by Hans Christian Andersen. I was obsessed with the palace at the bottom of the sea and the magic and mystery of the little mermaid's world. I remember reading that book over and over again, examining each illustration and convincing myself that it was all real. And even though I never saw myself in that story, I wanted to be a little mermaid, too.

Representation matters. There is no escaping the fact that readers engage in stories where they see themselves. I witness this as a mother, as a teacher, and from my personal experiences as a reader, and so, as a writer, this is an important focus of any story I tell. In 2017, I began researching Black mermaids and fell instantly in love. Quickly, I came across Mami Wata (Mother of Water). Commonly thought to be a single entity, the name has been applied to a number of African water spirits and deities. I chose to focus on Yemoja, often depicted as a Black woman with the tail of a fish, who is a Yoruba deity within the Ifá spiritual system and is believed to be the mother of all, giving birth to the waters of the world.

Skin of the Sea is set in the mid-1400s, when the Portuguese first began abducting and then buying West Africans and taking them back to Europe and colonized islands. Yemoja was said to have followed the first people who were taken from the West African coast and enslaved. This continued with the expanded transatlantic slave trade, and stories of Yemoja spread across the African diaspora.

Aside from Yemoja's role in the Ifá spiritual system, there are stories of the comfort she gave Africans while they were on the slave ships. Some speak of Yemoja wrecking the vessels, while others say she brought back home the souls of those who died. This last concept is the one that inspired me. What if she created seven Mami Wata to help her bless the souls of those who pass in the sea? What if one of them was a teenage girl who managed to save a life? Simidele (whose name means "follow me home") was born.

African mythology is integral to this story. Learning about Senegalese fairies, the African version of a unicorn, the bultungin shape-shifters of the Kanem-Bornu Empire, and the Ninki Nanka river monster only added to my motivation. Black gods, goddesses, mermaids, and other creatures both deadly and magnificent . . . and all with African origins. Creating a story blending these and West African history became a passionate obsession.

Black history doesn't start with slavery. An important aspect of *Skin of the Sea* for me is the positive depiction of ancient African knowledge, culture, and history, which are often insidiously and incorrectly presented as primitive. One example that added to my obsession was the conscious and deliberate use of fractals (repeated patterns) in hairstyles, art, cloth, and architecture across the continent. Ron Eglash, an ethno-mathematician, proposed that when Europeans came across these examples, they thought they were chaotic and therefore primitive. It didn't occur to them that Africans might have been using mathematics that Europeans hadn't yet discovered, suggesting that African knowledge of the concept of infinity was prevalent well before it was "discovered" by European mathematicians hundreds of years later. Fascinated and empowered, I knew I needed to add as many of these details as I could.

Skin of the Sea is a blend of history, myth, and fiction. It portrays an alternative version of mermaids and their origins, but also touches upon a dark time in history where resistance, courage, and ingenuity were shown. For me, writing *Skin of the Sea* has allowed me to tell a story of Black characters from ancient empires, showcasing their power and magnificence. It has pushed me into learning more about my father's country, my ancestors, and West African civilizations. It has shown me powerful images of Black deities and has expanded my knowledge of African history. My hope is that *Skin of the Sea* will spark readers' interest in discovering more, too. That their understanding and empathy will grow, and that they will be enthralled by and in awe of the magnitude of African history, culture, and stories.

FOR FURTHER READING

Adi, Hakim. "Africa and the Transatlantic Slave Trade." BBC. bbc.co.uk
/history/british/abolition/africa_article_01.shtml. Last modified
October 5, 2012.

Cuoco, Alex. *African Narratives of Orishas, Spirits and Other Deities.*
Parker, CO: Outskirts Press, 2014.

Dabiri, Emma. *Don't Touch My Hair.* London: Allen Lane, 2019.

Davidson, Basil. *The African Slave Trade.* Oxford: James Currey, 1996.

Diouf, Sylviane. *Fighting the Slave Trade.* Athens: Ohio University Press,
2003.

Eglash, Ron. *African Fractals: Modern Computing and Indigenous Design.*
New Brunswick, NJ: Rutgers University Press, 1999.

Elbl, Ivana. "'Slaves Are a Very Risky Business . . .': Supply and Demand
in the Early Atlantic Slave Trade." In *Enslaving Connections: Changing
Cultures of Africa and Brazil During the Era of Slavery,* edited by José C.
Curto and Paul E. Lovejoy, 29–55. Amherst, NY: Humanity Books, 2004.

Elbl, Ivana. "The Volume of the Early Atlantic Slave Trade, 1450–1521."
Journal of African History 38, no. 1 (March 1997): 31–75.

Graham, James D. "The Slave Trade, Depopulation, and Human Sacrifice
in Benin History." *Cahiers d'Études Africaines* 5, no. 18 (1965): 317–334.

History.com Editors. "First Enslaved Africans Arrive in Jamestown,
Setting the Stage for Slavery in North America." History. history
.com/this-day-in-history/first-african-slave-ship-arrives-jamestown
-colony. Last modified August 13, 2019.

Karade, Baba Ifa. *The Handbook of Yoruba Religious Concepts.* Boston:
Weiser Books, 1994.

Vogt, John. L. "The Early Sao-Tome-Principe Slave Trade with Mina
1500–1540." *International Journal of African Historical Studies* 6, no. 3.
(1973): 453–467.

Walker, Robin. *Before the Slave Trade: African World History in Pictures.*
London: Black History Studies Publications, 2008.

ACKNOWLEDGMENTS

Skin of the Sea gripped me from its inception, and I am filled with gratitude that others have felt the same. I am thankful for the support of friends and family, the #DVpit community, and Twitter and early readers.

Thank you to my family, who talked about the plot of *Skin of the Sea* over and over, even though most discussions ended in arguments. To my oldest son, who took special interest in reading the fight scenes.

Thank you to the children in my year 4 class of 2017–18 for your support and encouragement. A special shout-out to Daniel, Daniel G., and Oliver, who spent their weekends researching sea creatures and West Africa as well as asking me endless questions that kept me thinking and inspired.

Thank you to Nigel, who let me use his hot spot in the staff room when I ran out of data and #DVpit was popping off! Thank you for also reading endless drafts and quietly championing me from the beginning. Penny, who has kept my work from our university days and has encouraged my sense of voice since we were nineteen.

Thank you to Clare, Tricia, and Fran. You all kept me sane with your encouragement and cheerleading.

Thank you to Charlene and Siana for providing a safe and supportive space when it comes to sharing our work.

Thank you to Efosa Oviawe, who took up the mantle of making

sure I try every Nigerian dish he loves, and to Abayomi Odubanjo, who helped with my Yoruba and name suggestions. A massive thank-you to Ogunlade Ifamuyiwa, whose extensive knowledge of the Ifá spiritual system and orisas gave *Skin of the Sea* so much depth. I hope your church enjoys reading the book!

Thank you to the Yorùbáizm Team for translating the Yoruba spoken in *Skin of the Sea.*

Thank you to Beth Phelan for creating and running #DVpit on Twitter. Your campaign for diverse voices in publishing is phenomenal. Without this platform, I wouldn't have connected with my amazing agent. To Brittney Morris, who read my Twitter pitch and boosted me no end. Thank you to Tomi Adeyemi, who took time out to give me advice on submitting to agents and next steps.

Thank you to Jodi, who is not only a super agent but an amazing and clever person. I am in awe of you constantly.

To my editors, Chelsea Eberly, Tricia Lin, and Carmen McCullough, who have worked tirelessly to help make *Skin of the Sea* what it is and who have answered every question I can possibly think of. I am immensely grateful for all that I have learned from you.

Thank you to everyone at Random House who championed my book from the very beginning, including Michelle Nagler, Caroline Abbey, Mallory Loehr, Jasmine Hodge, Barbara Marcus, Regina Flath, Ken Crossland, Janet Foley, Alison Kolani, Tracy Heydweiller, John Adamo, Lili Feinberg, and Dominique Cimina. I feel so thankful for all your support and hard work.

Finally, thank you to the readers, for keeping stories alive.

WHAT DOES FATE HOLD
FOR SIMI?

READ ON
FOR A SNEAK PEEK
AT THE
NEXT BOOK.

Excerpt text copyright © 2021 by Natasha Bowen. Published by Random House Children's Books, a division of Penguin Random House LLC, New York.

The bones are buried deep, white against the velvet of dark water. I shudder in the cold press of the sea as I swim beneath giant rib cages. The chill has burrowed into my core, where it nestles in the pit of my stomach, settling next to the promise I made to Olokun. The promise I must keep, even though it colors my days in shades of midnight, of misery. Sometimes I let myself think of the sun, the perfect pink and orange rise of it, the fire of the way it sets. But then my mind always goes to Kola and the heat of his skin, the slice of his smile, and the way one touch can make my chest tight.

My choice.

My sacrifice.

I blink away curls from my eyes, trying to rid myself of thoughts that only make the lightless water harder to bear. Release them, I tell myself. Release what you cannot have and accept the present.

I adjust my grip on the terra-cotta pot I found resting in the sand, an offering from above that made its way down to the deep. At least I will be able to bring evidence that *someone* still worships Olokun. Flicking my caudal fin, its blush and gold pleats barely visible, I pass slowly under the last of the skeletons, their ivory arcs protruding from the silt.

When I emerge from the bones, I pause for a moment in water that grows warmer. The heat is a balm, and I spin once in the hot silk of a current, almost smiling at the relief it brings. Almost.

Ahead, on either end of the coral reef, the earth is split, emitting searing gases that bubble into the sea. A blue glow spreads over my skin as I draw closer to a large carved opening lit up by firefly squid. Smaller seeps of gases cause the water to shimmer and glitter, feverish swirls that escape, framing the entrance in the coral. The squid illuminate an archway draped with glowing sea moss and studded with mollusks.

I swallow thickly. The soft light makes my heart ache with its gentle beauty, but it's only a pale imitation of what I crave. Six months without the scald of a full sun and I find it hard to imagine the feel of sweat sliding down warm skin. I want air, even though I don't need it, even when it is dense with a coming storm or cut through with the chill of night. I want to see the stars again, their scattered flares puncturing the sky. I want to feel the earth beneath my feet, the rich black soil that turns to soft mud when the rains come.

Floating closer to the entrance, I run a finger over the etchings of fish, whales, and the peaks of the seabed. The last image is one of scales, curls, and the telltale beauty of Yemoja. My maker, my second mother, the most gracious of orisa. A sadness coils within me, but I don't let it settle. Instead, I focus on Yemoja's safety, of Folasade and the other Mami Wata, fulfilling their task of gathering the souls of those who die in the sea. If I hadn't asked Olokun for help, then the fracturing world would have broken entirely.

I am here so that they can be safe. And this is the price I must pay.

I touch the sapphire at my neck, its cold blue brighter than the rock around me. I think of blessing souls with Yemoja, honoring their journeys home to Olodumare. A different kind of service than the one that Olokun demands of me now.

But my choices were the right ones, and they don't change what needs to be done. I grasp the pot tighter and glide through the gases, chin tipped up, shoulders back. More warm water flows over me as I pass under the arch, giving way to much cooler currents when I emerge into a tunnel that stretches ahead. No firefly squid here.

My heart beats quicker, and I hold a cold hand to my chest. This part used to scare me, but months of making this journey has allowed me to swim through the passage with faith, though there is still a slither of dread in knowing what awaits. I slip into the gloom, skin grazing against the smooth black sides as I head toward the vague light in the distance.

The rock widens into a circular space. Hundreds of larger firefly squid are draped over the coral walls, their glow reflecting on the iridescent insides of cracked-open shells studded among them. The moss grows in abundance here, its thick glistening arcs looped around the walls. I squint through the dazzle of light, eyes narrowed against the sudden brightness.

A current tugs me farther inside and I let it, clasping the offering to my chest, allowing myself a glance upward at a ceiling peppered with more moss, its trails pulsing with soft white lights.

"I see that you have decided to grace me with your presence." The deep tone of the voice trickles out from the back of the hall, where the light stretches to reach. I feel a faint flicker of pride when I don't flinch.

A flash of a metallic gaze, and then Olokun leans forward, his mouth curled up at the edges. I swim toward the murkiness until I can make out the coil of the orisa's great tail curved beneath him. Olokun sits on a black coral throne, fingers curling over the armrests. He flicks his abebe back and forth, the silver fan creating ripples in the water. Shadows cloak the muscled bulk of Olokun's body, but his eyes shine in a face with sharp angles. A thick golden chain wraps around his waist, its end tailing off into the sea.

"It's not yet time," I answer, the words slipping out like stones settling around us. The pot is cool in my arms, and I grip its handles firmly, teeth clenched so tight that my jaw aches. I want to remind the orisa of what I gave up to be here, but I bite it down.

Setting the vessel before Olokun, I touch my fingertips and forehead to the ground as a sign of respect before moving backward. The orisa's cape trails down to the floor, black pearls bulbous and gleaming.

Olokun peers at the clay pot, a finger held against the cleft in his chin. "What is that?"

"An offering," I say, hands hovering over the tribute. "Shall I open it?"

"Let me." The water swirls, rocking me slightly as the orisa lunges forward and snatches up the pot.

Olokun wrenches the lid off and reaches inside, bringing out a bundle of waxed cloth that he slowly unwraps. The whitish belly of the raw yam is exposed. The orisa's smile disappears as he covers the peeled vegetable and settles it back inside.

"Another reminder of those who worship you," I say, my annoyance forming at the downward tilt of his lips. I know what he is thinking—that he will never be able to taste iyán this deep in the sea. Will never be able to dip it into ẹ̀gúsí, dig his feet into the hot earth, take sips of palm wine between each bite. He finds something lacking in every offering I bring.

Olokun shoves the pot against the wall with the others, and the golden chain around his waist rattles, its links clinking against the throne. He turns his gaze away from the discarded tributes I spend my days searching for, a frown puckering his forehead.

"Are you not pleased?" My voice wavers, the question shooting out before I can swallow it back down.

The orisa doesn't answer, but he kicks out at the pot this time, sending it crashing against the wall, where it smashes into pieces. I edge backward, welcoming the rise of my anger, using it to keep most of my fear at bay.

"It is not enough. You should be bringing me more. Find more!" Olokun roars, surging from his throne, tall in the glitter and gloom. When I don't speak, he sits back down, fingers testing each sharp point of his abede. "I do not ask much of you. Searching for tributes, your company at times, and overseeing the dead. These are small things."

My chest swells with anger. I think of the hours spent combing the bedrock until my fingers are numb, the relief when I do find something, the days when I dread returning empty-handed. The times when thoughts of Kola make me sink to the blackest part of the water, letting the freezing currents wash away my tears, when missing him hurts so much that it burns.

"You will never be sated!" The words fight their way up my throat, and I can't hold them in. "There's too much bitterness in your heart. It's not the people's fault that you are chained down here, and it certainly isn't mine!"

Olokun freezes, his abede held high. He slashes it once, twice through the water, and then looks directly at me, a muscle in his jaw twitching. "If I had been shown proper respect from the beginning, then I would not be trapped down here."

"You sent wave after wave to destroy Ife!" I answer, a sneer in my voice. Obatala created land in the middle of Olokun's waters and gave life to humankind. But he did not consult Olokun, whose outrage at his shrunken kingdom and lack of worship grew. Lurking in the depths, the orisa became twisted with spite and jealousy, until he tried to erase the earth and its people by battering them with the sea. "Obatala had to chain you to save humanity. You have no patience. No care. You are here because of what you did!" I glare at him, my frustration taking over. There was a part of me that used to feel some sympathy for Olokun, banished so deep, but his vanity is exhausting. "Was it worth this? The weight of water above us. A life without sunlight, the gnawing cold that settles in your bones?" This is the most I have ever said, and I brace myself for his fury, my hands in fists.

The gentle swish of water is the only sound in the chamber. I hold Olokun's gaze in a way I never have, my heart thumping.

"You made your choice, and now you dare to complain?" Olokun's voice is low, laced with menace. He snaps his fan shut and swims over to me, his eyes as icy as the water that presses down around us. "Tell me, did I force you to come to these depths?" I stare at the orisa, swallowing down more words, my shoulders quivering. "You offered me your service. I did not demand it from you, Mami Wata." His words are soft, winding through the water like ribbons. "The anger and pity that you feel is for yourself. Remember this and show your *respect*."

His last word catches at me. Olokun stood by his promise to help bind Esu, thereby saving those I care about. That deserves my deference, even if his past actions do not.

"Besides . . ." Olokun swims close enough for me to make out the twist of his short curls. "Do I not show compassion now?"

My shoulders slump, and my spine curves over once again. I think of what is expected of me next, and I nod. It doesn't matter how I feel—we must do what needs to be done. *I* must do what needs to be done.

"We will put your outburst down to tiredness and the cold," says Olokun, flicking the chain behind him. His eyes are shuttered now, any displeasure swallowed by the silver and black. "Come."

The last shreds of my anger dissipate as Olokun turns to leave, his tail a sinuous twist of purple. Behind the throne is another tunnel, and with a flick of his fin, Olokun disappears within it. Quickly, I follow.

The passageway splits off into a dozen others, some to areas I have never seen. Before long, we are outside and swimming into lighter water, the frigid depths bringing a numbness that seeps inside me. Olokun soars upward out of the black blue, and I follow him as he skims along the reef, golden chain trailing in his wake, seemingly infinite but never long enough for him to reach the surface. I follow the glints of metal, chest tightening with every stroke I make.

We are close.

Olokun doesn't look back at me, so he won't see the glaze of near tears, but as I move nearer to him, I can see his lips are pulled tight, chin held up.

"There are . . . more. This much I know from what the squid have told me." Olokun's words are cushioned in the indigo satin of the water.

I close my eyes and nod once, and then I am propelling myself up, drawing level with the orisa as we crest the reef.

Before us stretch the burial sands. The half-moon curve of pale silt spreads out as far as I can see, its surface littered with mounds that range from whale-sized to smaller than me. I swallow, heart beating faster as I make out the new bodies.

All who die in the sea end up here in Olokun's kingdom.

"Another ship?" I ask quietly, squeezing my words around the lump in my throat.

Olokun keeps his eyes on the people who have come to rest in his realm. Slowly he nods his great head, caudal fin waving in the water. Together, we scoop the silt from the bottom of the sea, covering each hand, each foot, smoothing sand over open mouths and sightless eyes. Burying the people who were taken, who could not be saved. I tuck wrappers over chests, touching a hand to scarred cheeks and tangled hair. I cry as we create new graves. Every time, it tears at me, and every time the pain grows until I think I can't take any more.

Once we are finished, we return to the reef, silent as our gazes sweep over the dead. My hands form fists, nails digging in, breaking the skin of my palms. Small crescents and bursts of blood are spawned, only to dissolve instantly.

"Before, you and your sisters gathered their souls, and I prayed over the bodies I buried." Olokun's eyes fix on the blue of the sapphire hanging around my neck, his words quiet. "Now, *we* bury them and pray together." He turns to me, holding out his hand. "Keeping their remains safe and blessing them. I know it is a hard burden to bear, but your service and added prayers are an honor to the dead, Mami Wata. Something special. I am glad to be able to offer them that, not just the actions and words of an orisa who seeks redemption."

I look down at his large palm, with its faded brown lines. My anger is gone, replaced with the melancholy that now accompanies me everywhere. I slide my fingers over his, intertwining bones and flesh, letting him pull me next to him. I am grateful that I can offer the last words over these stolen people, that we give them more dignity.

"A ṣe ẹrí nípa pé a rí ibi à ti sùn yín, a dẹ ṣe ìwúre pé kí ìrìn àjò yín sí ọdọ̀ Olódùmarè jẹ́ ìrìn àjò ìbùkún." We look down together as the prayer streams from our lips. "Ara yín á tún áyé wá; ẹ̀mi yín á sì jẹ́ ọ̀kan pẹ̀lú àwọn alálẹ̀. Pẹ̀lú àwọn ọ̀rọ̀ wọ̀n yí, a gbée yín pọ́n. A ò sì ní gbàgbé ìgbésí aiyé yín."

I don't cry anymore. Instead, I try to think of the lives they lived and the peace they have now.

"We witness your final resting place, and we add our blessings to your journey home to Olodumare," I murmur again as Olokun releases my hand. "Your body will rejoin the world, while your spirit will be at one with the ancestors. With these words we honor you and your life. Your death will not be forgotten."

The orisa gazes at the mounds, large and small, before he turns away, his tail propelling him through the dark. I do not follow—I know by now that he will not speak. He will meditate on the loss of life that the tides bring to his realm.

I shut my eyes and try to calm the tremble in my hands. Still, I can't stop the darkness that pulses against my closed lids. I've helped bury them, have spoken the prayer, but if I do not feel this pain, then who will? I think of how I could have been in one of these graves if Yemoja had not remade me. Despite yearning to be human, I had been given another chance at a different kind of life. One that I should still be thankful for.

I slide my arms around my waist, but I am too cold to offer myself any comfort. Instead, I clutch at the jewel of my necklace and think about the souls of the people I gathered. Those golden and silver threads of life, their memories, echoes of their joy. I imagine their ghosts rising up from the silt, brushing sand from remnants of patterned wrappers, out of the whorls of their ears and the blackness of their hair. They will look around them, at the heavy layers of the water above and the maw of the deep just outside Olokun's kingdom, and they will wonder what happened, where they are. And then realization will crash down on them—their life, their death—and just when they think that they cannot stand it, the ghosts will regard the bodies we have buried. Some will crumple in despair, while others will make fists of their vague fingers, smashing them against chests that can no longer feel, press against hearts that no longer beat. A fury felt even beyond life.

My lips flatten into a line. I will the ghosts in my mind to follow their souls and return home, to welcome the embrace of Olodumare. I send my apologies to them, clasping a hand to my own breast, fingers splayed over a heart that still beats, even though it feels shattered and cracked by loss.

Then the water rushes in a sudden current. Fear, as quick and vivid as a sea snake, darts in. I sway, bursts of ghosts still blooming on my eyelids, as small icy fingers slide around my wrist.

I really enjoy drawing. Not only is it relaxing, but it also helps me bring the characters and settings in my mind to life. I spent a lot of time exploring the forms of mermaids, the curve of a tail meeting the spine, underwater movement, and stretched-out curls. This sketch was a way for me to work out how Simi would change from Mami Wata to human, and decide that her scales would transform into her wrapper.

OYO Empire — ~~oriṣa~~ oriṣa religion became more widespread
(1837 collapsed). (1400–1800s)

- A powerful Yoruba state in the modern Nigeria began in the 1300s in the west African savannah north of the tropical forests where the Yoruba peoples lived.
  ALAFIN ORUNBOLI – 8th king ?

- Capital city – Oyo-Ile. By 1550 conquered two neighbouring kingdoms, Borgu and Nupe, & become the most dominant political entity in the region.

Oyo was ruled by an ALAFIN (king) who shared power with the Oyo Mesi, aristocratic leaders from each of Oyo city's seven wards. The Oyo Mesi were responsible for the selection of the alafin. They could also call for an alafin's suicide if he abused his power.

Under Alafin OBALOKUN, Oyo expanded small works & the Atlantic coast, and became part of the ATLANTIC OCEAN TRADE SYSTEM. — trading mainly

For me, one of the best parts of writing is the research. Building my knowledge of West African kingdoms before the sixteenth century was so rewarding. These notes are on the Oyo Empire. I was very interested in the intricacies of the ruling elite, how they gained power, and the reasons for their initial trade with Europeans.